SEPARATE LIVES

Mervyn Corwen first meets Moira Sheldon when she's a schoolgirl and he's her art teacher. At the time Mervyn believes Moira's affection is little more than a schoolgirl crush, but meeting her again at an evening class, Mervyn realises he isn't as indifferent to her as he first thought. When Moira agrees to her new husband's plans to move permanently to his beloved Greece, she misses her close-knit family, her friends, her home. Marriage to Mervyn is all she has ever dreamed of, but should she have been more careful what she wished for?

SEPARATE LIVES

SEPARATE LIVES

by

Sara Hylton

Magna Large Print Books
Long Preston, North Yorkshire,
BD23 4ND, England.

British Library Cataloguing in Publication Data.

Hylton, Sara
Separate lives.

A catalogue record of this book is available from the British Library

ISBN 0-7505-1591-0

First published in Great Britain by Judy Piatkus Publishers Ltd., 1999

Published in Large Print 2001 by arrangement with Judy Piatkus Publishers Ltd.

Magna Large Print is an imprint of Library Magna Books Ltd.

Printed and bound in Great Britain by T.J. (International) Ltd., Cornwall, PL28 8RW

To Mavis and Cyril

Remind Me

Remind me that this was the month
 I promised to remember.
The misted hills and purple shadows,
 the scent of woodsmoke in that far September.
The sea rippling in over the white sands,
 the air filled with birds' cries.
How strange that I should remember all these
 things when I have forgotten the colour of your
 eyes.
Remind me that there was love and tenderness
 in the warm night,
and how we owned the earth until the morning
 light.

Anon.

BOOK ONE

MERVYN

Chapter One

Mervyn Corwen had never known what it was like to be part of a real family. His parents had been killed in a motor accident when he was four years old and his mother's brother, a widower with one daughter, became responsible for his upbringing.

Uncle Bertram taught Latin and Greek at one of the West Country's more prestigious public schools. During term time he lived in a large old-fashioned house crammed with memorabilia of Ancient Greece and Rome. Marble statues stood cheek by jowl with urns and bronze weaponry and Mervyn and his cousin Athena were left largely to amuse themselves.

Athena was three years his senior: a remarkably self-possessed and very striking girl, and one singularly unconcerned that she seldom spent time with her father but who was, nevertheless, sure about how her life was going.

When the school closed for holidays Bertram and the two children went to a small Greek island where Bertram rented an unpretentious villa from the people who owned a vastly superior one further up the hillside.

Here Athena and Mervyn amused themselves, exploring the meadows perfumed with wild flowers, or searched for shell pools along the tiny bays and rock-strewn coves. Bertram spent his time writing his memoirs which he hoped would one day be published. Few people on the island knew him since he was a strangely solitary man but the islanders accepted the two beautiful children, Athena with her blonde curls and enchanting face, and Mervyn with his dark hair and direct, green-eyed gaze.

They made friends with the village children and in the way of the very young were quick to pick up the language. Bertram was happy to let them do as they pleased while he sat in the garden with the blue Aegean Sea before him and the scent of herbs all around him. For Bertram and the children those six weeks every summer were bliss, something to be remembered in the long English winters while they waited impatiently for two short weeks at Easter when they opened up the villa once more.

Bertram endeavoured to instil some of his ancient knowledge into the children from time to time, including Greek and Latin. He had little success. Athena wanted to dance. He would stand dourly on the cliff top while his daughter performed her graceful arabasques across the sand.

His nephew was an equal disappointment. All Mervyn wanted to do was sit with his watercolours at the table under the window in the evenings when the sun had gone down. He wasn't too sure what he wanted to paint, but he gloried in the colours and the intricate shapes they made when they mingled with the water on the paper in front of him.

The summers came and went, the children

grew, and Bertram retired to a cottage he had bought in the West Country for the winter and spent his summers on the Greek island. He was still writing his memoirs, but by this time he had lost all hope that they would ever be published: it was simply something for him to do.

Athena had singing lessons, went to dancing classes, spent long summer holidays on cruise liners with girls richer than herself and married at the age of seventeen an extremely rich Scottish landowner seventeen years her senior.

Mervyn was not academically minded. He applied himself to the study of painting, and, after three years at an art school in Bristol, managed to obtain a post as art master in a private girls' school. This allowed him to teach during the day, paint his own pictures in his leisure time and spend long summer holidays with Uncle Bertram at the villa in Greece, where he worked on his paintings.

After a while he acquired a small studio on the island and succeeded in attracting tourists only too willing to buy his pictures. He didn't make a fortune but it did enable him to maintain the place, purchase the best materials and enjoy every day the thing he liked doing most.

Moira Sheldon had been one of his pupils. He remembered her coming into the art room on that first morning carrying her paints and brushes in a small oblong box, looking round the room diffidently before taking her place at one of the easels.

Moira was not one of his brightest pupils but she was the most diligent. Mervyn had long been of the opinion that art could not be taught, that it was something that came from within and more and more, when he looked at the efforts of some of his pupils after long months of tuition, he was filled with despair.

Just occasionally one or other of them would display rare talent: then he would feel that all his hard work had been worthwhile. Moira, however, was not one of them.

She painted the sort of pretty watercolour some Victorian gentlewoman might have been proud of: bland and unoriginal. Moira was happy to copy from picture postcards and calendars. Painting *en plein air* – out of doors – was something she hated: she was either bitten with midges or hated the wind messing her hair. Why was it then that of all his pupils she was the one he fell in love with?

Was it because she had patently adored him, gazing at him enraptured as he brought her efforts to life, listening to his patient voice as he explained the intricacies of colour blending and shading? Was it because when he looked up from her painting, he caught the warm blush on her exquisite face, and felt the sudden racing of his heart?

Mervyn was well aware of the dangers of young adolescent girls falling in love with their teachers. He did nothing to encourage her infatuation; instead he betrayed an aloofness that unnerved and puzzled her. He spent more time with his other students, convinced that when she left in the summer, he would be relieved.

He went reluctantly to the end-of-term party:

he was only going to stay for a short while. But it was there that he saw her young face struggling with her hurt pride, as she tried to enjoy her last day at school. Her eyes studiously avoided meeting his, and it was seeing her sitting alone watching the dancing that, against all his better judgment, drew him to her.

When he asked her to dance he felt her hurt withdrawnness melt away. That evening they talked about themselves for the first time. Moira learned about his lonely childhood with a self-absorbed uncle and a precocious cousin, his love of the beautiful Greek island, the pictures he painted in the summertime and the people who hung around his studio and wanted to buy them.

He watched her eyes shining with delight as she told him how much she would love to see the island. She had never been further than Bournemouth, she said. That was where she went every summer with her parents. He learned that her father was a printer with his own small business, her mother a florist with a shop in one of the small villages. Moira had two sisters and innumerable cousins, aunts and uncles and they were a very closely knit family, spending time together every Christmas and in the summer holidays.

She told him that after the summer break, she would be working in her father's office over the workshop.

In a few days, he would be back on his Greek island, and no decision was made to meet again. As she left the party with her friends, she had waved to him from the door, which had prompted giggles from the other girls. It would soon be forgotten. Come September they would all be leading different lives and he would be facing a class of new students.

He thought about her now and again as he painted in his studio on the island or on the cliff top looking out across the sea. His uncle sat reading in the garden. He seemed older, shabbier. Athena never came. She would telephone from some faraway place she and her husband and daughter happened to be visiting and Bertram looked fondly at pictures she sent him of the little granddaughter she had called Cassandra. She knew that had pleased her father: anything to do with Ancient Greece had always had the power to delight him.

Mervyn sat on the clifftop watching the holidaymakers make their way from the small boat that plied between the islands, and along the harbour wall before they climbed the hillside. Soon a small group would gather round his painting and watch it come to life. They stood in silence, and eventually one or two drifted away to look inside his studio where there were pictures for sale. The morning looked promising.

The visitors were in love with the Greek islands, with the sunshine and the scent of herbs, with the azure sea below them and the short sun-baked grass beneath their feet. They wanted to take something home to remind them of those long idyllic summer days and they seldom haggled about the prices he charged.

It was late in the afternoon when he closed his

studio and walked up the hillside to the villa. His uncle was still sitting in his favourite chair looking at his favourite view and Mervyn went into the house to count his takings.

He poured himself a glass of wine and sauntered outside to drink it.

Bertram sat with his head leaning back against his cushions and when Mervyn spoke to him he did not open his eyes. One slim brown hand rested on his knee, the other trailed languidly over the arm of his chair, but his face had a greenish pallor that made Mervyn suddenly afraid. His uncle was dead.

Only two weeks of his holiday remained and there was much to do. His uncle had long ago established a desire to be buried on the island and his friendship with the local priest had assured him it would be possible, but there was the urgent task of informing Athena.

Two days later she arrived on the island alone. He went down the hillside to meet her off the boat and he wondered why in the midst of a group of people she stood out like an orchid in a field of clover.

She was dressed like any other holidaymaker, except that her simple blue cotton dress had an elegance that had never been purchased from a chain store. Her legs were bare but her blue sandals matched the colour of her frock exactly, as did the blue chiffon scarf she wore to tie back her hair, hair that shone gold in the morning sunlight.

Her face lit up with a smile and she came

forward with outstretched hands to meet him.

'You came alone?' he asked softly.

'Yes of course. Ian said he would come but there was Cassie. Funerals and children don't go together.'

'No, I suppose not.'

'Is everything arranged, Mervyn? What a good thing you were here. Thank goodness Daddy gave most of his treasures to the school and the local museum. At least we won't have those to think about.'

'No. There's very little here. His books I suppose, and his memoirs. He was still writing them you know.'

'Was he really? Poor darling. No one would ever have published them you know, who, these days, wants to read about some old dear going on about Ancient Greece and Rome?'

'Some of the villages might be glad of the furniture, there are one or two very nice pieces.'

'Oh we'll leave them here. After all, I intend to hang on to the villa, Cassie might like to come here one day with some of her friends.'

'But Uncle Bertram didn't own the villa, Athena.'

'He did, Mervyn. Didn't he tell you? He bought it years ago, when he decided to come to live here.'

'I didn't know. He never told me.'

'I think they were glad to sell it. After all, we never did see them, did we? Weren't they Italian or Sicilian? Why would Italians want to come to Greece when they have such beautiful places in their own country to go to?'

'Well, I suppose it's true to say they don't need to come for the sunshine.'

On the morning of the funeral they were surrounded by villagers. All had known Bertram for many years and he had been well respected, though never really one of them.

Athena put it into words as they walked back to the villa. 'Poor Daddy, he would have been surprised to have known how many of them came. I looked in his strong box last night and found his will. He was always terribly frugal, but he had a good salary for a long time. He gave so much of it away to all sorts of odd causes.'

'Well, you don't need it, Athena.'

'That's the artist in you – money's of no great importance to you. But it is to me. I do need money, we all do. He's left me some, and some for Cassie, he's left you his memoirs and £10,000.'

Mervyn stared at her in surprise.

'Well, surely you expected him to leave you something, he practically brought you up?'

'It always seemed to me that I was thrust upon him.'

'What will you do with it? Refurnish that poky little house you have?'

'It's big enough for me.'

'Never thought of getting married?'

'Not seriously.'

'Well, one day you might. £10,000 could come in very useful then.'

He smiled. 'I suppose so.'

'You can still come here to paint in the school holidays Mervyn. I shan't want to come and you can keep the villa in some sort of decent repair.'

'I'll do that gladly, Athena. How long do you intend to stay here?'

'Just a few days. There's nothing to keep me here, you'll be leaving yourself soon anyway.'

'Yes, next week.'

'I'd ask you to spend a few days with us on your next break but we never know where we'll be. If Ian isn't with us, I like to get away.'

In the early morning, a couple of days later, he stood with Athena on the rickety wooden jetty waiting for the first load of tourists to be brought over from Rhodes.

There was a strange primeval stillness with only the gentle sound of the sea lapping against the wooden struts of the pier, and the whistling of a fisherman. As if she followed his train of thought, Athena said, 'It is beautiful Mervyn. This morning I can understand why Daddy never tired of it but he never put anything into words, did he?'

'Perhaps he thought he didn't need to.'

'Oh but he did. I knew he loved his treasures, I used to watch him stroking a piece of old marble, gazing enraptured at a crumbling statue, counting the days until he could come back here, and I used to want to go on up to him and say, "Look at me, Daddy, I'm just as beautiful as your old statue".'

'But you never did?'

'No, pretending I didn't care was easier. There are only the two of us now, Mervyn.'

'I know. And if you ever need me, you know where to find me.'

'The same goes for me. There aren't many

people getting off the boat this morning, it looks as if you're going to have a quiet day.'

'It's too early. There'll be more of them coming in on the later boats.'

She smiled and put her arms around his neck, kissing his cheek swiftly.

'Take care Mervyn, be happy,' she said, then with a wave of her hand she was stepping lightly up the gangplank, and he stood at the end of the pier watching the boat slip silently away.

There would be Christmas cards and holiday postcards, birthday cards if she remembered, and if he took the trouble the odd telephone call. Athena had thought her father aloof, it was something that was bred in her.

He spent his days, packing his things and closing his studio, then he started on the villa. His uncle had always been meticulously tidy; at the same time, he was amazed at the empty cupboards and drawers – it was almost as though his uncle had realised that he should set his house in order.

He gave several little things away, like fruit bowls and bookends to the women who had looked after the house. They were received with smiles and gratitude far in excess of their value and on the last night the village priest appeared and they sat in the garden with a bottle of wine.

He spoke excellent English and it was obvious he had been a great admirer of Uncle Bertram.

'What will you do with his memoirs?' the priest asked him. 'Try to get them published?'

'He never completed them, and quite honestly interest in them would be very limited.'

'It is a great pity, all that work, all those long lonely hours. From my living room I could see the light burning in here, sometimes it was almost daylight when it went out, and I thought about him pouring over those memoirs.'

'Have you read any of them?'

'No, but I would like to read them. Did he leave them to his daughter?'

'No, he left them to me and I will gladly leave them with you. You are probably someone who would appreciate them.'

The priest smiled. 'I will take good care of them. When may we expect to see you again?'

'Probably at Eastertime. My cousin tells me Uncle Bertram bought the villa. I didn't know.'

'I'm sure he didn't intend to keep it a secret. The Contessa has not been to the villa for some years, not in fact since her husband died, too many memories I expect. When they came here at first they were a very happy family. The Conte was a charming man and the Contessa very beautiful, two rich young people fate had smiled upon. They had two children, a boy Alex, and a girl, Sophia. It was a happy time for them in that beautiful place with the large garden and the sea sparkling at every window. The air was filled with their laughter.

'I only remember seeing them once and that is some years ago. Two very young children and their mother sitting in the gardens. She waved her hand to me and I remember thinking that she was very beautiful.'

'Yes, and now her husband is dead and the island no longer sees them.'

'They'll come back I'm sure, grief doesn't last for ever. It isn't meant to.'

'No, you are right my friend. Life has to go on. We do not forget, but the initial pain goes. I have enjoyed our talk and look forward to seeing you next year. I will keep an eye on your villa and the studio, if you will let me know when you intend to return here I will send some women to clean the house in readiness and attend to the garden.'

'You are very kind. I'm not sure if my cousin will come here. Athena lives in Scotland and they travel a great deal. I shouldn't think the island is her husband's idea of a holiday.'

'Why do you say that?'

'They prefer the flesh pots, the South of France, America, cruise liners – things I've never been able to afford.'

'Ah well, each to his own. But you my friend will come back here. One day you will bring your wife here and your children.'

Mervyn laughed. 'Perhaps. As yet I have no wife and no thoughts on one. I'll walk down the hill with you, I need to stretch my legs.'

They walked in companionable silence and the perfumed breeze fanned their faces with gentle benevolence. In the dark indigo-blue vault of the sky a full moon silvered the waves along the shoreline and a myriad of stars glittered.

As Mervyn walked back alone he felt suddenly aware of a deep feeling of gratitude that Bertram had made it possible for him to return to the islands. He had been a man of few words, never demonstrative, but he had been a benefactor to that lost lonely boy. He had given him a home, an education and, in the end, a sanctuary where he could paint his pictures and enjoy the sort of life he loved most.

Chapter Two

There was the usual air of frantic activity on the first morning after the long summer holiday. New girls, looking a little nervous, anxiously gathered together in small groups waiting to be told where they should go. Old pupils over-confident, greeting old friends, scanning the notice-boards, and as Mervyn crossed the entrance hall on his way to the art room Marian Adcock, the biology mistress, caught up with him, favouring him with a broad smile.

'Managed to tear yourself away from your island then?' she greeted him.

'Reluctantly,' he replied.

'Sell many pictures?'

'Quite a few.'

'Aren't you the least bit lonely on your own? Surely you'd be happier with a companion?'

'I might not get as much work done with a companion.'

'Oh well, if you ever feel like inviting somebody you'll spare me a thought I hope.'

He smiled. Marian was the last person he would have thought of inviting. She was boisterous, rather pushy and desperate for a man. For several months the music master had been her quarry until she discovered he was something of a Romeo and was already involved with two other females on the staff. Eric Johnson had warned Mervyn not to become involved, adding that Marian was becoming somewhat desperate.

'I hope you're appearing at assembly,' she said at the art room door. 'You know Miss Borley has a thing about assembly, particularly on the first day of a new term.'

'I'll be there.'

'Have you seen Martin Starkey?'

'No. I've only just arrived.'

'Well he's looking for you, I've no idea why.'

He looked round the room with interest. It had been redecorated during the school holidays and several new easels added to those already there. The long windows looked out across the playing fields and towards the distant hills and he stood for a few moments looking out to where girls strolled towards the school until from the hall below he heard the distant sound of the gong calling them to assembly.

Footsteps were hurrying along the corridors and down the stairs and, leaving his case on top of the long table under the window, he let himself out of the room. The hall was already filling with girls and he went to take his place with the rest of the staff on the dais.

They greeted him with welcoming smiles and he took his place next to Martin Starkey, the history master, who had held up a hand to call him over.

There was no time for conversation. The girls

were on their feet for the morning hymn and after the first few bars on the piano they were launched into *Jerusalem*.

Margaret Borley, the headmistress, delivered her welcoming speech which altered hardly at all from one year to the next, and Martin managed to whisper, 'Before you go into class I'd like a word with you, Mervyn.'

Mervyn nodded.

The sermon and the prayers came to an end and then in orderly columns the girls made their way to their respective classrooms. The teachers exchanged greetings and followed them while Martin and Mervyn brought up the rear.

When they paused to chat the headmistress said, 'I'm sure whatever you have to say to each other can keep until the break. We have to be seen to be efficient on the first morning in school.'

Martin favoured his companion with a resigned smile before marching off.

In the art room the girls were milling round searching for easels and Mervyn encouraged them to settle down quickly.

These were girls who had been at the school some time. He knew one or two of them but had not taken any great interest in any of them.

For the first time in weeks he thought about Moira. A small dark-haired girl was sitting where Moira had liked to sit, near the window, where the morning sun made a golden halo of her hair and he found himself remembering the frown of concentration on her pretty face and the sad droop of her lips when things were not going well.

The girls were summing him up. By and large they were precocious, streetwise and pretty sure of themselves. Every year they seemed to be more sophisticated, audacious.

He dragged a small table into the middle of the room and placed on it a large blue and white bowl in which he arranged some apples and pears then he asked them to draw a pencilled sketch so that he could refresh his mind about their individual potential.

As he moved around them in spirits sank. There was no one who could be called outstanding. When the bell came to announce the morning break he experienced the utmost feeling of relief.

Martin was waiting for him in the hall.

'Ever felt like teaching evening classes?' he greeted him with.

'No. Don't they have their own teachers in further education?'

'Steven Matthews is a friend of mine and I know he's laid up for several months after a heart attack. They're looking for somebody to take his place until he's well enough to return.'

'I rather think I'll have had enough after I've soldiered on here. I don't think I'd feel very much like teaching art to adults.'

'They'll be different. Some of them are very good, I went to their art exhibition in the summer, you'd have been agreeably surprised I think.'

'They're people who really *want* to draw and paint,' Martin continued. 'Not schoolgirls who are having it thrust upon them. They need a teacher for two evenings a week, we could all do with extra cash. I don't suppose you're any different.'

Mervyn thought about the £10,000 his uncle had left him. Athena had suggested he look around for a classier place to live. £10,000 would hardly touch the surface of a new flat or house. Martin was right, the extra money would come in handy.

'All right then. If they haven't managed to get somebody I'll take it on for a few months.'

The college was adjacent to the civic buildings in the Town Hall Square and from the outside it looked imposing. Inside it was a hotchpotch of cookery rooms, lecture theatres, the art room, a small canteen and a large hall where end-of-term exhibitions were held as well as student get-togethers. All he was aware of when he walked into the room on his first evening was that there were about twenty easels in the room and all of them occupied by men and women. Some of them were elderly, some of an uncertain age. And then he saw Moira. She was sitting next to a woman of ample proportions and she was looking at him with wide-eyed delight. Most of them were already started on some project or other and he quickly realised that all he was expected to do was walk among them and help them with a few hints and suggestions if they needed it. By the time they broke for coffee his spirits had revived.

Some of their work was good. True they were amateurs but they were enthusiastic, willing to learn, and keenly responsive to his efforts to advise them. Only one elderly gentleman seemed averse to criticism and Mervyn quickly realised whatever he suggested he would go his own way.

When eventually he got around to Moira he was not surprised to find she was copying a calendar picture of a bunch of carnations and mimosa. Her painting was adequate but when he suggested that she should bring flowers into the classroom and endeavour to paint them she merely smiled, the sweet hesitant smile he remembered so well. She said, 'I've tried painting flowers at home but somehow I never get them right.'

'Well, I'm here to help you,' he said.

At the end of the evening he asked his class if they would like him to bring something for them to paint, but by and large they said they would prefer to paint their own thing. If that was what they wanted, the money he was being paid was hardly being earned.

As he left the building to walk to his house he saw Moira getting into a car with the large woman and driving off. It was possible they were neighbours, or the woman could be one Moira's numerous relatives. It had started to rain, so putting his head down he hurried towards the narrow road where his house stood surrounded by a small lawned garden and a short path edged with privet bushes.

He didn't like the house, and as he stood surveying the hall and kitchen beyond he felt suddenly depressed. A smell of stale fried food lay about the kitchen and the entire house had an unlived-in severity that he had never thought much about until this moment. Frequent visits to the island had made him like a bird of passage.

He felt restless as he switched on the electric fire in the living room. Here too the room felt strangely impersonal. There were no flowers, no ornaments: it was simply a bachelor pad devoid of taste. There was just one picture over the mantelpiece: a view from the terrace on the island. He had painted it when he first went there; it was a boy's painting, and he couldn't think why he'd never replaced it with superior work. He couldn't bring a woman into this house, she would think it was terrible. Why, though, had that idea suddenly come into his mind?

He made himself a coffee and went back to the living room to drink it. He switched on the television to watch the news but it was largely political and Mervyn had never had any interest in politics or politicians. Uncle Bertram had always maintained that you voted for them because you thought they'd listen to you. They never did, so why bother?

He began to wonder what Moira did when she got home. He could picture her in that suburban home, her mother bustling around getting super ready, her father either watching television or sunk into a book, her sisters doing their homework or chatting about their boyfriends. He smiled to himself. In all probability they were doing none of these things. He didn't really know anything about them and was not likely to find out.

All the same he knew when he sat at her easel to demonstrate how the picture should take shape, he was aware that she was looking at *him* rather than her efforts, and when he looked up he surprised a shy awareness in her eyes, covered immediately by a display of attentiveness he felt sure she was not feeling. Weeks passed. Mervyn continued his classes, Moira continued to give him that ambivalent smile. He wondered absently if she'd be going to the Christmas party. It was still some weeks away but already he'd heard the younger students discussing it, and one of them had asked pertly, 'Will you be coming Mr Corwen? We have a great time, you'll enjoy yourself.'

In the event, he had nothing better to do on the night of the party so he went. The students had organised groups who sang, performed sketches and played instruments; they had decorated the hall with balloons and streamers. The cookery classes had organised the food and it was plentiful and imaginative and as the evening progressed he came to the realisation that he was enjoying himself.

Moira was in the group that sang, dressed in a long black velvet skirt and a frilly white blouse which he felt sure she had borrowed from one of her older sisters since he'd never seen her in anything like it.

In the interval he mingled with the students and, after they had eaten, the musicians took their places on the platform and the dancing began.

He danced with one girl after another and it

was getting late when, finally, he asked Moira. They spent the remainder of the evening dancing together and, when the party was over, he asked politely how she was getting home.

'Oh, somebody will give me a lift,' she said lightly. 'I live out towards Brenton. Dad gave me money for a taxi.'

'Well my car's in the square so I'll give you a lift.'

'That is kind of you, if you're sure you don't mind.'

They ran through the rain to the car. It was a rather old and battered sports model but there was still something racy and romantic about the long bonnet and rakish lines. At least Moira seemed to think so from the bright expectancy with which she regarded it.

As she sank back beside him in the front seat, she said, 'Oh I love this car. I used to look at it when you parked it at the school. None of the other teachers had one like it.'

'No, but its getting a bit ancient, I should exchange it but it runs well and I'm not even tempted by another model.'

She smiled.

'Did you enjoy yourself tonight Mr Corwen?' she asked. 'We're not in school now Moira, why not call me Mervyn,' he said, smiling back.

He heard her quick intake of breath, then nervously she asked, 'I used to see your name at the school, I always thought it unusual.'

'It's Welsh. My grandmother was Welsh. Apparently she chose it.'

'Is she still alive?'

'I'm afraid not, nor my parents.'

'I'm sorry. Did they die recently?'

'No. I hardly remember them, my uncle brought me up.'

'Was he the one who lived on the island?'

'You remember that, do you?'

'Oh yes, I thought it was so romantic that you went there for holidays. It must be wonderful to be able to spend all summer on a Greek island.'

'Yes, but it wasn't exactly all summer, just the month of August I'm afraid. Now we're getting into Brenton. Where exactly do you live?'

Through the windscreen wipers, she directed him through a maze of avenues, curving and tree-lined, with predictable names like Acacia and Poplar, Chestnut and Willow until eventually she pointed to a large semi standing at a corner.

'There,' she said with a little laugh. 'Number one Sycamore Drive. They've left the porch light on for me. Would you like to come in for a cup of coffee?'

'Thank you Moira, but it's getting rather late and it's such a lousy night I should be getting back.'

Evidently the occupants of the house had heard the sound of the car drawing up at the front gate and in the next minute the front door was opened and the light from the hall streamed out into the darkness. A man appeared on the drive holding up a large umbrella and Moira said, 'There's Dad.'

In the next moment her father was at the door of the car opening it and peering inside saying, 'I'm glad you got a lift home love, it's a rotten night. Now who have we here?'

'This is Mr Corwen, Dad, our art master.'

'Nice of you, Mr Corwen, to bring Moira home, she's been in good hands. I know my wife would like to meet you. Do come in and have coffee with us.'

In some dismay Mervyn said, 'Well, it is rather late and a very wretched night, I should be getting back.'

'Somebody waiting up for you then?'

'Well no…'

'Then do please come in, and have a coffee to warm you up.'

To refuse would be churlish so reluctantly Mervyn followed Moira and her father up the path to the front door.

Her father was a tall thin man, spectacles and sparse grey hair. Her mother was small and plump, her smile warm and friendly, her younger sister stared at him, non-committally, assessing him from behind horn-rimmed spectacles.

He surmised that she was around seventeen and studious from the look of the table littered with exercise books and heavy volumes. Seeing him glancing at them, Mr Sheldon said proudly, 'Norah's swatting for her exams, we're confident she'll get a good place at university.'

Moira smiled. 'She's far cleverer than ever I was,' she said diffidently.

'And I work harder,' snapped Norah.

'Now girls,' her mother remonstrated. 'Moira has qualities you don't have.'

'What sort of qualities?' Nora asked pertly.

'She's a better help in the house and around the

shops, and she's tidier.'

'Sit here near the fire,' Mr Sheldon invited. 'You get the coffee, Mother, and we'll have some of Moira's sponge cake. I don't suppose the refreshments were up to much.'

'Actually, they were very good,' Mervyn said. 'Far better than I'd anticipated.'

'But not as good as Moira's sponge I'll be bound,' her father said firmly.

He was pressed into eating a large slice of Moira's sponge cake which was excellent, even when he was too full to do justice to it.

Norah was hunched on a pouffe near the fire, hugging her knees. Mervyn sat next to her on a comfortable easy chair while the other three were together on the velvet-covered settee.

After they had eaten, out came the photographs, since the conversation had largely been about holidays in Bournemouth or Torquay. Moira said plaintively, 'they'll not interest Mr Corwen, Daddy, he spends all his holidays on a Greek island.'

'I can't understand why people choose to go abroad for their holidays when we have such lovely places in England. I had enough of abroad during the war,' her father said firmly.

'That was different dear,' his wife said. 'Mr Corwen evidently enjoys foreign travel. Do you never holiday in this country, Mr Corwen?'

'Of course, but I do tend to go to the island at Easter and again in the summer. My uncle had a villa there, he died there.'

'I see. Here's a nice one of Moira in the New Forest last summer. We're a very close family. We have another daughter – she's married – and they usually join us for summer holidays. We rent a large house in Bournemouth, we've been going there for years.'

Next came family photographs, wedding photographs and Moira, pretty in a bridesmaid dress for her married sister's wedding.

Thinking that he should comment, he said to Norah, 'You're not a bridesmaid then?'

'Yes of course. She's only showing you the ones of Moira.'

'That's because he knows Moira better than he knows you,' her mother answered firmly.

'Are you in Moira's painting class,' she asked him.

'I'm her teacher,' he answered. 'I also taught her at school.'

'You're the Mr Corwen she was always talking about?' Norah asked with a smile on her unduly cynical lips.

'I told you he was a very good teacher,' Moira said hastily. 'Art was always my favourite subject.'

'Moira paints some lovely pictures,' her father said proudly. 'We have most of them framed and give them around the family at Christmastime. Do you think she should have gone on to do something with her art, Mr Corwen?'

Four pairs of eyes were regarding him expectantly and he had to choose his words very carefully.

'A great many people wish to paint, Mr Sheldon. Some of them starve in attics to get their work acknowledged. I rather think a safe job is preferable and to make painting a pleasing pastime. If your work is good enough, as in many other professions, the cream rises to the top.'

'I wasn't meaning as an artist, Mr Corwen. I meant as a teacher like you.'

'Not many schools employ a teacher simply to teach art,' he said and hoped that would bring the subject to a close.

He stole a surreptitious glance at his watch, dismayed to see that it was after one o'clock and he said hastily, 'Gracious, I'd no idea it was so late. I must be getting home. Thank you so much for the coffee, but I do have a fairly crowded day tomorrow.'

'Hasn't the school broken up for Christmas then?'

'No, two more days to go.'

He shook hands all round and Moira accompanied him to the door and stood there waving her hand to him as he drove away.

His thoughts were strangely bemused as he drove back along the empty rain-soaked streets.

Chapter Three

Moira closed the front door and went back into the living room where the family were making ready to go to bed. Her father gave her a smile.

'It was very nice of Mr Corwen to give you a lift home, love. I told you to take a taxi.'

'I know, but we were dancing together and he offered.'

'And you've had a crush on him since you were in the sixth form,' Norah said with a sly smile.

'I like him because he's a good teacher, I liked the others if they were good teachers too,' Moira said firmly.

'How old is he?' her father asked curiously.

'I really don't know, Dad, early twenties I think.'

'Late twenties or early thirties, you mean,' Norah said vehemently.

'I don't know how old he is,' Moira said testily. 'Does it matter? I'll help Mum in the kitchen, I notice you haven't offered any help,' she added, looking at her sister with some irritation.

Her mother was putting the crockery away and with a bright smile she said, 'I thought he was a very nice young man, Moira. How old is he?'

'Why is his age suddenly so important?' Moira cried. 'I don't know, I haven't asked him, but I will ask him if you really want to know.'

'Don't get so upset, Moira. Naturally your father and I are very concerned who you bring home. He's very nice, good-looking too, but a good few years older than you.'

'He's my teacher, Mum, not my boyfriend.'

'But you always talked about him a lot. Girls do quite often develop crushes on their teachers.'

'All right, Mum, I had a crush on Mr Corwen when I was at school, I'm not at school now, I've grown up. If there's nothing needs doing, I think I'll go to bed, goodnight.'

When Norah joined her a little later she pretended to be asleep. She wanted no more backchat from her. The younger girl said irritably, 'you're only pretending to be asleep, I know you're not.'

Moira didn't stir, and Nora said slyly, 'Mum'll be asking you to invite him to tea now that he's broken the ice. That's what happens when we bring boyfriends home.'

Moira sat up in bed and glared at her sister, 'He isn't my boyfriend,' she said angrily.

'Alec Rostron wasn't Janet's boyfriend the first time she brought him home, but it developed after Mum invited him to tea.'

'You're too old for your years,' Monica said sharply. 'You're still a schoolgirl but you think you know it all.'

'I know more than you do. You were always the quiet one, we all thought so.'

'If I'd known you were going to be around, I wouldn't have invited Mr Corwen in at any price. Goodness knows what he thought about you.'

'That I'm grown up and sophisticated, I expect.'

'That you're impudent and precocious, more likely. Why don't you shut up and go to sleep.'

She snatched the covers and pulled them over her head, but from the next bed came Norah's mocking laughter.

Moira didn't go to sleep, instead she lay staring up into the darkness. Her feeling for Mervyn Corwen was more than a crush – she believed it had been that at school – but it had not gone away. Now he was back in her life and the crush had become an actual physical pain that taunted her day and night. She knew that he liked her. There were times when she caught him looking at her when he should have been giving another student his full attention, and he spent longer at her easel than was absolutely necessary. There were better artists in the class, and miserably she wondered what Mervyn had thought about her father's praise of her work.

Mervyn sat in front of his electric fire, a whisky and soda on the small table beside him, his thoughts on the family he had just left. He thought about the lived-in comfortable room with its warm-toned carpet and velvet cushions. The Christmas tree standing near the window surrounded by gaily wrapped parcels, the closeness of a loving family.

His thoughts went back to Christmas times at his uncle's house. There had never been a tree with fairy lights flickering in the firelight. There had been presents of books, educational tomes that had never warmed the heart of the boy he had been.

He had gone just before Christmas in the company of his uncle to Athena's dancing class where the children were performing in front of their parents. The children were exquisite in their costumes, and Athena had danced her solo with poetic grace, her enchanting face alive with joy.

After the concert was over they had listened to her teacher's enthusiasm for her performance and the many hopes she had that Athena would continue with her dancing with a view to making it a career. His uncle had been coldly scathing.

In no uncertain terms he had informed her

dancing teacher that his daughter was a classical scholar, that she would go to university and do honours in classics and then teach. After his outburst they had all left without staying for the buffet.

That night he had heard Athena sobbing in her room, and when he went in to comfort her, she had said bitterly: 'I shall marry the first man who asks me. He has to be rich enough to take me away from all this, and I shall do none of the things Dad expects me to do.'

When she meet Ian McFarlane at the home of one of her school friends she set out to capture him from the older sister of her friend and succeeded. They were married quietly and went immediately to live in Scotland. Uncle Bertram nursed his acute disappointment and seldom spoke of her.

There was a Christmas party at his school too. And, on the last day, he found small parcels on his desk, dolled up in Christmas wrapping paper. Handkerchiefs, a tie he would never wish to wear, sweets and even mince pies one of their mothers had made.

He accepted their gifts with warmth and a sentimental feeling of belonging to somebody which quickly vanished when he let himself into his empty house.

Most of the other teachers envied his holidays on the Greek island, but they never quite knew what he did for Christmas. If they asked him round for drinks he invariably said he was invited somewhere else, and if they invited him on Christmas Day or Boxing Day he said he would probably be going to spend Christmas with his cousin: something he never did.

He lived like a hermit over the school holidays, afraid that, if he ventured out, he would meet somebody who would say, 'I thought you were going away for Christmas,' and he wouldn't know what to say.

The term finished after lunch and he was packing his gifts and cards into his briefcase when Martin Starkey opened the door and stood surveying the room thoughtfully.

'No budding Constables this year, Mervyn?'

'I'm afraid not. Take a look round. Some of them aren't too bad.'

'I looked in the other day when you were outdoor sketching. I expect you were frozen.'

'We didn't stay out long.'

'Will you be off to Scotland as usual?'

'I'm waiting to hear from Athena.'

'It's not much use inviting you round then. The wife has invited three or four of the students from college.'

'Thanks Martin, but I probably will be away.'

'Have you heard how much longer you're likely to be taking the evening class?'

'Not officially, although I believe your friend's recovering.'

'Yes. I must make an effort to get round there. I'll be off then, all the best.'

Although it was only early in the afternoon, lights streamed out into a dull gloomy winter's day. A Christmas tree was already lit up in the Town Hall Square and fairy lights twinkled festively from office windows.

Off the Square the market was doing brisk business as people shopped for fruit and turkeys. Over all, in spite of the gloom, there was an atmosphere of excitement as people greeted one another and children darted here and there in search of stocking-fillers.

An old feeling of nostalgia washed over him as he paused at the fruit stall where people were buying nuts and raisins, boxes of dates and tangerines. He remembered sitting on a rug in front of the fire, sharing a box of dates with Athena. Now, for some quite inexplicable reason, he decided to buy one and was about to hand over his money when a voice at his elbow said, 'Why Mr Corwen, I can see you're stocking up for Christmas.'

He looked down to see Moira's mother gazing up at him, a bright smile on her face, while behind her Moira and her sister looked on.

Mervyn smiled. 'It's years since I ate dates, I suddenly felt I should relive the experience.'

'Oh yes, we always have dates, everything else too. We make such a big thing of Christmas. Will you be going to your island?'

'No. I don't go there at Christmas.'

'But you'll be going away somewhere, I suppose?'

'I expect so, probably to stay with my cousin and her husband.'

'If you don't go, Mr Corwen, you're really very welcome to come and eat with us. One more won't make the slightest difference.'

'Thank you, Mrs Sheldon. You're very kind but I probably will be going away.'

'Well, if you don't, do please come. You'll be most welcome.'

She smiled and moved away while Norah grinned at him and Moira hung back nervously. 'Don't mind Mum,' she said anxiously. 'She loves having people around, particularly at this time.'

'She's very kind, Moira. I appreciate it.'

'Are you really going away?'

'Probably.'

'Only probably?'

'Well I'm waiting to hear from my cousin.'

'And if you don't.'

'I'm sure I shall be, but if I don't I'll stay at home, eat the dates and all the other goodies my students have given me. I'll eat my turkey and drink my whisky and when it's all over I'll go back to school and forget about it.'

'You'd rather do that than come to us?'

He looked at her helplessly, 'Moira, I'd be an imposition. You have a lot of relatives and I don't know any of them. They'd wonder what I was doing there.'

'My mother invited you.'

'That was nice of her, but, like I said, I'm sure I'll be away.'

'It would be nice if you came again, oh perhaps not at Christmas but one day soon.'

'Yes, that would be nice. And now I must go Moira in case my cousin has been trying to get hold of me. Have a lovely Christmas, no doubt I'll be seeing you in the New Year.'

He smiled at her warmly and he dimly heard her sister crying, 'Come on Moira, we're waiting for you.'

There was a Christmas card from Athena, Ian and Cassie and a short note informing him that they were spending Christmas in Tenerife. 'The weather in Scotland can be dire at this time of year,' she wrote, 'and in Tenerife there will be sunshine, we shall be looked after and I've never been brought up to enjoy cosy Christmas days, nor have you darling.'

Mervyn cooked his small turkey, followed by the smallest Christmas pudding he could find. He sat in front of the electric fire and his television set, a whisky and soda on the table in front of him in the company of a box of chocolates and the box of dates.

In the early evening the telephone rang for a short period and kept on ringing on and off for the rest of the day. He didn't get out of his chair to answer it. Whoever was ringing would eventually realise that he was indeed away from home.

Soon after eleven he heard the carol singers from the local church singing in the road outside his house so he switched out all the lights. It could well be that people who knew him were with them and the house had to appear unoccupied.

After assuring himself that they'd gone he switched on the lights and settled down in his chair. It was a pattern he would need to adopt all over Christmas, and against all his better judgement his thoughts turned to Moira's house where he could imagine the sort of evening they would be having: paper hats and festive fare, probably parlour games and gossip, excitement over their

Christmas presents. He would have stood out like a sore finger. Oh, they would have made him welcome, but they would also have been introducing him as Moira's art teacher. Her precocious sister would have been smiling with taunting amusement, and the rest of them would be surmising on how deep his interest was in Moira, particularly when Moira made her interest in him very apparent.

The day before New Year's Eve convinced Mervyn that he would have to go out to replenish his larder and to his utmost chagrin he discovered that the small shop around the corner was closed all over the holidays, which meant that he had to go further afield.

It was snowing, fine powdery snow that clung to his hair and clothing, covering the pavements with a substance resembling talcum powder and it was so cold the snow lay like a white sheet across the market square and the tarpaulins that covered the stalls. People with the same idea as himself were doing their shopping and the wind had risen so that he collided with a figure holding an umbrella so low that she was unable to see where she was going. A swift apology was followed by a startled exclamation from a female voice saying, 'Mervyn, it's you.'

He stared down into Moira's startled face and his first feeling was of relief that she was alone.

Collecting his wits swiftly he said, 'What are you doing out on such a day?'

'Shopping for fruit. Mum was too busy to come with me, Dad's over there.'

'Did you have a nice Christmas?'

'Oh yes, we always do. Did you? I thought about you in Scotland, was it very cold?'

'It's very cold here this morning. Does your party go on into the New Year?'

'We go to my sister's on New Year's Eve and Great Auntie Agatha's on New Year's Day. I wish they came to us.'

'Oh, why's that?'

'Well, I don't mind going to my sister's but Great Aunt Agatha's a different matter. We have to be there on time, eat on time, leave on time, and there's nothing to do except talk about the past, when Uncle Egbert was alive and all the grandparents.'

'In fact, a really family party.'

'I suppose so. What will you be doing?'

'Nothing much, preparing my lessons for the next term, eating and drinking, perhaps visiting one or two friends.'

At that moment her father joined them, smiling affably. The two men shook hands and Mr Sheldon said, 'My wife told me she'd invited you to spend Christmas with us Mr Corwen, she loves a party, the more the merrier, but you were going away.'

'Yes, that's right.'

'We're out for most of New Year and Moira and I wish we were at home, don't we, love?'

'She's been telling me about it.'

'Why don't you come round the day after New Year's Day? We'd be very pleased to see you. A few drinks and something to eat, nothing too festive, but it's better than being on your own.'

'Mr Corwen may be going to friends, Dad,'

Moira put in quickly.

'Oh I'm sorry, it was only a thought.'

Mervyn never quite knew why he couldn't have left it there, but Moira's pretty face was displaying that gentle hurt look he had seen before and he found himself saying, 'I haven't anything concrete arranged, thank you, I'll be glad to come round in the evening, around eight o'clock, do you think?'

'Oh earlier than that. Do come for a meal, the wife will be delighted.'

As he walked back to his house he couldn't believe that he had actually agreed to go. Moira was infatuated with him, she would call it love, but he wasn't very sure what love was. His feelings for Moira were more obscure.

She was a nice girl, a pretty girl, from a decent family background, but at the back of his mind he could see Athena's face, hear her voice saying tantalisingly, 'But they're so bourgeois, darling. They're really not you at all.'

He liked them but he was afraid of them. They were too conventional, too close and they threatened the free spirit he believed he had become. If Moira had to fall in love with one of her teachers, why couldn't it have been one of the conventional ones, not one who made a god of his art, who spent money recklessly on canvasses and paints, and lived like a bohemian for five long weeks in the summer sun on a small Greek island.

They would encourage him to go to Bournemouth and concerts on the pier, dress in suits to dine in hotel restaurants, and go to church every

Sunday. He would be more regimented than he had ever been with Uncle Bertram who had only required him to make himself scarce.

He felt he should telephone to make an excuse, but he couldn't do it, and as he donned his one and only suit and knotted his silk tie, he gazed at his reflection in the mirror. He wasn't bad looking. He was tall and slender, his face had the remnants of a summer tan which made his eyes seem unusually green. His dark hair framed his face which had a sculptured leanness with its thin aquiline nose and firm straight lips. His face was arresting rather than handsome, and his mind went over the other teachers at the school, more conventional, possibly more ordinary. That's what art does to you, he thought.

As he stood on the front doorstep ringing the bell he found himself wishing fervently that they would not have invited the rest of their close-knit family to join them. The last thing he wanted was to be viewed by aunts and uncles and a host of cousins.

He was agreeably surprised to find that only Moira's parents and Moira were there to greet him. Mrs Sheldon explained that Norah was staying overnight with a school friend and his spirits revived considerably.

They made him very welcome. The meal was excellent, the bottle of Chardonnay that Mr Shelton produced most appreciated and if the usual assortment of photographs followed he had to admit that he had dined well.

When the photographs were exhausted, Mrs Sheldon said, 'Are you musical, Mr Corwen?'

'I like music but I'm not a performer, and please do call me Mervyn.'

She smiled with pleasure. 'We've always encouraged our girls to be musical. Kathleen, our eldest daughter, has singing lessons and she sings in the church choir, Moira had piano lessons and Norah plays the flute. When we all get together we have quite a little orchestra as you can imagine.'

'Yes indeed.'

'Why don't you play something for Mervyn, Moira, that score from one of your musicals, not one of your classical pieces,' she encouraged.

'Oh Mum, I'm sure Mervyn doesn't want to hear me play, I'm not all that good.'

'You're very good,' her father encouraged. 'Play that favourite of mine, that Chopin waltz.'

Moira complied and Mervyn realised immediately that her piano playing was like her art, adequate but hardly professional. Even so as he sat in front of the glowing fire in a comfortable easy chair he felt unusually content. Good food and good wine, easy conversation, light music, there had been nothing like it in his entire life.

They were standing in the hall to bid him goodnight when Mrs Sheldon said, 'We have enjoyed having you Mervyn, we hope you'll come again very soon.'

'Thank you. You've been very kind.'

Standing near the front door Mr Sheldon said, 'That reminds me dear. Why don't we ask Mervyn if he'd like a ticket for the concert next Friday in the Civic Hall. Neither of us can go and Moira isn't looking forward to going on her own.

Would you be interested Mervyn?'

'Well I don't know. What is the concert about?'

'It's a concert by the town's orchestra. Norah is playing the flute. They always put on a good show. Singers and soloists. I've got a Masonic do on, unfortunately, so the two things have clashed. Will you consider it?'

'Well I'm not quite sure what I have on next Friday…'

He was dismally aware of Moira's eyes shifting away from his with that gentle hurt look he had come to know, and in the next breath he was saying, 'Yes, why not. Whatever there is can be put off, I'm sure. Let me have the tickets and I'll call for you.'

Three beaming faces assured him he had done the right thing and as he drove home he felt acutely aware that things were moving too fast. He wasn't sure if he was ready for them.

Chapter Four

The Civic Hall was crowded on the night of the concert and Moira whispered as they took their seats, 'Mum got rid of her ticket to some woman she knows at church.'

She looked very pretty in a dark red coat edged with a pale grey fur collar and her eyes were shining with an excitement that wasn't entirely due to the forthcoming concert.

Mervyn looked around him with interest. Their

seats were good ones, four rows from the front, and several people were smiling at them and Moira explained, 'Most of them are friends of the family. They've known me all my life.'

His heart sank.

Turning his head he was aware of a woman waving from a few rows further back and he instantly recognised Marian Adcock, the biology mistress. It couldn't in his estimation have been anybody worse.

At the interval they moved into a side hall where coffee and biscuits were laid out and almost immediately Marian was beside him, her eyes agog with speculation and Moira was blushing furiously as Marian said, 'Why it's Moira Sheldon, I didn't recognise you at first, you've grown up a bit since we last met.'

'Why don't you come round for a drink when the concert's over Mervyn. Coffee is all we'll get here.'

'Sorry Marian, but I have to see Moira home.'

Her eyes narrowed. 'Oh I'm sorry, I hadn't realised you were together, I thought you were on your own like me.'

'Are you enjoying the concert?'

'Well, it's something to do on a cold winter's night. I'm not really very musical. I didn't know you were.'

'I like music.'

'Oh well, they're going back so we'd better join them. Are you still working for your father, Moira?'

'Yes, Miss Adcock.'

'And enjoying life with plenty of boyfriends?'

Moira smiled.

Drat the woman. It would be all over the school after the holidays. They'd be adding up two and two and making five and he'd probably get a rollocking from Margaret Borley who might assume they'd been involved in some sort of association before Moira had left the school.

He didn't enjoy the second half of the concert because his mind was plagued with other matters, and he deliberately avoided looking at Marian as they left the hall by another door.

On the way home Moira asked softly, 'Did you mind meeting Miss Adcock?'

'I didn't care either way.'

'I thought you minded but I don't see why you should. I'm not a pupil now and it doesn't matter that I'm in your evening class. They're all adults there.'

'Marian Adcock doesn't bother me one way or another, Moira.'

'That's all right then.'

When they reached the house she said, 'You needn't come in, Mervyn. Norah will be home soon. Thank you for taking me to the concert, it was lovely.'

'Yes, I enjoyed it too.'

She took his hand and pressed it, then before he was aware of it she leaned forward and kissed his cheek. He could smell her perfume, feel the soft texture of her skin, the brush of her hair against his cheek and before he was aware of it she was in his arms, her lips were pressed against his and it was only Norah's high-pitched laughter as she walked up the path towards the house that brought their embrace to an end.

As he drove away he heard Moira and her sister arguing at the front door and he could only think that the younger girl's sarcasm had caused it. It was evident that Moira had trouble with her streetwise younger sister and he had little doubt that Moira would be the butt of her cynicism during the next few days.

Mervyn never quite knew how quickly it moved on from there. The invitations to tea came frequently. He met her older sister Kathleen and her husband George who worked in a bank on the High Street, and Mrs Sheldon was quick to inform him that George was due for promotion, his superiors thought very well of him.

Norah slyly informed him that George had been up for promotion as long as she could remember but somehow or other it never materialised.

'Will you continue to teach at the evening class even when the other teacher gets back?' she asked him curiously.

'No. It will end then.'

'Will you go on teaching at the other school? Aren't you bored teaching girls who aren't much good at it?'

'One day I'll make a change.'

'Oh. What sort of a change?'

'Perhaps I'll dig up my roots and go to live on the island. Make a living selling my pictures to tourists.'

'They're not there in the winter though, are they?'

'No, but I could paint in the winter and sell

them in the summer.'

'Does Moira know?'

'No. Why should she?'

Several days later he set out to walk with Moira across the park and was instantly aware of her silences. Her face was reflective, strangely withdrawn, and after awhile he said, 'You're very quiet this afternoon. Is something wrong?'

'Why did you tell Norah you were going to live on the island and not say anything to me?'

He stared down at her doubtfully. 'What has your sister been saying?'

'Only that you'll be leaving in the summer to live there permanently.'

'It's something I've dreamed about for years and done nothing about it. It's a pipe-dream Moira, besides the villa isn't mine. It belongs to my cousin.'

'But you might just do it?'

As Mervyn had anticipated his evening out with Moira had lost nothing when he returned to his school after the Christmas holidays. Marian Adcock had done her worst.

There were sly innuendoes from the men, a frosty look from the head mistress and even Martin Starkey whom he considered to be his closest friend on the staff had a quiet word for him.

'Sailing a bit close to the wind, aren't you Mervyn?' he'd whispered.

There had been no time for him to say more at that moment but the matter cropped up during the coffee break when they met outside the common room.

Martin had looked at him quizzically and Mervyn had been forced to retort, 'The girl isn't a pupil here now Martin, for heaven's sake she's nineteen, I teach her in evening class.'

'But you know what they're like. They'll put the worst possible construction on it, convince themselves you were involved with her when she was here.'

'Well I wasn't, so they can think what they like.'

'Well I'm warning you to expect repercussions from the Head.'

'And I'll be happy to put her in the picture.'

The opportunity came later in the day when he was leaving the art room at the end of the day. Margaret Borley was waiting for him at the end of the corridor and was met by his frown of impatience.

'You know what I want to talk to you about, Mervyn,' she began.

'Yes and I have to tell you Miss Borley that what I do in my own time is nobody's business but mine. Moira Sheldon is not a pupil in this school now and I am friendly with her parents. I've dined in their home and the tickets for that concert were given to us by her father. If Marian Adcock wants to make more of it that's up to her, but the whole thing is ridiculous.'

'I'm not interested in your association with Moira Sheldon now Mervyn. I am merely asking if anything was going on when she was here as a pupil.'

'And I am telling you that there was nothing beyond teacher and pupil.'

'I'll take your word for it, but you do understand I have to be very careful. The senior girls are almost adult, some of them too adult. Many of them are old beyond their years and crushes on the men teachers are bound to occur. I just didn't want people to think liaisons were going on in school after seeing one of my teachers with an ex-pupil.'

In all honesty Mervyn had to admit that Margaret Borley had a point. Some of the girls were precocious but Moira had not been obviously so. The teachers would remember her as a pretty, quiet girl, a middle-of-the-road girl with no academic distinctions, but someone who was diligent and gave no trouble.

The Moira he was coming to know would have surprised them. The Moira who was in love with him was a warm, passionate woman who had left girlhood behind when the doors of the school closed behind her.

He was well aware that she wanted more from their lovemaking. He was wary, unsure about where they were going, where he wanted to go.

The invitations from her parents were increasing as were the sly amused glances Norah subjected him to.

His class had been sketching in the local art gallery and now they were on their way back to the school in the middle of a grey January day, while Miss Adcock was bringing the girls back from a nature walk. He was hailed by a high-pitched voice saying, 'Hallo Mervyn,' and turning he saw Norah in the midst of a group of girls who were all eyeing him with great interest.

Marian Adcock joined him, observing with a

little smile, 'That's the sister I believe.'

Mervyn didn't deign to reply but unperturbed she went on, 'She's the clever one in the family, destined for university to study law.'

'How do you know?'

'My friend Emmie Standish lives in the same road.'

So, her friend would know how often his car stood outside their house and how long he stayed. How long they sat in the car before Moira ran into the house, but Marian was going on, 'Emmie quite likes the Sheldons, she says they're good neighbours, but that one's a minx, you've got the nicer of the two.'

'Your friend Emmie's assuming quite a lot.'

'Oh, come on, Mervyn. You're seeing a lot of the girl, you can't stop people talking.'

'Perhaps not, but why are they talking? Why don't they simply mind their own business?'

Marian grinned. 'If you didn't have a guilty conscience, it wouldn't worry you.'

'It doesn't worry me, it annoys me.'

From behind them came Norah's voice calling, 'Bye Mervyn, see you Sunday.'

Marian smiled at him with raised eyebrows, her parting shot being, 'I'm not sure that domesticity suits you Mervyn, and what price the villa in Greece? Is that going to go, along with your independence?'

Sunday had now become a regular occurrence. Mrs Sheldon cooked an excellent lunch and they talked about the family, holidays and what the town had to offer for entertainment. Along with talk of holidays came the question of whether

Mervyn wished to spend August in Greece when he had already stated his intention of spending Easter there.

'We were rather hoping you would join us in Bournemouth this year,' Mr Sheldon said hopefully. 'You'd enjoy it Mervyn, there's plenty to do; ever driven in the New Forest?'

'No.'

'It's beautiful, and in the evening there are shows in the various theatres. It would make a nice change from being on your own on your island.'

'I do go to work, Mr Sheldon.'

'Well of course you do, and you have a very nice job but it would be a very nice change from that island you go to, and you'd have a lot of company. You've never met any of our relatives and they're very anxious to meet you.'

'I have commitments in Greece Mr Sheldon. It's a working holiday. I paint and sell my pictures. It puts the jam on my bread-and-butter, so to speak.'

'Well you could paint in the New Forest, the scenery is just as beautiful as anything you would find in Greece I'm sure. Moira quite often does some painting in the garden, don't you, Love?'

'I'll think about it, Mr Sheldon. I have to go to the island at Easter, to open up the house and see if the studio is still standing.'

'But you will think about Bournemouth in the summer?'

Mervyn made no promises and it was Moira several days later who said, 'You won't come to Bournemouth will you?'

'Moira, I don't see how I can.'

'Couldn't I come to the island with you?'

'I doubt if your parents will allow it.'

'If I'm old enough to have a baby, I'm old enough to spend a holiday with you.'

He stared at her in appalled amazement.

'I haven't told anybody, and I'm not going to until I'm sure, then I won't be able to hide it, will I. Mervyn, I'm sorry, I didn't want anything like this to happen. My parents will be horrified and you probably won't want to marry me.'

For several minutes he sat in silence. What a fool he'd been. Now his world was tumbling around him and she sat sobbing quietly beside him. He reached over and put his arms around her. 'Moira, we'll sort something out when I get back from Greece. We'll have to tell your parents and ask for their blessing.'

'You mean you'll marry me.'

'Yes of course.'

'Can't we tell Mum and Dad we want to get married before you go to your island. While you're away we can start preparing for the wedding and in the summer we can both go back to Greece for our honeymoon.'

'You mean you're prepared to forget about Bournemouth?'

'I'm fed up with Bournemouth! Besides, I know you don't want to go and I want to spend time with you on your island.'

Moira didn't have an easy ride with her parents. She was too young to marry, she'd had little experience and if Mervyn insisted on spending every holiday abroad they'd lose touch with her.

'Daddy, that's nonsense,' she'd said adamantly. 'I'll talk him round to taking holidays in England with you and the others. Don't spoil things for me now.'

Her sister Norah had been rather more perceptive.

'How come he suddenly wants to marry you and whisk you off to Greece? He'll spend all the holiday painting pictures. You won't have any fun.'

'Well of course he won't. Besides I love to watch him paint, I might do some myself.'

'Yours are hardly in the same league.'

'They will be. I'll have my own private teacher.'

'I wonder what Aunt Agatha will say about your wedding? She's sure to say you're far too young.'

'I don't care what she says. She's old and fussy. I'm glad Mervyn hasn't met her, she's our great aunt anyway, even Mother grumbles about her interfering.'

'I suppose you're going to ask me to be your bridesmaid?'

'I might, if you behave yourself.'

'Mother will insist. Will you be wearing white?'

'Of course. Why shouldn't I?'

'I just wondered with all this haste.'

'You have a nasty mind, Norah Sheldon, you don't deserve to be my bridesmaid.'

With Marian Adcock's friend residing in the same road Mervyn had little doubt that news of his approaching marriage would soon be common knowledge around the staff.

In his absence they aired their suspicions. None of them thought it a good idea: he was too old for her, and when he pointed out that thirteen years was hardly a lifetime, they suddenly remembered that she'd been very young for her age.

Margaret Borley openly disapproved, indicating that people would talk and the goings-on at the school could become suspect. Marian Adcock was rather more spiteful, asking archly, 'I hope you haven't been doing something you shouldn't Mervyn? Time will tell.'

In the Sheldon household the talk was all of wedding dresses and wedding presents. Where they would live? Who would they invite? Who would be their attendants?

Moira studiously avoided any discussion about the baby, but when Mervyn said she must tell her parents immediately or allow him to do it, she said tearfully, 'Not before Easter Mervyn please. We can talk to them together when you get back from Greece.'

Since they had decided to marry in July, Mervyn said she could hardly expect to hide her pregnancy until then, whereupon she had burst into tears and he had been glad to take her home and drive away.

His thoughts were grim as he drove the distance to his home. Standing outside his house stood a new expensive car and, as he walked round it, he could only surmise it belonged to somebody visiting one of his neighbours. As he reached his front door, however, he was surprised to see that it stood ajar and he opened it gingerly and called out, 'Hello, who's there?'

To his astonishment the lounge door opened and a young girl came rushing out followed by his cousin Athena.

She embraced him warmly saying, 'I got a spare key from the woman next door. I've switched on the electric fire and I've tidied up the kitchen. The place was a mess Mervyn.'

'I know. I have an evening class tonight, I never seem to have much time for the house these days. What brings you here Athena? I can't remember the last time you visited me.'

'I know. I went to pick Cassie up at her school for Easter so I decided to make a detour and call round here. What do you think about my daughter?'

'She's very pretty. Isn't she rather young to be boarded out at school?'

'She's seven and a half and it's a very nice prep school. You love it, don't you darling?'

Cassie smiled.

She was a very pretty child with a wealth of auburn curls and wide blue eyes. She resembled Athena and there was about her a slender coltish grace.

'I looked in the cupboards but all I could find were tins. Is there somewhere we could go for a meal?' Athena asked.

'There's The Bull, it's not bad. How long do you propose to stay?'

'Only tonight Mervyn, and we're not staying here, we'll ask The Bull if they can put us up, but we do need to talk. Easter's coming up so you'll be off to the villa, and I want to hear what you've been doing since we last met for father's funeral.'

'I'm engaged to be married.'

Her amazement was very apparent. 'But who to

Mervyn? I didn't even know you were interested in somebody.'

'Her name's Moira Sheldon, I used to teach her at school and she's in my evening class.'

'So she's considerably young than you?'

'Around twelve years.'

'Is she pretty?'

'I think so.'

'Well do go and get spruced up, darling, then we'll go out and you can tell me all about her. When's the wedding to be?'

'July.'

'And then what?'

'We'll spend our honeymoon on the island, if that's all right with you.'

'Why me?'

'Well, it's your villa Athena. I have to ask your permission.'

'Oh Mervyn why should you? We never go there, you're the one who loves it and looks after it. I often wonder why you don't give up teaching. You could live permanently at the villa and paint.'

'Don't you think I'd be giving up the substantial for a pipe-dream?'

'Isn't that what artists do? You could charge more for your pictures, people would still buy them.'

'I'm not so sure.'

Well, we'll talk about it over dinner. We're starving, aren't we Cassie?'

Chapter Five

Mervyn chatted to Cassie while her mother booked their accommodation for the night. He found her lively and intelligent, a little assertive for a seven-year-old and when her mother joined them she said brightly, 'Well how have you two been getting on?'

'Very well,' Mervyn assured her. 'She reminds me of you when you were a child.'

'Yes, well, I've brought her up to be independent. I had to be, either that or succumb to Daddy's morose domination. I'm bringing Cassie up to put Cassie first, to think that she's the most important person in the universe and no man is going to persuade her otherwise.'

'Aren't you in danger of making her selfish and egotistical?'

'Perhaps. But I remember how we were. At the mercy of Daddy's sulks and moods. His absorption with times that have gone for ever. Surely you haven't forgotten those afternoons when we had to listen to him going on about Ancient Egypt, Greece and Rome.

'I borrowed *I Claudius* out of his library and read it under the bedclothes by torchlight. When I told him the Caesars were a bunch of depraved imbeciles I got a lecture from here to eternity on their architecture, their roads, their empire.'

Mervyn laughed.

'I agree it wasn't easy, but aren't you bringing Cassie up to be as ruthless as they were? One day she could get badly hurt.'

'Not Cassie. She'll be able to give as good as she gets to any man, woman or child. Now let's talk about your bride and your wedding. I hope you're not wanting Cassie to be a bridesmaid. Children have no place at weddings, they get in the way.'

'I rather think Moira will make her own arrangements about attendants.'

'I'm not sure Ian will be able to be there. I don't know whether I told you, but he had a nasty fall from a horse and he's in and out of a wheelchair.'

'I'm sorry Athena, I didn't know.'

'He's very independent and he doesn't like a fuss. He doesn't mind where I go and what I do so he's hardly a big problem.'

'Even when he's your husband, Athena?'

'Ian knew the sort of woman I was when he married me. He knew the sort of upbringing I'd had and we both had to make adjustments. I'm very very fond of him. He's given me security, a daughter and a respectable and solid background, I sometimes ask myself what I've given him and I have to acknowledge that it's not nearly as much.'

'What have you given him, Athena?'

'I admire him, I respect him, I'd never leave him for anybody else.'

'And has there ever been anybody else?'

Mervyn had expected her to be indignant, but instead there was a small doubtful smile on her face, then she said calmly, 'Darling Mervyn, I was twenty-three and Ian was forty. I met a man on a cruise liner and I thought I was in love with him. He was handsome, charming, and he gave me an ultimatum: leave your husband or we're finished.'

'And?'

'We finished. I had to choose between the substance and the shadow, I chose the substance.'

'What happened to the charmer?'

'He got off the ship at Genoa without a backward glance. I never saw him again.'

'Were you very miserable?'

'Miserable, angry, unsure, but time passed and I stopped thinking about him. I'm happy enough with my life Mervyn, I wish I felt as confident about yours.'

'What do you mean by that?'

'This girl with the doting family. You've never been used to a doting family. You could feel suffocated.'

'I doubt it.'

'Well I'm not so sure. Are you going to start house-hunting?'

'I suppose we must sooner or later.'

She stared at him doubtfully. 'It all sounds so haphazard Mervyn. You haven't come to terms with it yet.'

'Well the wedding plans are going ahead, Moira's mother is having a ball and the time will simply flash past after I return from the island.'

'Doesn't she want to go to the villa with you?'

'No, she wants to help her mother with the

wedding plans. Besides her family are very circumspect I doubt if they'd agree to her going to the island with me, even with an engagement ring on her finger.'

'How perfectly droll.'

'It's the way they are Athena. Uncle Bertram never interfered with us because he preferred to be left alone to do his own thing. They think as a family and act as a family.'

'I'm beginning to think that Daddy didn't have much wrong with him after all.'

'I like being with them Athena. They're close, they enjoy being together, they care about what happens to each other. They have parties, go on holiday together, enjoy the closeness.'

'What will happen when you spirit her away to Greece for your honeymoon?'

'That's different.'

'But it won't always be different. In other years they'll want their little girl with them. If you have children they'll want their grandchildren with them too. Are you quite sure you've thought this through?'

'Yes, I'm quite sure. If you could stay on a day or two you could meet her.'

'Not possible darling. Ian's expecting us home. Poor dear, he's not too well right now and he's looking forward to seeing Cassie. Remember what I said Mervyn, I don't want you to suggest turning her into a bridesmaid, she'd hate it and so would you. I expect there are a good many children in the family.'

'I'm not sure.'

Mervyn looked across the table at Cassie

quietly eating her pudding. She had taken no part in their conversation but he felt sure nothing had escaped her.

He smiled at her, and as she pushed her plate away she said 'Why can't I be a bridesmaid Mummy? Jayne Anderson was a bridesmaid last summer, she had pale pink roses in her hair and a long pink dress.'

'I'm sure the bridesmaids have already been chosen dear, and we are a rather long way away in Scotland.'

'Does that mean we won't be coming to the wedding?'

'I really think you should keep your father company while I'm away Cassie. He sees you so seldom now that you're at school.'

'You're always telling me I make excuses not to do things, now you're making an excuse.'

'No darling, I'm stating a fact. Now if you've finished your dinner perhaps I should take you up to your room and see you settled down for the night. Now say goodnight to Uncle Mervyn.'

Cassie held out her hand in a very grown-up manner and did not attempt to embrace him. She appeared too grown up, too mature, but, then, when he thought about the girl Athena had been, he realised how much like her Cassie was.

When Athena returned to the table about half an hour later she smiled as she took the chair opposite.

'I know what you're thinking about Cassie, Mervyn, that she's too adult, just as I was.'

'Something like that.'

'Did she say any more about wanting to be a bridesmaid?'

'No. She knows it wouldn't do any good. I can't see my daughter running round with a host of other children all dolled up in silks and satins. She's bossy and precocious, they'd probably resent her and she'd be hurt. Only children get all the attention, Mervyn, and I have to admit that Ian and I have spoiled her a little. We knew she'd be an only one.'

'How does she get along at school then?'

'Well enough. She figured prominently in a recent school concert. She's like me: what other people think about her doesn't unduly worry her. Surely you must have taught girls like that.'

'Some. Most of them were rather unpopular, they didn't much care.'

'That's what I've just been telling you, Mervyn. I never cared; Cassie won't care either. I have to admit I've mellowed considerably: I've had to, being married to Ian, but Cassie'll probably marry an altogether different sort of man. I hope so.'

'I thought you were happy with Ian.'

'I am, happy enough.'

'But you're not averse to lecturing me on my choice of a wife.'

'You're not like me, Mervyn. You're sweeter, you could be brain-washed into anything. I never could. Have you thought about it, Mervyn? There are going to be a host of people on your bride's side of the church and hardly anybody on yours.'

'It isn't important. I shall invite one or two

members of staff and their wives, and you'll be there I hope.'

'Come wind or high water, darling, I'll be there.'

At the door of the hotel she embraced him warmly and stood looking through the glass doors watching him walk across the car park to his car. His meeting with Athena had disturbed him in some strange, inexplicable way. He couldn't see Moira and Athena ever becoming friends. But, then, it hardly mattered: they were not destined to meet very often.

Moira's attitude to the impending marriage was also giving him some concern. He wanted to tell her parents about the baby but she was refusing adamantly. 'We'll tell them together when you get back from Greece,' she argued. 'After all, it's only three weeks and I don't want them going on and on about it while you're away.'

He had to accept it, but when he listened to them going on and on about the wedding arrangements he became increasingly worried.

The subject of attendants came up constantly and Mrs Sheldon was anxious to make sure that he had nothing to complain about.

'We have such a large family, Mervyn. We simply don't want to offend anybody. Obviously, our elder daughter will be Moira's matron of honour and Norah will be her other grown-up bridesmaid. There are five little cousins, four girls and a boy, they'll want to take part.'

'So many,' Mervyn murmured.

'Well yes, and doesn't your cousin have a daughter? She'll want to be included, I'm sure.'

'No, Cassie will be remaining in Scotland with her father who isn't very well at the moment. Only Athena will be coming to the wedding.'

Moira and her parents stared at him in some surprise.

'But aren't they the only relatives you have?' Mrs Sheldon persisted.

'Yes, but we've never been a family like yours.'

'There'll hardly be anybody on your side of the church, we'll have to tell our friends to sit on your side, I'm sure they'll understand.'

'Well, I'm inviting one or two of my colleagues and their wives, I've asked Martin Starkey to be my best man.'

'It'll feel like being back at school with all those teachers there,' Moira complained.

'I was your teacher too, Moira,' Mervyn said evenly.

She blushed. 'I know, you were different.'

He had thought that she would try to persuade him from visiting the island but to his surprise she accepted it.

'You won't want to bother with all the wedding arrangements,' she said logically. 'Mum has everything in hand, and when you get back there'll be very little to do.'

'Except tell your parents what we should have told them much earlier,' Mervyn said stolidly.

Her eyes had filled with tears. 'I wish you wouldn't keep going on about it, Mervyn.'

He flew out to Athens on a cool windy morning two days before Easter. He had bade a tearful farewell to Moira the evening before. Her family had wished him well and Mrs Sheldon had been more than kind, handing him boxes packed with home-made cakes and a large cooked chicken.

'I'm sure foreign food isn't nearly as good as you get here,' she'd said. 'Moira made the sponge cake and I made the rest. Do you have friends there?'

'Yes. The village priest and I have a good woman who comes to clean the house.'

'A priest did you say? Is he Catholic then?'

'Greek Orthodox, I believe.'

'Oh well, we don't know much about that, do we, dear? How old is the woman who cleans the house?'

'Around fifty, I think.'

'Does she have children?'

'Yes, several daughters and two sons who are fishermen.'

She was staring at him with narrowed eyes and he hastened to say, 'Most of the children are married.'

'And how old is the one who isn't?'

'Around twelve.'

Her curiosity both irritated and amused him. Athena would have thought it intrusive and hilarious. In her opinion the Sheldons would be dubbed bourgeois and hardly her sort.

As he stepped off the boat that plied between the islands he was glad of the fleece-lined coat he had elected to bring. Easter there could be unpredictable, sometimes verging on the heat of summer, sometimes as cool as the land he had left behind him.

Every time he came back he was of the same

opinion that nothing ever changed: he believed the island had looked exactly the same for uncounted centuries.

He looked round the small living room appreciatively. It was spotlessly clean and kindling had been gathered and stacked up in the fire grate ready for lighting. In the kitchen milk had been left, and bread, and in the centre of the table was a large basket of fruit and a flowering plant.

He had left a supply of tinned fruit and meat in the larder and there was Mrs Sheldon's chicken for his evening meal. He unpacked quickly, putting his things away in the bedroom before making up the bed with clean linen and blankets. By the time he had finished, the sun had disappeared and a chill wind was rustling through the shrubs in the garden so that he was glad to put a match to the fire and settle down in front of it with a tray of food on his knee.

He was clearing away when there was a knock on the door and he hurried to open it, expecting to see the woman who looked after the house, but it was the priest who stood there smiling and waiting to be invited in.

'Already the house looks lived in,' he said looking round him.

'Yes, Maria has looked after it very well, even laying me a fire. Do sit down, Father. Would you like coffee or a glass of wine?'

'Wine I think. Try this one, the year was a good vintage.' He produced a bottle of wine from the canvas bag he carried and, thanking him warmly, Mervyn placed two glasses on the table.

'Has anything changed since I left here at the

end of August?' he asked.

The priest smiled. 'Two of the old people have died, one or two of the young ones have moved away to the cities and tomorrow I have two wedding ceremonies to perform. You are invited, one of the girls is Maria's eldest daughter.'

'Are you sure I'll be welcome?'

'Most certainly. I was asked to invite you by Maria and her husband. What has life been doing to you my friend?'

'I am engaged to be married.'

The priest raised his eyebrows and his smile was one of delight.

'And when is the happy event due to take place?'

'Sometime at the end of July and then we shall be coming here for the whole of August.'

'That is good then. Will your new wife love the island as much as you do?'

'I hope so. She wants very much to see it.'

The priest sat back in his chair smiling and Mervyn filled up his glass, then went to add more kindling to the fire.

'I have another message for you,' the priest said softly. 'I showed the Contessa into your studio, I didn't think you would mind. She saw a picture you painted of my house and she admired it, I thought it would do no harm to show her round your studio.'

'No, I don't mind. But most of the canvases I have there are unfinished, I'm sure the studio was a disappointment.'

'On the contrary, I have a commission for you.'

'A commission!'

'Yes. Apparently her husband had a favourite place in the garden where he spent all his time the summer before he died. It is a little arbour surrounded by his favourite shrubs, from where he could look out across the stretch of cliff to the blue sea beyond. She showed me a photograph taken in the garden that last summer and she is hoping you can copy it.'

'I've never done much with portraits I'm afraid, I'm a landscape artist.'

'Nevertheless, my boy, you will look at it and tell her what can be done.'

'Is she here for some time?'

'I'm not sure, but I told her you would be here for two weeks and would call to see her. She is charming.'

'Are her children with her?'

'They are coming here for Easter. Alex is eight, Sophia is seven. The little girl is talkative, the boy more reserved.'

'I never met either the Contessa or her husband. My uncle purchased the villa and when I was here it was shuttered up and empty.'

'Yes, unfortunately, it has been like that for several years. When their father died the children were little more than babies.'

The day after his arrival was filled with music from the two wedding ceremonies in the morning to the late evening when the wedding guests went to their homes. It had been decided to make it a joint affair and the wine flowed freely throughout the day.

The young men danced in shirt sleeves rolled up over bronzed arms, the girls wore pretty white dresses and none of them were averse to dragging Mervyn into the stream of merrymakers.

Moira would love this, he kept thinking. The music and the scented breeze were as intoxicating as wine and there was plenty of that. Never in her life would she have seen anything like it, the joy, the spontaneous exuberance, the music that echoed over the countryside long after the sun had sunk in brilliant crimson behind the distant hills.

He couldn't help thinking about the plans being made for his own wedding ceremony. The grey stone church with its squat square tower, the throng of Moira's relatives he had not met, and Moira, beautiful and happy in her wedding finery. Though, he thought, with a sudden stab of guilt, wouldn't she look rather larger by then? What would Athena make of it all? Athena who was so discerning and sophisticated, and his friends who had all known the girl Moira.

What would she think of the tiny villa with its old-fashioned kitchen and ancient cooker and cooking vessels. He sat looking round the living room with some anxiety. Instead of painting he should think of having somebody choose new curtains and cushions, new rugs for the floors, new plant pots for the wide windowsill, but surely Moira would want to choose these for herself.

It was true the room had a charm about it, but Moira was accustomed to the niceties of English living: the delivery of the morning milk, the shops filled with everyday necessities, the whistling of the newspaper boy bringing the morning paper.

They were things he hadn't missed. That was home, this was different, and because it was different, he saw only the charm and never the deficiencies. He'd grown up with them, Moira had grown up with holidays in Bournemouth and a more orderly existence.

His thoughts turned to his promise to visit the Contessa in her villa but he was none too happy with the arrangement.

He had never concerned himself with portrait painting and he had visions of the interior of the villa with its priceless pictures and ornaments. Perhaps he would be able to convince the lady that he would be unable to accept the commission she was offering.

Chapter Six

It was mid morning when he climbed the hill leading up to the huge ornamental iron gates set before the villa above. He hesitated, peering uncertainly along the twisting drive edged with intricately laid-out shrubs and flowerbeds.

A long marble terrace stretched in front of the house and behind the marble pillars the villa rose with exquisite symmetry against the cloudless sky above.

He heard the sound of children's voices and as he climbed the steps a little girl came running along the terrace followed by a boy. They paused to stare at him and he smiled, unsure if the children spoke English. He need not have worried because immediately the girl said, 'I'm Sophia, who are you?' in perfect English.

'I am Mervyn Corwen from the villa below, I have called to see your mother.'

'Does Mama know you are calling?'

'I believe so.'

'Then if you will ring the bell on the door, Mario will take you to my mother.'

He smiled his thanks and the children stood to one side to allow him to pass and he looked down into the dark brown eyes of the boy. He was tall, his eyes serious and there was a grown-up gravity about his expression that gave a sudden maturity to his size. His sister was evidently precocious, the boy was more distant.

'Aren't you going to tell me your name?' he asked gently.

'Alexander.'

'But that is a wonderful name, a very famous name. My old uncle would have been delighted to hear it.'

'Was that the old man who sat writing in the garden below?'Alexander asked curiously.

'Yes. Did you ever meet him?'

'No, my mother told me about him.'

'He was a scholar who loved ancient history. That is why he would have liked your name.'

The boy smiled, and his sister pouted prettily.

'Why would he like Alexander and not Sophia?' the girl asked with a frown on her pretty face.

'My uncle liked any name connected with ancient history.'

'And Sophia isn't?'

'I'm really not very sure.'

'Oh well, he isn't there any more. Did he go away?'

'I'm sorry to say he died.'

'Really. My dog Bubbles died, we all die sometime, don't we?'

She gave a sharp tug to her brother's hand and together they ran along the path towards the beach below.

He continued his climb up the steps and when he looked along the terrace he saw that a woman walked towards him from the entrance. She smiled and his first instinct was to think that hers was a face he might want to paint. She was incredibly beautiful. Her dark brown hair framed a face of classical proportions, and dark blue eyes smiled at him and he realised instantly that he had been staring at her.

She held out her hand saying, 'I am Leonora, the Contessa Andoineto. Before we talk perhaps you would like coffee, or a glass of wine.'

'Coffee would be very nice.'

'Then we will drink it on the terrace at the side of the house, it has the most beautiful view, the one I would like you to paint for me.'

He was surprised how easy it was to chat to her. She had travelled extensively and could talk knowlegeably on a great many subjects. After they had finished their coffee she said, 'Now I think we will walk down to the little balcony overlooking the sea where my husband liked to spend his time in the summer before he died. It is very beautiful there, it will be easier for me to return there with company.'

They stood on the jutting piece of rock in front of the tiny summerhouse and looked across the expanse of water towards the island beyond. It was as beautiful as the photograph had led him to believe and he looked down at it while he pictured the sick man sitting staring out at his favourite view, securely wrapped in blankets to cut out the soft winds.

'The view is lovely,' he said. 'I can paint it but I'm not sure about the figure of your husband. I have never painted portraits professionally if that is what you want.'

'No no, I want you to concentrate on the scenery, the figure on the photograph is not too detailed, an impression of him would suffice.'

'Suppose I do what I can with it and allow you to tell me if you are satisfied.'

'Yes, I think that's a good idea. How often will you need to come up here?'

'I'll make sketches and take photographs, then I can work on the canvas in my studio or elsewhere. Did Father Cristofson tell you I am only here for two weeks?'

'The picture couldn't be completed before you return home?'

'I doubt it. I could finish it at home but I would lose the colours, I shall be returning here at the end of July.'

'Then you could finish it then. Will you be alone?'

'No. My wife will be with me.'

'Oh, I'm sorry, I did not realise you were married, the priest did not mention it.'

'He didn't know. I am getting married in July.'

She smiled. 'Then how can I ask you to work on my picture when she will need you to show her the island and spend all your time with her?'

'Moira will understand I'm sure. I'm hoping she will paint a little herself, in any case we shall work something out.'

'In the meantime Mr Corwen I will look for you here during the next few days.'

'Of course.'

Mervyn did most of his painting sitting in the summerhouse because a chill wind blew constantly across the headland and the colours were frequently changing, so that more and more he had to refer to the photograph to enable him to capture the colours of summer.

Occasionally the Contessa would join him, sitting silently, engrossed with his sketches. Servants from the villa served them with coffee and light refreshments and the children would join them, sitting with their mother watching him work.

It was always the girl who tired of watching him first, then she would start to chatter, or race away across the grassy slopes of the garden, but the boy stayed, as totally absorbed in Mervyn's artistry as his mother.

On his last evening she invited him to dine with her at the villa after the children had gone to bed, and he hesitated, saying that he had brought only casual clothes with him, clothes that were hardly suitable for eating dinner with a contessa.

She laughed.

'When my husband was alive we always dressed for dinner because he was a traditionalist. It was the way he had been brought up.'

'But not you?'

'I like dressing up, I enjoy beautiful clothes and the grand occasion but I enjoy informality too, particularly here when there is nothing to dress up for. Please have dinner with me, and I promise I shall enjoy the simplicity, the delight in being completely relaxed.'

They dined alone where the long windows looked out into the darkness where a little wind rustled the leaves of the trees and overhead stars shimmered in a midnight blue sky. True to her word she wore a short simple silk dress that showed off her slender tanned arms and the dark lustrous hair framing her exquisite face. He listened to her voice, low and only faintly foreign to his ears, and she talked about her family, her childhood in Italy, her children, but not her husband, and later she showed him round the rooms of the villa and the treasures it contained.

When they stood at last looking out across the moonlit gardens it seemed to Mervyn that her thoughts were on other years, that there was nothing more to say.

He looked down at her hair touched by silver moonlight and the gentle curve of her cheek and he felt an inexplicable urge to take her into his arms. It was not passion that prompted it, merely a desire to comfort a woman who seemed strangely alone and lost. She looked up at him and smiled but he was unprepared for her words.

'You have told me very little about the girl you intend to marry, Mervyn. Most men would have talked of little else.'

After his first embarrassment he said evenly, 'I thought you wanted to talk about your husband, it seemed more logical somehow.'

'I must apologise, I have probably bored you terribly.'

'No, no, I understand. Your grief is still very real, you must miss him terribly.'

'It is five years since my husband died, Mervyn.'

'Even so.'

'Most people grieve because they have loved, others grieve out of a sense of guilt, a feeling that they could have loved more, given more, this is how I see myself.'

He stared down at her, it was an admission he had not expected, and one she could not expect him to reply to.

'I have surprised you,' she said quietly.

When he did not reply she said, 'I did love Giorgio after a fashion, but it was never the love he wanted, which I was unable to give.

'When I married him I was desperately in love with somebody else, a man my parents disapproved of. He was a boy I met on a summer holiday in Portofino when I was sixteen. He was handsome, charming, full of life and exciting as only the young can be exciting. My family told me that I would forget him, that Giorgio was eminently more suitable, older, richer, wiser and every bit as handsome. I come from a very powerful family where money talks and at seventeen I was rushed into an engagement with a man I did not love. I respected Giorgio, he was a good man, but after Lorenzo he was dull, unimaginative, but I believe he loved me.

'At eighteen I was married and we were living in Rome, then the troubles started.'

She was silent, staring out unseeing across the garden and he was reluctant to break the train of her thoughts. He waited, aware that there was so much more she wanted to tell him.

'If you have never been afraid you will find it hard to understand what happened next but I can assure you I began to fear for my sanity, even my life. Lorenzo would not let me go. He came to Rome, he followed me wherever I went, and when he did not see me he pestered me with letters and telephone calls. I was living on my nerves, and when Sophia was born he wrote letters threatening what he would do to her. That was when Giorgio brought in the police and Lorenzo was arrested.

'It was a terrible time for us. Our friends knew, people all over Rome knew, and to get away from the scandal Giorgio bought this villa so that I could spend the summer here. Lorenzo was serving a prison sentence and he had been warned that when he was released he must stay away from us.'

'Did you still love him?'

'No, how could I? But I understood him and I pitied him. I had betrayed Lorenzo and my husband, I was a very unworthy wife and when Giorgio became ill, I really believed that it was I who had brought so much unhappiness into his life that had caused it.

'When he died, so young, with so much to give

the world, I was desolate with grief and with guilt. The good priest comes here and tries to comfort me, he sees only the loss of love, I can never tell him how very different it could all have been.'

'Don't you think it's time now to forget the bad and remember only the good?'

'I'm sure you are right. Are you wondering why I have told you all this?'

'The need to confide in somebody I feel sure.'

'Not entirely. It is because you have never talked about your love, and I have wondered if you are like I was, marrying somebody because you feel you must instead of because you cannot live without her.'

'Perhaps we English are rather more reserved, I'm sure that has something to do with it.'

'Perhaps. We Italians are possibly more volatile, we show our emotions instead of hiding them.'

'What happened to Lorenzo? Did you ever see him again?'

'No, and yet there are times when I find myself thinking he is behind me on a crowded street, or hiding behind the rocks on the beach when I walk down to the sea. I hope he has forgotten me. I feel he must know that Giorgio is dead and that I am alone living the life he would wish for me. I do not think we shall meet again.'

Later that night as Mervyn walked down the hill to his villa he found himself listening to the wind stirring the trees and the sound of the breaking surf on the sand and he could imagine how every sound in the night brought a sense of fear into the heart of the woman he had just left.

He had known her only two weeks and yet she fascinated him, her beauty and her charm, even the haunting sadness that occasionally chased the vitality from her face.

If he loved Moira, how could he feel this sudden enchantment for another woman? Of course it was foolish to think there could ever be anything between Leonora and himself: they were poles apart, two very different people from different cultures, but what she had said was true. He had never once felt the urge to talk about Moira, and yet it was Moira he was going home to, Moira and a marriage he had never envisaged.

Ahead of them was the prospect of her parents' anger, the snide comments of his colleagues, and life with a girl who may or may not want what he wanted. In August they would return to the island, but would it be the same. He very much doubted it. With those thoughts in his mind he closed the door of the villa behind him and finished packing his suitcase for the journey home.

It was early afternoon when he unlocked his own front door and he stared down the long hall with something like dejection. It felt cold and although he had only been away two weeks there was a thin film of dust on the hall table and the plant which he had thought he had watered hung its leaves accusingly.

He switched on the electric fire in the living room and went through to the kitchen to put the kettle on. He was about to take his suitcase upstairs when the telephone rang shrilly in the hall and he went immediately to answer it. He was not surprised to hear Moira's voice with a certain relief in it.

'You're back. I rang before but there was no answer. Did you have a nice time?'

'Yes thank you. What sort of an Easter have you had?'

'Oh hectic. I'll tell you all about it when I see you. I did some shopping for you Mervyn, I thought you might not have anything in.'

'That was kind of you dear, I'll pick it up in the morning.'

'No. I'll bring it round tonight. I want to see you. Don't you want to see me?'

'Well of course. But by the time I've unpacked and warmed up the house and had a meal, it will be rather late.'

'It doesn't matter. Dad will drive me over and you can drive me back, or I'll get the bus.'

'Do we need to trouble your father tonight, Moira?'

'You don't sound very pleased to see me. If you don't want me to come round, then I won't.'

'Yes of course I do. I'll see you later then.'

He felt irritated by the telephone call. It was too pushing. He didn't want to see her father so soon, they had to talk before they spoke to her parents, couldn't she see this for herself?

He found a tin of soup in the kitchen and there were a couple of eggs which he hoped were fit to eat. Moira was a good kid even to think of shopping for him, why couldn't he be grateful?

Mr and Mrs Sheldon sat facing each other in

their living room listening to their daughter's voice on the telephone in the hall, and they eyed each other apprehensively.

'It sounds as if he's back,' Mrs Sheldon said. 'Moira's very edgy, I've asked her if anything's wrong but she says she's fine and why don't I leave her alone. Do you suppose she's having second thoughts?'

'Well, of course not. It's because he's been away and all these wedding arrangements going on. I'm not surprised she's edgy, I'll be glad when it's all over.'

'Well arrangements do have to be made. We can't let things get out of hand. I'm the one who's had to do most of it.'

'I know dear, and you've done well. She should be grateful instead of being snappy with you. Don't say anything – she's coming back.'

When Moira entered the room her mother was leafing through the pages of a magazine and her father was doing his crossword. Her mother looked up with a smile and Moira said, 'Mervyn's back, he's had a nice time. I told him I'd go round with his shopping tonight. Can you give me a lift, Dad?'

'I can drop you off when I go to my meeting. Will Mervyn bring you home?'

'I expect so, unless you call for me.'

'I'll call for you love, the meeting should be over around ten thirty.'

They heard her humming to herself as she ran upstairs and Mr Sheldon said, 'There, she seems happier already, you've been imagining things, love.'

In her bedroom Moira decided to change into something more attractive than the slacks and sweater she was wearing. Her hands were trembling as she buttoned her blouse and she was dismally aware of the fear with which she viewed the evening ahead.

Over and over again she thought about the words she would say to him, thinking up new ways to say them, new excuses, afraid of his anger, his accusations. Tomorrow her life might be completely changed, her dreams shattered irrevocably. There would be hysteria, tears, pleas for forgiveness, but would they be enough? She had never been more afraid in her entire life.

Her father viewed her silence on their drive to Mervyn's house with something approaching anxiety. He put it down to pre-wedding nerves, but Moira had never been a worrier and of late the sunny smile had gone from her face and they were treated to long silences and fretful tears.

'Not getting cold feet, are you, love?' he asked her anxiously.

'No, of course not.'

'Well you don't have to marry him if you don't want to. It's better to find out now rather than later. Don't you be worrying about the wedding arrangements, all your mother and me want is for you to be sure and happy.'

'You can drop me here on the corner, Dad, have a good meeting,' was all she offered, and before he could answer her she had opened the car door and stepped out into the road.

'Around ten-thirty,' he called to her, and with a wave of her hand she was away running along the road towards Mervyn's house.

She stood for several seconds outside the front door before she was able to pluck up enough courage to ring the bell, then she waited anxiously for Mervyn to open it.

He was smiling, reaching out for her, holding her gently in his arms, then taking the shopping bag from her he led the way into the kitchen.

She knew that she was babbling. Asking questions about the island, about what he had done there, about his journey home, suddenly aware that he was gazing at her oddly.

She was talking too much, too aware of her sticky hands clenched at her sides, and aware of the tremor in her voice as she said, 'Dad's calling for me around ten-thirty on his way back from the meeting.'

'Then we'll go and sit in the living room where it's warmer, I can put the shopping away later.'

'I'll do it for you,' she said hurriedly.

'Later Moira, I want to hear what's been happening while I've been away.'

'My sister and her husband came for tea on Easter Sunday, and we went over to see Great-Aunt Agatha. She hasn't been well. We didn't go anywhere to stay, Mother's been so busy with one thing and another…' Her voice faltered and he said gently.

'What's wrong, Moira? Don't you think we should speak to your parents now, as quickly as possible I think.'

She dissolved into tears and he took her into his arms, soothing her gently. In the next moment she had struggled free and was saying, 'I'll go into the kitchen and make a cup of tea.'

'Tea can wait Moira, we have to talk.'

'I know, but later Mervyn.'

He watched with dismay as she ran out of the room and he heard her opening and shutting cupboards in his kitchen.

Chapter Seven

She came with the tea and made a great show of pouring it and passing his cup to him. Her face was tear-stained, and, nonplussed, he watched while she took her seat in an armchair at the other side of the fireplace. That she was afraid was evident, but he put her fear down to the fact that they could not delay speaking to her parents any longer.

At last he said, 'We don't need to speak to your father tonight Moira, we'll speak to both your parents as soon as possible.'

The tears increased and perhaps more impatiently than he intended he said, 'Moira please stop crying, it isn't the end of the world, and we're not the first people it's happened to. I'll talk to them, you can leave it to me.'

'That's just it,' she sobbed. 'You don't have to any more.'

'What do you mean?'

'You don't have to marry me. There isn't any baby.'

What was his first reaction? Relief, dismay,

suspicion and before he could say anything she said, 'I was wrong, and now you don't have to marry me. We can tell them we've changed our minds, that we're not suited, that you've found somebody else, anything, but you don't have to marry me now.'

'Does this mean that you've changed your mind, that you don't wish to marry me?'

Her eyes opened wide in agonised astonishment. 'Oh Mervyn no, I love you, but I don't want you to think I was trapping you into marriage, some girls do it I know, I know girls who have, but we can tell my parents we've changed out minds, it doesn't matter about the wedding arrangements. Dad said only tonight that they weren't important.'

'So you have discussed it with your parents.'

'No. No. He thought I was unhappy about something. I was, I was unhappy about having to tell you about the baby and having you think I'd said there was a baby just to see if you'd marry me. Dad won't mind so much, it's Mum who'll mind most, the reception and the dresses, the relatives, even the church, but it'll only be a nine-day wonder, it's nobody's business but ours.'

'So everything has been arranged?'

'Well yes, before I knew. We booked the church for the last Saturday in July, and the wedding reception at the Royal Hotel in Durbridge, you know that large hotel at the crossroads. I've been going to the dressmaker's and everything is in hand.'

Mervyn's head was spinning with talk of bridesmaids and dresses. He had been away for two weeks but the arrangements had gone ahead and something like anger showed in his eyes, so that Moira cried, 'Mervyn, I told Mum not to be in such a hurry but she said the dressmaker was a busy woman and we had to get in early. You must know what it's like, so many people get married in the summer and the Royal Hotel already have three booked in for the same day.'

When he didn't answer the tears started afresh and she said, 'I don't think I want to wait for Dad, I'll go home on the bus and I can telephone him from home to tell him he needn't bother.'

'You can't go home on the bus, Moira. I'll get the car out.'

'No, I want to go home on the bus. I don't think you want to talk to me any more tonight. I want to go out of here alone, if you want to see me again you know where I live.'

She was out in the hall, grabbing her coat, fumbling with the lock on the door and he took hold of her hands and held them close. 'We'll talk tomorrow Moira, you're in no fit state to talk tonight. I don't like you going off like this, you're being very silly.'

'Yes, well, I am silly, I've made a mess of everything and now you'll hate me. I won't blame you if you never see me again.'

She went, running blindly down the path and out through the gate. He heard the sound of her flying footsteps on the pavement until he could hear them no more.

He returned to the warmth of the living room and sat staring in front of him. He didn't have to marry her, but had anything really changed? Things had gone too far, her mother's involvement with the wedding arrangements, everybody in the town must know by this time that Moira Sheldon was engaged to one of her old school teachers. Then there was the minister at the church, the retinue of ushers and bridesmaids, the guests and the reception, the bridal gown and the flowers.

As Moira had said, weddings had been cancelled before and become a nine-day wonder, but she had also said that she loved him. At that moment he didn't ask himself if he loved her.

Moira sat on the bus staring miserably through the misted windows. For days she had been dreading her meeting with Mervyn and now it was over, how he would react when he had had time to think about it was another matter. She had no doubt that he would come to the house to discuss things normally, he was an honourable man, at the same time she had always known in her innermost heart that she had been the besotted one. Now there was an opportunity for him to tell her parents they had made a mistake, they were no longer in love, if he came to tell them that, she would die, she would simply die.

Surprised when she entered the house her mother said sharply, 'Isn't Mervyn with you?'

'No. I told him not to get the car out, he's only just got back. There was a lot to do.'

'Didn't your dad say he'd pick you up?'

'Yes, but I didn't want to wait for him. He's

always late. I'll telephone the club and leave a message for him.'

'When shall we see Mervyn?'

'You will, Mum, when he's sorted himself out. Are you on your own?'

'Yes, your sister's in her bedroom doing her homework. Have you been crying?'

'Of course not. It's started to rain.'

Her mother looked at her pointedly, but Moira escaped by going into the kitchen.

Mrs Sheldon was troubled. All over Easter her daughter had moped about the house, and when she was questioned was close to tears. If she didn't want to marry Mervyn then she had to say so. It would be difficult, informing the vicar and the guests, cancelling the reception, and the dressmaker. It would cost them a great deal of money but Moira's happiness came first. Resolutely she marched into the kitchen to confront her daughter.

'Something's wrong, Moira, and I want to know what it is,' she demanded.

'Nothing's wrong.'

'You're hardly speaking to any of us, you don't want to do this, that or the other and you hardly said a word to Great Aunt Agatha.'

'I never know what to say to her, she's always telling all of us what we should and shouldn't do.'

'She was very nice. It was natural that she should be interested in your wedding. Have you quarrelled with Mervyn?'

'No, of course not.'

'Well, young couples are traumatised just before a wedding and he's been away. Your father and I thought he ought not to have gone so close to your wedding.'

'It's months off, I told him to go. Besides he had to see that everything was all right there.'

'I can't think why he has to take you there for your honeymoon, you'd think he'd want a change.'

'He has people there who want to buy his pictures. Besides, I want to go there.'

'Well, just remember, if there's anything I need to know I'd rather know sooner than later. When are we seeing Mervyn?'

'Probably over the weekend. He starts back at school on Monday.'

'Yes well, the sooner we see him and get everything sorted the better. We're not at all happy with your attitude, Moira. It's worrying your father and me.'

Mervyn sat slumped in front of his fire. His thoughts were a mixture of freedom, relief and a more insidious feeling that he had been manipulated.

It was all very well for Moira to tell him he needn't marry her after all, but in the next breath had come talk of the arrangements already made for their wedding. Before he went to Greece he had been certain that he loved her, now he felt more and more unsure.

He found himself remembering Leonora, her beauty, her charm, the sophistication of an older more worldly woman. How would he feel in Greece with Moira when he had to see Leonora?

His thoughts turned to Athena. If he told

Athena he knew exactly what she would say. 'Don't go through with it, Mervyn, you don't have to. She's been devious, she's tried to trap you.' But he wasn't sure that she had.

He found himself remembering the girl who had sat at her easel with the sunlight from the window gilding her hair, a girl with a shy smile that lit up her face whenever he stopped to speak to her. That girl's face had been innocent and free from guile, he would not believe that Moira had tried to trick him into marriage.

He had been tired when he returned from Greece, but he found that sleep eluded him. For hours he tossed and turned in his bed, but it was almost dawn before he sank into a troubled sleep.

It was Saturday. Moira usually went shopping with her mother on Saturday morning so he decided to drive over to their house before they left for the market. The dull rainy morning matched his mood exactly and his mood was not enhanced when Norah opened the door with a pert smile on her pretty face.

'I'd forgotten what you looked like,' she said with a grin.

'Surely not in two weeks.'

'Mervyn's here,' she called along the hall and both Moira and her mother came out of the kitchen to meet him.

Mrs Sheldon was smiling, but on Moira's face there was that look of uncertainty he had seen the evening before.

Mrs Sheldon did most of the talking, asking him about his holiday, then she was launched into the preparations for the wedding and Moira escaped into the kitchen saying she was going to make coffee.

As soon as she'd gone, Mrs Sheldon said, 'I don't know what's happening with Moira, Mervyn, she seems so nervy and withdrawn, she's close to tears whenever we mention the wedding. Is something wrong? If there is, it's better to find out now rather than later.'

'Would you like me to have a word with her, Mrs Sheldon?'

'Oh, would you, Mervyn?' she breathed with something like relief.

Moira was setting out cups and saucers at the kitchen table but as soon as he opened the door she busied herself at one of the cupboards and he could see that her hands trembled nervously as she closed the cupboard door.

He sat down at the kitchen table, but when she stood with her back to him he said evenly, 'Come and sit down Moira, we have to talk. Your mother is very worried about you.'

'I don't see why.'

'She has every right to be concerned, you're a bag of nerves. We no longer have to tell your parents why we should marry, I would have thought that would have removed some of the reasons to worry. Am I right in thinking you've gone off the idea?'

She spun round to face him, her eyes wide with fear, and with tears in her eyes she muttered, 'It's not me. It's you who've gone off the idea.'

'Have I said so?'

'No, but you must have. You think I've tricked you into it, that I was holding a pistol to your head, and now the preparations have gone on too long for you to get out of it. I told you you needn't marry me now, we can tell them today.'

'Moira, I have never said I didn't want to marry you, I have never said that I thought you tricked me into it, but we do seem to have been catapulted into it with unnatural haste. You're really very young, in spite of all the wedding arrangements, wouldn't you like to postpone the wedding until you're absolutely sure?'

'I am sure, I've never been more sure of anything in my life. I'll never want to marry anybody else. It's you who wants to postpone it.'

'No, Moira, it isn't. You're feeling guilty and you've too much imagination. We'll go and tell your mother that she's done splendidly and agree to everything she's done.'

He stood up and went to take her into his arms. She clung to him like a lost child and he dried her tears.

'What's your mother going to think when she sees you've been crying?' he asked gently.

'I'll make the coffee and be in with it in a few minutes. You can tell her everything's fine.'

So to Mrs Sheldon's utmost relief Mervyn reassured her that it was pre-wedding nerves that had brought on the trauma, and she accepted his explanation gratefully before launching into a list of the arrangements that had been made.

'The dressmaker is booked up for months so we had to tell her immediately what was required. Three grown-up bridesmaids and four small children. I was a little bit bothered about your cousin's little girl but you did say she wouldn't want to be a bridesmaid Mervyn.'

'That's right. Cassie won't be coming to the wedding, she'll be in Scotland with her father. Ian isn't well, he won't want to make the journey.'

'But your cousin will come?'

'Yes I'm sure she will.'

'There are going to be a lot of us and hardly any of you.'

'That doesn't matter. I was never a part of a large family, there was always just Athena and me.'

'What an unusual name she has. What is she like?'

'Beautiful, fashionable, easy to talk to.'

'I wonder what she'll think of me,' Moira said.

'She'll think that you're pretty and sweet and I'm sure you'll get on like a house on fire.'

More doubtfully Moira said, 'She'll think I'm too young for you, too unsophisticated.'

Mervyn squeezed her hand and smiled down into her eyes. 'You worry too much, darling, about everything. If you're going shopping with your mother I'll give you a lift into the town.'

Mrs Sheldon wouldn't hear of it.

'Norah will come with me to the market, you and Moira take a walk in the park. I think you both need to talk, it's only a few months to your wedding.'

So they set off together to walk through the park which was just around the corner. They walked hand in hand, and as they walked down the street they encountered some of the Sheldons' neighbours including Marian Adcock's friend who was in her front garden pruning some of the bushes. She smiled, and came towards the gate, but Moira decided they should cross the road and all Mervyn could do was smile in return.

'She's terribly nosy,' Moira said feelingly. 'Every time she sees my mother she's asking questions about the wedding and anything else she feels she should know.'

They were walking along the path towards the children's boating lake when a black labrador came bounding towards them, his tail wagging exuberantly, and with a wide grin on his face. Mervyn recognised the dog instantly as Martin's dog Bruce and he bent down to pat him, whereupon the dog rose on his haunches to lick his face. Then they were hailed by Martin's voice calling, 'Down boy, Mervyn doesn't want you to eat him.'

Moira greeted him with a shy smile. She only knew Martin as her old history teacher and history had never actually come easy to her, and as he fell into step beside them she ran on ahead with the dog.

'She's a nice kid,' Martin said. 'I'm not surprised she's a bit overwhelmed by the two of us, even if you're the man she's going to marry.'

'Anything been happening I should know about over Easter? Mervyn asked.

'Like what for instance?'

'Well I rather gathered before the break that changes were afoot.'

'I don't think they will affect me, are you thinking they may affect you?'

'Well yes, the art teacher is usually a sufferer, any teacher that doesn't have much of a say with the three R's.'

'Well, I shouldn't worry before you have to. Come Monday and you'll be informed. Enjoy the island over Easter?'

'Very much. I got a commission from a titled Italian lady to paint a picture of the coastline from her summerhouse.'

'Nice. Young or old?'

'Young. Beautiful.'

'But you came home to Moira?'

'Italian Contessas are hardly in my league.'

'But you're still spending your honeymoon on the island?'

'Well yes. Moira would like to see it, and summer can be very beautiful there. What will you be doing?'

'We'll be off to France as usual. My wife never seems to want to go anywhere else. Two weeks is enough for me, and I don't like to leave my dog for longer.'

Mervyn had never had a dog. Uncle Bertram had not been an animal lover so he was hardly eligible to comment on Martin's affection for Bruce.

'I take it it will be a dressed-up affair, Mervyn. I don't possess a morning suit, I'll have to hire one,' Martin said glumly.

'Well I do rather think Mrs Sheldon will want a very formal affair. I've left all the arrangements to them and from what she's said they seem to be going to town.'

Martin groaned. 'Is your cousin coming down

for the wedding?'

'I do hope so, she's the closest relative I have, but they do go away a lot.'

'Mmm well, you've around three months to change your mind and for the bride to change hers. I doubt if she will, though.'

'Why do you say that?'

'Because for a girl of her age you're the ultimate catch, a bit different from the lads her friends are entangled with. Nothing wrong with that dear boy, a lot of men will be envying your good fortune. I know one or two who've said as much.'

Mervyn laughed. 'Really, and who might they be?'

'It's not the men you need to worry about, it's the women. Marian Adcock for one. She's had plenty to say.'

'I'm sure she has.'

'Well, you have to admit she was pinning her hopes on you, the one member of staff who was unattached, and to have you snaffled from under her nose by a mere pupil takes some getting used to.'

'She'll survive. Marian would never have been my cup of tea with or without Moira.'

Martin smiled. 'Well, see you on Monday then. She seems to be enjoying herself with my dog. Here boy, time to go home.'

The dog bounded towards them followed more slowly by Moira, who responded to Martin's smile with a shy blush.

The rest of the weekend was spent in a flurry of wedding plans. Bridesmaids and dresses, the reception, the flowers and the church and the guests on the Sheldons' side who seemed never ending.

'You're sure your cousin will be coming?' Mrs Sheldon asked anxiously.

'Yes I'm sure she will.'

'Why won't she bring her husband?'

'He isn't at all well, and Cassie will be staying at home with him.' He was trying to remember what Ian looked like: he had only met him twice and seen his name on Christmas cards. It was difficult to explain to people like the Sheldons who were such a large close-knit family that their daughter was marrying into a family so totally different.

He had brought the Contessa's picture back with him, and, on Sunday afternoon, he set up his easel and worked on it while Moira sat nearby, plying him with cups of tea, yet totally absorbed in his work.

She'd never be able to paint like Mervyn: he was a genius, she totally mediocre, she thought. It embarrassed her when her father went on and on to Mervyn how they could become a team on the island and that people would want to buy her paintings too.

Mervyn always received his comments with a gentle smile but offered no reply.

'I'll get off home after tea,' she said. 'It will give you a chance to get ready for school in the morning.'

He did not induce her to stay, and as he drove back to his home he reflected that there was still a constraint between them that exiled those heady moments of passion they had known.

There had been more tenderness in their goodnight kiss than passion, and he put firmly out of his mind the feelings Leonora had aroused in him at their last meeting. The urgent need to take her into his arms, the wild beating of his heart, the desperate need for more.

Chapter Eight

They were half way through the first morning of the new term and Mervyn surveyed his pupils with practised tolerance. There was no one outstanding, and the morning had progressed uneventfully.

Perhaps Martin had been wrong about problems afoot and no doubt he'd learn more in the staff room.

Marian Adcock met him at the door, and with a coy smile on her face said, 'Back to normal Mervyn, two weeks fly by, don't they? Enjoy the break?'

'Yes thank you, did you?'

'I didn't do anything much, the weather wasn't good. We don't all have an island retreat to go to.'

He was spared from saying anything else as Martin passed him a cup of tea and nudged him over to the window.

'Heard anything?' he hissed.

'About what?'

'Well, she's had Jeffries in, so I reckon you're

the next on her list.'

Jeffries was the music master. He gave singing lessons, and looked after the school choir. Mervyn felt sure that music and art were probably the two subjects the powers-that-be would regard as expendable.

'Jeffries isn't here. Is he still with the Head?'

'I don't think so. He's probably thinking over what she's been saying to him.'

'You don't know anything for sure, Martin.'

'No, that's true. But rumours have a way of circulating.'

At that moment the door opened and Andrew Jeffries came into the room. They watched him helping himself to coffee from the side table, but from his expression there was no way of knowing if he had received bad news or good.

When Marian Adcock crossed over to his side he drank his coffee quickly and escaped. Martin grinned. 'He's obviously no intention of letting Marian grill him,' he said. 'If I don't see you this afternoon I'll wait for you after school.'

The summons came to the Head's office half way through the afternoon and even before he closed the door he could hear the hiss of conversation from the girls.

He found the headmistress standing at the window, staring down at the tennis courts with an absent frown on her face. She turned to face him with a brief smile and took her chair behind the desk.

'Did you enjoy the Easter break, Mervyn?' she began.

'Yes, very much.'

'I suppose you did quite a bit of painting?'

'Some, but Easter doesn't bring in many visitors to the island. Did you get away at all?'

'I went to stay with my sister in Norfolk. The weather wasn't good. I suppose you're wondering why I have sent for you so soon after the break?'

Mervyn didn't speak but he watched her fingers playing nervously with the pencils on her desk.

'I don't quite know how to put this, Mervyn, but the school governors and the parents are having serious thoughts about art and music in the curriculum. They think there's too much of it and you have to admit we have no budding Leonardos or Joan Sutherlands.'

'True.'

'So you admit they have a point?'

'Of course. I have to ask you how it will affect me.'

'Well the art classes will have to be cut down obviously, and in their place will be more classes on subjects regarded as more important to the girls' futures.

'The cuts would mean your art teaching would be cut to two mornings a week. I see you have only your art school qualifications, so it might be difficult to ask you to take on teaching another subject, other than games, I suppose?'

'I was appointed as the school's art master.'

'Well of course, and now things have changed. I had Jeffries in this morning and we talked on similar lines. He has adamantly refused to teach anything beyond music, says he'll retire and teach privately if the worst comes to the worst.'

'That might work with music. It wouldn't work with art.'

'No, I can see that.'

He stared at her glumly, and she said quickly, 'Could you try to get additional work, Mervyn, by teaching in further education? Adult students go to evening classes because they seriously want to paint, they don't have it thrust upon them. You would have to shop around for a post. The man you covered for is back at work, I believe.'

'Yes, and the pay for teaching adult students will not be nearly so good.'

'And you do have to think about your forthcoming marriage. You will have a wife to keep, rather different than being on your own, I think.'

Silently Mervyn agreed and the Head went on, 'The changes will not be made until after the summer holidays, so I'm not asking you to decide today. Talk it over with your fiancée Mervyn.'

He was dismissed, and on the way to the art room he was glad that the corridors were empty and he reached it unmolested.

The girls were chatting in groups, and in some annoyance he snapped, 'Get back to your easels and try at least to pretend some interest in what you're doing.'

They took their places nervously. He was not usually so caustic, that was the reason for his popularity, after school they would no doubt be speculating as to what had annoyed him.

Martin was waiting for him after school and his heart sank when Marian Adcock caught up with him.

'You got your pep talk, did you?' she enquired.

He nodded.

'Oh well, I shouldn't worry about it too much. She'll no doubt ask you to help out on the playing fields. Jeffries, I rather think, is past the rough and tumble.'

'Nothing is settled yet.'

'Well, she won't hang about. The powers-that-be have to be seen to get their money's worth.'

Martin lowered the window of his car and called out, 'I'll give you a lift Mervyn, it's coming on to rain.'

'And he's curious,' Marian added.

He climbed into Martin's car, and Marian strode off to her own. 'I thought she'd jump onto the band wagon. Did Borley have you in?'

'Yes. Art is going the way of music. The kids are having too much of it. She wants me to cut right down, and fill in by teaching games. Jeffries has refused and is talking about leaving.'

'I thought he would.'

'Well he has a point. He specialises in music. I specialise in art. When she saw I wasn't enthusiastic about the alternative, she suggested I teach adult students in some adult education college.'

'Well, you filled in very well here.'

'In the short term, but there isn't anything here now. I'd have to shop around.'

'And you have a wedding coming up and from what I know of the Sheldon family they would prefer to keep their little girl close by.'

Silently Mervyn agreed with him while he worried about what his news would do to Moira.

He was half way through cooking his evening

meal when the telephone rang and Moira's voice said, 'You are coming round tonight, Mervyn? There's so much we have to discuss with Mum and Dad.'

He could hardly believe that it was his voice saying, 'I'm sorry Moira, I can't manage tonight. There's a beginning-of-term meeting at the school and I don't know what time we'll be through.'

'Oh dear, that's awful. Do you have to go?'

'I'm afraid so. It's not something I can get out of.'

'It will have to be tomorrow then.'

'The entire week promises to be very hectic. You and your parents go ahead, darling, I'll fall in with everything you suggest.'

'But when will I see you?'

'I'll telephone as soon as I can see daylight.'

'All right then.' The line went dead.

She was annoyed and she had every right to be. He should be talking to her about their wedding and about his job but somehow he couldn't bring himself to.

He looked along the length of the hall where smoke was pouring out of the kitchen and he hurried to turn down the gas. The steak was burnt. It really didn't matter: he wasn't hungry.

He made a cup of tea and helped himself to cheese and biscuits which he took into the living room on a tray then he turned on the television and sat slumped in front of it with the tray on his knees.

It would have done him good to talk about things, but not to Moira. He wished Athena lived nearer. Athena's mind was clear-cut and uncomplicated; she would offer suggestions, see beyond tomorrow, discover alternatives. He discarded the idea of telephoning her, but it would not go away, and later in the evening he decided it was worth a try. She was probably away from home. That Ian was a semi-invalid didn't seem to interfere with their holidays abroad. All the same, he was glad to hear the sound of her voice.

'How was the island?' she greeted him, 'Did you do much painting?'

'Yes, I have a commission for the Contessa.'

'Well done, darling. You're moving onwards and upwards.'

'I need to talk to somebody Athena. You seem the best person.'

'Not your little bride?'

'Not for this.'

'Then what is it?'

'I wished you lived nearer, it's difficult to carry on a conversation on the telephone about something like this.'

'Would you like me to come down?'

'Could you?'

'I don't see why not. Ian won't mind if I leave him for a few days. Book me in at the hotel, I quite enjoyed staying there the last time I was with you.'

'You can stay here.'

'Mervyn darling, I hate your house. When you move into something more up-to-date after your marriage, I'll probably be pleased to stay with you for a few days, but until then I'm happier at the hotel. I'll get away tomorrow morning, see you in the evening. How's that?'

'That's marvellous Athena. Thank you for coming, and give Ian my best wishes. How's Cassie?'

'She's fine. I'll give you all our news tomorrow evening. How's your fiancée?'

'Very well and busy with wedding plans. Everything seems to be happening too quickly.'

She laughed. 'You can tell me all about the wedding Mervyn, I've been thinking about it a lot, I can't quite see you married.'

'This time next year I'll be an old married man.'

'That's what bothers me darling. See you tomorrow.'

Athena had decided they should have dinner together at her hotel, and then go back to his home later in the evening. He looked at her now, curled up in a corner of the settee, like some beautiful exotic patrician beauty of ancient Rome.

She was wearing long black velvet trousers and a brilliantly patterned velvet tunic. She wore her blonde hair in a gentle page-boy style that framed her delicately tinted face with its arched brows and eyes the colour of an azure sea.

He watched her inserting one of the black cigarettes she favoured into a long ebony cigarette holder and he asked himself what the Sheldons would make of his one relative.

He thought about Mrs Sheldon with her stout walking shoes and country tweeds, her dark felt hat pulled down firmly over her permed hair, and

Moira whose mother hated to see her wearing slacks, preferring to see her daughters in the skirts and blouses, and pretty afternoon frocks they had grown up in.

He became aware that she was looking at him with a tantalising smile on her lips, saying softly, 'You never did approve of my style Mervyn.'

'I never questioned it Athena.'

'Perhaps not in so many words, but just then you were asking yourself what your new in-laws would make of me.'

'Well, you're certainly different.'

'I like being different. Now tell me what's so pressing that you wanted me down here.'

So Mervyn poured out his troubles and she listened gravely without interrupting until he suddenly realised he seemed to have been talking for hours.

He stared at her helplessly, and she said, 'I thought you wanted to talk to me about your wedding, not your job. You don't want to be an ordinary school teacher Mervyn, you never did.'

'No I don't. Uncle Bertram wanted it for me, something academic, never art. I never wanted anything else. Not particularly teaching, but teaching was a starting point.'

'But you've often felt frustrated teaching girls who had no aptitude.'

'I know, but at least I felt I was teaching something I had an affinity with, now I don't know what to do. This couldn't have come at a worse time.'

'Because of your marriage, you mean?'

'Well of course. It's three months off, we should

be house hunting. Now I'm not even sure that I shall be staying on here.'

'What's the alternative?'

'Some other school where I would teach art, perhaps even in further education, there must be something somewhere.'

'Another place, another job, teaching inferior talent when you could be painting yourself and selling your pictures.'

'Hardly something that would keep us in some degree of affluence Athena. Most painters earn very little during their lifetime. They're only acclaimed after they've been dead some years.'

'You do very well on the island.'

'Well yes, for a few weeks in the height of the summer.'

'Have you never thought of moving there permanently?'

He stared at her in some amazement. 'Athena you can't be serious. I shall have a wife to consider, she would probably hate it, particularly in the winter, and there would only be the locals living there.'

'But you told me yourself! People asked you to do paintings for them and they would pick them up here. Besides, now that you're doing this one for the Contessa, couldn't she find you other customers?'

'You make me sound like a grocer Athena.'

'I know, but we are talking about money at the end of it, aren't we Mervyn? Artists, grocers, doesn't everything all boil down to money?'

He watched her reaching out to refill her wine glass and he felt suddenly exasperated. With her cigarette holder and the long shimmering earrings. With her mode of dress which seemed too alien and exotic for his modest living room, and irritably he said, 'You're not taking this at all seriously Athena, perhaps I shouldn't have asked you to come.'

She was immediately contrite.

'I do think it is serious Mervyn, but shouldn't you be telling your bride instead of me? I haven't been able to understand all this haste to get married, unless of course there's some reason I don't know about.'

She fixed him with a half smile and he snapped.

'There isn't a reason.'

'Then why so soon? She's only just out of the schoolroom, your schoolroom. Without this wedding, you'd have been able to think in the long term about your job. Now you have to think about it too quickly to accommodate everything else you've planned.'

He knew she was right.

'Are you asking me to tell you what I would do in your position?' Athena asked.

'Well, yes.'

'I would talk to your fiancée, tell her what has happened at the school, tell her you both need to put your wedding on hold until your job is sorted out. You really don't want to have other worries at this time. On the other hand, you can go right ahead and go on with it. After all you do have a job, you're not being sent packing – well, not quite. You could get married, buy a new house, do the reduced lessons, and the games periods.'

Of course it all sounded so simple. Jeffries

hadn't been able to accept it but then Jeffries was nearing retirement age anyway. Retirement for him was a long way off.

Athena had presented him with two alternatives. Reason told him which he should take; his heart told him the other.

Moira ran down the road to the bus stop impatiently eyeing the empty road until she saw the bus lumbering round the bend. There was anxiety in every line of her waiting figure and she went to sit at the back of the bus twisting her gloves nervously in her hands.

She had thought Mervyn would telephone her immediately she arrived home from work but there had been no word. After seven o'clock she telephoned the school to ask if he was there but the caretaker answering her call had said the staff had all gone home.

She telephoned his house but there was no reply from that, and Moira was not to know that he was sitting down to dinner with Athena at the hotel.

He was having second thoughts. He was angry with her, believing she had tricked him into marriage. It was his way of letting her down gently. It wasn't fair, she had to know, her parents had to know.

She got off the bus but instead of going immediately to his house she walked along the row of shops in the next road, looking in their windows. She had to know, and yet she was afraid of meeting him. At last she turned into his road, surprised to see an unfamiliar car parked outside his front door. The car was new and expensive. It probably wasn't a visitor at Mervyn's house at all, but there was a light shining through the curtains in his living room and she hesitated at the gate.

Mervyn would not like to think she was checking up on him, particularly if he had a visitor. Some other teacher, perhaps the headmistress. At that moment she was wishing she was older, more confident. After all she was his fiancée, she had every right to visit his house and enquire why he hadn't bothered to telephone her.

She was still hovering on his doorstep when the woman who lived next door came out, regarding her curiously. Moira smiled, and the woman said, 'Is the bell off love, I should try knocking. Mr Corwen has a visitor, I saw them going in together around eight o'clock.'

Moira smiled and pressed the bell button again, and then through the glass in the door she saw a figure moving to open it.

Mervyn looked down at her in surprise and the words tumbled over one another as she said, 'I telephoned you Mervyn, I telephoned the school, I thought something had happened to you, I hope you don't mind my coming. Is there somebody with you?'

'My cousin Athena, Moira. Come in and meet her, she wants very much to meet you.'

Chapter Nine

Moira sat on the edge of her chair and had never felt more uncomfortable in her entire life. She felt bemused by the elegant smiling woman sitting curled in the corner of the settee and uncertain about the pleasantries they were exchanging when she felt sure something more serious had been going on before she arrived.

Athena was charming. Saying how much she'd been looking forward to meeting her, questions about the wedding arrangements, saying how much she was looking forward to it, but Moira was aware of the anxiety in Mervyn's eyes, the dismal feeling that she should not have come.

'Are you staying here with Mervyn?' she asked at last.

'No, I'm staying at the hotel. After all, Mervyn is at school all day but we can meet up in the evenings.'

'How long are you staying?'

'I'm going home before the weekend. Why don't you and Mervyn dine with me at the hotel tomorrow evening? We really should get to know one another, Moira.'

Moira looked at Mervyn anxiously, and he was quick to say, 'Yes why don't we?'

'My mother would like to meet you. Perhaps you'd like to have a meal with us,' Moira said hopefully. But with a little smile Athena said,

'Actually dear, the hotel would suit me better – as I shall have to be off early the next morning, but I shall look forward to meeting all your family in July.'

'Mervyn didn't tell me you were visiting him.'

'It was all arranged very quickly. Mervyn has a problem at the school, and we always talked about everything and helped each other out, he thought I might be able to give him an opinion.'

Moira looked at him sharply. 'What sort of problem, Mervyn?'

'Well I had every intention of discussing it with you too darling, but Athena offered to spend a few days here and I thought it would be nice to see her.'

'But what's wrong at the school?' she persisted.

'New arrangements, upheavals of one sort or another, I'll tell you all about it later. Now what do you both say to a cup of coffee?'

There was an odd smile on Athena's face, and Moira felt shut out. Why couldn't Mervyn tell her about the school now? He'd discussed it with his cousin, surely it was more important that he should discuss it with her.

She felt strangely inadequate, too young, in the face of the sophisticated woman eyeing her with something like compassion.

Mervyn produced the coffee and once more he and Athena were discussing family matters. Athena's husband and Cassie, Cassie who was having singing and dancing lessons, Cassie who's examination results were giving cause for some annoyance from her father.

Athena laughed. 'After all Mervyn she's so

much like me. Daddy always complained bitterly about my prowess at school, but I loved to dance. Instead of getting married out of the schoolroom I should have gone on with my dancing. Miss Howlett said I had great potential.'

Mervyn laughed. 'Even dancing requires some dedication, Athena, and that was something you never had.'

'Do you have a job?' she asked Moira.

'I work in my father's office.'

'Oh well, that's nice. Did you ever have dancing lessons?'

'No. Dad thought it more important to have shorthand and typing lessons. He was probably right.'

'I'm sure he was. But you paint, don't you? Mervyn said you were one of his pupils.'

'Yes, I go to evening classes now, but I'm not all that good.'

'That's probably because you measure your work against Mervyn's. When we meet again you must show me some of your work.'

'I wouldn't dare. You've seen Mervyn's and mine is rubbish compared to his.'

Neither Mervyn nor Athena disagreed and the conversation lapsed into silence while Mervyn refilled their cups.

Athena consulted her watch saying, 'I'll be getting back to the hotel, Mervyn. Shall we say around eight tomorrow evening? I'll look forward to seeing you both.'

She rose to her feet and Moira looked in some dismay at the picture she presented. What would her mother make of this beautiful, exotically dressed woman and what would she be wearing for the wedding?

Moira rose to her feet and Athena kissed her on both cheeks. She could smell Athena's perfume, feel the velvet softness of her cheek against hers, the silken texture of her blonde hair against her face, and then Mervyn was escorting her out of the room. Moira sat back in her chair, a bemused expression on her pretty face.

At the door Mervyn said, 'I wish you hadn't mentioned the school, Athena.'

'I know. You have to talk about it, Mervyn. She's very pretty, and she's sweet. Now that I've met her I can understand her appeal, but it's not going to be easy for you, darling, I wouldn't like to be in your shoes.'

He watched her drive away, then, with a sinking heart, he returned to Moira.

He was aware of the sulky expression on her face, but he said brightly, 'I'm so glad you've met Athena at last. She does live some distance away so I don't see very much of her.'

'I wouldn't have met her if I hadn't decided to come,' she said quickly.

'Why do you say that?' he prevaricated.

'Well, I didn't know she was here, did I? You said you were busy with meetings at the school. You didn't say she was coming.'

'No. When I told you about meetings at the school, I didn't know she was coming.'

'Why do you need to talk to Athena about the school when you don't talk to me?'

'I had every intention of discussing it with you, Moira.'

She bit her lip nervously. It was all going terribly wrong. She was nagging him, and he was already distrusting her. Why couldn't she be nice, why was he looking at her in exasperation?

She jumped nervously to her feet. 'Perhaps I'll get off home now Mervyn. Will you call for me tomorrow evening? Do you really want me to go with you?'

'Well of course I do. Moira, what is this?'

'Well, wouldn't you prefer to be meeting your cousin without me?'

'Come along, I'll drive you home and I'll call for you tomorrow evening around seven-thirty.'

'I can easily get the bus.'

'And I can just as easily drive you home.'

The silence on the way to Moira's home was oppressive and neither of them knew how to break it. He brought the car to a halt outside her front gate and she said, 'Are you coming in, Mervyn?'

'Not tonight dear, I am rather tired. I'll see you tomorrow around seven-thirty.'

He kissed her gently and drove away.

Inside the house she put her coat away in the hall cupboard and ran upstairs to her room, while in the living room her parents looked at each other in some dismay.

'Now what's the matter?' her father said sharply.

'Shall I go after her?' her mother ventured.

'No. Better leave her. The way things are at the moment I'll be surprised if this wedding goes ahead. We want some straight answers from both of them before we make any more arrangements.'

'The arrangements are already made,' Mrs Sheldon said dolefully.

'Ay well, we're making no more until we're sure things are all right.'

Norah eyed her sister with malicious humour as she changed her dress yet again.

'What's so special about Mervyn's cousin that you've got to doll yourself up in your Sunday best?' she enquired.

'She's very fashionable. I want to look right. Which do I look the best in, the red skirt and blouse or the blue dress?'

'I don't like the dress, I never did.'

'Then you think the skirt and blouse are better?'

'I've never had dinner at the hotel so I don't know, do I?'

'You're hopeless.'

At that moment the front doorbell rang and Moira said anxiously. 'That's Mervyn, and I'm not ready yet.'

She heard her mother letting him into the hall and the sound of their voices coming from the living room.

Her parents saw nothing different in Mervyn's greeting of them. He was much as he'd always been. Courteous, friendly, and when Moira came at last into the room he was carrying on a conversation with her father on the merits of Rotary versus Masonic activities.

Moira looked very pretty in her new red skirt and white silk blouse and in some anxiety she said, 'Do I look all right for the hotel?'

'Well, of course you do,' her mother said and Mervyn said, 'You look lovely Moira. Don't let Athena influence you, she's always way out in my opinion.'

Reassured, Moira donned her camel coat and after kissing her parents said, 'I don't suppose we'll be late Mum, Mervyn's cousin is leaving in the morning.'

They waited for Athena in the hotel lounge and she came towards them with outstretched hands, kissing them both. She was wearing a black dinner gown, exquisitely cut and sophisticated. A beautiful foil for her pale blonde hair. There were pearl earrings in her ears and a three-row pearl necklace round her throat and Moira felt juvenile and gauche even when Athena ushered them into the dining room chattering brightly.

Moira remembered very little about the conversation in the dining room, and very little afterwards about the meal, but it was in the hotel lounge later that Athena said, 'I think now is the time Mervyn to chat about your current predicament and see what solutions Moira has to offer.'

'Is something wrong?' Moira asked anxiously.

'Things are happening at the school that I don't like, Moira. There have been rumours flying around for years, but last Monday they became reality and now I have to think very seriously about where I want to go from here.'

Moira was looking at him fearfully and Mervyn decided not to beat about the bush, however unpalatable his words might be.

'They have given me a choice of staying on at the school, but in a reduced capacity. I'd have to take games – or else I have to look elsewhere.'

Moira breathed a sigh of relief. 'But that's all right then Mervyn. You can still stay. You surely won't mind that, will you?'

'Yes, I'm very much afraid that I shall mind. First and foremost Moira, I'm an artist, I like to paint more than I like to teach, but I will teach, and paint in my spare time, I can't, however, see myself taking games lessons.'

'What will you do then?' she asked, staring first at Mervyn then at Athena who sat back in her chair quietly listening.

'Look for another art teaching job in another school, possibly another area, or get out of the profession altogether.'

'But what will you do then?'

'Athena has shown me an alternative. I have to know if you agree its feasibility. Unfortunately, Moira, it's only three months away from our wedding, so decisions will have to be made very quickly.'

'What alternatives?'

'To live on the island and paint fulltime. We can spend five or six months there, all the summer in fact and tourists will buy my pictures. I already do quite well in the one month I'm there, I can do much better if I'm there longer. It's also possible that the Contessa can find customers for me, she has as good as said so. It's up to you Moira, could you bear to live for more than half a year on a Greek island watching me paint?'

All Moira could think about at that moment was that the marriage was still on. He wasn't trying to get rid of her, and yes it would be wonderful to live on the island. None of her friends had the remotest chance of doing anything like it. She would be married to an artist. She'd been proud of marrying a school teacher, but an artist was something else.

One look at her shining eyes told Mervyn that at least for the present she was for it. He very much doubted if she would still be for it when she'd had a chance to discuss it with her parents.

When he deposited her at her front door she said, 'Do you want to talk to Mum and Dad about it, Mervyn?'

'Not just yet Moira, there's still a lot to think about. Perhaps over the weekend.'

'Oh yes, you'll have a better idea then what's happening. I liked Athena, she's very nice. I wish I could look like her but I don't suppose I ever shall.'

'You're not in the least like Athena, Moira. She's quite unique, she always was.'

'But you think I'm just as nice?'

He laughed. 'I never thought of Athena as being nice, she was always too controversial. I'm glad you two have met. You'll be able to prepare your family for her, that way they'll not be too dumbfounded.'

She laughed. She loved Mervyn when he was funny. Everything was going to be fine, her mother could press on with all she needed to do, she could tell Norah to shut up when she was being peevish and there was so much to look forward to, so much that was different.

Over lunch the next day Mervyn talked to his friend Martin, and Martin in his usual logical fashion proceeded to offer his fors and againsts, while paying due respect to what he felt Moira's views would be once she had fully taken in the idea.

'You won't have an easy passage,' he said. 'By this time her parents will have had their say and they won't want their little girl to be living abroad. They obviously thought she'd done very well for herself, a school teacher with a steady job and a pension at the end of it. Don't artists reputedly starve in garrets? Don't they become famous when they've been dead 300 years?'

'It's a bit different these days,' Mervyn said adamantly. 'People are holidaying abroad, they see artists painting views they like and they buy them to remind them how beautiful abroad can be. I've got quite a reputation on the island. They come to look at my pictures, to walk round my studio. I think it can work.'

'And what will she be doing while you're working?'

'She can go to the market, look after the house and the garden, do some painting herself. Other women do it, most women would enjoy the life, the scenery and the sunshine. Why should Moira be any different?'

'And her family?'

'What's to stop them coming out for a few weeks in the summer. Her sister could spend the summer holidays with us.'

'And this is the family who are tied to Bournemouth and the whole conglomeration of them holidaying together?'

'People can change. Once they've had a taste of

foreign travel they could take to it.'

'I hope so, for your sake, dear boy, but if they don't, you could have a moaning wife on your hands, hankering after home and family, then what?'

'I don't know. I'm talking to her family over the weekend. I'll have a better idea, then, of how they're taking to the idea.'

Excited by the idea Moira had been quick to tell her parents, and now she was suffering the backlash of their alarm.

'What is he thinking about?' her father complained. 'Giving up a steady decent job as a school master for something that might or might not work out. He's got qualifications. And what's so special about art anyway?'

'He loves art, Dad. He's brilliant.'

'Well, we all know you think so, but what sort of money is he going to make? How can he even think of going to live permanently abroad, how can he expect you to tear yourself away from us to go with him. It's a different world, a different life. Your mother and me don't want him to do it, Moira. We'll have words to say to him on the subject, never fear.'

'You can't tell Mervyn what to do with his life, Dad, it's his business.'

'Not entirely. Not when it concerns my daughter.'

'I'll be his wife. He will come first.'

'Like I said, we'll talk very seriously to him about it. I suppose that cousin of his has had something to do with it.'

'I liked her, she was very nice.'

'Doesn't the villa belong to her?'

'I don't think that matters. They've obviously come to some arrangement. Athena's a woman of the world, I don't want her to think we're all country bumpkins.'

'She can think what she likes. I don't know the woman. All I know is that you're my daughter and we don't want you living in Greece or anywhere else abroad for that matter.'

'Dad, it's Mervyn's job we're talking about. He's unhappy with the way things are going and he's worried with the wedding coming up. I don't think you should interfere, after all it's his life, mine too.'

All she was aware of in the days that followed were the whispered conversations from the living room whenever she was out of it, her mother's tear-stained face and her father's obstinate condemnation.

Sunday lunch had been a silent meal with an atmosphere you could cut with a knife.

Mrs Sheldon gave her husband several warning looks, Norah looked on expectantly and Moira looked from one to the other anxiously. Mervyn was well aware that very soon they would express their opinion forcibly but he was prepared for them.

He decided to be the first to raise the issue.

'I expect Moira has been telling you about matters at the school,' he began.

'She has, Mother and I don't know what all the fuss is about. It's not as though you're in danger of losing your job. If you give something like that up, there'll be a dozen or so teachers itching to take your place.'

'If the job wasn't changing, I wouldn't be thinking of leaving. If I could step into a similar job to the one I already have at some other school I'll give it a try, but there are far more art teachers than jobs, and with the cutbacks, an art teaching job is going to be hard to find. I'm not qualified to teach other subjects. And I know nothing about games, and care for them even less.'

'Have you tried to find another school?'

'No. If I do, the same problem is likely to occur wherever I go. Art is not deemed to be a subject likely to endow a child with a career at some future date. Most of the pupils I teach are disinterested, apathetic even, and at the end of the day what does it do for them when other subjects mean so much more? If a painter wishes to paint he will do so, lessons or no lessons.'

'But to live abroad, away from your friends and family,' Mrs Sheldon said.

'I have no family.'

'No, but Moira has. She's got us, a lot of us, and we don't want her to go.'

'I can see that you will miss Moira, Mrs Sheldon, and she will miss you, but this is my life, my work. I have to do the best for me and for Moira. You can come to stay with us, and in the winter we'll be glad to come back for several weeks each year. You're not going to lose your daughter, and Moira herself has offered no objections.'

'She's dazzled by the idea, that's why. It's something none of her friends are doing. She thinks she's got one over them, I doubt if she's really understood how it's going to change her life.'

'Well, I do understand how you feel about it, but when all is said and done, it's Moira and myself who have to decide.'

'And if Moira decides she doesn't want it, will the marriage be off?' her father demanded sternly.

'No Dad no,' Moira cried. 'I am going to marry Mervyn whatever you say, and if he wants us to live abroad, then live abroad we will.'

Chapter Ten

The last Saturday in July dawned bright and sunny and Mervyn's heart lifted. It was a good omen.

Moira had been obsessed with the weather for her wedding day. July had been wet with grey skies and sudden bursts of rain, and every time they had met she was fearful that their wedding day would be suitably unpredictable. Now the sun was shining out of a clear blue sky and he cheerfully cooked bacon and egg and waited for the kettle to boil.

Everything was going well. He had sold his house to a young couple, who would be setting up home together, and they had bought his furniture and everything else he had no further use for. They would be moving in the following week.

Athena had arrived yesterday and was staying at the hotel. Last night he had invited Martin and his wife to dine with them there and the evening had been pleasant and amusing. Moira had decided that she would hold a party for a few of her girlfriends: dinner in a small hotel where the food was good and not too far from where they lived. She told Mervyn it was unlucky for the bride to see her fiancé the evening before the wedding.

Athena had presented him with the deeds for the villa in Greece, which Mervyn had accepted with some reluctance.

'Oh come on,' she'd said with a smile. 'You've always loved it and we'll probably never get there again. Ian is hardly fit to travel anywhere and I'm not sure about Cassie.'

'You know that you and Cassie can always come to us.'

'I know darling, but Cassie is growing up so fast, I'm not sure what ideas she's got buzzing around that head of hers. Take the villa and enjoy it. I've also brought you a wedding present.'

'Surely not. The villa has to be enough.'

'I'm giving you that Grecian urn Daddy was so fond of. He insisted that it was valuable and I should treasure it. I hate it and so does Ian. I'd have to be a historian to love it, but you always liked it. Now it's yours.'

Mervyn was remembering the Grecian urn which had been his uncle's most prized possession. Beautifully shaped in terra-cotta, slightly grazed here and there due to its antiquity, but Uncle Bertram had assured him that it would one day be priceless.

'It is a family heirloom,' he told Athena. 'Shouldn't Cassie have it?'

She trilled with laughter. 'Darling Mervyn, my daughter is a small child. She has no interest in ancient history or modern history either.'

'She's so young yet. She could change.'

'Not Cassie. I never changed Mervyn, and she's like me.'

'Did you bring the urn down with you?'

'Yes, it's in my room. I'll get it, and Martin can have a look at it.'

Martin admired the urn. If Athena had offered it to him he'd have snatched her hand off and couldn't understand why Mervyn was wavering. His wife was of Athena's opinion. It certainly wouldn't go with any of her décor, she'd be hard pressed to find a home for it.

The two women discussed their attire for the wedding ceremony, while Martin and Mervyn discussed what tie they needed to set off for the church the following morning. At the end of the evening Athena had promised to collect Martin's wife, and Martin was calling at Mervyn's where a wedding car would pick them up.

Mervyn's sleep had been dreamless, due largely to the excellent wine they had drunk over dinner and the satisfaction that he had shelved a job he had lost interest in and was embarking on an entirely new life.

Moira had assured him that she was the envy of all her friends: to be marrying the dishiest teacher at her former school and starting her married life on a Greek island set in the Aegean.

Her friends envied her, she'd done better than any of them with their motley crowd of boyfriends who'd grown up in the same neighbourhood.

In the main they were cocky young men with long hair and exaggerated opinions. Most of them were more interested in football and rugby than the girls they tagged along with, but none of them were reluctant to discuss their conquests, and none of them were destined for early rise to fame.

Moira was well aware of her friends' admiration and in some cases their jealousy. Unconcerned she prattled on about the island, the villa and the immediate future which she viewed through rose-coloured spectacles. And in the main they likened her story to the films they saw of glamorous palm-shaded beaches and pink-washed villas in sun-washed gardens.

Her parents wished they could be so confident. All they could feel was a sense of loss that their daughter was leaving home, not for the next road, or the next town, but another country, living with foreigners.

It was only just light when she stood at the window looking out over the back garden towards the wood beyond. It was going to be a fine day.

There was a cross, fretful sound from Norah's bed and she grumbled, 'What are you doing standing there? It's only just light.'

'I wanted to see what the weather was like.'

Norah betrayed no interest and Moira returned to her bed to sit hugging her knees. She was not going back to sleep, there was too much to do, too much to think about. Her two suitcases lay on the floor already packed and in the spare room her wedding dress hung outside the wardrobe, the beautiful delicate veil covering the spare bed.

Noiselessly, she slid out of her bed and tiptoed across the room to the door. There was a slight click as she turned the knob and once more Norah said crossly, 'Where are you going now?'

Without answering Moira let herself out onto the landing. She padded along the short corridor to the spare room and then stood entranced, looking at the white lace wedding dress hanging from its hanger, the tiny bodice and long sweeping skirt, the long transparent sleeves and the halo of chiffon roses that would adorn her veil. A pair of white satin shoes stood near the dressing table and she picked them up and stared down at them with a smile on her lips.

Draped over the arm of a chair was a long satin slip and if she opened the wardrobe door she knew she would find Norah's bridesmaid's dress hanging there. It was of pale peach taffeta, with deep peach roses set on a velvet band for her hair.

There was such a lot to think about. The hairdresser was coming at nine o'clock, the remainder of her attendants were to be here for ten, and she hoped the children would be well-behaved. The three little girls were looking forward to it with great excitement, the one boy was a bit of a handful. He wouldn't like being kitted out in peach satin trousers, white silk shirt and frilled cravat.

She could hear sounds coming from their parents' room so she hurried back to her room and waited to hear footsteps going downstairs, then she followed to find her mother in the kitchen putting the kettle on.

Mrs Sheldon looked round with a smile. 'There was no need to get up so early dear. I was awake so I thought I'd make a cup of tea and take one up for your father.'

'I'm too excited to sleep, Mum, and there's so much to do.'

'There's nothing to do, only get ready for the church and that's hours off yet.'

'I know. Oh I do so hope it stays fine. We've had so much rain lately.'

'Well the forecast was good. Here, I'll pull back the curtains.'

Moira fled to the window and looked out. A pale watery sun struggled in the eastern sky. The puddles had dried up across the drive. Oh, surely it was a good omen?

Norah came into the kitchen rubbing the sleep out of her eyes.'

'You're up early,' her mother commented.

'Well, she was staring through the window, then she was out of the room, I couldn't get to sleep after that, I thought I might just as well get up.'

'Well you can make yourself useful, get out the cups and saucers and a tray for your father.'

'Is he having breakfast in bed then?'

'No. Just a cup of tea and I'll make him some toast.'

'I'll bet you went to look at your wedding dress,' Nora said with a sly smile at Moira.

'What's wrong with that?'

'You've seen it a dozen times already.'

'You'll probably do the same to yours if ever somebody asks you to marry him.'

'Well, it won't be straight out of the schoolroom, or to a man a lot older than myself.'

'You're only jealous,' Moira snapped, and, exasperated, her mother said, 'Now then girls, we don't want any of this today of all days. You're getting to have quite a nasty tongue in your head, Norah.'

Norah remained silent and Moira said, 'I'll take Dad's tray up Mum.'

When she had left the kitchen, Norah said, 'When she's gone, can I move into the spare room Mum? I don't want to sleep in a room with twin beds in it, it's silly.'

'We'll see if you behave yourself,' her mother replied calmly.

'I'm only joking most of the time, Mum? She's too touchy, particularly about him.'

'Well, I'd rather you kept your opinions to yourself. Everybody thinks she's done very well for herself, we're only doubtful because she's going so far away. We like Mervyn, he's charming and good looking, and he does have a lot of talent. We'd have had doubts about any man she wanted to marry. If your father had his way his girls would have been marrying over thirty, young men who lived in the next road.'

Norah laughed. 'That'll be me. I want a career first, then a man in his forties, some chartered accountant or factory owner.'

'You've always been the one with big ideas,' her

mother said sharply.

'No bigger than Moira's,' Norah answered pertly. 'She's the one with a villa in Greece and an artist husband. I wonder what his cousin will be wearing.'

Mervyn was having similar thoughts. Athena could be relied upon to create a stir. She had never wanted to paint pictures, but her artistic ability was reflected in her style and the clothes she wore. Today she would have thought very carefully about her attire.

He looked at himself in the mirror. Mrs Sheldon had insisted on morning dress for the men who had a part to play, her husband, the groom, his best man and the groomsmen. Mr Sheldon had struggled into the suit he had worn for his own wedding and only worn once since – for his eldest daughter's marriage. It no longer fitted, so he had been forced to hire one.

The groom and his best man were rather more fortunate since the morning suits they possessed still fitted. The groomsmen, with sulky dismay, hired from the men's outfitters in the town.

The carnation button-holes arrived at the same time as Martin and the two men surveyed each other, well satisfied with their appearance.

'Do you have to come back here?' Martin asked.

'No. The luggage is at the hotel. I'll lock up and leave the key next door. Somebody will drop you off for your car later on.'

'Right. Well, it looks as if the wedding car's here.'

Mervyn took a quick look round the hall. It had

been his home for many years, even when it had never felt like home. Athena had hated it and never lost an opportunity to say so, consequently he had viewed the house through her eyes, the too lofty rooms and steep staircase, the draughts through the long windows. Now he was leaving it for ever and he had no regrets.

They were very early at the church, but, even so, as they walked down the centre aisle a great many of the pews were occupied, by girls from the school and certain members of the staff, by parents and old girls, and Martin muttered, 'They've shown up in some force, I expected it.'

They took their places in the front pew but after a while Martin murmured, 'There's ages to wait. What do you say if we go out through the side door and wait in the churchyard? It's a warm sunny day, we can watch some of the arrivals until it's time to come back.'

Mervyn agreed. Anything was better than sitting in isolation in the front pew listening to the low murmur of conversation from the rear.

Outside in the sunshine Martin handed him a cigarette and they stood where they could look down the long path towards the lych-gate and were soon rewarded by seeing groups of people walking through it.

The wedding guests were beginning to arrive now, conspicuous by their large hats and floating draperies. The men were wearing buttonholes, the women sprays of carnations. There were a great many of them, and Martin said, 'Do you know them all?'

'I don't know any of them. Moira warned me

they were a large family and they've invited a great many friends.'

'A wedding like this must have cost a bob or two.'

Still they came. Excited children in frilly dresses and young boys in their Sunday suits. Then there was a sudden stir and a large elderly lady was being propelled along the drive, assisted by two stalwart young men and watched anxiously by their women folk.

'Who's the old girl?' Martin asked.

'I can only think it's Great Aunt Agatha, the family *grande dame.*'

She was a large lady by any standards and she was wearing a large black hat pulled down firmly over her iron-grey hair. She had a large red face and was puffing with exertion. Although it was a warm day she was wearing a black fox cape over her beige dress and half way along the path she stopped to admonish the children who were running in front of them.

'Oh well,' Martin murmured philosophically. 'You'll not be seeing much of her in the near future.'

Mervyn grinned. 'No. That is a consolation.'

'Here I think come my wife and your cousin. I suggest we get back into church, it'll be interesting to see the effect Athena has on the congregation.'

Mervyn followed his gaze to where Athena and Martin's wife Anne were walking slowly along the path. Anne was wearing a pretty beige suit and cream flowered hat. Athena, however, was in black and white: an outfit that would have done credit to Ascot with her stark white gown and short black silk jacket, topped with a very large black hat decorated with white chiffon flowers. The outfit was exotic, but it was undeniably elegant and suited her blonde fairness and shapely figure.

At their entry into the church silence descended on the pews behind them and they could distinctly hear the sound of two pairs of high heels walking down the aisle and entering the pew behind them.

They both turned to smile at the two women and Mervyn could see that every eye in the pews around them was staring in amazement. Athena smiled serenely while Great Aunt Agatha adjusted her glasses to get a better view. Marian Adcock had grinned at him cheerfully from a few rows further back and he could see that she was accompanied by the friend who was a neighbour of the Sheldons. He had no doubt that a great many of his old colleagues would be in the church but he did not turn round again. He sat listening to the organist playing a selection of Kettelby's melodies.

Then there was another stir and Mrs Sheldon entered the church alone, wearing the pale blue dress and jacket her daughters had urged her to choose, with the navy and pale blue floral hat her husband had told her was too young for her.

A waiting silence seemed to have descended on the congregation until the welcoming strains of Lohengrin's Wedding March filled the church and Mervyn and Martin stepped out of their pew to greet the bride.

Mervyn had known she would look beautiful, but in those first few moments when their eyes met he knew that this would be how he would remember her always, no matter what came after in their lives.

He was aware of her standing beside him in floating white lace and there was the scent of roses from the flowers the bridesmaids carried behind them. They were people in a play. The sonorous voice of the clergyman, the music and the singing, Moira's voice, little above a whisper making promises that were binding and sacred, and his own voice, more resonant and below him her eyes looking into his filled with trust and deep abiding love.

Almost before he was aware of it they were following the vicar to the high altar and he was pronouncing them man and wife. She was in his arms, her soft lips against his, and then they were being ushered into the vestry followed by a retinue of attendants, her parents, Aunt Agatha and Athena, kissing him gently and wishing him well.

There was so much conversation, so much laughter, so many well wishers and then from the body of the church the music swelled and they were forming a procession to lead them along the aisle and outside into the sunshine. It was over. He was now a married man, come rain or shine.

In the hotel those who had something to say had said it all. Martin had been witty and flattering to the bridesmaids. Mr Sheldon's voice had cracked with emotion when he talked of his little girl going to live abroad and how she had given them so much joy in their time together. Then the telegrams and good wishes had been read out, the toasts had been drunk and they were getting into the bridal car for their journey to the hotel in the town where they would change out of their wedding finery. Moira was flinging her spray of white roses into the waiting crowd but neither of them knew who had caught it.

It had been a wonderful day and everything had gone smoothly. Mrs Sheldon had wept a little, but Moira had felt few guilty qualms. Ahead of her lay excitement. Two days in London, and she had never ever been there, a plane journey to Athens and she had never flown in her life, and then life and love with Mervyn in a dream villa on a dream island.

She felt a few pangs of regret on that first evening in London as she looked round the hotel restaurant. Her parents would be sad, but in time they would come to realise that she was happy with Mervyn and they would visit them for holidays, and she and Mervyn would return to England many times to see them.

Mervyn smiled across at her, well aware that her thoughts had been miles away, and she blushed. 'I was thinking about my parents,' she admitted. 'They'll be feeling very sad tonight but as soon as we arrive on the island I'll write to tell them how wonderful it all is.'

'I hope you'll think it is wonderful, Moira.'

'I shall, I know I shall. I hope they'll come to see us, and we'll come back often to see them, won't we?'

'Well of course.'

'They could come for the summer Mervyn, particularly when we have children.'

He didn't answer. To talk of children disconcerted him. He hoped Moira was in no hurry to have children but he thought it wiser to ignore her words at that moment, instead he said, 'What do you want to do tomorrow, we have another day in London before we leave for Greece?'

'I don't honestly care, Mervyn. I've never been here before, you must know what we can do with our day.'

'Well, I'm sure you'd like to look round the shops in the morning then we can take a city tour in the afternoon or spend it on the river. We're going to a show in the evening.'

Her eyes lit up with delight. It was all too wonderful to take in but more than anything would be the nights of love when there would be no unspoken feeling of guilt.

Tomorrow Mervyn had said she could choose her wedding present and he asked her to think of something she had always wanted more than anything else. She did not tell Mervyn that she had never really wanted anything that indulgent parents had not provided, and when she was older what she had really longed for had been Mervyn. From that first moment when he had walked into the classroom, and even now, she couldn't believe that he was really hers. Life had been too good to her and she found herself remembering something her grandmother had once said to her, that everything in life had to be paid for in one form or another.

Moira had asked her what she meant and the

old lady had looked at her rather sadly saying, 'Well love, life is a mixture of joy and sadness. Sometimes sorrow knocks early, sometimes later, but we all have to have a taste of both before it's all over.'

To be honest Moira hadn't thought much about it. Granny was old, she rambled on a bit, but as she sat looking into Mervyn's eyes and thinking her world was perfect, she was aware of a faint shadow shading her joy.

Oh surely not, she thought. Nothing could be so cruel as to take away her happiness when she'd done nothing sinful to deserve it.

Chapter Eleven

They were sitting in the airport lounge waiting to board their plane. Excitedly Moira looked around her at fellow passengers in holiday mood, at others destined for exotic places she had never heard of, and laughter and light-hearted conversation. Mervyn was vastly entertained by her wide-eyed delight as she sat clutching the cream leather vanity case which he'd bought her the day before and which contained the gold bracelet she'd wanted.

Mervyn's holdall sat on the floor at his feet and with it was a large cardboard box containing the Grecian urn Athena had given him as part of her wedding present. Now Moira eyed it curiously.

'What's in the box, Mervyn? You've been

looking after it so carefully.'

'Our wedding present from Athena.'

Her eyes lit up. 'What is it? It's sure to be something wonderful.'

'I very much doubt if you will think so.'

'Why is that?'

'Well it's a vase, and very, very old. My uncle prized it because it was authentic and came from Ancient Greece. Neither Athena nor I thought much of it.'

'Then why has she given it to you?'

'Because she doesn't want it and because she thinks I'll look after it. It is very valuable.'

'Why didn't you like it then?'

'Shall we see what you think about it when we arrive on the island.'

'And that was her wedding present?'

'Along with the deeds to the villa. Athena has been very generous, to tell the truth I was reluctant to take the deeds, what do you think?'

'I think it's wonderful of her. Oh Mervyn, life is going to be so wonderful, we own our own villa, you have the money from your house and my parents have been very generous. We really are very lucky, aren't we?'

He put his arm around her and hugged her.

'Yes, I really think we are.'

It was true. He had a young, beautiful wife, a villa he had always loved on an island he had always wished he could live on for ever. At that moment there was not a single cloud on their horizon.

To Moira it had been the adventure of a lifetime:

the plane journey, the sea and the sunshine, and finally their voyage to the island on the motor-boat that plied between the chain of islands.

Not even the dilapidated taxi that drove them to the villa could dispel her enthusiasm for her first sight of the white villa and the gardens that swept down to the top of the cliff. Dumping her luggage on the steps she ran across the grass until she could stand staring out across the coastline and the turquoise Aegean sea.

Mervyn joined her and she looked up into his face with shining eyes.

'Oh Mervyn, it is beautiful, isn't it? I can understand your wanting to paint pictures here, I can understand how much you care for it.'

Taking her hand he pulled her towards the villa. He had written to his friend the priest asking if he would arrange for his villa to be cleaned and got ready for them, and he looked round to see that fresh flowers had been placed on the windowsill and that the room looked cheerful and tidy.

Moira stood looking around her, at the tiled floor with its assortment of well-worn rugs, and the plain whitewashed walls and ancient fireplace where the cleaner had placed a plant to rob it of its starkness. He could not tell from her face whether she was pleased or dismayed, and he went forward to open the kitchen door so that she could follow him in.

Again her expression was comical as she surveyed the white sink and old cooker, the array of large heavy cooking utensils hanging from a wooden beam and at that moment he knew she was thinking of her mother's neat new kitchen with its refrigerator and new cooker, the dishwasher and washing machine and all the sophistication of modern living.

She looked up at him in some dismay.

'I know what you're thinking,' he said with a smile, 'but we can shop now for new stuff. I thought you'd like to choose them for yourself.'

Her face brightened.

'Shall we open your parcel and look at the vase,' she said with a smile.

He laid the vase on the table and looked down at her expression. She didn't like it. She went forward to take a closer look, and after a few moments she said, 'It's scratched on this side Mervyn, and there's a crack in the handle. I don't suppose Athena knew.'

'That crack's been there for centuries, my dear.'

She stood looking down at it with evident disappointment.

'You don't like it?' he asked.

'Not really. I don't think it's as nice as the vase Aunt Sophie gave us. She said it belonged to Granny and it's Spode. I didn't like that at first but Aunt Sophie said it could be valuable one day.'

'But not I suspect as valuable as that one, Moira.'

'Because it's so old, you mean?'

'Exactly.'

'Where are we going to put it? I'll be afraid of it getting broken.'

'Well my uncle had it on display where his fellow teachers could admire it. Athena kept it hidden, I suspect you'll want to do the same.'

'But wouldn't that be awful, Mervyn?'

'Yes, it would be terrible, but it will probably keep the vase intact and stop you breaking it accidentally.'

She laughed. 'You really think I might do that?'

'Well I always had suspicions that Athena might.'

'Can we have a look at what's upstairs.'

Together they walked up the curving stone steps towards the upper regions and he allowed her to wander into the two bedrooms alone and the tiny bathroom off the main bedroom. Moira's first impression was that they were spartan and not at all how she'd imagined they would be. The views from the windows were superb and as she returned to the main bedroom where Mervyn stood looking out of the window her spirits revived. She loved him so much, she had to love his villa and his island. They'd shop for new cushions, curtains and rugs for the floor. She'd throw out all those antiquated cooking pots and pans and in no time at all everything would be wonderful.

The Sheldons received a series of colourful picture postcards each one showing different views of the island. Clusters of white houses huddled at the top of limestone cliffs above an azure sea and they passed them among their friends who marvelled at the deep blue sky and the sparkling sea.

Her letters to them were filled with delight about the villa, the gardens and a way of life none of them could relate to. They were happy that Moira was happy and that she had settled down to her new life in a foreign land.

Mervyn couldn't imagine how she managed to fill postcards and several sheets of writing paper almost every day with details of her new life. He was not to know that truth and imagination were both involved, and as the days passed imagination took over from the truth.

The villa in Moira's letters would have been more in keeping with the one sprawling across the cliff top at the top of the hill. The terraced gardens, the romantic summerhouse that resembled some Greek temple, the scent of oleanders were fashioned by the dreams in her heart, reality was far away.

She refused to admit to herself that she was bored. Every day she wandered down to Mervyn's studio to watch him paint, and occasionally she took her watercolours and sat in a corner of the studio trying to copy one of the views from an array of picture postcards.

Occasionally a visitor would pause to watch her, and one day a woman visitor stood behind her for rather longer than usual and when her husband joined her she said, 'I rather like the picture this girl is painting, there isn't one of this view here.'

'It's from the other side of the island,' her husband answered.

'Of course. Do you like it?'

'Well, it isn't an original, is it? We're not interested in buying a copy of something.'

That was the last time Moira took her

watercolours to the studio. Her work was inadequate.

This was not married life as she had pictured it. In the evenings they dined at one of the tavernas along the coast, the rest of the time they lived off fruit, and it was one morning in sheer desperation that she said, 'Tonight I want to cook our evening meal. I'll shop for fresh vegetables and I'll have everything ready for when you come home this evening.'

This was what Mervyn had hoped for, that at last she was thinking in terms of being a real housewife instead of merely a visitor.

He had had a good day. Four of his pictures had been sold and none of his customers had haggled about the prices he had placed on the paintings. He watched them going off to board the ferry carrying their pictures, entirely happy with what they had bought and as he locked up for the night he reflected that life was going to be very good for them. He was becoming known, and Moira was settling down to domesticity.

It was already dusk when he climbed the hill up to the villa. Lights were lit along the road and as he closed the garden gate behind him he was suddenly aware that smoke was streaming out of the kitchen and there was a strong smell of burning. He rushed through the garden and the smell became stronger, then Moira was rushing out of the house and into his arms, her face streaked with tears.

'The meal's ruined,' she cried. 'It's that wretched stove and I can't lift the pans, they're so heavy.'

He stared at the scene that met his eyes when he stepped into the kitchen. A pan filled with potatoes lay on the floor with the contents steaming out over the flags. A burnt-out roasting tin lay half in and half out of the oven, its contents filling the kitchen with acrid smoke, while another pan containing vegetables had been pulled clear of the gas jet.

He went forward to switch off the oven and Moira cried, 'I was trying to empty the potato pan but it was so heavy I couldn't hold on to it. I don't understand the cooker, I hate the pans, I hate everything about the kitchen.'

She was sobbing now, and as he attempted to comfort her she cried, 'I'll never cook in this kitchen with these old things, I didn't think it would be anything like this.'

'Don't worry about the meal,' he told her. 'We'll either eat at the taverna or I'll make an omelette. We can clean the kitchen up later.'

'The pan'll be ruined. I bought a chicken but it's burnt to a cinder. How have you managed in that awful kitchen all these years?'

Mervyn had never thought about the kitchen. It was like it had always been and he'd never considered it a problem. He'd been selfish, unimaginative and very much a fool. He'd married a child bride from a cosseted background, he'd brought her to an island far from home, and expected her to settle down to a primitive existence far removed from anything she'd contemplated.

Scenery and sunshine were not enough. If he wanted his wife to be happy, he had to spend some money on the villa, particularly on the kitchen, but it would take time.

She sat, a picture of misery, on the window-seat staring out into the garden, and shivered delicately. The smell of burnt cooking lingered everywhere, but the room felt cold in spite of the heat of the day.

He had been looking forward to their meal together, now he realised he wasn't hungry. All the same he had to ask her, 'Are you hungry darling? We'll walk down to the taverna if you like.'

'I'm not hungry, I don't want to eat.'

'Then I'll light the fire, it feels cold in here.'

The tears started afresh, and he went to sit beside her, taking her hands into his. 'It isn't the end of the world, darling,' he said. 'We'll do something about the kitchen and pans. We'll talk to the priest, he'll know where we can find something you like and we'll get workmen in to modernise the kitchen.'

'But when? How long will it take?'

'I don't know, but as soon as possible, I promise.'

'I suppose all the kitchens are like this one and they don't mind. They don't know any better. They'll think I'm being silly, that I haven't tried.'

'They won't think anything, Moira. It's nothing to do with anybody else.'

'Maria would have been able to cook in that kitchen with those wretched pans.'

'Maria hasn't known anything else, she's always cooked with pans like that.'

'I'll clean it all up. I don't want Maria to see it

looking like that.'

'We'll both clean it up. Then we'll go to the taverna and get something to eat.'

'I'm not hungry, I don't want anything.'

'Then we'll have coffee and try to forget about the whole wretched episode.'

The sobs started afresh and Mervyn thought she should be left alone so that he could start on the cleaning-up process. It did not take long to clean up the floor but the pans were a different proposition so he left them soaking in hot water. He opened the door and window to get rid of the smell of burning and when Moira appeared in the doorway staring around her dejectedly, he said brightly, 'You see, it's all cleared away. Are you sure you don't want to go down to the taverna?'

She nodded.

So he made coffee and they sat in the living room drinking it and, to take her mind off the disaster in the kitchen, he told her about the pictures he had sold and the money that had been paid for them.

Later that night they made love more sensually and passionately than before and she lay at last listening to his even breathing beside her. She believed him to be asleep but sleep was a long way off.

Mervyn was a deeply worried man. He knew in his heart that life with Moira on the island was not going to work. His beautiful child bride had never really left her parents' house. For what remained of the summer she would tell herself that she was content and happy, but in her innermost heart it would be a lie, and when the visitors left and the island became her own again there would be nothing on it for Moira.

He had to think carefully of their future here, and their future together. He was not to know that the girl lying awake beside him was thinking on similar lines.

None of it was like she thought it would be. Of course the island was beautiful, people were envying her, the visitors were saying how wonderful it must be to live there, but they were soon going home to shops and theatres, to concert halls and decent houses with dish-washers and decent cookers.

Back home in England life with Mervyn had seemed so wonderful. She loved him of course, she would never love anybody else, but she'd thought marriage to him would mean a nice house in England, with a lovely garden; Mervyn would be in a secure profession, coming home every evening to a beautifully cooked meal she had enjoyed preparing; they would watch television or visit her parents or friends, or the cinema, or maybe a concert at the school.

There would be the island to come to for a few weeks in the summer, while other holidays could be spent in Bournemouth or Torquay. They would bring their children up near her parents, and thinking of children brought her suddenly to realisation.

How could she possibly have children on the island? Children needed nursery schools and decent education later on. There was no way her children were going away to school in England while she stayed here: she had to be with them, see them grow up. Her parents had to see them grow up.

She had seen the children on the island running carefree across the cliff top, Greek children, in their raggle-taggle clothing, none of them knowing a word of English. What would her children have to do with them?

That was the moment the idea was born. She had to get away from the island, and get Mervyn away too, and the way she could do it was to have a child. Mervyn would understand that she needed her parents, proper medical attention, civilisation. Mervyn had said they should wait for a while before they had a family, until he was sure that sales of his pictures had really taken off. She knew that he didn't really mind whether they had children or not, but she would stop taking precautions, tell him they hadn't worked, tell him she had forgotten.

With her future firmly resolved she felt happier than she had felt all day.

They were awakened by the sound of Maria working on the burnt pans in the kitchen and Mervyn ran downstairs after dressing hurriedly to find her with her arms immersed in the sink as she scrubbed away the burnt remains congealed in the pans.

Her eyes met his and she smiled. He smiled ruefully in return and when Moira arrived in the kitchen later Maria had put the pans back on the shelves and was busily cleaning the burnt oven plates.

Moira avoided meeting the younger girl's eyes,

but if she had she would have been surprised at the sympathy in them. Maria was aware that her employer's wife was not happy in the villa. She knew that she hated the kitchen and its primitive furnishings and she understood why. She had seen the glossy magazine photographs Moira had brought from England with their beautiful homes and gardens, their furnishings and wonderful bathrooms and kitchens. How could she ever be happy with this life when there would be so much more in the country she had come from?

She took their breakfast out to the little terrace where they could sit and look out across the sea, and while Mervyn thought how beautiful it all was, Moira sat back relaxed and happy, relieved that there was a way out.

She walked with Mervyn to the garden gate and he said smiling down at her, 'What are you going to do with your day?'

'Oh there's sure to be something to do at the villa, then I'll shop for fruit and take a walk down to the studio.'

'Don't attempt to cook a meal, darling, not until we've replaced those awful pans.'

'I won't. We can eat at the taverna.'

She stood at the gate watching him walking across the cliff top and then he descended the hill and he was lost to sight.

In the villa the flowers could do with changing and she went around the garden choosing a selection of favourite blooms. She was walking back up the path when a large white car swept past the side of the villa, up the steep road that led to the large villa above. She stood staring after it. She could see it come to a standstill outside the wrought-iron gates before one of the gardeners came to open them, then it swept on to come to a rest below the terrace.

A woman sprang out of the driver's seat, a woman who was tall and slender with a bright chiffon scarf tying back her long dark hair. She closed the car door behind her then ran lightly up the steps and vanished inside. The Contessa had returned. Moira sauntered back through the garden, faintly troubled.

Mervyn had talked about the Contessa, told her something of the other woman's life, and when she had asked him what she was like, he had said she was sophisticated and beautiful. Moira didn't want to meet her.

They would have nothing in common: after all she was foreign. They spoke different languages. It never occurred to Moira that the Contessa would speak perfect English, but it did occur to her that Mervyn might admire the Contessa and wish Moira was more like her.

The day passed slowly. There was nothing to do in the villa: Maria had done everything. They didn't really need Maria, but at least she was somebody to smile at, somebody who knew the odd word of English, somebody who would clean the villa for Mervyn when he was here alone.

She paused to consider her thoughts. Well, of course, Mervyn would want to come here in the summer to sell his pictures, and he might well have to stay for a while to dispose of the property. She had little doubt that if and when she returned to England Mervyn would go with her. Surely that was what husbands did?

It never occurred to Moira for a single moment that she was being selfish. She was her daddy's little girl, she'd been brought up to expect the best, wasn't that how her father had always behaved towards her mother? That her life with Mervyn was different never seemed to matter.

She stood looking round the living room: undeniably, it was charming. She had arranged the flowers in two vases and plumped up the cushions, and outside the sun was shining on a deep blue sea and the scent of herbs was powerful on the breeze.

The summer would linger on until the warmth of the autumn which Mervyn assured her could be beautiful. There was no immediate rush to leave, time was on her side.

As she left the garden she looked up at the villa above: the car had gone. Maybe it had not been the Contessa after all. Or maybe she was visiting friends? She decided against going to buy fruit – it could wait until later – instead she would walk down to the studio.

She enjoyed chatting to the British tourists, hearing their praise for Mervyn's paintings, their openly expressed envy that they were lucky to be living on an island the tourists regarded as paradise.

As usual the ferries were disgorging their array of passengers and their first stop was Mervyn's studio where they stood in groups admiring his work. Mervyn was standing in the middle of a group of people. But suddenly, he left them to greet a woman who took his outstretched hand, then they stood apart chatting easily together.

Moira paused, staring down at them, then she saw the white car standing near the wall, and without a second's thought she turned and retraced her steps towards the village.

Chapter Twelve

Moira made sure the white car was parked outside the villa before she walked down to the studio. The visitors were already leaving for the ferries and Mervyn greeted her with a bright smile, well pleased with the day's events.

His pictures were selling well. Those who had bought his pictures showed others and he was concentrating on watercolours which did not take so long to finish.

'I can see you've had a good day,' Moira said.

'Very good, darling, one of the best I think. You've missed the Contessa, she's here for the rest of the summer.'

'Is she here alone?'

'She's arrived alone. At the end of the week her friends are coming with the children they were collecting from their schools.'

'Did you tell her you'd finished her picture?'

'I promised we'd take it up there this evening. She invited us for dinner but I said we'd go up later. When you didn't arrive I wasn't able to consult you.'

'I did some shopping for fruit. I told you I would.'

'It will be all right, darling. It's nothing formal. You needn't dress up.'

'I shall have to wear something decent, I'm sure she will.'

Later Mervyn watched in some exasperation as she threw things out of the wardrobe and onto the bed. She was disdainful of the pretty cottons he suggested, saying they would not be nearly grand enough, and when at last she chose a dress she had worn for her sister's wedding he made no comment. Moira would have to learn by her mistakes.

They walked up the hill in the cool scented night, under a sky brilliant with stars, and all around them was the chirping of the cicadas to disturb the stillness. Mervyn carried the Contessa's picture under his arm, while Moira tripped beside him in her high-heeled shoes, her satin skirt gleaming in the moonlight.

The Contessa came out on the terrace to meet them and immediately Moira knew that she should have taken Mervyn's advice. She felt over-dressed. The pretty pale-blue bridesmaid's frock looked girlish beside the Contessa's casual dress: a colourful voile skirt and pale-cream blouse. Her legs were bare and suntanned, her feet encased in cream sandals, strappy with flat heels.

Her dark hair fell onto her shoulders in large waves. The older woman was beautiful and exotic to Moira's English eyes.

Her welcome was warm and friendly and she drew Moira into the villa, expressing her delight at their meeting and with good wishes for their future happiness. How young she is, she was thinking, as young as I was when I married, and with so much to learn.

Mervyn was busy unwrapping the picture which he propped up against the wall and the Contessa went forward to look at it.

He watched her expression, waiting for her words, and when they came they were filled with delight.

'It's beautiful, Mervyn. I thought you said you'd never painted figures?'

'Well the figure isn't very prominent as you can see. I enjoyed painting the scenery.'

'But it's beautiful, I love it. Don't you think it's beautiful, Moira?'

'Yes. It's very nice.'

Both Moira and the Contessa were aware of the banality of her reply but by this time Leonora was holding it up to catch the light, saying, 'I must find the perfect place to hang it, somewhere that will do the picture justice. At the weekend I have the children coming and friends, I thought I would hold a dinner party, invite Father Cristofson and one or two people I know who live on the islands. I do hope you and Moira will join us, Mervyn.'

'Thank you Leonora, we'd love to.'

Leonora laughed. 'We'll make it a festive occasion and dress up for it.'

Moira's heart sank. This woman looked wonderful in casual clothes. What would she look like dressed up?

When the Contessa saw Moira's gaze flitting

round the room she said, 'Would you like to see round the villa Moira? Mervyn's been here before so we'll give him a glass of wine and you and I shall take a tour around.'

Moira thought she had never seen anything more beautiful in her life. The marble stairs and the crystal chandeliers, the carved gilt balustrade and the furnishings in satin and velvet.

Whenever she had thought about Mervyn's villa she had imagined something like this, oh not so grand as this one, but on the same lines, like the villas she had seen in films and read about in books. Large gracious rooms and terraces overlooking marble arbours. She was aware of a feeling of resentment. Mervyn had misled her, he had made her believe in a fairytale and the reality was nothing like it. If they spent a small fortune on the tiny villa it could never be like this one, and she'd written to everybody at home to tell them how wonderful it was. Her parents and her sister would hate the villa, the kitchen with its awful pots and pans, and the cooker that was a nightmare.

Leonora was aware of Moira's pensive expression, and the envy she read in her blue eyes was disturbing. Mervyn should not have married this girl, she was a disaster, and yet there was something appealing in her pretty face, something childlike. She could have been so right for another man – a younger, less intelligent man.

She felt a vague sense of pity for them both. She knew what would have happened. If there had been no Moira she and Mervyn would have drifted into some sort of an affair, something that might have lasted as long as they spent their summers on the island. Now it would never happen.

'The villa's so beautiful,' Moira murmured.

'Yes it is. I had thought to sell it. Now I don't think I could bear to live without it. You are happy here Moira, you love the island, don't you?'

'Yes, it's very nice.'

There it was again, the banality of her reply, 'Very nice!' A beautiful island steeped in history set in an azure sea. Was there anything in Moira's life that could be described as more than very nice?

Moira was obsessed with what she should wear for the Contessa's dinner party. She had already worn her party dress. She had left her wedding dress at home to be altered for some future grand occasion and she deemed everything else in her wardrobe to be totally unsuitable.

Mervyn assured her she looked beautiful in whatever she wore, but, even so, she persuaded him that they should take the morning ferry to Rhodes to look at the shops. Rhodes was busy with well-dressed tourists, and some of them assured her the shopping was excellent.

One morning on Rhodes convinced Moira that she wished she was living there. Rhodes was sophisticated, the shops were wonderful, and the morning they had promised themselves stretched into the early evening.

Moira bought two dresses, expensive, more sophisticated than any she had ever worn, and

Mervyn was unsure about liking them.

As they stepped ashore from the ferry taking them home, Father Cristofson was the first person they encountered, and he came forward to meet them with a warm smile and the news that many of the tourists had been unhappy to find the studio closed since they would have no means of visiting it again before returning home.

Mervyn decided to be philosophical about it. Others would come, tourists came and went, if they were sufficiently interested, they would come back.

At least Moira was happy. She spread the dresses out across the bed and stood admiring them.

'I shall wear the black with the white beading round the neck,' she decided. 'My mother would never let me wear black. She said it was too old for me, but I'm a married woman now, it's time I was able to please myself.'

He smiled.

'I thought you would have wanted to look at kitchen furniture,' he said dryly. 'I rather think it will have to come from Rhodes.'

'We'll have to look at that some other time,' she assured him.

Moira was no longer concerned about kitchen furniture, she did not expect to be living on the island all that long. She had planned her future too well. A baby and a return home to England, then Mervyn would follow her and they would only return to the island for brief holidays. If Mervyn could sell pictures on the island he could sell them at home.

Mervyn felt that there was something secretive about Moira these days. When he talked about things that had seemed important, she was quick to change the subject. She made no more offers to cook a meal. She made toast and boiled eggs. She developed a passing interest in the cooker that enabled her to warm up pasta dishes they bought from the taverna and she seemed happy enough with her plants and flowers from the garden.

She noted that several cars stood on the driveway above them. She did not want to go to the Contessa's party. Neither of them would have anything in common with the Contessa's continental friends and in spite of the new dress and high-heeled strappy shoes she wished they could have made an excuse not to go.

Seeing Mervyn in his white tuxedo did nothing to calm her fears. He looked so handsome, but this was an alien Mervyn who had stepped out of a world she had not known.

As they walked through the gardens above they could hear music and the sound of laughter, and Mervyn put his hand under her arm and drew her up the steps. Lights from the chandeliers inside the villa shone across the terrace and inside the room Moira was aware of men and women standing around in groups in laughing conversation, and then the Contessa was coming forward to greet them, beautiful in tawny chiffon, her dark hair piled on top of her head and there were jewels around her throat and in her ears. She was smiling, charming, and then they were taken to meet the others who spoke with them in faultless English.

How easily Mervyn greeted them while she stood stiffly beside him, a glass of wine in her hand, her smile stretched taut on her bemused face.

All the fantasies of her youth were being enacted in this room. As a dreaming schoolgirl she had imagined herself amongst people like this in a villa like this one. She had been the centre of attention, young, beautiful, in a white satin gown with jewels round her throat and a tiara on her hair. Now here she was, wishing the ground would swallow her up, and painfully pleased to see Father Cristofson standing in the doorway with a calm smile on his face.

When she thought about it afterwards there was nothing she could remember about their conversation until Mervyn was despatched to bring back the urn that had been their wedding present.

They stood around it in delighted awe and two of the men bargained with Mervyn as to how much he should sell it for. The amount seemed incredible and Moira thought he could hardly refuse to sell it but he did.

Seeing her expression of dismay Mervyn smiled. 'My wife is thinking I'm all sorts of a fool not to part with it,' he said. 'She really doesn't care for it.'

Their expressions were polite, but she knew that they were all thinking she must be a fool not to know its real worth.

The Contessa put a gentle arm around her shoulders, saying lightly, 'Well, I agree with

Moira. Giorgio would have filled this villa with relics from the past if I had let him, If she has it on display she'll be afraid of it getting broken; if she hides it away she'll feel guilty. Either way she can't win, any more than I could. Now come along all of you, dinner is served and you can meet the children.'

Moira thought the little girl was pretty and with a lot to say, the boy was tall and handsome but more reserved. He bowed over her hand and murmured a greeting and she looked into his dark grey eyes and felt that if anybody in the room understood her naïveté it was this boy with his calm straight gaze and the gentle smile on his handsome face.

There was dancing along the terrace in the warm night air and it was later when Mervyn was in conversation with the two men who had wanted to buy the urn that Moira saw the boy standing alone on the terrace gazing out to the sea shimmering in the moonlight.

She went to stand beside him and although he looked up with a smile he did not speak. She was a grown-up married woman but she felt she had far more in common with this young boy than with any of the people in the room behind them. At last she said, 'It is beautiful, isn't it? Do you like coming here?'

'Yes very much. Do you?'

'I suppose so. I think I'm a little bit homesick.'

'Is England as beautiful as this?'

'It's different. Have you never been there?'

'I've been to London, but I was too young to remember. That was when my father was alive.'

'I'm so sorry that he died so young.'

He nodded, but did not offer a reply.

'Are you here for the rest of the summer?' she asked.

'I think so, unless Mama decides to spend time in Italy with my grandparents.'

'Where do they live?'

'In Rome.'

'How wonderful, I've never been to Rome. This is the first time I've been abroad.'

'You should go to Rome. There is so much history in Rome.'

'I was awful at history at school.'

He smiled.

'I suppose you're awfully good at it?'

He smiled again. 'So I'm told.'

'What do you want to do when you leave school?'

'My father's family are bankers. I think that is what I shall do.'

'And your sister?'

He laughed. 'Sophia will want to go to parties and have a very good time. She has told me so.'

That was the moment Mervyn joined them on the terrace and with a little smile and correct bow Alexander said, 'Thank you for talking to me, I think Mama will want us to go to bed now.'

Mervyn put his arm around her and asked, 'Enjoyed yourself darling?'

'Yes, it's been very nice. How grown up he is.'

'Alexander! Yes I suppose he is. He was only a little boy when his father died.'

'That's terrible. Will she marry again, do you think?'

He stared down at her, strangely startled by her question. 'I don't know. Perhaps, if the right man comes along.'

'Who would have to be the right man?'

'Somebody rich, intelligent, worldly. I don't think she's in any hurry.'

'She's very beautiful.'

'Yes. And so are you, my dear.'

'But not like her. I'm like a thousand others, she's different.'

'And you're being silly. How do you feel about going home? It's getting late and I'll probably have a busy day tomorrow. If you'd rather stay to dance some more, you only have to say so.'

'No. I think I'd like to go home.'

They took their leave and the Contessa walked along the length of the terrace with them. A small breeze ruffled the trees and the Contessa shivered slightly and drew her wrap closer about her shoulders.

Mervyn looked down at her with some concern. 'Was that chill or fear Leonora?' he asked gently.

Her face was strangely sad as she looked up at him and Moira waited, troubled by the expression on her face and the inexplicable meaning of his words.

Leonora smiled, 'It is so foolish, Mervyn, but there are still moments when I feel fear. Oh not here, surely, when I am with two friends in my own garden on a summer night, but when I am alone and every rustle of the leaves makes me feel that the past is not done with me and that there is more to come.'

'It is done with you, Leonora. Over and done with a long time ago. We'll wait here until you return to the house, you have nothing to fear.'

'What is she afraid of?' Moira asked curiously.

'Old ghosts, darling.'

'Her husband, do you mean?'

'No. Some man she was in love with a long time ago, a man who wasn't very kind to her.'

'Is she afraid he will come back into her life?'

'Something like that. It's all in her imagination, I'm sure. He's probably a much married man by this time and living in Italy.'

'But suppose he isn't?'

'My dear girl, don't you start looking for ghosts. What time did Father Cristofson leave the party?'

'I don't know, I didn't see him go.'

'Well, it was hardly his sort of scene.'

'They all spoke English. Why do we always expect foreigners to speak English when we don't know a word of their language?'

'I know, it's awful. But I think, perhaps, it started with frontiers: theirs are land boundaries, ours are seas.'

How small their villa seemed after the one above it. While Mervyn made coffee she undressed and snuggled into her robe. It was a full moon, and the sea stretched before them like a sheet of rippling silver.

Moira wondered to herself why she'd never really appreciated the beauty of a full moon at home – probably because it had to compete with so many street lights and lights pouring out of windows, but here on the island the moon came into its own. The light of the sun was powerful, golden and glowing but this moonlight was gentle, caressing and incredibly romantic. She went out into the garden and stood on the lawn, and dimly on the breeze she could hear the sound of music from above and then footsteps passing their gate until they receded into the distance. Lone footsteps walking down to the harbour, but where had they come from when there was only the villa above them and the guests at the villa were in their cars? She shivered delicately. Of course she was being stupid, it was probably some fisherman or some village lover taking a late-night stroll.

The cars had gone from outside the villa above when Moira went out into the garden the next morning. She could hear the laughter of children and then she saw Sophia and Alexander running down the cliff path to the beach. Those children loved the island, but her child would be born in England and only rarely come back to it, she told herself adamantly.

She hardly ever shopped for food since they invariably ate at the taverna, but she loved walking round the market and looking at the fruit and vegetables, and the fish that had been brought in that morning. They were like no fish she had ever seen and it was on one of her excursions to the street market several days later that she met Leonora chatting animatedly to one of the stallholders.

'They will tell you anything,' Leonora said with a laugh.

'What are you shopping for?'

'Nothing particular, perhaps some fruit.'

'The fish is wonderful. Sea bass is my favourite.'

'We usually eat at the taverna. I'm terrified of the stove in the villa.'

Leonora laughed. 'I know, mine too is fearsome. And the pans and pots are incredibly heavy. Mervyn tells me he is having your kitchen transformed.'

Moira smiled. By the time the kitchen was transformed she hoped to be back in England. A new stove and new equipment would not make her change her mind.

'Why don't you come up to the villa this afternoon? I do miss the company of other women and I would like to get to know you better.'

Moira smiled. 'I'm not sure what time Mervyn will get back from the studio. I'll ask him.'

'I'm sure he would like you to make friends with me. Shall we say you'll come about three o'clock?'

'Thank you, yes. I'll be there.'

Moira didn't want to go to the Contessa's villa, but she didn't know how to get out of it, and if she tried, Mervyn would think she was a silly spoilt brat who would rather hurt somebody's feelings in pursuit of her own way.

She walked down to the studio so that she could tell Mervyn of Leonora's invitation and she saw his face light up with delight.

'That's marvellous, darling. I do want you to be friends with Leonora and you need somebody beside me to talk to.'

They sat in the summerhouse on the cliff top where a servant served them afternoon tea. Tiny almond cakes and chocolate gâteau, and china tea served in delicate transparent Noritake cups.

When she admired them, Leonora said with a little smile, 'My husband bought them for me in Japan, I use them for special occasions.'

Moira's eyes opened in surprise and Leonora laughed, 'Well, this is a special occasion, isn't it? I am delighted to be welcoming Mervyn's young bride into my home.'

'Do you miss your husband very much?' Moira asked her.

'Very much, when I am here, because he loved this place. When I am in Rome I miss him less because there I am surrounded by family and friends.'

'Why were you so afraid in the garden last night?'

Leonora didn't answer immediately, instead she stared pensively along the cliff top. Her smile was sad when she answered her. 'I was being foolish. There is nothing to be afraid of, everything terrible happened a long time ago, it has no place in the present.'

Moira wanted to ask more, but something in the other woman's expression forbade it.

Chapter Thirteen

Elizabeth Sheldon sat at her kitchen table staring down at her daughter's letter with a bemused expression on her face. Her first instinctive feelings had been of delight. That was before she went to a kitchen cupboard to retrieve all the other letters she had received from Moira since her departure for Greece.

There had been so many of them. Letters that were gay and filled with sentimental nonsense. She was having a wonderful time. The island was paradise and Mervyn was so busy selling his pictures, they'd be rich before they knew it.

The last letter had described the large villa where the Italian Contessa lived and where they were constant visitors. Her letter read like one of those glitzy novels she got from the library, or some Hollywood movie she went to see when Norah was home from university.

The letters from Moira came constantly and they were all filled with the same sort of news. Letters from Norah came spasmodically, they were lucky if they got one a month, and always with the excuse that she was working very hard and, when she wasn't, she was partying with a host of friends. She didn't know why she believed in them more than she believed in Moira's.

She picked up her latest letter and read it through again. Moira was pregnant and wanting to come home. There was no hospital on the island she would have to go to Rhodes or even further, and she knew hardly any Greek. Mervyn had agreed that home was the best place for her but she had to ask if that would be all right with her parents.

Moira already knew that they would be delighted to have her home. She could stay with them until the baby was born and afterwards if she felt like it, but Mervyn would have to be consulted and Moira said very little about Mervyn in her letters. At least not Mervyn in his role as her husband.

When she heard her husband's key in the lock she hastily scooped the letters together with the latest one on top and waited for her husband to enter the kitchen. He smiled, then his eyes went immediately to the letters and in some exasperation he said, 'You're surely not reading them again. You must read them every day.'

'I know, it's because she's so far away.'

'Well, reading her letters isn't going to bring her any closer. She's with her husband. Heaven only knows who Norah's spending her time with.'

'Norah was always better at looking after herself than Moira.'

'And Moira's got somebody else to look after her now. Really Liz, don't you think it's time to let go of the apron strings.'

Solemnly she handed over Moira's latest letter and watched his face while he read it. There was doubt and uncertainty in his expression. 'I thought they'd have had the sense to wait to have children before they were properly settled? Moira told me they would be in no hurry.'

'Well, it's happened, hasn't it? And now we have to think about having them home.'

'He may not want to come.'

She stared at him in amazement. 'But of course he'll want to come. He surely won't allow her to come back on her own.'

'I didn't say that. He may want to go back. After all, that was the idea, wasn't it – to sell his house and live there permanently.'

'Well, things have changed now.'

'Have you thought where we're going to put them?'

'Moira's large bedroom is still here and Norah is at university. We can turn her room into a nursery.'

'And when she comes home? Are we going to ask her to sleep in the garden?'

'Well of course not. There's no problem until the baby's born, then, we'll just have to get on with building that other bedroom over the garage – after all we got planning permission some time ago. In any case, Norah has said she wants a job away from here, so she'll hardly be coming home for good.'

'I don't think we should be making plans right now. We have to see what Mervyn thinks. It's much too soon to do anything else.'

'Well, we have to think ahead. I have to write and tell her they'll both be welcome. What more can we say?'

He picked up his newspaper and walked out of the kitchen. In the living room he sat slumped in front of the fire in his favourite chair: it was all going to change. They were too old to have a new baby in the house. Since the girls went, they'd become set in their ways.

They didn't have to listen to the girls squabbling over ridiculous things. He didn't have Liz worrying if everything was all right with her daughters. Of course he loved them both, and he'd always be glad to see them and have them stay for holidays, just as long as they were happy and moving back into their own lives. Never in a thousand years had he bargained on being saddled with the return of two adults and a new baby on the way.

His wife entered the room, carrying a tray laid out with tea and china. She was cosseting him, showing him that he was the important one, but he read the signs well: Liz was happy, she wanted them home.

Moira too was happy. She had dropped her bombshell to Mervyn and suffered his amazement that she had forgotten to take precautions. He had yet to absorb the full implications of her confession.

Leonora was aware of it.

'You're not happy about the baby, Mervyn?' she asked.

'Not entirely. I think it's too soon. I've had a very good summer, but we have to live in the winter. I'm not sure how long people are going to be interested in my pictures.'

'I'm working very hard for you, Mervyn. I have a great many people who are waiting for the winter so that you can paint for them.'

He stared at her in surprise. 'Who are they?' he asked curiously.

'Well there's Thesapolous, the shipping magnate. He saw the picture you did for me and he wants you to paint the scenery on the other side of the island. It's wild and beautiful. You should drive over there one day and take a look at it.'

'Is he serious?'

'Of course he is, and there are others. Besides, work for him and you're in business. Other work will follow, so much, you will begin to wonder why you were afraid.'

'Moira is wanting to go home for Christmas and stay there.'

'When's the baby due?'

'June.'

'But that's ages away. Surely she doesn't expect you to stay with her until the baby is born. Why can't she return with you for a little while?'

He didn't answer. He had already raised these questions with Moira and been met with her string of reasons. Proper doctors, a good hospital, her need to be with her mother.

'How do you suppose the girls on the island go on when they have their children?' he had asked her, only to be confronted with tear-filled eyes and the logical answer that they were Greek girls and had known nothing better.

Mervyn managed to buy an old car from the man who ran the garage in the village and drove across the island one sunny morning in early October. On the way, he explained to Moira that he had a commission to paint that side of the island from a wealthy shipping magnate.

She sat in the car while he strolled across the headland and watched him taking photographs. He could imagine this coast in the winter when the sea broke in across the rocks and precipitous cliffs. Leonora had been right, it was beautiful, wild and untamed and totally unlike the side where most of the islanders lived.

He was quick to notice her glum expression when he returned to the car.

'Don't you think it's beautiful?' he asked her cheerfully.

'I'd rather have the other side. It reminds me of Scotland, we went there once when I was younger, I didn't like that either.'

Mervyn got into the car and reversed onto the road. 'Are you going to paint it from those photographs?' she asked. 'You discouraged us from painting from photographs and other pictures.'

He smiled. 'I know. I'm going to do some sketches from the photographs. I can do those when I take you home before Christmas, and when I come back I can do some serious painting.'

She stared at him in amazement. 'You mean you'll be coming back before the baby's born.'

'Moira, you knew when we left England, that this was to be our life. I have no home in England. This is my home, and here too is my work. Surely you understand this?'

'Yes, yes, I do, but to leave me in England alone to have the baby while you're here on your own?'

'You'll hardly be alone, Moira. You'll be surrounded by that very extensive family of yours, all of them prepared to look after you. Besides, we're talking about a great many months when I shall need to be here. When the birth is imminent I'll fly back to England and stay with you until it's born, then we'll all come back together.'

Her thoughts were chaotic. To come back here, even in the summer time was something she had not bargained for. She had thought they would return to England and Mervyn would realise he had to do something more concrete than paint pictures for holiday visitors. He had to get another job, preferably in teaching. Her father would have to talk to him, explain that the island was no place for his wife and child, make him understand that he was being selfish, putting his love for painting before his love for his wife.

Her silence on the journey home troubled him. He was discovering a side of Moira he had never seen before. She had been so enthusiastic about their future, so thrilled that he was making money selling his pictures, so proud to be his wife, now all she could think of was home and her parents. Athena had called her his child bride and he had resented it – now he saw the logic of her reasoning.

It would be lonely in the winter on the island. Leonora would not be here, her villa would be closed up until the spring, and there would only be the Greek priest to chat to. All the same there would be his work and it was his work that guaranteed their future.

The Sheldons faced their youngest daughter in

grim silence. Her tirade was over and she sat with compressed lips and heightened colour, staring at them furiously.

'Don't you think you're being very selfish, dear,' her mother said mildly. 'If it was you, we'd do exactly the same, want you to come home, make you welcome. What else can we do?'

'She was so full of herself when she went away,' Norah said sharply. 'She was doing better than anybody, marring her teacher, living abroad, making everybody pea-green with envy, and now she's only been away a few months and she's coming back. There's no room for her here.'

'There's her old room, dear. She's not likely to be worrying you. Besides, you're away most of the time at university.'

'I do get holidays. There'll be the baby screaming its head off and where is the baby going to go? Not in my bedroom.'

'We thought of having another room built over the garage.'

'Does that mean she's not going back?'

'Of course not, but if she goes back they'll be coming back for visits, Norah.'

'And what about me? I spend weekends with friends and I won't be able to invite them back because we'll have no room for them. She's always had all her own way. She's always been the favourite.'

'Now Norah, that isn't true,' her father said at last. 'We've never made a favourite of any one of you, we love you both equally.'

'Ask the rest of them, my cousins and my sister said it was always Moira, and when she married

Mervyn you were all so thrilled by it. Her wedding cost three times as much as Kathleen's and George's.'

'That's not fair, dear. Kathleen didn't want a big wedding, we gave them money for their house. Moira didn't need that. They had a house in Greece to go to and Mervyn had the money for his house here.'

'It's not fair. They have a house there, and money, and they're both coming back to live here. Kathleen and George will be furious when they hear.'

Kathleen and George showed no surprise in front of Kathleen's parents, what they said in private was a different matter.

The neighbours quickly got to hear about Moira's pregnancy and that she was coming home to have the baby, and from one of their neighbours Marian Adcock was nothing loath to spread the news in the common room at the school.

They were quick to put two and two together to make five. Martin was quick to defend his friend.

'It's no use your speculating like this,' he said tartly. 'We don't know when the baby's due, probably not until the summer.'

'Then why are they coming home for Christmas?' Marian asked.

'Probably because it's Christmas.'

'Time will tell,' she answered archly.

'Yes it will, and in the meantime we'd do well to keep our thoughts to ourselves.'

Marian didn't particularly like Martin. She'd always thought of him as a stuffed shirt, and he'd always thought she was an embittered old maid who'd fancied Mervyn Corwen who had never fancied her.

The Sheldons called in the local builder and work was started on the bedroom over the garage.

The neighbours put their heads together. Were the Sheldons thinking their daughter and her husband were coming back for good? Wasn't he supposed to own a villa in Greece? Wasn't he supposed to be going out there to paint? Was he coming back to teach school again?

Speculation was rife and it continued because the Sheldons were unable to satisfy their curiosity.

Meanwhile in Greece Moira was happier than she'd been for months. She had something to look forward to, she was going home. She watched Mervyn setting out with his artist's materials every morning for the other side of the island and she dressed prettily for him in the evenings so that they could dine at the taverna.

She saw little of Leonora. The children had returned to Italy and school and Moira was surprised that Leonora lingered on at the villa.

She had presented Mervyn with a list of people who were anxious to have him paint pictures for them and Moira was impatiently wishing she would mind her own business. When she said as much to Mervyn he had answered her with some asperity. 'Moira, isn't this what my life is about? I'm an artist, this is what I'm here for, this is what I do best.'

'I know, darling, but they'll be somewhere over here and we'll be in England.'

He had stared at her in astonishment but she had refused to meet his eyes. Did she really think they were going back for good, or was she simply not thinking straight.

Neither of them were to know that Moira's attitude was exasperating Leonora to such an extent that she felt troubled. This was a marriage that was going one way, Moira's way, and she was reluctant to admit that she cared too much about Mervyn.

She knew if there had been no Moira they would have drifted into an affair. The long summer was coming to an end and she had to think about leaving for Rome. She had stayed on the island longer than usual because friends she knew in the area were anxious to meet Mervyn to talk about the commissions they had for him.

She always invited Moira to visit with Mervyn, but Moira never came, and she had to listen to Mervyn making excuses for her. She was tired, she needed to rest, she wasn't sleeping well.

She accepted his excuses with a gentle smile and felt relieved that he was alone.

'Have you decided when you're leaving for England?' she asked him.

'I think Moira would like to go sooner rather than later, but I have promised Andreas I'll finish his picture by the end of November, that will mean we shall be home before Christmas.'

'And is she agreeable to that?'

He had looked at her with a wry smile. 'No Leonora. She would prefer to go home tomorrow but it isn't possible.'

'I have decided to close up the villa and return to Italy at the beginning of next week. I intend to invite some of my friends who live on the island to a farewell dinner, I hope you and Moira will come. After all, we're not likely to meet again until next spring.'

'Thank you, I'll look forward to it.'

'And Moira?'

'Well of course. I'm sure she'll come to your farewell party.'

Moira knew the people who would be at Leonora's party. Father Cristofson, the doctor who was Italian, highly respected, and who had lived on the island for a great many years, an American author who wrote historical novels and who Mervyn found amusing and worldly and his wife who talked incessantly about her flower garden and their travels before they came to reside in Greece.

Moira described many of Leonora's friends as snobbish, theatrical, too foreign, but surely she could find no fault with the ones she had invited this time.

When he told Moira of the invitation, she smiled, saying, 'That will be nice.'

Nice was Moira's stock in trade, her word to describe everything that was not diabolical or disliked.

She was not looking her best, but then she seldom wore makeup these days, preferring to sit in the garden or lounge about the house with her hair tied back from her face with a chiffon scarf, and he felt a faint antagonism when he thought about the pretty girl who had sat in the classroom with the sunlight shining on her blonde curls through the long windows.

He sympathised with her morning sickness, but bravely she assured him she'd be much better when they returned home.

The bedroom over the garage was almost finished. The plasterers were in and Elizabeth felt relieved that it had been completed before the rain set in.

Norah surveyed the room with narrowed eyes. It was much larger than her bedroom and she suggested it should be her room. She'd be well away from a crying baby and the baby would be nearer it's mother.

Elizabeth was anxious to appease her youngest daughter. She wanted no quarrels between the girls and Norah had an acid tongue in her head and Moira could be easily upset.

The Sheldons felt unsure about how they were going to cope with Mervyn. As a visitor to their home he'd been charming, friendly and appreciative of Elizabeth's cooking; as a resident he could be very different. For one thing it had been Mervyn's wish to live abroad with his art. Would he really settle for life in England with his wife's family?

Moira assured them in her letters that they were both looking forward to coming home. She no longer wrote about the beauty that surrounded her, the Italian Contessa or Mervyn's customers. Now all her letters were in the same vein, England and family, familiar sights and sounds, and Mervyn and his pictures were seldom mentioned.

'I wonder if things have dried up out there?' Arthur Sheldon said curiously.

'Well most of the tourists will have gone home. I suppose it will be quiet at this time of the year.'

'Do you suppose they'll be staying on here until the summer then?'

'I don't know. I only wish I did.'

She had asked Moira in one of her letters how long they intended to stay in England, and would Mervyn be looking for work.

Moira had ignored the question and continued to ignore it.

Questions were being asked in the common room at the school.

'There's no vacancy for him here,' the headmistress said adamantly. 'I gave him every opportunity to take on more classes to enable him to stay on, but he wasn't interested. I know for a fact there's no job going at the college.'

'I think you'll find Mervyn won't even think about coming back,' Martin had said quickly.

Marian Adcock had sniffed derisively. 'Well, the Sheldons have had their house extended. Why would they bother doing that if it was only for a week or two, or even a few months?'

Martin had to agree that it seemed very strange, but the Sheldons were doting parents, nothing had ever been too much trouble for their children.

It was silly to speculate. Come Christmas and all would be made clear.

Chapter Fourteen

It was hard to remember that it was the end of October when the sea rolled in like a turquoise carpet and the sky above was decorated with delicate white clouds.

Mervyn was delighted with the way his picture was going. He had found a comfortable place hollowed out in the rock face and there was room for him to spread out with his equipment. The sun felt warm on his face and there were no sounds beside the distant bells round the necks of goats.

He had come to love this side of the island. It was dramatic and stark but there was a wild beauty about it that captured his imagination and he worked effortlessly, only stopping to eat his sandwiches and drink the flask of coffee he had brought with him.

Tonight it would be Leonora's farewell party and he had told Moira he would get back in good time to change and make himself presentable. He was aware in the late afternoon that the day was changing. The sky was darkening and a few light drops of rain fell on his face. Hurriedly he wrapped up his canvas and packed away the rest of his things. Then he clambered up the rock and ran to where he had parked the car.

He had not gone far when the rain came down with a vengeance and the road was awash with water. He had to stop the car to allow a flock of goats to pass in front of him then he drove on thinking that Moira would hate having to go out on such a night.

By the time he reached the villa, however, the rain had almost stopped and he remembered that Leonora had said this was the predictable side of the island. He let himself into the villa expected Moira to be dressed and ready to go, instead he found her curled up on the sofa wearing slacks and sweater and fast asleep.

He shook her gently, smiling down at her, and when she opened her eyes he said, 'I thought you'd be ready Moira. I'm afraid I got held up on the road and it was raining heavily. I'll have a shower while you change into a party dress.'

'Mervyn, I don't want to go.'

He stared at her in amazement, meeting her stubborn gaze and the spoilt-little-girl expression on her face.

'What do you mean, you don't want to go?'

'I don't know why she's asked me. I really don't know any of them. They talk about things I don't know anything about and they're all a lot older than I am.'

'I'm older than you, Moira.'

'I know, but you're different, you're my husband.'

'Then don't you think that, for once, you can put your own feelings on one side and go to this party? Or are you so obsessed with your own feelings you're prepared to hurt somebody else's?'

She stared at him in hurt surprise. He had

never used that tone of voice with her before. He was her teacher again, somebody who could rubbish her work, somebody who had authority enough to tell her to stop chattering and apply herself to her studies.

'I haven't felt very well,' she stammered. 'Anyway I don't want to go, you'll have to make some excuse for me.'

'Oh no Moira, you'll make your own excuse. If you don't go you must write a letter of apology and tell Leonora exactly why you don't feel able to say goodbye. Tomorrow she's leaving for Rome. This is the least you can do.'

'I shouldn't have to write a letter. You're going. You can tell her I'm not well.'

'You're perfectly well, Moira. You simply don't want to go and I have no excuses to offer on your behalf. I can tell her, of course, that you simply didn't want to come.'

'You can't say that.'

'But it's the truth, Moira. Stay away if you must, but don't expect me to cover for you. You're behaving like a spoilt child.'

He left her to her own devices, feeling angrier with her than he had ever felt. While he showered and dressed his anger didn't evaporate.

He heard her go into the bedroom and for one moment he wondered if she had changed her mind and was getting changed. He waited in the living room, looking out into the darkness. A pale crescent moon had risen and a gentle wind stirred the leaves on the hibiscus. He heard her coming down the stairs and he turned to meet her.

She was still wearing the slacks and sweater and there was a closed-in expression on her pretty face. She came towards him holding out the envelope in her hand.

'I've written her a letter,' she said stonily. 'You can read it to see if you approve.'

He took the letter, then, without reading it, put it into his pocket and without another word left the room.

He was the last to arrive and Leonora welcomed him by asking. 'Are you alone, Mervyn?'

'Yes, Moira hasn't been feeling very well today.'

She looked at him with a half-smile and the expression in her dark eyes made him reach into his pocket and hand over Moira's letter.

She read it without speaking then she folded it and placed it behind an ornament standing on a small table.

'Did you paint today, Mervyn?' she asked him.

'Yes. It was beautiful over there, then the rain came. I had lost count of the time, I'm afraid.'

'Come and meet the others. You'll be ready for a meal.'

He had been in the company of the others several times in the past and conversation was easy. At the same time while he tried to chat normally he was aware of his feeling of anger against his wife. These were delightful people, making him feel one of them as they would have made Moira feel one of them. If Leonora had refused to go to his house after they had invited her, Moira would have been furious. He would have been treated to a display of tantrums and tears, but she was capable of doing it to others.

It was after midnight when Leonora walked with her guests to the gates. She had thrown a soft wrap over her dress and the wind blew her long dark hair entrancingly around her face. The author and his wife had given Father Cristofson a lift home and the doctor and his wife were already driving out onto the road.

Mervyn and Leonora paused near the gates and she said gently, 'You've been rather silent this evening, Mervyn. Please don't mind so much that Moira didn't want to come to my party. I had all sorts of strange notions in my head when I was pregnant.'

'The baby isn't due until the summer, Leonora.'

'I know, but men seldom understand these things.'

'Are you glad to be going home?'

'Very glad. After all, you will soon be leaving for England and I should have been up here completely alone except for the servants. In the summer I'm happy here, but not when the darkness comes early and the summer visitors have gone.'

'But you're not afraid any more, surely?'

'Afraid no, fanciful yes. You would have had to know what it was really like to understand my fears. Never to feel alone, to feel constantly watched, to listen always for footsteps behind.'

'But not now, surely?'

She shrugged her shoulders, an entirely alien gesture, and with a little smile, she said, 'Get off home Mervyn, and make your peace with your wife. I'm not offended, you came, I really didn't mind that she didn't.'

'It's the principle of the thing, Leonora.'

'I know. She's young, obviously spoilt. She has a lot of growing up to do.'

She paused.

'I wonder if you will come back here?' she said.

He stared at her in amazement. 'Well, of course we shall. This is our home. Besides, I have a lot of work waiting for me.'

'Yes, of course.'

'Why do you even think that, I wonder?'

'When I go home to Italy I am surrounded by people who love me, but I am by myself and they cannot understand why I need to come here alone when I could be in Rome or elsewhere surrounded by friends and family. You are going home to friends and family, and from what I know of your wife she will prefer it there.'

'They are not my family, Leonora. There is only Athena in my family and I may not even see her. The others are Moira's family, but I am her husband.'

'Of course. You will come first, I'm sure. Goodbye Mervyn, good luck with the baby and a pleasant journey.'

He looked down at her face etched in moonlight, and he put his arms around her and kissed her gently. The scent of her perfume was in his nostrils, the feel of her softy body in his arms, and he felt her arms steal upwards around his neck and the kiss became warm and passionate for them both.

It was only when he released her and they stood

for a long moment staring into each other's eyes that she smiled gently and turned away. He waited while she walked back along the path and climbed the steps up to the terrace. She entered the villa without looking back, and slowly he walked down the hillside.

Moira was in bed but she was not asleep. She had heard the cars leaving the villa above and her ears strained to hear Mervyn's footsteps along the road. He was the last to leave. What was he doing with Leonora? Why did they have to talk so late after the others had left? Were they discussing her?

She heard him enter the living room and waited for his footsteps to climb the stairs. Time passed and he did not come. In actual fact Mervyn sat slumped in a chair, a bottle of wine on the table beside him and with no wish to go to his bed. At last and after what seemed like hours, Moira rose from the bed and, shrugging her arms into a light robe, she crept downstairs. Mervyn was asleep in his chair. There was half a glass of wine on the table and she stood hesitantly in the doorway. One half of her wanted to rouse him, the other was afraid of the condemnation that she might still read in his eyes.

Moira slept fitfully until the early morning sun invaded the room. Mervyn had not joined her and she took it as a sign that he was still angry with her. In actual fact Mervyn had slept peacefully in his chair throughout the night and as Moira showered and dressed she heard the sounds of crockery from the kitchen below.

She stood in the kitchen doorway watching as

he arranged cups and saucers before returning to the stove and the whistling kettle, then he looked up and saw her.

She smiled, hurriedly asking if she could help him get breakfast, and he knew instantly that she was nervously offering the olive branch. 'There's nothing to do, Moira. What would you like for breakfast?'

'Coffee and toast, nothing more. Please, Mervyn, let me get it. You didn't come to bed. Were you very tired?'

'I must have been. I slept in the chair.'

'Was that because you were angry with me?'

It was her gentle little-girl voice she always used after the mildest argument and he felt irritated by it. For the rest of the day she would be sweet and malleable, desperate to please, painfully affectionate, and while he struggled with his feelings, she repeated her question.

'No, Moira, I simply drank a glass of wine and went to sleep.'

'Did you give Leonora my letter?'

'Of course.'

'What did she say? Was she very cross with me?'

'She read it and laid it aside. Nothing was said.'

'Then she was cross with me.'

Instead of answering her, he applied himself to buttering the toast and carrying it across to the breakfast table.

'Come along,' he said, 'I'll pour the coffee.'

'Mervyn, I really am sorry, I didn't want to go to the party with you, I wasn't feeling well and I thought it would go on so late. There'll be other parties.'

'Have you forgotten that she's returning to Italy today?'

'But she'll come back, there'll be other times.'

He smiled. 'Of course,' he said pouring the coffee.

There could well be other times, and other excuses he thought, and he would have been surprised if he could have read Moira's thoughts. She was going home. England was a long way from Leonora and her parties, and she would persuade Mervyn to stay in England. After all, she was his wife.

'Are you painting today?' she asked him.

'Yes, I'm driving to the other side of the island. I hope to finish the picture today if the weather holds good.'

'I'll come with you. It will be a nice change and there's not much to do over here.'

He stared at her curiously.

'You don't like the wild part of the island, Moira. You always say it depresses you.'

'Well, it won't depress me today. I can watch you paint and we'll be together.'

'We won't be together. I scramble down the rock to a ledge I've found there, you will spend your time sitting in the car waiting for me.'

'Isn't it dangerous to scramble down the rock?'

'Not in that place, it isn't. I do it all the time, but it wouldn't be safe for you.'

'I don't mind sitting in the car. I can take a book. I'm knitting things for the baby, the time will soon pass.'

'Moira, I'd really rather leave you here. I shall feel obliged to hurry with my work when I think of you sitting on the cliff top alone. I really don't think it's a good idea.'

'You're punishing me for last night.'

'No Moira, I'm being sensible. I'll leave you to clear away so that I can get off. I'll be back before it gets dark and we'll go out for a meal. If you haven't been feeling well, it's a good idea to rest up.'

His thoughts were in turmoil as he drove along the narrow road to the rugged west coast. He could hear the tinkling sound of goat bells and he sat for a while in the car looking down on the sea pounding against the rocks. The sun was shining, the sky was a bright azure blue and he should be sorting out his equipment prior to climbing down the rock. Instead, all he could think about was the fact that he no longer loved his wife.

From that first moment when she had walked into his classroom he had loved her, and now, after four months of marriage, love had died. Why? he asked himself angrily. It had nothing to do with that wretched party, nothing to do with the fact that she didn't care much about the island. It had all to do with the difference in their age, their entire upbringing. He should have seen it from the beginning, other people had seen it, his friends, Athena, even his acquaintances. It wasn't Moira's fault. She had wanted him, but she had been too immature to understand that she was in love with love. She had made a perfect suit of clothes and expected him to fill them. If he asked her to be honest, she would surely have to admit that she had fallen out of love with him.

Intellectually, emotionally, they were miles

apart. He did not hate her. He felt an affectionate kindness towards her, but that was all.

What were they going to do with their lives? There was the child to consider, and Moira wanted to return home. Back in her parents' house she would come to hate the island even more. Sunshine and scenery were no substitute for cinemas and concert halls, shopping in the High Street and a return to holidays in sophisticated hotels dotted around the coast.

That life was not for him, but what could he do?

He had to think seriously about their future and the only way he could do it was logically and at some length. He got out of the car and wandered aimlessly across the cliff top. It was breezy on the headland and it helped to clear his head. Moira was his wife, he had to take care of her, but that shouldn't mean burying every dream he had ever had. Painting was his life, he had to earn money, even if it meant their spending time apart. Some women would follow their husbands to the ends of the earth, Moira was not built in that mould.

He knew he would do no painting that day. A young boy came onto the cliff top with a herd of goats. He was wearing a simple, pale-green smock and the sunlight lit up his smiling face and shock of curly hair, so that he seemed to Mervyn like a vision from ancient Greece, a young God on the slopes of Olympus in the dawn of the world, with only the sound of goat bells and the distant sound of the sea. In his imagination he peopled the hillside with mythical creatures, flying horses and unicorns. Aphrodite and Adonis, all watched over by a benevolent Zeus. What a picture it would make, and even as he thought it, he brought himself suddenly down to earth.

Life was real and urgent: there were sterner things at stake than the painting of paradise. Without a second's thought he returned to his car and drove back to the villa.

He found Moira curled up on the couch with a magazine in her hands. She waited avidly for them to arrive from home and her mother kept her well supplied. They both interested her and disturbed her. She looked up in surprise when he entered the room asking, 'Was the weather bad?'

'No, actually it was a lovely day but I realised I wasn't really in the mood for painting, after all: We have a lot to talk about Moira. I think we should do it sooner rather than later.'

She stared at him, and in her eyes was the first hint of fear.

'Talk! What is there to talk about? What have I done?'

'Nothing, my dear, but I do realise that you're not very happy here. I've been selfish. This is the sort of life I've grown up with, the island, the villa, my work, but it isn't your life Moira. Have you been very homesick?'

'No, no, of course I haven't.'

Her reply was too quick, there hadn't been time for her to think.

'We have to be honest with each other, Moira. I suspect we've never been truly honest, either of us. We were in love, we wanted to get married, my life changed. It wasn't the sort of life you thought you would have with me. I suspect you want to go home very much, Moira.'

She was not quick enough to hide the sudden fleeting look of joy that illuminated her face, then quickly it was gone and she asked breathlessly, 'Mervyn, how can I go home and leave you here? Will you come with me?'

'So you do want to go home?'

'Well, to have the baby yes, and we were going home for Christmas anyway. Oh yes, Mervyn, we do have to talk. Can you paint at home? Can you find a new job there? We can still come back here for holidays.'

He knew now that she had been planning their future for some time, a new house not too far away from her parents, a new school for him, a new job, and perhaps, if they were lucky, a month here in August.

'I'll make arrangements for us to return to England as soon as possible. It will probably be at the end of November.'

'Oh Mervyn, that will be wonderful. You can paint at home, in the conservatory or the new bedroom until the baby is born, and we can both look forward to coming here in the summer, perhaps bring Mum and Dad.'

He decided he would not tell her yet. He had no intention of living the sort of life she had planned for him. He would see her settled in with her parents, then he would come back. He would leave it with Moira how their future would evolve.

Chapter Fifteen

All morning Moira had been happy. He had heard her humming while she packed her suitcase, running to the gate whenever she heard the sound of a car on the cliff road. They were waiting for the taxi to take them to the ferry.

'I hope he isn't going to be late,' she cried. 'Have you used them before?'

He assured her that he had.

'I do hope the plane won't be late. Mum and Dad will be sure to be meeting us at the airport.'

'I told them they needn't bother. I would hire a car.'

'But it won't be any bother darling. They'll want to meet us.'

The taxi arrived and they picked up their cases, after reassuring themselves that everything in the tiny villa was in order.

She waited impatiently while he locked the door but when they reached the waiting taxi, there was no sign of the driver, and looking up the path they saw him staring into the garden of the villa above.

Mervyn opened the door for his wife, slamming it behind her so that the driver turned and walked towards them.

Mervyn was looking at him curiously and with a grin he said, 'I like to look at that villa, it's beautiful.'

His English was good enough to surprise Mervyn who said quickly, 'You're new here?'

'No, I've worked on the island before, but I've been on the boats during the summer.'

'But you're not from these parts?'

'My home's on one of the other islands. I move around a bit.'

'Your English is surprisingly good.'

'I worked in England at one time. Is this all your luggage sir?'

'Yes.' He stood watching while the driver placed it in the boot. Something about the man disturbed him. He was affable, about Mervyn's age and good looking, but he was remembering Leonora's eyes when she had looked out across the gardens the night before. Somehow he didn't think the man was Greek and casually he asked, 'Why are you so interested in the villa, I take it you've seen it many times?'

'Yes sir, and every time I wish it was mine. I'll never afford one like it. Do you know the people who live there?'

'Yes. They're our neighbours.'

Through the driving mirror their eyes met, and, as if he thought Mervyn was waiting for an explanation, the driver said, 'I've always thought it sad that nobody ever seemed to be there. When my wife comes here she looks at that villa. I can't get her away from it.'

'I've never seen a woman up there.'

'Small dark woman, very pretty.'

Mervyn didn't answer him. His English was too perfect with hardly a trace of a foreign accent, and even then it was not the accent of the islanders. Nor did he believe in the wife.

He was becoming paranoid. In his heart he'd accused Leonora of being so, and some of her anxieties she had transferred to him. Moira was looking at him strangely, but by this time they were arriving at the jetty and already a small queue had formed at the gangway.

By the time they had collected their luggage and he had tipped the driver, they were the last to board the boat and were lucky to find seats together.

'Why were you asking him all those questions?' Moira asked.

'I wondered why he was so interested in the villa. I've had other taxi-drivers, they've never given it a second glance.'

'Well he said he wasn't a local man.'

'I know. There was just something about him that didn't ring true.'

'I think Leonora imagines things.'

Their arrival in Rhodes meant an end to the discussion. As always the harbour was bustling with visitors and market stalls and they were lucky to pick up another taxi to take them to the airport.

Not even England on a grey November day could quench Moira's high spirits as her eyes eagerly scanned the crowd of people waiting for travellers, then she picked up her parents standing anxiously just inside the doors and she ran towards them and Mervyn watched while they swept her into their arms.

More decorously Mervyn shook their hands and Mr Sheldon informed them that the car was parked in the car park. He helped Mervyn push their trolley through the crowds and waiting taxi-drivers.

'Did you have a good flight?' he asked.

'Quite good,' Mervyn answered, while Moira said, 'It wasn't bad, I've come to the conclusion that I don't like flying.'

'Neither do I,' her mother agreed.

'Is Norah home?' Moira asked.

'Not until Christmas, and we don't really know if she's coming then.'

'Oh. Why's that?'

'Well, she's made a lot of new friends at university. She seems to get a great many invitations to visit their homes.'

'Well, surely, she'll want to be with us. After all, she hasn't seen me since the end of July.'

The end of July, Mervyn thought savagely. Was that really all the time they had had?

Mr Sheldon was saying, 'We've furnished the bedroom over the garage, love, but Norah's put in a claim for it. Says the baby will be better in the small bedroom and nearer to you.'

'I suppose she's right,' Moira admitted grudgingly.

'And the happy event is due in the summer?' he asked.

'Yes, early July.'

'So you'll be coming back in good time for that?'

'We have to talk about it, Dad,' she replied.

She was unsure how they would respond to her suggestion that she was staying until the baby was born, what came afterwards would have to wait.

Mervyn knew what was passing through her mind. Moira would not go back to the island, but how would it affect their marriage? They would all be ranged against him but in the end he too had a life to live.

The weeks leading up to Christmas were busy ones in the Sheldon household. Moira was happy. This was her world, shopping in the market, in the high street, drinking coffee with her mother and friends, attending church and concerts in the evenings.

He was bored. He tried some sketching but his thoughts were bitter when he remembered the canvases that he had left unfinished on the island, and one day Mr Sheldon said, 'What about your painting Mervyn? The room over the garage is well lit, and there are two radiators in it. We can move the furniture to make room for your equipment.'

'I have nothing here. The canvasses were far too large for me to bring and in some cases the paint was still wet.'

'When will you finish them then?'

'When I go back.'

'And when will that be, after Christmas? Does that mean Moira will be going with you?'

'You will have to ask her that, but I must go back. The paintings have been commissioned.'

'Well really. I thought you'd have been staying on for a while, particularly in the winter. What about the baby, surely you'll come back to England for the birth?'

'Of course.'

When they were alone Arthur Sheldon confided in his wife. Her eyes filled with tears.

'Really Arthur, how can he even think of going back and leaving her here? What sort of a marriage do they have? Does Moira know he's going back?'

'She must do, love. Don't take on so, it's got nothing to do with us.'

'But it has. She's our daughter, the baby'll be our grandchild.'

'And she's Mervyn's wife.'

'I know. What does he do with himself all day while Moira's shopping with me?'

'How do I know? I'm at work aren't I?'

To Mervyn the days seemed endless. He looked in the bookcase for books but found few to his taste. He did the crosswords in the daily paper and watched television. Most days the rain came down from leaden skies and it was dark by half past four in the afternoon.

He had been back in England two weeks when he decided to visit his old school during what he knew would be their break. Nostalgia filled him as he walked across the familiar path from the iron gates, looking at the lights blazing from every window, picturing the hall being got ready for Christmas festivities, and the camaraderie within the common room. Most of them he had liked – there had only been the odd one or two who had riled him, like Marian Adcock with her thinly disguised taunts, and her more annoying attempts to flirt with him.

They were chatting over the coffee cups when he opened the common-room door and immediately all conversation ceased and he was greeted to cheery greetings and a swift look round the room assured him that Marian was not present.

Shaking hands, Martin said affably, 'She's off with a chill, you've picked a good day. The Head's off too, some virus that's going around.'

Mervyn spared a swift rush of gratitude for the virus.

'I suppose you're here until after Christmas,' he said.

'That's the idea.'

'And when is the happy event due?'

'Next July.'

'What a pity Marian isn't here. She was convinced it was imminent.'

'I was sure she would be.'

'So you'll be coming back for the summer?'

'Yes. Moira'll be staying on here.'

Martin raised his eyebrows. 'You mean you're going back alone after Christmas?'

'Will you be seeing Athena?' he continued.

'I thought I'd give her a ring, if she's at home I might go up there for a day or so.'

'And will Moira go with you?'

'Perhaps, perhaps not.'

Athena was at home and wanting to see him. Moira, however, did not wish to go to Scotland so soon before Christmas: she preferred to help her mother at home. 'After all, darling, Christmas is always so hectic here. The family are popping in and out half the time.'

'With a house full of people, Moira, perhaps you won't miss me if I stay on with Athena?' he asked quietly.

'Mervyn, I think that's awful. Our first Christmas as husband and wife and you're thinking of staying on in Scotland. Mother will be horrified.'

The entire outcome was solved by providence, just before Christmas, there were blizzards all over the north, and all trains were cancelled. There was no chance that Mervyn could rejoin the Sheldons in time for Christmas.

He was appalled that Athena's husband looked so frail, spending most of his day sitting in front of a roaring fire in the chair he had become adept at propelling around the house. Athena was her usual enigmatic self, her expression saying far more than her words.

Outside the wind raged fiercely around the large stone house and beyond the churning waters of the loch the mountains loomed dark and forbidding. Inside, however, there were logs burning in huge grates filling the air with the scent of pine, and he got to know Ian, finding him calm and sensitive, a man afflicted with great pain, yet a man with a wry sense of humour, surprised that they had many things in common.

Cassie was much like her mother. A self-contained child whose dancing feet echoed along the winding corridors and lofty rooms of the old house. She was Ian's joy, and one day Mervyn felt saddened when he said, 'I shan't see her grow up, Mervyn.'

He sat staring into the fire, before he looked up with a wry smile saying, 'I'm deteriorating, I know it without them telling me. There was a time when it was no trouble to move my chair about the house. Now more and more I am finding it difficult.'

'Athena tells me you're much the same,' Mervyn ventured.

'I try not to worry her. I was always too old for her Mervyn. I've never asked her to slow her steps to match mine, but when I've gone she'll bloom again. There is life for Athena after me.'

'I don't like to hear you talking like that, Ian. I'd like to think you'll be here to see Cassie grow up.'

Ian merely shook his head.

'That would be unfair to both of them Mervyn. There was a time when we would never have been in Scotland over Christmas. We'd have been in some foreign place where the sun was shining and the sea was blue. She tells me she doesn't miss those days, but I know she does. She's a young, beautiful woman with so much living to do. I don't want to be a burden to either of them, and I'm very much afraid I have been over these last few years.'

'I'm sure Athena doesn't think so.'

'Perhaps not, but one has to look at these things honestly.'

The storms died out and the loch calmed. It was a time for him to return to his wife but he was aware of a great reluctance. He was happier listening to Ian's wry humour and Athena's vague promptings about his future. He walked with Cassie along the banks of the loch and gave her lessons in watercolour painting. Before New Year however, he decided it was time to leave.

The Sheldons' greeting was less than rapturous, although they knew about the blizzards and that it would have been impossible for him to travel.

'Did your cousin wonder why I didn't go with you?' Moira asked.

'They would have liked to have seen you, Moira. You would have loved the house on the banks of the loch.'

'I've only been to Scotland once and that was when I was very young. I didn't like it. There was a lot of mist and it was cold.'

Mervyn didn't pursue the subject, and Moira asked, 'Did Athena want to know when we were going back?'

'Yes. I told her you would be staying on.' It was out now and he looked at her hurt little-girl face and accusing eyes.

'You didn't say very much about the school, Mervyn. Did they get somebody in your place?'

'They have another woman teacher.'

'Teaching art?'

'Amongst other things.'

'You could have done that, Mervyn. I thought I was marrying a school teacher, I never thought I was marrying an artist.'

'I did keep you fully informed, my dear.'

Moira's parents were unhappy with the situation because they could not help but be aware of the undercurrents.

'Why doesn't he get a job here?' Mrs Sheldon grumbled. 'There must be a great many teaching jobs going, there are enough schools and there's the college.'

'We can't interfere, Elizabeth.'

'I blame that cousin of his, giving him that villa

as though it was a piece of furniture, he thinks he has to go back there.'

Things didn't improve that evening when one of Moira's schoolfriends called to say that her parents were moving into a new house being built across the park.

The following day Mrs Sheldon and Moira made it their business to inspect the new houses and one look at Moira's face told her mother that they were exactly what she would like. Why, oh why, couldn't Mervyn have kept his job at the school? They could have moved into one of these and they'd have been nearer her parents.

'You must try to persuade him to stay here,' her mother said.

'He's a married man, about to become a parent, he should put you and the baby first.'

'He hasn't got a job here Mum.'

'And whose fault is that?'

'He made a lot of money selling pictures on the island, more than he could have hoped to make teaching.'

'Money isn't everything.'

They were not to know that at that precise moment Mervyn was sitting in front of the fire in Martin's house, a whisky and soda in front of him, while Martin and his wife occasionally exchanged glances when they became increasingly aware of Mervyn's morose silence.

The labrador came into the room and stood hopefully with his ball in front of Mervyn's chair and Martin said, 'He's in no mood for you, old lad. Bring your ball over here.'

Mervyn shook himself out of his reverie and,

with a wry smile, said. 'I'm sorry to be such poor company. I've a lot on my mind. I should have walked it off before I intruded on you two.'

'If you want to talk about it, we're good listeners,' Martin said. 'But we didn't want to be the ones asking questions. I take it that all is not too rosy with your life at the moment?'

Mervyn nodded.

'I don't know what to do. I love the island and I'm making money. It's what I've always wanted to do, paint, sell my pictures, and Moira did assure me it was what she wanted too. Now I'm aware she hates every moment she spends in that place. She and her parents are doing all they can to persuade me to stay here, find another teaching job, buy some property here.'

'And what about you?'

'I'd stagnate. She's my wife and there's the baby. I don't know what the answer is.'

Martin didn't want to tell him that marriage with Moira had been a disaster waiting to happen. Everybody in that common room with the exception of one or two had thought so. They had all taught the Sheldon girl, a nice pretty girl, a small-town girl who should have married a local boy like the one her older sister had married. A boy who would have enjoyed going for tea every Sunday, sharing a family holiday for two weeks at the coast, and celebrating birthdays and Christmases together until time ran out.

Mervyn should have been the one to know it couldn't work. He was marrying a child bride who would have made some other man an admirable wife, but not Mervyn, never Mervyn.

Instead he said, 'But you'll have to go back there if you have commissions to do. Surely Moira can see that?'

'I suppose so.'

'It's your work Mervyn. Didn't you explain it to her when you got married?'

'I thought I'd explained it very fully. She's not entirely to blame. After all, she hadn't seen the island for herself. It's very beautiful, but there are no shops as such, no cinemas, and I was kept very busy. Everything about it was wrong from the outset.'

'Most people would enjoy spending their summer on a Greek island.'

'The summer wasn't too bad, but then the holiday people left and the days shortened. She hated the villa, particularly the kitchen, she had nobody to gossip with, and the one person she could have talked to she didn't particularly like.'

'Who was that then?'

'Leonora, the Italian contessa who lives at the large villa above us.'

'Beautiful?'

'Yes very. And delightful, very delightful.'

'I can well understand that your pretty child bride wouldn't take to Leonora. Beautiful, sophisticated, aristocratic. Wasn't her husband there?'

'She's a widow.'

'Oh dear. She probably looked on her as a husband stealer.'

'What are you going to do, Mervyn?' Martin's wife asked curiously.

'Obviously I have to go back and obviously it's going to be a difficult decision to make. I'll be leaving a tearful wife behind as well as her family who will most certainly be condemning me for everything.'

He took his leave and, at the door, Martin said, 'You'll let us know when you're leaving, Mervyn?'

'Yes of course. I'll be back well before the baby's born.'

Martin stood at the door watching his friend walk to the gate. He seemed somehow like a man surrounded by a great loneliness and strangely solitary. He wouldn't like to have Mervyn's problems on his shoulders, but then he'd have had more sense than to marry one of his old pupils, particularly one as cosseted as young Moira Sheldon.

Chapter Sixteen

Wind-swept clouds hung low in the threatening sky that covered the English countryside. It was bitterly cold with flurries of snow erupting across the tarmac and Mervyn had been glad to sink into his window-seat from where he could gaze at the lights from the airport they would soon be leaving behind them.

They were ready to taxi along the runway and he was now aware that there was nobody joining him and that there were many empty seats in the plane. He would have nobody to chat to, leaving him plenty of time to think about the last few days he had spent with his wife.

It had seemed to Mervyn that a spectre had hung over the house. There had been no spoken reproaches from Moira or her parents; at the same time they had made him feel like a deserter. They had all accompanied him to the airport and Moira had smiled bravely, saying, 'Don't worry about me darling. I'll be perfectly all right. I'll write often and tell you how the baby's faring. July will soon be here. Do you mind if it's a boy or a girl?'

'No, just as long as you're both well and happy.'

'I hope it's a girl. Girls care so much more for their parents and their home. I want to call her Margaret, I always wished they'd called me Margaret. What do you want to call her?'

'I'm quite happy with Margaret, dear.'

'No, no, she has to have another name, one your uncle might have chosen.'

He stared at her in surprise. She had never mentioned his uncle before, and she had often said that Athena and Cassandra were fanciful.

'There must be something,' she urged.

'My uncle always said if he'd had another daughter he'd have called her Selene.'

'Really. Was she a goddess? I've never heard of it.'

'And if it's a boy?'

'I'd like to call him Peter. Peter Arthur after my dad,' then hurriedly, 'Unless you'd like to call him Peter Bertram?'

'Perhaps we should wait and see, Moira. You

might change your mind.'

'I shan't. I like Peter, and I do want to call him after Dad, because he was blessed with three daughters and never had a son. You do see, don't you?'

It was time to leave. Time to put his arms around her and look into her tear-filled eyes, time for their reproach to manifest itself once more as he took her father's outstretched hand and kissed her mother's cheek.

He despised the feelings of relief that swept over him, relief tinged with remorseless guilt, guilt that lingered long after the plane soared above the low, sleet-filled clouds into the sunlight above.

His spirits revived when he viewed the island of Rhodes beneath them, as the plane banked ready for its landing. A watery sun was shining but in late January there was little warmth in it. One had to go further south to escape the winter chill, the coast of Africa, Egypt and beyond.

Only a handful of local people waited at the jetty for the ferry that plied between the islands and they greeted him with cordial smiles. He felt one of them after the years he had spent coming and going to the island.

It was choppy on the water and the small ferry that did duty in the winter months tossed like a flimsy cork in the swell but the crew and the passengers treated it with good humour and laughter. Mervyn's spirits soared: he was coming home.

He was helped onto the jetty by a member of the crew who handed him his luggage and he walked across the road to the garage on the quayside. He knew the garage-owner well, had bought his old banger from him and the man greeted him with a bright smile and warm handshake. He looked around and seeing that Mervyn was alone looked at him curiously and with a wry smile.

'My wife's staying on in England. It's too cold for her on the island at this time.'

The man was not to know that it was infinitely much colder in England.

He went to the open garage door and called out to whoever was inside and after a few minutes the man Mervyn knew as Demetrius came out. He took Mervyn's luggage, indicating the ancient taxi standing near the wall and Mervyn asked the proprietor, 'Who was the man who brought us to the ferry just before Christmas?'

The two men looked at one another, then Demetrius said in Greek, 'That would be Paulus,' and Mervyn's Greek was good enough to understand him.

'Doesn't he work here now?' he asked.

The older man said, 'He come, he go. He not live on the island.'

'But he works for you from time to time?'

He shrugged his shoulders. 'Yes, yes, him good workman, but he likes to work the boats. Next year he'll be back, always he comes back.'

'Does his wife live on Rhodes?'

Again the two men exchanged glances and shrugs and from their expressions Mervyn gathered that a wife was something none of them talked about or knew much about.

'What did you say his name was. Is he Greek?'

The two men looked at each other in perplexity. They didn't know much about him, that much was apparent and the proprietor said, 'You not like this man, not satisfied?'

'Oh yes, I just didn't think he lived here. He was very interested in the Contessa's villa.'

He laughed. 'He has no money. I not pay him enough to buy that, however interested.'

Mervyn smiled, deciding to leave well alone. He didn't like to think that the garage owner might consider him over interested in a casual employee.

There were no flowers in the garden of the villa and he was glad that Moira was not seeing it like this.

The living room was scrupulously clean with the fire laid and ready for lighting and the plants had been cared for, standing erect and green in their containers. Absentmindedly he glanced at the small pile of letters Maria had placed on the table, art circulars most of them, with the exception of one in Martin's handwriting. He had not known that Mervyn would be leaving for England so soon.

He felt suddenly cold, and after putting a match to the fire, he looked in the kitchen and saw that fresh milk had been left there as well as bread and eggs.

Picking up his suitcase he went upstairs and into the bedroom. Nothing of Moira remained: it was as though the few months of their life together had never been. Haphazardly, he opened one or two of her drawers but they were empty.

Moira had known she would not be coming back and yet she had not wanted their marriage to end. He knew that she loved him, but she wanted the marriage on her terms.

He had no doubt that they would journey on together. If he was lucky she and the baby would join him in the summer for a few weeks when the weather was hot and the island busy with holiday crowds. Perhaps she would persuade her parents to join them and they would agree that the island was beautiful but they would also see the ancient stove and the heavy crockery, the whitewashed walls and the great open fireplace.

They would understand why Moira couldn't settle here, a primitive paradise, and they would add their persuasions to hers for him to return to England.

Mr Sheldon had been quick to tell him about the art exhibitions in the town where unknown artists were selling their pictures for fifty pounds or even more, and these were people painting in their spare time. Why Mervyn would be able to charge double that, and Mervyn had not bothered to tell him that he was already selling his pictures for twenty times that amount.

Almost every day letters came from Moira, she was as prolific in her letter-writing to him as she had been to her mother. She wrote about the concerts they were attending and how much he would have enjoyed them. She wrote about one they had been to at the school where the children were enchanting and where so many people had asked about him.

'I didn't hear from you at all last week,' she

wrote. 'Do please write soon and tell me how you are and what is happening there.'

There was little to tell her. He told her he was well, had finished two of his pictures and they were being collected within the next few days. Maria was looking after him very well and he was dining often with the priest.

He had the feeling that every letter he sent to her was the same, while hers were filled with family, friends and there was always so much to do.

Athena wrote to say that Ian's health was deteriorating and she wished they could get away from the damp and the low-hanging mists. Cassie was well and was taking the lead in her school's concerts, a fact that didn't surprise him, a girl with so much of her mother's flair and confidence.

It was the end of March and he had left his studio early and was cooking his modest evening meal in the kitchen when he heard the sound of a car on the road and then a sharp knock on his door. He was amazed to see Leonora smiling at him, and laughing at his surprise she said, 'I came back early Mervyn. I'm hoping you would come up to the villa with me to see if everything's in order. There's a taxi waiting.'

He looked sharply at the driver of her taxi, relieved to see that it was Demetrius who greeted him with a cheerful grin.

'Moira won't mind you coming with me?' she asked.

'Moira isn't here. I came back alone.'

'You said she might stay on until the baby is

born. Is she quite well?'

'Very well, and with much to do. How could you tear yourself away from Rome at this time?'

She didn't answer him immediately and there was a thoughtful frown on her face. At last with a little smile she turned to say, 'Even Rome has its disadvantages, Mervyn. My mother thinks it's time I remarried, I've been on my own long enough.'

By this time they had reached the front of the villa and Demetrius was lifting out her luggage.

'There isn't much of it,' Mervyn said. 'Don't you intend staying long?'

'I didn't take very much away. My wardrobes here are full of clothes.' After telling Mervyn where to find the fuse-box she stood in the dark waiting for the lights to come on, then she went into the salon and pulled back the drapes at the long windows.

Mervyn had followed her into the room and stood beside her gazing out across the gardens.

'This is the first time I've ever been on the island in March, Giorgio would never come and there was always so much to do in Rome. This time there wasn't enough to do.'

'I can't believe that, Leonora.'

'Well, there were the shops of course, the opera and the fashion shows, but then everywhere we went there was Marco.'

'Marco?'

'Yes. I've known him for years, he was a friend of Giorgio's, he came to our wedding. He's handsome, very rich and he thinks like Giorgio and acts like Giorgio. He's also a banker.'

'He sounds eminently suitable to me.'

'Of course, perhaps that is why I find him entirely unsuitable. I would be marrying for the sake of getting married. Marco and I have known each other too long, we would not be marrying for love.'

'That too might not be a bad idea.'

'Oh dear Mervyn, are you really so disillusioned?'

'Perhaps I am. Love blinds one to so many things. I was in love with Moira. It stopped me thinking about all the things that would divide us, things that are now so apparent.'

'And now you are saying that you are no longer in love with her?'

She looked up into his face, brooding and reflective and she knew that he was thinking of Moira and the state of his marriage.

'How long did it take you to realise you didn't love Giorgio?' he asked her.

'I told you that I never really loved him. I loved somebody else, somebody quite unworthy, somebody who didn't deserve my love. Giorgio was a good man, it was sad that I didn't love him. It wasn't like that with you and Moira. You thought you did love her and she loved you.'

'But neither of us are prepared to make a sacrifice to stay together. My life and my work are here. Moira's life is with her family and familiar things. Which one of us should be the one to bend?'

'Have neither of you heard of the word "compromise"?'

He didn't answer, there was no answer.

'Don't you mind being here alone?' he asked her.

'Yes I mind. I will find myself looking for shadows, listening to footsteps, seeing eyes peering at me through the trees and bushes in the garden. There won't be anybody of course, it will all be in my imagination.'

And of course it would be, he told himself, the taxi-driver was just that, a man who did casual labour and worked on the boats, a man who liked the look of the villa, not some long-lost lover looking for revenge.

'You know where to find me when you need me,' he said looking down on her with gentle irony, and they both knew what his words could mean. They were two lonely people – she beautiful and appealing – two people who found each other attractive: it was a situation waiting to be exploited.

Moira's letters continued to arrive almost daily, each one filled with her everyday activities and each one conveying thoughts on all that he was missing, including prospects of employment in the area. She'd been talking to Marian Adcock who had told her there would soon be another opening for a teacher at the school.

When Mervyn replied to her letters he ignored such matters, but he found it increasingly difficult to tell her anything she wanted to know.

He punished himself by staying away from Leonora, even when he knew that one day they must meet. She came into his studio one afternoon and sat for a while watching him paint. He turned to smile at her asking. 'How do you think it's coming along?'

'Very well. Is it something you started in the summer?'

'No. I'm painting from photographs. I thought it was too dull to paint outside.'

'Why don't we drive over there in the morning very early? This morning there was the most beautiful red sky out there. If you can capture that I will commission you to paint it.'

He laughed. 'You're not serious of course.'

'But I am very serious. I will hang it in my bedroom in Rome and I will think about the day you painted it, and how beautiful the day was.'

'Tomorrow it could be different.'

'We could try?'

'We?'

'Why, yes, I will go with you. We can take a picnic and I'll be very quiet, just watching you paint.'

'And we shall probably freeze.'

'Well of course not. That little niche in the rocks that you found is a wonderful shelter.'

'How do you know about that?'

'Moira told me. She thought it was dangerous.'

'It may be if we go there together.'

Their eyes met and held, then, with a light laugh, she said, 'I'm going home now, Mervyn, I'll pack a picnic hamper and I'll drive. Suppose I pick you up around ten o'clock?'

Before he could answer she was letting herself out of the door and he called out, 'Suppose it's raining?'

'It won't be, I promise.'

He watched her running to her car, reversing it

out onto the road, and driving fast up the hill. When he left the studio later to go to his car, he met Demetrius walking down the road. He favoured Mervyn with his usual cheerful grin and Mervyn surprised himself by asking, 'When is the other mechanic coming back?'

Demetrius shrugged his shoulders. 'Who knows, he come, he go, in the summer perhaps.'

'What did you call him?'

'Paulus.'

He tried to remember the name of the Italian Leonora had loved years ago but he couldn't. Maybe she had never told him his name.

The prospect of spending the next day with Leonora filled him with anticipation, mingled with self-doubt. They were getting into deep water. Who knew what the outcome might be?

When he got into her car the next morning her face was alive with smiles. 'You see,' she said. 'I told you the day would be beautiful. Did you see the colour of the sky?'

'I did, and now the colour will have gone.'

'But the scenery is still there and you will remember the colour. I always thought artists were very good at carrying colour in their minds.'

She drove fast along the narrow cliff road and the powerful car completed the journey in half the time it took him in his elderly tourer.

'You drive too fast,' he cautioned her.

She laughed. 'I know. Giorgio always told me that. He said that one day I'd take a nose dive over the cliff.'

He helped her to climb down the narrow path onto the ledge below and there was ample room for Leonora to sit curled up in a corner so that she could watch him sketch. It was a view he had drawn many times but this morning there were seabirds and spray on the rocks below.

She did not chatter as Moira always did when she watched him work, she sat in her corner hugging her knees entirely wrapped up in watching the picture take shape, and occasionally when he looked up to look at her she smiled.

He lost all sense of time and it was Leonora who said, 'There is food in the car, Mervyn. Surely you must be hungry.'

He looked at his watch and gasped with surprise: it was two o'clock.

'Why didn't you tell me it was so late?' he said with a smile.

'It doesn't matter. You'll have to help me up, I'm a little stiff after sitting so long.'

He pulled her to her feet and stood with his arms around her, her head resting on his shoulder, then reluctantly he released her to help her up the cliff.

She had packed a veritable feast for them and there was a bottle of Orvieto to drink. By the time they had finished their meal spots of rain were covering the car windows and overhead storm clouds were gathering.

'I thought you said it would be glorious all day,' he said teasingly.

'But it has, and it will be. Now it is time to go back. We have had the best of the day.'

'I'm not a bad cook,' Mervyn said, 'If you don't mind eating like a peasant, I can cook a meal for us.'

She didn't answer but the rain was coming down in torrents and she was giving the road all her attention.

The storm was bringing rocks and pebbles down the road with it and even Leonora was unable to drive with her usual élan. They were both glad to see Leonora's villa on the hill above them, and she brought the car to a standstill outside Mervyn's gate.

He got out of the car and started to collect his equipment from the back seat, then he turned to look at her. She was sitting in the driver's seat with her hands on the wheel, and it was evident that she was not getting out of the car.

There was an expression on her face he couldn't read, but he said quietly, 'Thank you for today, Leonora. It was nice of you to come and the picnic was an inspiration. You don't want me to cook for us, then?'

She shook her head. 'I don't want you to make love to me in your wife's house and on your wife's bed, Mervyn. That is where it would lead to. Why don't you come and dine with me. There are no memories of Giorgio in my bedroom and even if there were he is long dead. If you don't come I shall know you don't want there to be anything for us Mervyn. I shall understand.'

He stood in the rain listening to the car's engine until he could hear it no more.

Chapter Seventeen

Mrs Sheldon surveyed her youngest daughter across the kitchen table with an unhappy frown on her face. She had hoped Norah would come home for Easter, now she wasn't so sure. The two girls had already had words, and Norah had always had a sharp tongue in her head. The point was that in many respects she had to agree that Norah was right but Moira had always been the gentle, delicate one.

Moira had hated sport which Norah had excelled in. Moira had been the dreamer with her head in some book or other, painting her pictures, living her life with her head in the clouds, while Norah had been streetwise, the one who knew where she was going.

When everybody thought Moira was doing remarkably well for herself in the marriage stakes, Norah had been the one dissenting voice: he was too old, too different, too totally wrong for her.

'I don't want you and Moira quarrelling while I'm out, you've only been home three days and you've already reduced her to tears,' Mrs Sheldon warned her.

'That doesn't take much.'

'Have a bit of patience. She's having a baby and obviously has a lot on her mind.'

'She's got the stupidest marriage I ever heard

of. She's here and he's in Greece. If they're so much in love, why aren't they together?'

'It's very difficult. She wants the baby to be born here and he has his work on the island. I thought he might have come back for Easter but Moira says Easter is just when people are starting to arrive on the island and he will be far too busy.'

'She doesn't want him to see her looking fat and plain. She says he's coming over for the baby's birth, then she'll be able to show it off and dress herself-up to look beautiful for him. She's a silly cow.'

'Norah, I don't like you to speak like that about Moira. She's being very brave to face it all here without his support.'

'Oh Mum, if she said the moon was made out of green cheese you and Dad would agree with her.'

'I've got a friend at Uni who was born in Nigeria. She has three brothers and a sister all born out there where her father was a doctor. Most of the time they lived on a compound surrounded by wild animals and they had a tin bath and an old pump to pump out the water. Her mother never complained: she knew the sort of life she'd have when she married, and she stuck it out. Moira stuck it for a few months and it's my bet she'll never go back.'

'Well, of course, she'll go back. She loves him and he loves her.'

The expression on her daughter's face unnerved her. It wasn't the sort of love Norah believed in.

'You wouldn't have behaved any differently if you were unhappy. Moira said the cooking facilities were primitive. The girl who helped around the house only knew a smattering of English and she had nothing in common with the Italian woman. Mervyn was too wrapped up in his work to be able to spend much time with her, what would you have done?'

'I sure as hell wouldn't have left him to come back here. He was the one earning the money, and he explained everything to her before they went to live there.'

'Then I don't think she fully understood him.'

'No, she didn't. She thought she'd be living on an island where the sun always shone, the palm trees waved along the beach and they'd dance to bongo music every evening. I don't think the marriage will last.'

'That's an awful thing to say.'

'Well, I don't Mum. It'll last if he comes back here, takes up a teaching job and paints pretty pictures in his spare time. Can you see him doing that?'

'I can if he loves her.'

Norah favoured her mother with a cynical smile. Her mother'd been reading too many romantic novels where the hero was always willing to give everything up for love and the heroine was duly grateful.

Nonplussed, Mrs Sheldon bit her tongue. Norah was wrong of course, she was too canny for her own good, but the prospects of a peaceful Easter seemed to be too much to hope for.

'Well I have to go to the shops,' she said.

'Remember what I said, I don't want you two quarrelling while I'm out.'

'Well, she isn't down yet, is she?'

'She has to rest and she hasn't to be upset.'

Norah grinned as her mother marched out of the kitchen.

Norah went to stare out of the window. It was one of those mornings in early April that had started by promising much in the way of sunshine. Now a thin drizzle of rain covered the windowpane and the sun had retreated behind the clouds.

There was always so much to do at university and she had made a host of good friends there. Here the prospect of the day ahead didn't exactly fill her with elation. She could study, but a holiday was a time to forget work for a while. She could have gone to the shops with her mother but Moira had always been the one to do that while she had had to be forced into it. The sound of the opening door made her turn to see her sister entering the kitchen.

She looked tired and there was a greyness about her face that made her seem drawn and older than her years. She sat down heavily at the kitchen table and Norah said, 'There's some tea in the pot but I'll brew some fresh, unless you'd prefer coffee.'

'No, I'm not drinking much coffee.'

Norah set about brewing a fresh pot of tea and Moira sat lethargically with the morning paper spread out in front of her. Norah looked at her in some exasperation. She was a young wife, about to become a mother, and yet there was nothing in her appearance to remind her of the beautiful young girl who had departed for Greece only months before. What sort of disenchantment had done this to her?

She poured out two cups of tea, taking them over to the table and placing one in front of Moira.

'What are you doing with yourself today?' she asked her.

Moira lifted her eyes and gazed at her dully for several seconds before answering. 'What is there to do? What are you doing?'

'I'll think of something.'

'Has Mum gone out?'

'Yes, to the shops. Do you ever go with her these days?'

'Occasionally, but I'm feeling so tired.'

'Why doesn't Mervyn come home for Easter? Don't you want to see him?'

'Well, of course I do, but not looking like this.'

'Other women's husbands see them looking as you do. Why is he so different?'

'I don't want him to see me like this, it's got nothing to do with him.'

'I don't understand anything about your marriage. I used to listen to you going on and on about him when you were in his class. He was the most marvellous person in the world, even then. Then you got him and everything was perfect. Now you're miles apart and you don't even want him home for Easter. What's happened to your marriage?'

'Nothing. I want to see him in the summer when I'm back to normal and we have a baby.'

'And, then, you're going back with him, and living like any other married couple?'

Moira's eyes refused to meet hers, and Norah said flatly, 'You're not going back with him, are you? If he wants a normal marriage he has to come back here, teach, buy a modern house round the corner, and paint pictures in his spare time. He won't do it, Moira.'

'Won't he if he loves me?'

'And if you loved him, you wouldn't be asking.'

'You'll see. I know my husband rather better than you do.'

Elizabeth Sheldon did not linger over her shopping. She was reluctant to leave her two daughters together because their animosity towards each other worried her. Norah was too outspoken and Moira had changed from the sweet gentle girl she remembered. Now she was withdrawn and secretive, answering Norah's barbed remarks with snide assurance.

Whenever she voiced her opinion to her husband he merely said that she was reading more into the situation than it warranted. Of course Moira had changed, she was a married woman expecting a baby, a married woman whose husband was miles away and no doubt she was missing him.

Of course he was refusing to see any change in his favourite child: it would take something drastic to make him see it. She listened nervously for the sounds of a quarrel as she opened the front door, but there was silence and when she went into the kitchen only Moira sat at the kitchen table with a magazine spread out in front of her. She was still wearing her dressing gown and as she looked up Elizabeth was dismally aware of the dark shadows under her eyes and the unhealthy pallor of her skin.

'Where's Norah?' she asked.

'She's gone out.'

'Will she be in to lunch?'

Moira shrugged her shoulders, and more sharply than she intended her mother said, 'Surely she said where she was going?'

'No. She's probably gone to the tennis club, that's where she spends most of her time.'

'Aren't you getting dressed?'

'I suppose so.'

'I'm worried about you, Moira. Why don't I go with you to the doctor? Perhaps you're sickening for something?'

'Mum, I'm pregnant.'

'I know that, dear, but there's something else. You don't seem to have any interest in anything these days. You need Mervyn to come home, a first baby could arrive sooner rather than later.'

Moira jumped to her feet. 'Mother I've told you I don't want Mervyn to come home and see me like this,' she said irritably. 'I don't want him worried. Besides we shall need all the money he can make.'

'Well, you're worrying me and your father, or doesn't that matter?'

'You're worrying about nothing, Mum. I feel you're always watching me, looking for things that are wrong with me, you never did before. I'm going to get dressed.'

That she had had words with her mother

worried her. What was wrong with her? Once this had been such a happy household, she'd been loved, cosseted, made to feel wonderful, and Moira was unable to understand that the only person who had changed was herself.

Irritably, she hunted in her wardrobe for something suitable to wear. She hated the maternity dresses she was wearing and she looked at the things that no longer fitted her with impatience. She had loved pretty feminine dresses and her parents had enjoyed seeing her looking pretty and fashionable. They had not been rich, but whatever money they were able to spare had been spent on their daughters, and Moira had benefited more than the other two, largely after her elder sister married and Norah was still wearing school uniform.

She peered at her reflection in the mirror. It was true her eyes were sunken and she felt so tired. All pregnant women must feel the same, she mused, it was simply her mother fussing as usual.

She applied some blusher to her cheeks and lightly powdered her face. Satisfied that she looked better she went back to the kitchen where her mother was busy at the oven.

'What had Norah to say for herself?' her mother asked.

'Nothing much.'

'I hope you didn't quarrel.'

'I wish she'd mind her own business, Mum. She's jealous because I'm here, she's always going on about my going back to Greece, or Mervyn coming here.'

Her mother didn't speak. Norah voiced the same questions she longed to ask, but in a rather more intrusive way. When she turned she saw that Moira was sitting at the table writing one of her almost daily letters to her husband.

'What do you find to write about?' she asked curiously. 'Nothing much happens around here.'

'But of course it does, Mum. I tell him about the family, the lovely gardens. England is so pretty in the springtime.'

Not pretty enough to bring him home, Elizabeth thought. If England was so pretty, why couldn't Mervyn paint pictures here, why Greece? And sensing her thoughts, Moira said, 'Mervyn painted lots of pictures when he taught at the school and he sold some of them, but he didn't get nearly as much money as he gets now. There are art classes everywhere with people painting pictures of England, they're amateur artists as I was. Mervyn is a professional, he can command more money for his pictures.'

Elizabeth didn't understand why. She'd been to the exhibition in the local art gallery and some of the pictures by local artists had been very good. What made Mervyn's so different? After all Moira had painted some very nice watercolours herself.

'I think I'll make sandwiches for lunch,' she said quietly. 'There'll probably only be the two of us, we'll have something more substantial this evening.'

Moira didn't look up. Letters to Mervyn were becoming harder to write. How often could she write about the gardens and the people he might or might not know? How could he be interested in members of her family he would not remember? Her letters were becoming stilted, and his in return came spasmodic and were increasingly shorter. She understood. After all, how could he hope to interest her in an island she had been happy to get away from, and people she had hardly related to?

Her mother remonstrated with the way she picked at her food. 'You're eating less than a sparrow,' she complained. 'You seem to be forgetting that you are eating for two.'

In the early afternoon Moira set out to post her letter and decided to take a short walk in the park. The sun had come out. The flower beds were bright with winter pansies and people were out and about enjoying the bright sun. She had not gone far when she saw their neighbour, Miss Adcock's friend, walking with her Yorkshire terrier and the older woman stopped to speak to her.

'How are you Moira, and how's your husband?' she asked.

'We're both fine, thank you. I've just posted a letter to him.'

'That's nice, but it would be nicer if he could come home.'

'Well, he's awfully busy, but he will be home soon.'

Fortunately, Moira knew nothing about the remarks that were buzzing around the common room at the school the next morning, when Marian Adcock informed her colleagues that Mervyn's wife was looking quite poorly and

Mervyn was in no hurry to come home.

'She looked fine the last time I saw her,' Martin said. It wasn't true, but Martin would have said anything to disprove Marian's words.

'Well, I'm only saying what my friend told me, and Mrs Sheldon herself is worried. She's said as much.'

'Is she likely to go back with him when the baby's born?' another teacher asked.

Martin shrugged his shoulders, but Marian said emphatically, 'It's my bet she won't. She wasn't happy on the island and it's my bet in the long run she'll persuade him to come back here. He'll be glad to find a teaching job anywhere, and not be too fussy about teaching art.'

When nobody spoke she went on, 'He could get a job at the other end of the country. It'll be interesting to see if she leaves her parents to live with him there.'

Martin didn't like Marian, he thought her a poisonous, vindictive, embittered spinster who had set her cap at Mervyn and been repulsed. There were several unmarried women on the staff, women who hadn't particularly wanted to get married but who were nice, unresentful souls, but not Marian with her acid tongue and obvious jealousies.

He repeated Marian's words to his wife that evening. 'She's right about the girl looking ill, but I wouldn't have given her the satisfaction of agreeing with her,' he said firmly. 'She's willing for something to go wrong with that marriage from the word go.'

His wife didn't comment. She had seen Moira

in town with her mother on several occasions and noted the girl's lethargy and unhealthy pallor. She was no more fond of Marian than was her husband but she had to admit in her innermost heart that she viewed Mervyn's marriage as a disaster waiting to happen. She had wished them well and hoped that it would work out, but she had had little faith in her wishes being granted.

Several days later, Mervyn stared down at his wife's letter and his thoughts turned to his memories of an English spring. Lilacs and cottage gardens, coarse grass blowing on rolling moorland and the sound of lawn mowers and bird song. In spite of himself, a feeling of nostalgia swept over him. Which was home? That island lapped by northern seas or this one already warmed by the sun, red-roofed white villages and the persistent sound of goat bells.

The ferry's plying between the islands was busy now. Every day his studio was crowded as they came from Rhodes and other, smaller islands, and they bought his pictures and gave him enough work to keep him busy for months. Most of them were coming back, they loved the islands, they'd been visiting for years, so why couldn't Moira have loved it? Why had everything turned sour?

He looked up at the sound of the garden gate closing and then he heard Leonora's swift light footsteps on the garden path, then she was in his room and in his arms. They were lovers, their days were filled with companionship, their nights with passion and neither of them had any thoughts beyond the here and now. They asked no questions of each other, they were simply two people who lived for each day as it came and with no thoughts on the morrow. They came from different worlds. They had commitments neither wished to acknowledge, and yet they both knew that in the end decisions had to be made.

There were times when Leonora asked herself if she had ever really been in love. That first misguided young girl's romance had been doomed from the outset. They too had come from different worlds, even though they shared a common nationality. She had been an aristocratic rich girl, he had been a student with little money. All they had had was passion and flaming youth. Then there had been Giorgio.

Giorgio had been so suitable, rich, kind, decent, too suitable, and she had not loved him. She had respected him, liked him, but missing had been that vital spark that they were both aware of. They had adored their children, and now she adored Mervyn, even when she asked herself if what they had together would last.

She was a rich woman. She did not need any of the money he might make selling his pictures, and in the end her life was in Rome. Rome with its sophistication, the eternal city where her family were old and known and she knew that in the eyes of her family Mervyn would be considered as unacceptable as that first misguided passion had been.

What did she know of England, that cool green land where Mervyn already had a wife who was expecting his child?

Neither of them was looking beyond the present when their days were filled with comradeship and laughter and their nights with passion. Neither of them were aware that around the corner tragedy was waiting to strike.

The letter from Moira's parents came early in June urging Mervyn to return to England without further delay. Moira was ill in hospital and matters were very grave.

He flew out from Rhodes on a warm morning, golden with sunlight, and he was thinking of Leonora standing on the jetty watching him sail away on the ferry. 'Don't worry about the studio. I'll go down every day and sell your pictures,' she'd said. 'I'll explain that you've been called away. I'm sure Moira is going to be fine.' Her smile had been warm, encouraging, and for a long moment, they had looked into each other's eyes before he boarded the boat.

It was early evening when the plane flew into London and immediately he had collected his suitcase he telephoned the Sheldon's house. There was no reply, so he decided the best thing to do was hire a car to drive to their home. Although the traffic was heavy in London it became lighter as he drove towards Gloucester and just before eleven he was ringing their front-door bell.

He could see a light through the glass door coming from the rear of the house and urgently he rang it again. The light became stronger as somebody opened the kitchen door, and then through the glass he saw Norah hurrying towards the front door.

They stared at each other for several minutes before she opened the door wider and he followed her into the hall.

'Are you alone?' he asked her.

'Yes. The hospital rang for Mum and Dad to go there. They told me to stay here in case you came.'

'I rang earlier, there was no reply.'

'No, we were at the hospital.'

'How is she?'

He stared at her as her eyes filled with tears. 'She's very ill. She doesn't know us.'

'But what's the matter with her?'

'It's her liver. She's so yellow. Mum and Dad know what's wrong with her. She's in St Clare's. Do you want me to come with you?'

'No. Stay here, Norah, I'll go alone.'

It was only when he was on the way to the hospital that he realised she hadn't said which ward Moira was in, and St Clare's was a huge hospital. His mind refused to accept that Moira was dangerously ill.

Chapter Eighteen

It was pouring with rain when Mervyn drove into the hospital grounds, and the lights from the huge building penetrated into the wet misery of the night as he ran from his car to the hospital doors. Only one woman was sitting behind the central desk and the lights were dimmed in the corridors beyond. He realised, with something like shock, that it was after midnight.

He made enquiries at the desk, but if he had hoped for reassurance from her expression, he was disappointed. It was bland and incurious.

The corridors seemed to go on for ever and he met only two people, a boy pushing a trolley and a nurse engrossed in reading a leaflet.

He reached the ward he was looking for and opened the swing doors to reveal a large square hall with corridors leading off it. Two people were in the hall, sitting like statues, staring straight in front of them, oblivious to everything beyond the torment inside.

He strode across the room and was almost upon them when Moira's father looked up and rose to his feet. Her mother stared at him dully before she put her head in her hands and started to sob. The two men exchanged glances before Mr Sheldon shook his head, saying in a strangled voice, 'You're too late Mervyn. She's gone.'

Mervyn stared at him in disbelief, and, pulling him to one side, Mr Sheldon said, 'We were with her when she died, but she didn't open her eyes, she hasn't spoken for days. They did everything they could: it was her liver, malignant. They told us last week they could save the baby but not Moira.'

'The baby…?'

'Yes. A little girl. Caesarian, Moira knew nothing about it.'

'And the baby?'

'She's beautiful.' His voice broke and the tears coursed slowly down his cheeks so that Mervyn stood quietly beside him until he could regain his composure, then he said, 'We're waiting to see the doctor. If you want to see her she's still in her room.'

Four days later he stood in the window of the Sheldons' house staring through the window at the groups of mourners leaving their cars to walk into the house. He knew that he must have met them all at the wedding but he could not remember them, all except Aunt Agatha that is.

The old lady was being helped from the funeral car. She was wearing a large black felt hat that was knocked awry by the car door, and as she hastened to straighten it her handbag fell into the road to be retrieved by the funeral director.

It seemed unreal, like a scene in a play or a film, with actors playing parts and he himself only an onlooker. He thought about his last moments with Moira when he had stared down at her beautiful face etched in gold caused by the disease that had killed her, and in that still golden face he had been unable to remember that other face of the girl sitting underneath the window with her easel in the school art room, a girl whose smile had been warm and gentle, whose hair had shone golden in the sunlight.

They had talked about his daughter Margaret and at first he had stared at them bemused and with the realisation that in a few short days his life had changed. He also knew that he would never think of her as Margaret, she was Selene.

They were flocking into the house now, standing in groups, eyeing him curiously as someone alien and they were doubtful how to approach him.

Somebody announced that there was food laid out in the dining room and almost guiltily they sidled out feeling that food was the last thing they should be thinking about, and yet it would be churlish to refuse it.

The vicar approached Mervyn and held out his hand.

'This is a sad occasion, Mervyn,' he said gloomily. 'Such a lovely girl, so young and with so much to live for.'

Mervyn nodded wordlessly.

'I suppose it's far too soon to ask what you intend to do now. Obviously there's the baby to think about.'

Hastily he went on, 'Of course you and the Sheldons will have to do some serious talking when all this is over. If I can be any help please don't hesitate to get in touch.'

They were doing full justice to the repast the caterers had provided but Mervyn felt that any morsel of food would have stuck in his throat. Great Aunt Agatha sat in a high-backed chair at the table surrounded by her relatives who were plying her with food and listening to her strictures.

His father-in-law joined him saying, 'I should get some food while there still is some, Mervyn.'

'Thank you, but I'm not hungry,' he answered.

'Nor me. I could never understand why food was on offer at funerals.'

'I think it originated for people who had had some distance to travel.'

'You're probably right.'

'Elizabeth's gone up to sit near the baby so that the nurse can come down to eat.'

Mervyn looked at him helplessly, and the older man, red-eyed, shook his head sadly. 'I know son, it's a hopeless situation. None of us expected this.'

In his innermost heart Mervyn was wishing he could have turned the clock back two or three years, used what little common sense the fates had given him, and been wise enough to see the perils that confronted him.

Now here he was, a widower with a baby daughter, a home in a foreign land and a career that relied entirely upon the whim of others. There was too the feeling of guilt that while his young wife had been desperately ill he had been passionately involved with another woman.

He had written to Leonora to tell her about the death of his wife and that he was the father of a baby girl. She would not write back and he had no means of knowing how she would view the situation. He realised that their future did not lie together but he could not get her out of his thoughts, not even when there were so many more pressing things to worry about. The memory of her warm, pulsating body lying in his arms intruded upon the sadness he faced every day. They were Leonora's eyes he saw, Leonora's full passionate mouth, the texture of her shining blue-black hair against his face, never Moira's, and though he despised himself for feeling this way he couldn't help it.

Arthur Sheldon too was burdened by too many

thoughts he was unable to express to the man standing beside him. What would he do? Go back to his island to paint his pictures? But what about the child? They hardly knew him. His beautiful head-strong daughter had never counted the cost, and it was true they had spoiled her, more than they had ever spoiled the other two.

The baby's nurse was at the table helping herself to food and seeing the two men standing together she came over to them. She was a capable young woman and Elizabeth had heard only good things spoken about her. Fortunately, she was free to look after the baby for several weeks until the family were able to resolve matters. She smiled. 'Baby Margaret hasn't been any trouble,' she said brightly. 'She's a good little thing.'

The two men smiled. She felt able to pose the question the men felt unable to talk about.

'I'm going to enjoy looking after her for the next few weeks. Have you had any thought about what's going to happen when I leave?'

'It's something we shall have to talk about very soon,' Sheldon said evenly. 'These last few days have been so awful, we've had too much on our minds.'

'Yes of course.'

'I understand you've been living in Greece, Mr Corwen?' she said.

'On one of the Greek islands.'

'How wonderful. I spent two weeks with my sister in Corfu, it was a wonderful holiday. We're going back to the islands one day. I expect you know it well, Mr Corwen.'

'I'm afraid not.' After he had said it Mervyn realised that he knew very little about the islands, other than his and Rhodes which he knew reasonably well. He had promised Moira that they would discover the others over the years, now it would never be possible.

'The old lady seems to have a very good appetite,' the nurse said with a smile.

'Yes,' Arthur said wryly, 'We can rely on Aunt Agatha to do justice to what's on offer.'

The guests departed at last, shaking his hand and murmuring their condolences. In the main their eyes refused to meet his, and Norah standing beside him said caustically. 'Thank goodness they've gone, now perhaps we can get back to normal.'

He stared at her curiously. 'Normal, Norah? What is normal?'

'You know what I mean. If you're staying on with the baby I'll have to start looking for a flat, the house isn't big enough for us all.'

Meeting his shocked gaze the warm colour flooded her face and she said hurriedly, 'I'm sorry, I didn't mean to sound so mean, but while you've been in Greece, this conversation's cropped up more than once.'

'I don't see why, Norah.'

She couldn't hide the malice behind her smile. 'Well, Moira and I talked about when you would come back here, where you and Moira would live until you got a new job and a new house, it could have been months. Now if you decide to come back for good, it's all going to be discussed again.'

'I've no intention of turning you out of your bedroom, Norah, nor have I any intention of coming back here permanently.'

'What about the baby?'

'Something will be sorted out. I hardly think it will upset any of your arrangements.'

He couldn't believe that his words to Norah had made up his mind, but he knew when they settled down together in the evening that her parents had been made aware of his words when Elizabeth said sharply, 'How do you propose to care for Margaret on your own in Greece, Mervyn? She's only a baby, she'll need a good nurse. Moira said the island was primitive.'

'I've no doubt that I can obtain a very good nurse from among the families on the island. They look after their children very well and whether the island is primitive or not, Greece was civilised when we were only just emerging from primeval life,' he retorted.

'All the same,' Arthur said testily, 'things are different now. They probably don't speak any English, and Margaret is our grandchild, we only want the best for Margaret.'

'And what do you think would be the best for her?'

'I've had nothing else to think about for days,' Elizabeth said sharply. 'I think she should stay here with us until she's older. You know you can come here to stay whenever you wish. After all, we're better able to cope with a young baby than you and in some ways she'll take the place of Moira.'

'That's what I'm afraid of,' Mervyn said softly.

'What do you mean by that?'

'The time will come when I shall want to take her away from you. She'll grow up, go to school, realise that I'm her father and you're her grandparents.'

'That shouldn't pose any problem.'

'Not even your reluctance to see her go?'

'We wouldn't be reluctant, after all she'll only be on loan to us, won't she?'

Meeting Elizabeth's eyes Mervyn knew that she had won. Her reasoning was entirely logical. The child would be loved and cared for by Moira's family, and he would retain the freedom that he regarded as so precious. At the same time Mervyn promised himself that one day his daughter would live with him. The situation with the Sheldons was only a temporary measure.

'When will you go back?' Arthur asked curiously.

'Next week probably. This is the time of year when the island is crowded with tourists. They stay on the island and come in on the ferries, and they come to buy my pictures. I need to make money, for myself and for Selene.'

'Selene?'

'That's the name I chose for her, Moira wanted Margaret, but in my heart I think of her as Selene.'

'I never heard of it,' Elizabeth said. 'Is it something your cousin would have chosen?'

'Perhaps. She called her daughter Cassandra because she thought it would please her father. He would have been happy with Selene.'

'It sounds foreign.'

'It's Greek.'

'I thought as much.'

Across the room he saw Norah grin and he realised that she was relishing this exchange of words between them.

'How does Norah feel about a baby in the house?' he asked curiously.

'Norah'll be very good. She'll help me a lot I know.'

Mervyn wasn't so sure. He thought Norah would resent the baby and the pampering she would get from the rest of the family. One day he would take Selene to the island, perhaps when she was three or four and ready for school. He'd shop around the English people who lived on the islands, they had children, they obviously had tutors for them.

When he visited his old colleagues at the school he found that they too were interested in what he intended to do about his daughter. Marian Adcock, as usual, had her opinions.

'I thought the Sheldons would take over,' she said. 'Mrs Sheldon's been worried sick in case Moira and the baby wanted to go back to Greece with you.'

'That friend of yours gossips too much,' Martin had said sharply.

'Well Elizabeth Sheldon talks to the neighbours, gossip hasn't entered into it,' she retorted.

'I don't know why you don't come back here,' she went on. 'You could get yourself one of those new houses near the park and get another job.'

Mervyn ignored her.

'Come and join us for a meal,' Martin said.

'Heaven knows when we'll see you again.'

'Oh soon. I shall be coming to see my daughter.'

'Margaret?'

'Selene.'

Martin laughed. 'So you're sticking to that, are you?'

'I hope to.'

Athena too was amused by his insistence that this was how he wanted his daughter to be named.

'She'll be totally confused darling,' she said over the telephone. 'Her grandparents calling her Margaret for many months out of the year, and then the advent of this strange man suddenly appearing to call her Selene.'

'The confusion will soon disappear when I take her to live with me,' he answered.

'And when will that be?'

'As soon as I can manage it.'

'I was sad about Moira, Mervyn. She was beautiful and sweet, would it ever have worked out?'

'I doubt it.'

'Whose fault?'

'Mine for not seeing the dangers, hers for wanting it too badly.'

'I wonder if there'll be somebody else.'

'A lifetime is a long time, Athena.'

'I know, too long to live it on your own.'

'We'll see. How's Ian.'

'Suffering, poor darling.'

'And Cassie?'

'Blooming. So terribly mature and confident.

She's talking about visiting you on the island. Would that be a problem?'

'No. Let me know when she's coming.'

'It would probably be in August.'

'Can't you come with her?'

'No. I can't leave Ian. I haven't been the best wife in the world, I'm trying to atone for past mistakes.'

'I want you to get to know Selene, Athena. Will you?'

'Of course darling. I'll be her eccentric, glamorous aunt who descends on her from time to time with gifts her grandparents will deplore.'

'That would be a mistake.'

'Not really. I'm part of that strange difference about you that Moira fell in love with. Don't let it disappear from your daughter's life.'

'Don't you think it was that part of me that Moira came to distrust, simply because she didn't understand it?'

'You're probably right. You know, dear, as the months pass, and the years, the Sheldons are going to discover you in Selene and they may not know how to cope, just as Moira couldn't cope.'

'Hopefully by that time she'll be living with me.'

'I hope so. But she's a part of them too, they'll always be there for her.'

'I know.'

That evening he stared down at his daughter sleeping peacefully in her cot. She was beautiful with soft golden hair against the white pillows, gold-tipped lashes making crescents on her cheek, one tiny hand clenched above the blanket and he stroked her cheek as gently as a butterfly's touch. A strange feeling of searing love swept over him. This beautiful child would lack for nothing. He would paint every hour of every day to make money for her future. He would ensure that his name was known all over the Greek Islands and further afield.

He bent down and placed a light kiss on the baby's head, then he left her room closing the door quietly behind him.

Tomorrow he was flying home. Would Leonora be waiting for him in his studio as she had promised?

Leonora was in Rome. She had kept her word, going each day to the studio where she had shown people round, sold his pictures, encouraged people to buy, giving her judgement regarding their choice. It had been one night when she stood on the balcony staring out to sea that she had been aware of the setting sun shining on two round specks through the trees, binoculars, and she had become suddenly afraid. Somebody was out there watching her.

She knew that tourists walked across the headland, climbed the narrow paths to stare in admiration at the haunting beauty of the villa glimpsed through the trees, but somehow Leonora could not associate those binoculars with a random tourist. They were too concentrated, too intrusive, and she went back into the house quickly locking the doors behind her.

That was the moment she decided to return to Rome. She had no idea when or if Mervyn was coming back. She had received only one letter from him informing her of Moira's death and the birth of the baby. He had responsibilities, perhaps he never would come back.

Next day she went down to the studio and placed a notice on the wall to say it was closed, then she wrote to Mervyn to tell him what she had done. She would come back in August with the children, there would be many people around then, and there would be servants in the house.

On the day Leonora flew home to Rome, Mervyn flew back to Greece. He did not receive her letter before he left.

He stared at the notice on the wall of his studio with mixed feelings.

Had Leonora gone home because their affair had run its course? Because she thought he would not be coming back? Or for some other reason? When he spoke to the Greek priest, he merely said he believed she would be back in the summer with the children, and there had been a strange knowing expression on his face.

Mervyn had never thought to feel lonely on the island and yet he was. In the villa he could see Moira, sitting curled up on the couch with her magazine, sitting in the garden staring out at the sea, sulking when he tried to persuade her to visit some favourite place of his.

In the night he missed Leonora, Leonora who had filled every warm passionate moment, and in the darkness he could hear the sound of her light footsteps running from the gate to his house.

Could it be the same when she came back with the children in the summer? Children that were sophisticated, growing up too fast. Then he remembered that Cassie might be here.

In August Leonora would be back, if he remembered so vividly she must remember things too.

He made it his business to stroll round the gardens of her villa to assure himself that all was well and it was on one of those strolls that he discovered a set of footprints under the cypresses at the edge of the garden. Whoever had stood there had been well hidden by the trees, and there was nothing for gardeners to do there. A strange feeling of dread swept over him. Suppose Leonora had been right and somebody had been watching from the shrubbery?

Several times he went back to look at the footprints. It had been a favourite place for whoever had stood there, and he discovered no others. He also resolved to say nothing to Leonora. Surely it could only have been some curious tourist entranced by the beauty of the villa.

Several nights later a heavy sudden shower of rain obliterated those footprints as if they had never been.

Chapter Nineteen

The tourists were pouring into Rome and the rich habitants were moving out: to their villas on Capri and Ischia or the Amalfi coast. To their yachts anchored in exotic marinas or the Lido at Venice, anywhere to get out of the summer heat of Rome and the piazzas crowded with noisy guides and their processions of tourists.

The Princes Cabrodini surveyed her youngest daughter with a worried frown. As the years passed she understood Leonora less and less. She couldn't understand for instance why she had elected to go to Greece two months earlier than usual, particularly when the weather was still chilly and when the island was likely to be quiet. Then suddenly she was back, going here, there and everywhere, with the usual contingent of escorts who appeared whenever she was home.

The Princess had insisted that they leave for Venice. She liked Venice in June, she liked the Lido, but rarely went into the city, and Leonora had offered no objections. They would stay there for a month, then perhaps a few weeks on Capri before the children arrived.

Why they couldn't all stay on in Capri instead of Leonora whisking the children off to Greece, she couldn't imagine, but no doubt in time Leonora would decide what she wanted to do.

Her elder children had never been any trouble. Nino, the son of her first husband, was settled in Florence with a charming wife and children, Gabriella her daughter from her second marriage had married a Swiss banker and they lived happily in Geneva, but Leonora, her third husband's child had been too beautiful, too volatile, possibly too spoilt.

As far back as her schooldays there had been all that trouble with that terrible boy who had eventually made her life a misery. Giorgio had been so good for her, it was unfortunate he had died so young, but she had two children and enough money, nothing in her life to worry about, and a string of men with money and class, most of them desiring rather more than a platonic friendship.

'Wouldn't the children like a change this year?' she ventured. 'You've already spent several weeks on the island, why not stay on in Capri, allow the children to get to know it.'

'They do love the island, Mama.'

'They know very little else. I didn't think it was a very good idea when Giorgio bought that villa, but I did think after he died you would all tire of it.'

'You've never been there, Mama.'

'I know. It wasn't my scene. This is what I like, people dressed beautifully and good music. Oh I've no doubt the villa is charming, Giorgio would never have bought any old villa, but doesn't it have too many memories, memories you should be getting away from now?'

Leonora didn't answer but remained staring out across the sands to the sea beyond.

'Didn't you say some man was painting a picture of Giorgio?' her mother continued.

'Yes, he finished it. It's hanging in the hall at the villa.'

'Was it any good?'

'Yes Mama, it was very good. Mervyn is a good artist, his pictures are much sought after.'

'Isn't he English?'

'Half English, half Welsh.'

'How well do you know him?'

'He owns the small villa his uncle bought from

Giorgio. He's just lost his wife, and he has a baby daughter.'

'So he's likely to be sad and very vulnerable. You've gone through that phase very successfully, be very wary, my dear.'

Leonora smiled.

'You can smile,' her mother said sharply, 'but I do know a little bit about what it's like for a woman on her own, and a man on his own is even more desolate.'

Reflecting on her mother's life Leonora could only think that her mother had never allowed sad memories to inflict too drastically. She had married three rich titled men who had adored her even when they had died young. Leonora had never known her father, he died after a fall from his horse when she was three years old, and since then her mother had never lacked for escorts but had said adamantly that her third marriage had to be her last.

'I understood Marco to say he would be spending a few weeks here,' the Princess said artlessly. 'When is he coming?'

'I have no idea, Mama.'

Marco Ponti was a friend of her late husband's: rich, handsome and devoted. In his mid forties and a bachelor, Marco had a string of romances behind him but had been wary of marriage. Leonora had no doubt that he was changing his opinions, he very much wanted to marry her. The fact that her mother was aware of it unsettled her.

'Well I'd like him to spend some time with us in Venice.'

'We shall be going on to Capri soon.'

'Not necessarily. I decided on Capri before I knew Marco might be coming. Now I'd rather like to stay a little longer.'

She looked at her daughter hopefully. If they stayed on and Marco came perhaps they could all go on to Capri together and forget that villa in Greece.

Leonora knew exactly what was passing through her mother's mind.

She thought about Mervyn. Their time together had been wonderful but he would be a different Mervyn, grieving, guilty, ashamed of his affair with another woman when his wife lay dying.

Her mother pressed her opinions, seeing the doubt on her daughter's face, ignorant of what had put it there.

'You like Marco, don't you Leonora?'

'Yes Mama. Marco is very nice.'

'Nice! Most women would view him as a veritable treasure. He's handsome, well connected and extremely rich. You never cease to worry me, I've never heard you enthuse about anybody beyond that dreadful man years ago. You never enthused about Giorgio.'

'I know, Mama. Giorgio was your choice. He too was nice.'

'Is there somebody else?'

'You mean you wouldn't know about it?'

'No I wouldn't, not when you spend several months out of my sight.'

'In a lonely villa on a lonely island.'

'You have servants.'

'And children.'

'You haven't had the children over the last few weeks.'

'No Mama. I had things to do there, see to some decorating, the garden, nothing gets done in the winter.'

'So do you intend to take the children again in August?'

'I haven't made up my mind yet. I think I'll take a swim, the sea looks very inviting.'

'Who do you suppose that woman is, the one over there sitting with that elderly man? She chatted to me while I was waiting for you this morning, I believe she's American.'

'She's a film actress,' Leonora said briefly.

'Is that her husband?'

'I don't know, Mama. I shouldn't think so.'

'Really. Years ago when one came to the Lido it was filled with old royalty. They had beautiful manners and great style, now we are reduced to American film starts and ageing Casanovas.'

Leonora laughed. She remembered coming to the Lido as a child, meeting the hierachy of European nobility, most of whom had fled their war-ridden countries to find sanctuary in any place where they could still parade their style of who curtsied to whom; and whom they sat next to around the dinner table. She and Gabriella had laughed about them, their pretensions that in the end didn't really mater. Nobody cared any more.

The American film actress waved to her as she ran to the beach and the man she was with raised his binoculars.

That was when she thought about the setting

sun glinting on the two circles sheltered by the shrubbery. The setting sun was doing exactly the same thing to the binoculars raised to the man's eyes while he sat in his deck chair. She hadn't been wrong, somebody had been standing under the trees with his glasses trained on the villa and she ran faster until she reached the sea. In those few moments she believed she was running away from whatever danger lay behind her, but in her heart she knew that she needed to be afraid. If he had found her in Greece, he could find her anywhere.

She could marry Marco. He would be a good kind husband, she would have everything, love, riches, position. The world would be their oyster and he would be her protector from any danger from the past, but she wasn't ready for Marco. What she had with Mervyn was still real and unfinished. She would not go back this year, she'd give him time to get over Moira, come to terms with his child, then she'd go back.

That evening over the dinner table she said to her mother, 'I've made up my mind. We will spend August in Capri, it will be a change for the children.'

'What's made you suddenly decide on that?'

'Well I do listen to your suggestions Mama. Oh I know you say I never do but you're wrong. Alexander's been to Herculaneum and Pompeii with his school, he was very impressed so I'm sure he'd like to go there again. Sophia will love Capri.'

'Why don't you sell the villa in Greece? Wouldn't the Englishman like to buy it if he's doing so well with his pictures?'

'I'm making no decisions about the villa Mama. Giorgio wouldn't have wanted me to sell it and neither will Alexander.'

'I'm sure Alexander will tire of it, after all his friends are in Italy, his interests will be in Italy. One day he'll marry, some girl he meets in Rome from a good family, at least that's what I hope for.'

Leonora smiled. Her mother was happiest when she was arranging people's lives.

On Capri Sophia was in her element. She had playmates in plenty, girls she knew in Rome, children from similar backgrounds, and Leonora thought she was growing up too fast, she was precocious, a vain beautiful child, and Marco was enchanted with her. The children were asked to call him Uncle Marco.

Alexander enjoyed sailing on Uncle Marco's prestigious yacht, swimming in the warm sea that lapped gently along the rock-strewn coves, but in the evenings he was bored. His mother and Uncle Marco went to the cafés and listened to the haunting Neopolitan love songs, and Grandmama sat on her veranda entertaining other women of a similar age, old friends known to her in Rome.

The Princess was delighted that things were going so well. Marco would be an admirable son-in-law just as Giorgio had been. He got along well with the children, particularly Sophia whom he spoiled terribly. Leonora would come to see the value of a second husband in Marco's position. She would sell that villa on the island

and forget about it. After all there was nowhere as wonderful as Rome, nowhere as permanent.

The first two weeks passed quickly. Sophia was out with her friends, Mama was sitting in the garden surrounded by the scent of Oleanders but Alexander stood thoughtfully staring at the villa of Tiberias glimpsed through the trees.

Leonora put her arm round his shoulders asking, 'Happy darling?'

'Yes thank you Mama. How long are we staying here?'

'Aren't you happy here?'

'Well yes, but we always go to the villa in August and August is half way over.'

'I thought we'd have a change this year, darling.'

'Is that because Marco is with us?'

'Well, he has taken you sailing, you love his yacht and Sophia is very happy here.'

'I know. She knows people and she likes the shops and the music. I like the villa, there aren't so many crowds.'

Leonora's mother thought the idea of visiting the villa entirely ridiculous, as did Sophia.

'There's nothing to do there except play in the gardens and visit the market,' she stormed. 'There are no nice shops, no real fun anywhere.'

'Alexander likes it.'

'Oh well, he would, wouldn't he? He likes the sea and the coves. He likes the villa and the people. We've been going there for years, why can't we just stay here for once? Besides Grandmama thinks we should.'

Her tears of protest brought a swift rejoinder

from the Princess. 'Sophia is growing up, she needs this air of sophistication, not some rural setting that pleases Alexander,' she said adamantly.

'Giorgio loved the villa Mama, and he is after all Giorgio's son.'

'And very like him. Serious, too withdrawn. Marco has been good for him.'

'Mama, it's moving too fast, Marco has asked me to marry him, I'm not sure that I'm ready for another commitment.'

'Why ever not?'

'I'm happy as I am, just me and the children. There's plenty of time.'

'That is just where you're wrong. Let Marco slip through your fingers and somebody else will jump at him. The older you get the fewer the opportunities.'

'It never stopped you, Mama.'

'I never cease thinking that I was very fortunate, but that doesn't mean to say you'll be equally fortunate. Times are changing, older men are marrying silly young girls and women are becoming too independent. Go to your villa if you must, but ask Marco to go with you, I'm sure he will. Besides, I don't want Sophia here with me, she's too precocious for an old woman like me to cope with.'

'Mama, I doubt if you'll ever be old.'

Sophia brought the subject of the villa up that evening over dinner. Her pretty face was mutinous as she turned on her younger brother vindictively.

'Why do you want to go to Greece when we can

stay on here in Capri? You can have the sea and the boats here, but there's so much more here, I don't want to go to the villa this year, I'll stay here with Grandmama. You'll have me, won't you, Grandmama?'

Her grandmother looked at her with a half smile on her lips, then shaking her head she said, 'If your mother and Alexander go to Greece then you must go with them Sophia. I stopped looking after children a long time ago.'

'I'm not a child,' Sophia cried. 'I'm almost grown up.'

'What is all this about Greece?' Marco asked.

'The villa we have there on an island. Didn't you visit us once when Giorgio was alive?' Leonora said softly.

'Of course. A very charming villa, a pretty island. Don't you usually spend the summer months there?'

'We always have in other years and Alexander wants to go back there before he needs to return to school.'

'Do you want to go there?'

'I'd decided this year that we wouldn't, Alexander will be very disappointed if we don't. That's right, isn't it, Alexander?'

'Yes Mama. There's only two and a half weeks left.'

'Would you like to sail there, that is if your mother decides to invite me?' Marco asked with a smile.

Alexander's face lit up and even Sophia appeared a little interested.

He looked at his mother expectantly, then

urging her gently he said, 'Please Mama, that would be wonderful. We never sailed there, not even when Papa was alive.'

Leonora knew that he had won. She had no excuses to offer, particularly when Sophia said, 'Oh yes please Mama, it would be nice to sail there in Uncle Marco's boat, it will be nicer than anything we've seen in the harbour there.'

Her grandmother smiled derisively. Sophia would never make any of the mistakes her mother had made. Sophia already knew what she wanted from life and no impecunious boy without position would change things. She had watched Sophia in the company of the friends she hobnobbed with since they arrived on Capri, boys from monied families, cocky, brash, arrogant, totally unaware that her elder brother presented an aristocratic breeding that she cared little for.

Sophia would happily spend her life cocooned by riches. Breeding and money did not always go together and in her mercenary heart her grandmother applauded the girl's ambitions. Fortunately her first husband had been blessed with a great deal of money while her two titled husbands had been burdened by titles accompanied by debts. What was the use of living in a palazzo when there wasn't sufficient money to pay the gardeners?

She really didn't mind that her daughter and her children were leaving now that Marco was going with them. If Leonora had any sense she would accept his proposal and settle down in Rome to a sophisticate monied existence.

The next morning Leonora was helping Alexander with his packing when he surprised her by asking, 'Are you going to marry Uncle Marco, Mama?'

She stared at him without speaking for several seconds, then with a light laugh said, 'Darling, what a funny thing to say.'

'I think he would like to marry you. He's very nice.'

'You like him then?'

'Yes.'

There was doubt in his voice and after a few moments he said, 'I thought you liked Mervyn. You were very happy when I saw you together.'

'You knew that Mervyn was married, Alexander, you met his wife.'

'I know, but she went away, didn't she? She wasn't happy on the island, I don't think she will be going back there ever.'

'No darling. Moira will never be going back to the island. Now have we packed everything you will need, if so, I'd better see how Sophia is coping.'

Mervyn was eating breakfast on the patio with Cassie when she pointed out to sea excitedly and following her gaze he saw the white yacht moving slowly to its anchorage in the island's marina.

Cassie was running towards the cliff top but Mervyn had seen it all before. Visitors to the island came and went, the larger vessels didn't usually stay long, they preferred Rhodes or the other islands where there was more in the way of entertainment.

When she came back to the table she said, 'It's probably somebody who wants to buy your pictures Uncle Mervyn. I'm going down to the studio, are you coming?'

'Later Cassie, I have one or two letters to write. You can open it up for me.'

During the weeks she had been at the villa she had enjoyed showing visitors round the modest studio, wrapping the pictures they had bought, chatting to them, and they had laughed and joked with her. Cassie was an enchanting creature with her mother's beauty and vivacity and she left him wondering if his own daughter would be blessed with her humour and her charm.

He thought about her constantly, the tiny bundle of humanity that belonged to him. The urge to love her and protect her was so strong he was amazed by it. He wanted to bring her home and he wished Leonora was there to offer some feminine advice. He couldn't understand why she hadn't come to the island with the children in August as she had always done. Why didn't she write? Was it because she realised that their affair was going nowhere or had something frightened her in those days before she went away? He could not forget the footprints he had found in the garden, somebody had stood there watching her villa.

He was about to leave the villa when Cassie came running across the garden, her eyes wide with excitement.

'They've come to the villa, Uncle Mervyn, I saw them leaving the yacht, a man and a woman and two children.'

'I didn't hear a car.'

'Well they've come. They collected a white car from the garage and they drove up here. There's a boy a bit older than me and a girl. I'm going to go up there to introduce myself.'

'Give them time to settle in, Cassie.'

'I've met them before, a long time ago, when I was here with my mother.'

'Like I said, don't be in a hurry to go up there. You said a man was with them.'

'Yes, a tall man wearing a yachting cap. He probably owns the boat, the lady's husband died.'

Leonora had spoken of a brother and a brother-in-law, but then Leonora would know a great many men in Italy. All the same he felt strangely antagonistic towards the unknown stranger.

He spent the afternoon at the studio and was soon wishing that Cassie was with him since the afternoon proved to be exceptionally busy as well as lucrative.

It was late in the afternoon when she came into the studio and by this time the ferries were leaving and he was showing the last of his customers through the door.

'Have you been very busy?' she asked him.

'Yes, I could have done with your help, Cassie.'

Uncontrite, she perched on one of the trestle tables.

'I saw the boy and the girl in the gardens,' she said brightly, 'so I went to talk to them. The girl's called Sophia, the boy's called Alexander. I shall call him Alex.'

'You'll be the only one who does.'

'Well I prefer it. Alexander sounds so stuffy. He's nice, he's good looking and one day he'll be an Italian Conte like his father.'

'You found all that out in one brief afternoon, did you Cassie?'

'His sister told me. They've been staying in Capri with the Contessa's mother. She's a princess, Sophia told me that too.'

Chapter Twenty

In the days that followed Mervyn was made more and more familiar with the comings and goings at the villa above. Sophia and Cassie had struck up a firm friendship, and Cassie was invited to go sailing on Uncle Marco's yacht. She talked about it endlessly; she also talked about Alex as if he was her soul mate.

Mervyn asked no questions, he didn't need to.

'They're going back to Rome at the beginning of September to school like me,' she informed him. 'Uncle Marco is taking them back, he has business in Rome.'

It would therefore appear that Leonora was staying on at the villa but Mervyn had not seen her and she had not thought it necessary to see him. He felt angry even when he knew his anger was unjustified. They had enjoyed a love affair; they had never promised themselves that it would be more than that.

On the morning of Cassie's departure he accompanied her on the ferry to Rhodes, from where she was flying home. Cassie was accustomed to flying here, there and everywhere, and when he asked if she was nervous, she merely favoured him with a pitying smile, saying, 'Uncle Mervyn, of course I'm not nervous, I enjoy flying. Mummy will meet me. We're spending a few days in London.'

The next morning he stood in his garden watching Marco's yacht sailing away from the island and he knew Leonora would be alone. He had seen Marco walking along the cliff path, a tall, handsome man in immaculate white and wearing a yachting cap on his dark hair. A man from Leonora's life, from a past he had no part in and a world he did not know. Early in the evening two days later, she came to see him.

She might have seen him only the night before, she was smiling, her beautiful face warm and alive, holding out her hands and kissing him lightly on both cheeks.

'I'm so sorry about Moira. Tell me about your daughter. When will your see her again?'

So they talked about Selene and what the summer had done to them both. He was aware that she was nervous. There was a taut anxiety that he had never noticed in her before and, when there appeared to be nothing more to talk about, the silence between them seemed burdened with doubts.

At last he asked, 'You're staying on here, Leonora?'

'Only for a few days. I'm packing up the things

I want to take home with me, personal things. I don't want to leave them here.'

'You'll be closing up the villa for the winter early?'

She nodded.

'You're flying back to Rome?'

'Yes. Mervyn, I have to tell you and I'm not very sure how you're going to take it. We had something wonderful together but it was never meant to last, we both know that.'

She was looking at him expectantly but he was not making it easy for her.

'I'm going back to the world I know,' she said softly. 'This was never my world, it was Giorgio's and it will be Alexander's. One day the villa will belong to him. I won't be coming back here.'

'Isn't that very final?'

'Yes, it has to be. Marco has asked me to marry him and I've said I will. I've known him a great many years, he was a friend of Giorgio's and our families have always been close. He gets on well with the children and they like him. My mother likes him, she's been encouraging me for years to marry him. We shall live in Marco's villa in Rome. It's a life I know. We all have our own little niches in life. You have yours in which I would be an interloper. You have Selene, Mervyn. She is the most important person in your life. We have both to move on.'

'So I take it this is goodbye then?'

She smiled gently. 'It has to be, my dear. I leave you with so many memories and so much warmth. I'm flying to Rome in a few days and there's much to do in the meantime.'

'You don't want us to meet again before you go?'

'I've left my car at the garage to be serviced. After I pick it up, I shall take it over to the Hyams'. Millicent Hyam has been asking for it ever since I told her that I was leaving the island for good. I'll stay the night with them and they'll bring me back the next day.'

There was nothing more to say. Leonora seemed to have taken care of everything, even her car. She had had two weeks to inform her servants and her friends and he was probably the last to know what she intended to do from now on.

He did not touch her again. For several long moments they stared into each other's eyes, then with a little gesture she was gone and he heard the sound of her high heels beating a staccato rhythm across the path.

He stood for a long time staring out of the window but he was not seeing the sea gilded by the setting sun, his mind was filled with memories of days and nights that had been brief and filled with a warmth and passion he would remember in a future that only offered loneliness and solitude.

Then he remembered Selene. At the end of the summer he would see her, and one day she would belong entirely to him, one day, when she would be a little girl running across the sand in the warm sunshine. That day would come as surely as the dawn.

Leonora walked quickly up to the villa. It had not been easy to tell Mervyn of her future plans.

She could not tell him that she did not love Marco, although she liked and respected him as she had liked and respected Giorgio. Leonora had only ever been in love once, when she was young and foolish, when the man she thought she loved was unworthy and she had been too blind to see it.

She had never forgotten those heady days of youth and passion. She had been made to pay for them and she believed she was still being made to pay. Well, she was going back to Rome, back to the protection of a good man who would be her husband. If her past caught up with her in Rome, there would be those around her who would know how to protect her.

Mervyn slept badly on that hot August night. He was aware of the distant roll of thunder and lightning lighting up the room. In the early morning he heard the rain and he got up hastily to close the window. It was coming down in a steady downpour but his first thought was that the garden could do with it, he was accustomed to the sudden tropical storms that swept across the island.

He slept fitfully but the sun awoke him as it illuminated his room with all its strident splendour. He went downstairs to make coffee and, while he waited for the kettle to boil, he went to stand outside on the patio. The sea was calm and a file of fishing boats was sailing towards the harbour after a night spent riding out the storm. There was all the promise of a beautiful day.

He was locking the door on his way to the

studio when he saw Leonora walking down the hill towards the little town. She was walking quickly, and there was something carefree and joyously youthful in her tall slender figure. She was wearing white trousers and a red sweater, her dark hair caught back from her face and tied with a red chiffon scarf, and as she skipped daintily down the road Mervyn decided he would wait in the garden until she drove past.

She was going to collect her car and on her way to the Hyams' she would need to pass his villa. He went to stand on a grassy mound where he had a view of the road and where she would see him, and in a short while he was rewarded by the sight of her white Mercedes climbing the hill. He raised his hand to wave to her and she stopped the car. For a long moment they stared into each other's eyes, then with a smile and a wave of her hand she was driving away and he remained in the garden until the sound of her engine was lost in the wind.

By midday storms once more swept across the island and only a few people braved the crossing from Rhodes in the small ferry boat. They made their purchases and left, and in the early afternoon Mervyn decided to close the studio and return home. The wind was very strong as he climbed the hill and after eating a light meal he decided to spend the afternoon writing letters.

Before leaving England Athena had urged him to make a will and he was remembering her smiling face as she had said, 'Darling, don't look so surprised. You're not going to go any earlier, but you do have a daughter, and Ian has always said everybody should put their affairs in order.'

He decided to write to Athena to tell her he had done exactly that. He also informed her that in his will he had distinctly stipulated that, should anything happen to him, he wanted her to have a say in bringing up his daughter.

He wasn't sure how she'd react to this piece of information, or why he had wanted it. Athena was light-hearted and often mercurial, but underneath all that there was a certain relaxed common sense. In all probability if the fates were kind to him, she would never be called to do more for Selene than act the part of an indulgent aunt, but now it was done and by the same token he felt the need to write to the Sheldons to thank them for all they were doing for his daughter and to assure them that he would return to England as soon as possible to see her.

By the time he was sealing his last envelope the storm was over and a pale watery sun was gilding the sea. He decided to walk down to the village to post his letters, but as he was leaving the villa two police cars came screeching up the hill, one with its sirens blaring. He stared after them. Some impecunious wayfarer on the crumbling cliff top, some child caught in the storm and missed by a frantic mother: he didn't spare them another thought until he reached the edge of the town and caught sight of people standing around in groups staring up the road.

Outside the garage Artos and Demetrius were in earnest conversation with a policeman and Mervyn waited until he walked away before joining them.

'Has there been an accident?' he asked curiously. 'I heard the police cars on the coastal road.'

Artos shrugged his shoulders and Demitrius stared down at the floor.

After a few minutes the older man turned and walked away and when Demetrius was about to follow him, Mervyn repeated his question.

Demetrius too shrugged his shoulders and in a mumbled voice said, 'An accident the police say, on the coastal road.'

'What sort of an accident, a car accident?'

'Yes. A slippery road, a bad bend, a driver going too fast.'

'Do I know the driver?'

'I can say no more. The police have all the details.'

The small groups of people were staring at him curiously and then he saw Father Cristofson striding down the village street, addressing the groups sternly and advising them to return to their homes. Meeting Mervyn's eyes he joined him, shaking his head dismally and saying, 'This is a sad business my son, a very sad business.'

'Is it Leonora?' Mervyn asked softly.

The priest nodded his head. 'Always she drove like the wind, as though all the demons in hell pursued her, and this morning she drove over the cliff in a thunderstorm.'

'And?'

'She's dead, of course. Who could survive such a misfortune? The car is a burnt-out wreck at the bottom of the cliff. There was no chance she could have survived it. Those two children, and the man she hoped to marry, they will be devastated, and you too my friend.'

His wise eyes met Mervyn's clouded ones and Mervyn knew that he was aware of his closeness to Leonora.

The crowds had melted away and the priest had walked on to his church in the town. There was nothing for Mervyn to do except go to his home, and yet some strange nagging thought persisted. Leonora had driven along that road in thunderstorms many times, when the mist hung low across the cliff top and she had known every bend along that winding road. Artos was outside his garage talking to an old man, but when he saw Mervyn approaching him, he turned hurriedly as if to go inside.

Mervyn reached the garage door before he did.

'Who serviced the Contessa's car, Artos?' he enquired, and was immediately met by the other man's angry stare.

'I am an honest man. We do only good work here, the car was perfect. How can I help it if the Contessa drove like the wind? There was nothing wrong with the car.'

'But who serviced it, Artos? Demetrius?'

The garage owner pushed past him angrily and slammed the garage door behind him. There was no way he would divulge who had serviced Leonora's car, and Mervyn had to agree with him that he had no right to question him. There would be an inquest. Artos ran a reputable business and there would be no dissenting voices raised to say otherwise. He was a foreigner, Leonora had been a foreigner, and these small island communities stuck together through thick and thin.

He opened his studio, not because he anticipated visitors, but so that he could hang around the area. The garage doors remained closed. Nobody entered, nobody left, and after a while he closed the studio and walked home. He found it impossible to believe that the beautiful vital woman he had seen that morning was dead, and he sat forlornly in his chair staring into space, until a knock on his door startled him into activity.

Father Cristofson was standing on his door-step, and Mervyn felt a rush of gratitude that he was not going to be asked to spend the evening alone. The priest accepted a glass of wine he poured for him with a wry smile.

'I have come to tell you that they have recovered the Contessa's body and she is being flown home by private jet this evening. The car will be recovered sometime tomorrow. Life has to go on, my friend.'

'I saw her this morning. She seemed relaxed and happy, walking down for her car.'

The priest nodded. 'It happened very suddenly. I always remonstrated with her that she drove too fast. She would smile and say she knew the road well and she was a good driver. I shall miss her, but she was never coming back to the villa. She was going back to her world.'

'Was she happy, do you think?'

'Oh yes. She had made up her mind to be happy. A new start, a man who would be good to her, care for her children, a life in Rome. Have you ever been to Rome, my friend?'

'No. One day I promised myself that I would go there.'

'All roads lead to Rome, that is what I believed, when I was a young priest visiting Rome for the first time. I was enchanted with Rome, its vitality and its splendour. I often talked to Leonora about it, she could bring it alive for me. It was her husband who loved this place, Leonora only tolerated it because there was so much of Rome in her past, waiting to be rekindled.'

Mervyn didn't speak. In his heart he had always known their love affair was thistledown and that one day they would return to their separate worlds, and, as if sensing his thoughts, the priest said, 'We all have our own little space on this planet, Mervyn, I am not yet sure where yours will be, but I always knew where Leonora's was. Mine is here, I shall never leave it, but you have a daughter, you will discover your place with her.'

The priest finished his wine and left. It was dark when Mervyn walked up the hill and let himself in through the gates of the villa above. He walked along the terrace past the curtained windows and its darkness depressed him. Moonlight filtered through the trees, silvering the sea, lighting up the path and Mervyn walked through the garden, his footsteps taking him to that place in the shrubbery where he had found the footprints. He knew the rain would have obliterated any that were there, but he could not help himself. There were no fresh prints but still he searched around. He was about to turn away when he saw something gleaming on the ground, partially hidden by a clump of ferns. He bent to pick it up and stared down at a silver propelling pencil stained with soil and rain.

He put it in his pocket. Somehow or other he had to find out who that pencil belonged to; if he couldn't, he would hand it to the police.

He heard the gates clang to softly behind him and he stared up the road shaded by trees, where the moonlight made vague shapes and creeping shadows and he stood listening. The sighing wind sounded like somebody breathing but he pulled himself together sharply. He was becoming as apprehensive as Leonora when in all reality it was probably a gardener who had stood in the bushes to smoke a quiet cigarette. He didn't believe it even when he thought it.

It was almost midnight when he heard the sound of a helicopter and he went to the window to see if he could see anything. He could only think that this was taking Leonora's body home. He saw, momentarily, a light flickering in the sky, then quickly the helicopter moved across the sky and the sound of its engines became ever fainter as it merged into the night.

He made up his mind that tomorrow after he had left the studio he would drive to where Leonora had met her death. By that time they could have recovered her burnt-out car, but he would be able to see the tyre marks, and the broken trees as it had crashed its way down the cliff. He could not have said what good he expected the visit to do: he simply had to reach his own conclusions. In all probability she had been going so fast, she had lost control of her car on the wet road. And yet the doubts persisted.

He washed the propelling pencil in hot water. The rain and mud had taken its toll on the bright finish, the pencil could have been in the soil for many days and he searched in vain for any initials engraved on it. It was simply an ordinary pencil: its only distinguishing feature came from the place where he had found it.

As he walked down to the studio next morning, it seemed to Mervyn that Leonora's death was already forgotten. The little town had an air of normality, the market traders were setting out their stalls, and the bell from the church steeple tolled cheerfully over the busy scene. The garage door was open and Demetrius was outside arguing with a man as they peered into the engine of his van. There was no sign of Artos and no sign of any other mechanic.

Visitors were stepping off the ferry and even as he unlocked the studio door they were waiting to be admitted.

The last ferry left for Rhodes in the late afternoon and that was when he locked his studio door and left for home. He arrived just as Maria was leaving, and unable to help himself, he asked, 'Do you know if Artos has another mechanic at the garage besides Demetrius, Maria?'

He knew that Demetrius was married to Maria's older sister and that they were a very close-knit family.

The girl looked at him curiously, and he said hurriedly. 'My car needs servicing and I want to make sure Demetrius can do it.'

Her face cleared.

'If you ask for Demetrius, I'm sure he will do your car, Mr Corwen.'

'He does have a great deal of work. He could do with some help.'

'There is Artos.'

'Of course, but Artos isn't always available. Is there nobody else?'

She shrugged her shoulders. 'Sometimes perhaps,' she said, then with a brief smile she hurried down the road.

These island people would hang together. His uncle had said many times that if you offended one of them, the entire island would take offence – even the priest was not immune from such misplaced loyalty.

He was clearing away after his meal when there was a knock on his door, and on going to open it, he saw the Hyams standing on his doorstep. He invited them in and poured three glasses of wine. Millicent was tearful, her husband unconvinced.

'We stopped the car to look where Leonora's car went over the cliff,' he said evenly. 'There are definite skid marks on the road, but Leonora had driven along the road a great many times. She knew every twist and turn and she was a good driver even if she was a fast one.'

'She was to stay with night with us,' Millicent said, 'and we were to bring her back in the morning. She seemed so relaxed and happy that she had made up her mind to return to Rome to marry Marco. Lately she's been nervy, afraid of her own shadow, then suddenly her life was really falling into place. Those poor children will be devastated.'

Neither of the men spoke and Millicent went on, 'Alexander is so mature. One never really knew what he was thinking about anything, but Sophia could run wild. Leonora told me her mother was hopeless with her. She spoiled her terribly. Now who will look after them?'

'Well, they're at good schools,' her husband said. 'Do we know anything about Leonora's mother?'

'Only that she's been married three times and has a title. She's rich, so money won't be any problem. I'm not sure that grandparents are the best people to bring up their grandchildren. What do you think, Mervyn?'

'There are times when there's nobody else.'

'Oh yes, of course. That was insensitive, I'd forgotten about your baby daughter. I hope she's being well taken care of.'

'Yes, I'm sure she is.'

'Well, we're calling on some more friends in the town. Everybody is quite stunned by this tragedy. Leonora hasn't been herself these last few months. She had become so jumpy. I'm sure it was living in that big villa surrounded by trees and cliffs. I asked her what she was afraid of, but she just shrugged her shoulders and said "Nothing at all, I'm being very silly".'

After they had gone, Mervyn changed his mind about visiting the place where Leonora's car had left the road. Instead, he decided to wait to see if Maria had anything to tell him about the garage.

He had never before felt lonely on the island:

There had always been his work, the sound of the sea and the warmth of the sun to cheer him, then there had been Leonora with her beauty and her passion.

For the first time he felt an acute feeling of isolation, the sort of loneliness he had felt when Moira was with him, because he had known that she was unhappy and hating the island intensely.

Chapter Twenty-One

It was one of those hot dry days at the beginning of September when the colour seemed to have gone from the land and the sea moved slowly like molten glass. It was Sunday and there would be no ferry coming from the larger island and therefore nobody interested in looking at his pictures.

The sound of church bells floated stridently in the still air and Mervyn decided that today was the day he would visit the scene of Leonora's accident.

He now regretted having mentioned the servicing of his car to Maria. She had favoured him with a great many doubtful looks and he had felt obliged to ask her if she had mentioned it to Demetrius.

She admitted that she had, and Demetrius had said he was always available at the garage. He came no nearer to knowing if a third person was involved and deemed it unwise to question Maria further.

When he met Artos in the village there was a constraint between them, and he believed Artos thought that in some way Mervyn held him responsible for the crash, when really all he had wanted to know was who had serviced her car.

He left the house in the early afternoon, taking the familiar road along the coast. A thin mist floated on the sea obscuring the horizon and it was hot and sultry, the grass on the cliff top was dried and colourless and on such a day he found it difficult to remember the island's beauty.

A young boy sat on the hillside surrounded by his goats, and he was playing some sort of instrument. It seemed almost biblical. He waved to the boy and received an answering wave in return, then ahead of him was a bend in the road and beyond the long coastline with its numerous inlets and rock-strewn pools.

At one point he thought he heard the sound of another car and he stopped to see if it would pass him but, although he listened carefully, he could hear nothing, only the sound from the bells around the necks of the goats.

He came at last to the sharp bend at the top of the hill and he steered carefully to a small clearing at the edge of the road, where he got out of his car. He could clearly see the skid marks veering across the dry soil and the churned-up crater where the car had gone over the cliff.

He walked to the edge and peered over. He could clearly trace the path the falling car had taken by the broken trees and scarred branches, then below an area of scorched earth and blackened timber. They had been quick to remove what was left of the burnt-out car. The priest had told him that Leonora's body had been thrown clear but that she was probably dead when the car hit the ground.

He started to descend the cliff, hanging on precariously to broken branches as he went, his feet sliding dangerously on the slippery ground. He quickly realised that he had been unwise to attempt it, but something outside himself urged him on. He arrived at the bottom of the hill gasping for breath and in pain from bruising on the way down. For a long time he hunted round the churned-up area but there was nothing to find: it would seem the police had done their job well.

He could smell oil and burnt timber and when he looked upwards to the top of the cliff his heart sank at the prospect of climbing back.

He was half way up the cliff when something colourful fluttered along the branches in front of him and he reached out for it, recognising it immediately as the red chiffon scarf Leonora had worn to tie back her hair on the last morning he had seen her. It was so delicate he clutched it in his hand before holding it against his face. He could smell her perfume, feel her in his arms, see the warmth in her eyes, then quickly he thrust it into his pocket and started his climb upwards.

With relief he hauled himself over the last steep piece of rock onto the grass verge, his arms and hands aching with excruciating pain. There was blood on his knuckles where they had been grazed by the rocks and there were bloodstains on his jacket and rents in his trousers, but at least he was alive and with no serious injury.

He walked unsteadily towards his car, then paused when he heard the sound of a car's engine coming towards him on the road.

For a moment the car stopped on the bend, then with a sudden rush of acceleration it came on, veering swiftly off the road towards the cliff top. Unable to move Mervyn stared incredulously at the oncoming car and then he felt the full force of it knocking him sideways and he was falling through the broken branches until he was only aware of the searing pain tearing through his body before there was nothing.

The driver of the car got out and went to peer over the cliff. He was unable to see Mervyn's body through the branches and the undergrowth but he was taking no chances. Almost casually he walked over to Mervyn's car and tried the door handle, it was unlocked. He reached inside and released the handbrake, then with one hand on the wheel he pushed the car to the edge of the cliff then he closed the door, went to the back of the car and slowly pushed it over the cliff. He waited while it bounced down the rocks, churning up roots and trees, and finally coming to rest where Leonora's car had landed days before.

He walked back to his car and sat for several minutes smoking a cigarette. There was a strange smile on his face as he drove away. In his cold unforgiving heart, there was no compassion, only bitter memories of a woman he had once loved and who had not loved him enough. Now he had paid her back for those years he had spent in prison, her and her lover. Besides, he was becoming a nuisance, asking too many questions. He had promised himself that one day she would pay: now they had both paid.

After the sound of the car's engine had droned away there were no sounds on the cliff top except bird song and the distant tinkling of goat bells.

Chapter Twenty-Two

They stood around the tiny churchyard in silent, shocked groups. The priest conducted the service of his friend, and the villagers rubbed shoulders with the people who had not been born on the island but had chosen to live there because they loved it. Athena stood alone, still unable to comprehend fully that Mervyn was dead: a slender woman in a simple black dress, her blonde hair caught back in a black silk scarf.

The man standing alone under the trees looked at her curiously. He wondered if she had loved him, but she was beautiful, this daughter of England. The priest would know who she was and if she would keep the villa or sell it.

The service was over, they were milling around, shaking hands, offering condolences, then several cars were driving away and the blonde woman was walking up the hill towards the villa with Father Cristofson.

In the villa Athena offered him wine and sandwiches she had prepared earlier, then she went towards a cupboard and brought out a portfolio of Mervyn's private papers.

'He told me he had made a will,' she said gently. 'But of course it was like Mervyn not to tell me what was in it. I expect everything is in here.'

'He was an orderly man. It probably will be.'

'He has a solicitor in England, but there will be copies of everything, I'm sure. There's nothing at the studio. Immediately news of his death leaked out, they came in their droves to buy his pictures. Everything is for Selene, I feel sure.'

'That poor child will never know her father.'

'No. It's very sad, but to lose someone one has known and loved is perhaps more painful than to lose someone one has never known.'

The priest smiled gently.

Athena was pulling out a long white envelope, and looking at the priest, she said, 'This is his will, I should read it.'

'Yes, of course you should. And everything else you feel you should see.'

She sat down weakly in an armchair and started to read, then stopped and stared vacantly into space. For a long moment, he could not tell by her expression if she approved or disapproved. Then looking up she said, 'I haven't read it all, but it seems Mervyn knew exactly what he wanted to do if he died. I don't think he believed his death would come so soon or so suddenly, but he apparently didn't want any problems. There's a legacy for his daughter's grandparents, but largely his money will go to Selene. He has left some money for your church, Father Cristofson, as well as my father's memoirs to you.'

'That is kind.'

'You were his friend. He had great regard for you.'

'And I for him.'

'Do you understand any of this? First Leonora, then Mervyn, in exactly the same spot. They said Leonora had been driving too fast, Mervyn would never have driven too fast at the same spot.'

The priest shrugged his shoulders.

'I fear we shall never know the true story, Athena. Perhaps the inquest will come up with something.'

'I doubt it.'

'Why do you doubt it?'

'Nobody saw the accident, nobody heard anything. I think in the end it will remain a mystery.'

The priest got to his feet saying, 'I will leave you to your papers Athena. You are returning to England in the morning?'

'Yes. Maria has helped me to leave everything in order here and there's nothing to keep me here now. My husband is not well, I told him I would get back as soon as possible.'

'And will you come back here, do you think? Or will you dispose of the villa?'

For a long moment she stared into space, troubled by her thoughts, then with a little smile she said, 'He's left it for Selene, I don't think I shall do anything about it in a hurry.'

'Then I will leave and let you get on with it.'

She went with him to the door and stood until his tall figure had disappeared along the road, then she turned and went back inside.

She was not relishing the thought of going through Mervyn's private papers and yet it was a job that had to be done. She felt it was an intrusion, but laying the will aside she reached down into the file and brought out several other documents. They were mostly notes on investments, and then she found the envelope bearing her name. Tears pricked her eyes as she tore it open. What premonition of early death had prompted Mervyn to write to her?

There were several pages of it, and it began with the conventional greeting of 'Dearest Athena'.

Picture me if you will writing this letter in the fading light, enhanced by sudden bursts of lightning and distant thunder. The incredible thing is that I should be writing this letter at all, but memories of Moira's death and more recently Leonora's have helped to convince me of my mortality.

My thoughts are for Selene. Her grandparents will surround her with love and attention, so much so that she will know nothing of me and I am vain enough to resent it.

I want you to talk to her about me, take some part in her education, show her the world and what it offers, which is something I do not think her grandparents are capable of doing.

They are good people, but you and I lived a different life. I'm not saying that it was a better life, but it did make us think beyond the bounds of everyday living.

I have instructed my solicitor in England with regard to these matters but I felt an explanation was due to you. It may be that you will probably never need to read this letter, that we shall go on to live out our lives and die in gentle old age, but this was not something that I thought should be left to chance.

Your ever loving cousin, Mervyn

Tears rolled down her face and she sat with the letter in her hands for a long time before she folded it and put it back in its envelope. She stood looking out through the window, over a garden bathed in moonlight and beyond the silver line of the sea. In a gentle voice she breathed, 'I will talk to Selene about you Mervyn. I'll show her your pictures and I'll bring her here and show her our island. I promise I won't let you down.'

Mid morning found her waiting at the gate for her taxi to take her to the ferry. She was taking with her the file containing Mervyn's will and the other papers, a few mementoes of the villa and some photographs. Maria had helped her stack the cupboards with things that might not be needed for a long time, and she had wept a little as Athena pushed a wad of money into her hands. The Urn she had given to Mervyn as a wedding present was in the priest's safekeeping for Selene.

She did not look at the taxi-driver as he held the door open for her, and he knew he would remember the sadness in her face and the sense of loss. She turned in her seat to look back at the villa, then she sat staring out of the window until they reached the jetty.

He took out her luggage and she paid the fare, then without a word she turned to join the other people waiting for the ferry.

He waited, his face inscrutable, and as the ferry came to rest at the jetty, Demitrius joined him on the harbour wall.

'Do you know her?' he asked Demetrius.

Demetrius nodded. 'They came here as children, cousins they were.'

'Not lovers?'

Not answering, Demetrius walked away, but the other man continued to watch as the ferry sailed away.

BOOK TWO

SELENE

Chapter Twenty-Three

Norah Sheldon stood in the doorway of the kitchen, watching her mother busily icing a batch of small cakes at the table. She knew her mother hadn't seen her – she'd been too immersed in the task in front of her – and when she spoke, her mother looked round sharply.

'What a fright you gave me,' she said. 'I didn't hear you come in.'

'I see the red carpet isn't out yet,' Norah answered.

Ignoring her comment, her mother said. 'Have you come for tea? If so, you can help me lay the table. Your father's gone to the station to meet Margaret.'

'And she's going to be totally confused. At university, at her Aunt's and with her friends, she's known as Selene. Isn't it time you changed too, Mum?'

'I shall never change. Margaret is what Moira wanted.'

'Oh well, she'll soon be off again.'

'Why do you say that?'

'Well, she rarely stays longer than a fortnight in the summer. They'll be off on their travels.'

'Why are you always so sarcastic about her? She spends two weeks with us in Bournemouth, it's only to be expected that she spends two weeks with them.'

'You'd have thought, after her husband died, Athena'd have been fed up with travelling around. I thought she had bad arthritis?'

'Here's the tablecloth, Norah. Get the crockery out of the cabinet.'

'I remember that we used to eat in the kitchen, except when we were entertaining. I didn't think entertaining your granddaughter counted.'

Her mother didn't answer, and with a cynical laugh, Norah said, 'You're keeping up with Athena, Mum. All the niceties of afternoon tea with the Royal Doulton and the silver. What will you do if she brings a boyfriend with her?'

'She would have asked our permission first.'

'I didn't know they did that, these days.'

Norah's attitude towards her niece troubled Elizabeth. She had this deep-seated resentment that had only grown over the years and was a relic of what she had felt for Moira.

Norah had her own home, a small house at the other side of the park and, if she had had men friends, neither of her parents had known about them. As the years passed she grew more and more waspish and Elizabeth often wished she was the sort of daughter Moira had been.

Norah was a teacher now at the school she had attended as a girl. She was the head of the English department, respected but hardly popular, since she rarely attended school functions and was not on friendly terms with the rest of the staff outside school hours.

She could hear her removing crockery from the glass cupboard in the dining room, noisily, irritably, and, anxious for its safety, she went into the room to help her.

'Why don't you stay and have tea with us?' Elizabeth said. 'You're going home to an empty house and I don't suppose you've got anything prepared.'

'I have work to do, examination papers to mark. If I stay for tea it's going to be late.'

'When are you coming round again?'

'Oh, one day, when I have the time. I expect you'll be shopping for clothes. She'll be going off on holiday before long.'

'We'll all be going off on holiday to Bournemouth. Why don't you come with us?'

'Oh Mum. I left Bournemouth behind me years ago.'

'But you're going off somewhere surely?'

'I thought I might go up to Scotland for a few days, walking.'

'On your own?'

'I don't mind my own company. It's preferable to trailing around with somebody who doesn't like the things I like.'

'Why not ask Margaret if she'd like a few days in Scotland? Since Athena went to live in Devon she never gets to visit Scotland and she was very fond of it.'

Norah merely favoured her with a slow sardonic smile before closing the glass doors. 'Anything else you want before I go?' she asked.

'No. I can see you're anxious to get away.'

'Yes well, like I said, I have a lot of work to do this evening.'

She watched her daughter walking quickly down the path outside and striding out along the road. Why didn't she dress smarter? She looked so frumpish in that old mackintosh she'd had for years, business-like skirt and shirt blouses and flat brogues. She'd been pretty enough as a child, not so pretty as Moira, probably because she'd had to wear glasses, but she'd always been the clever one.

She went back to the kitchen to pile the trolley with thinly sliced brown bread, plates of cold chicken and a mound of iced cakes. Arthur had advised her against a hot meal in case the train was late, and in any case it was a warm summer's day.

She felt restless. Dusting furniture where there was no dust, straightening cushions that didn't need straightening, then going to stand at the window so that she could look along the road.

Her mind went back over the years to the tragedy of her daughter's death, followed so quickly by Mervyn's. It had traumatised them until that moment when Elizabeth looked down at the tiny baby sleeping peacefully in her cot and the sudden realisation that she belonged to them and only to them.

The shock had come later when they became aware of Mervyn's will and his wishes to have Athena involved in the child's life. She had been gentle with them, gentle but firm, and over the years they had found her co-operative, although inwardly Elizabeth resented it when her granddaughter enthused about the time she spent with Athena.

At last she was rewarded by the sight of her husband's familiar car rounding the corner and coming to rest in front of the house. Then they were getting out of the car and he was helping with the luggage.

Margaret looked towards the window and waved, then picking up one of her cases she ran up the drive and Elizabeth hurried to meet her on the doorstep.

Every time they saw her she seemed to have changed. She was tall and slender but her colouring was the same. Moira's colouring, Elizabeth thought as she enfolded her in her arms. Softly waving hair that framed a beautiful face, hair that gleamed golden in the sunlight and eyes like blue azure pools. There was so much of Moira in her, but Elizabeth had to admit it was mainly in her appearance. There was an independence about her that her mother had never had, a light gaiety that covered an underlying rare intelligence.

'I'm so glad to see you, Granny,' the girl said hugging her closely. 'You look very well.'

'I'm fine dear. Your Aunt Norah was here but she couldn't wait, she has examination papers to mark.'

'Well of course, she's always so busy. Perhaps I'll call round to see her one evening.'

'Oh yes, dear, you should do that. Tea's ready, your favourite cakes.'

The girl laughed. 'I told Grandy you'd be making a fuss, there was really no need. Can I help?'

'No, it's all ready.'

'Then I'll just take my case upstairs and help Grandy with the rest.'

Tea was a light-hearted affair. She kept them

entertained with talk of her life at university and the many friends she had made there. It was then when Elizabeth said, 'You know we've booked for Bournemouth Margaret?'

'Yes of course.' With the mention of her name the girl's face clouded and she stared at her grandparents doubtfully before saying, 'Granny, why don't you call me Selene? Everybody else does?'

'You mean your Aunt Athena does.'

'No I don't and she's not my aunt, Granny, she's my father's cousin, I call her Athena.'

'She's the one who calls you Selene though.'

'Everybody calls me Selene, all my friends do. I prefer it Granny.'

'Your mother wanted you to be called Margaret.'

'Granny, I know. I never knew her, I never knew my father, but I do prefer to be called Selene. Does it really matter?'

Her grandmother's face was impassive, but it was Arthur looking from one to the other who said evenly, 'No, of course it doesn't matter, if she wants to be called Selene, then we should agree to it.'

'Forget Moira's wishes, do you mean?' Elizabeth said flatly.

'Granny, you can think of me as Margaret, but there are times when I feel totally confused.'

'You needn't have been. You're only confused when you've been with them.'

'Come on love, your granny's made these cakes for you,' Arthur cut in hurriedly.

His granddaughter had had to grow up with

Elizabeth's resentment towards Athena, and now her intransigence was creating an atmosphere that was marring what should be a happy occasion. Elizabeth was aware of it, but she couldn't help it. She had to keep faith with the daughter she had loved. She resented Arthur's disloyalty.

Selene looked from one grandparent to the other, and in a resigned voice said, 'Very well, Granny, if that's really what you want, I suppose it's got to be. I just think it's silly, that's all.'

'Why is it silly? You were Margaret until Athena interfered in your life.'

'She's only doing what my father asked her to do. She explained it to me.'

'I'll bet she did.'

'Why don't you like her?'

'We don't really know her. She's never been our sort.'

The girl bit her lip and decided to change the subject, 'I'll help you with the dishes, Granny, then I'll get unpacked.'

'Can't your unpacking wait until later. Help me clear away, then we'll sit in the lounge and you can tell me what sort of clothes you want for your holiday.'

That was something else Granny would find fault with. She had yet to tell them that after they came back from Bournemouth she had promised to see Athena and spend some time abroad with her.

It was much later in the evening when she broached the subject, when her grandfather sat in his favourite armchair with a whisky and soda on the table in front of him and Granny worked on her embroidery.

'Six weeks' holiday is an awfully long time,' she began.

'Oh well, it'll soon pass,' Elizabeth said. 'We'll be spending two weeks in Bournemouth, then we'll be visiting Kathleen and one or two cousins. They're all looking forward to seeing you.'

'I have to see Athena, Granny.'

'Why, why do you have to see Athena?'

'She wants me to go abroad with them. Cassie will be home.'

'Why does she need you if she's got her daughter?'

'Probably because she made a promise to my father, Granny.'

'She made a promise to get involved with your education, not whisk you abroad whenever the spirit moved her.'

'Granny, I really do like to spend some time with her, Cassie too whenever it's possible. I'm twenty years old, I want to go abroad and see something of the world.'

'There's plenty of time. Your mother didn't like living abroad, she told me she hated every moment of it. Your father and Athena were brought up like bohemians.'

'I don't think so, Granny. Athena told me her father was very strict, sometimes too strict.'

'Not strict enough by all accounts. I expect they did run wild on that island. Where abroad does she want to take you?'

'To Italy. To Rome.'

'I don't want her taking you to that island

where your father died. Does she still have that villa there?'

'I don't know.' She wanted to remind her grandmother that it was her villa. She knew in her heart that one day she would go there but tonight was not the time to talk about it.

'Why are you going to Rome?' Elizabeth asked.

'Cassie has a friend in Rome, somebody she met a long time ago.'

'When is she going to marry that man she's been going around with all these years?'

'I don't know. Cassie says it isn't serious.'

'Not serious! Why they've been all over the world together, here, there and everywhere, I'm surprised her mother condones it.'

'Cassie's twenty-eight, Granny.'

'It doesn't matter, she's still unmarried and living off her mother's money.'

'She does modelling work, Granny, very successfully.'

'And we all know what they get up to, don't we?'

Across the room her eyes met her grandfather's and he smiled. Suddenly the atmosphere lightened and, jumping to her feet, she said, 'I'll make coffee, then we'll talk about Bournemouth.'

After she'd gone into the kitchen, Elizabeth said, 'Why don't you say something Arthur? Surely you don't want her going off to Italy with Athena and her daughter.'

'We're in no position to stop it, and we should stop interfering or we'll antagonise all of them.'

'I don't understand you, Arthur, she's our granddaughter. We should be consulted.'

'She's also twenty years old, Elizabeth, and Athena is merely doing what Mervyn would have wanted her to do.'

'I'll never forgive him, never. Why couldn't he just leave Margaret to us to bring up. We did a good job with our own children, why involve Athena? She's been no great shakes with her own daughter. Cassie's unmarried, and with I don't know how many affairs in her past.'

'You're only surmising.'

'Well, of course, I'm not. She's had that long-lasting one with that French boy, and who knows how many others in between.'

'That's it, who knows.'

'Well, I don't want Margaret to be like her, do you?'

Arthur had to admit that he didn't.

'I've only met the girl twice,' Elizabeth went on. 'She's overdressed and over-painted and I thought she was frivolous, didn't you?'

Arthur reflected on the last time he had met Cassie. Yes, she'd been frivolous, she'd also been fun, and she'd improved the atmosphere of that dull November day by her beauty and her wit.

'I can see you don't,' his wife said dourly.

'She was fun, Elizabeth. She didn't say anything out of countenance and nobody disagreed with anything she said.'

'Well, of course not, not in front of us anyway.'

Their granddaughter brought in the trolley and started to pour out the coffee. As she handed the cup to her grandmother Elizabeth said grudgingly, 'When are you going to Italy?'

'The weekend after we get back from Bournemouth, if that's all right with you and Grandy.'

'It'll have to be, won't it.'

'Don't you want to hear about the Uni dance last week?'

'Who did you go with? Was there a crowd of you?' Elizabeth asked.

'Yes, the girls I room with and four boys who live in the same flats.'

'What sort of boys?'

'Nice boys, Granny, all of them students with very little money and plenty of ambition. Nobody special for any of us, but nice.'

'I don't want you to get involved with anybody special, you're far too young. All that can come later when you have a good job and a bit of money behind you.'

Arthur smiled. It was like Elizabeth totally to ignore the money Mervyn had left for his daughter, which was considerable. She wanted Margaret to become a teacher like Norah, the teaching profession was eminently respectable, it was what they'd wanted for Kathleen and Moira, but only Norah had been clever enough to please them.

She never questioned her granddaughter on the future but took it for granted that she would want what they wanted for her. Now Arthur was not so sure. He recognised that she was not like her mother but had all Mervyn's independence. They would find out soon enough what she intended to do with her life.

Elizabeth was planning the next day's activities.

'Tomorrow morning we'll go into the town, there's a new dress shop opened in the High

Street, it's expensive, but you'll need to keep your end up with that Cassie,' she said firmly.

Her granddaughter didn't tell her that Athena had already said they'd do some shopping in Rome when they arrived there. Happily, she allowed her grandmother to go on planning their day, shopping in the morning, then lunch in her favourite restaurant. More shopping in the afternoon and tea in her favourite store until it was time to head for home.

In the evening out would come their purchases and they would discuss how the dress material should be made up and Grandy would try on his holiday sweaters and sandals. Granny had a good dressmaker, a Mrs Pilling, who she said was worth her weight in gold, while inwardly she deplored the fact that her granddaughter preferred to buy her clothes off the peg.

She had tut-tutted at one or two of the girl's purchases, they would have been Athena's choice, she thought silently – floating skirts and gay colours, shoes with too-high heels, too strappy, and scarves and brightly coloured beads.

Elizabeth was glad Norah wasn't there to see what they had bought, her snide comments would have endorsed what she thought about Athena in her heart.

The Sheldons didn't keep late hours. It had been the same for as long as Selene could remember, coffee and biscuits at ten o'clock, then after the news was over time to go to bed.

She knew the holiday in Bournemouth would be exactly like all the other holidays she could remember in different parts of the south. They would go to the concerts on the pier and in the pavilions, they would watch the dancing in the ballroom at the hotel and if some boy asked Selene to dance the grandparents would look on benignly admiring, as long as she was returned to their table as soon as the dance was over.

She had only ever brought one friend home for a week in the summer and that had been her best friend Polly Jamieson. Polly was lively, with an impish sense of humour. She had a fund of stories, some of them a trifle naughty and her grandparents hadn't approved. She lived with her mother who was divorced from her father and had a man friend. Her grandmother demanded the full story of how Polly and her mother lived and what had gone wrong with the marriage.

It hadn't really mattered that Polly had been bright and amusing, but it had mattered very much that in their opinion her lifestyle was somewhat bohemian. Polly had made other friends, and, although they never actually fell out, now they were merely on speaking terms.

Her grandparents liked her to themselves so that they could talk about her mother, show her pictures her mother had painted, deluge her with photographs of family outings to Bournemouth and elsewhere. Their faces would grow sad and reflective and they very seldom spoke of her father.

She had seen the sort of pictures her father had painted and they were beautiful, while her mother's had been pretty and amateurish. She never talked about her father's pictures to her grandparents – somehow any talk of her father seemed to upset them. If she needed to know anything about him, she had to talk to Athena.

She wouldn't have admitted it to anybody, but she hoped the two weeks in Bournemouth would pass swiftly and she could move on.

Dutifully she visited Aunt Norah and found her sitting at a large table in the dining room. Spread out across the table were numerous books and reference tomes and Norah greeted her with a swift smile saying, 'Sit over there, I need all the space on the table I can get.'

'You look awfully busy.'

'Yes well I am. You should remember that end of term is always busy. How do you think you went on with your exams?'

'Quite well, I think.'

'Have you had any thoughts on what you want to do – accountancy, law – I'd made my mind up what I wanted when I first went to university.'

Selene knew what she wanted but she also knew it wouldn't have the blessing of her grandparents. She wanted to paint or do dress designing. They would think it ludicrous but it was in her blood.

'I'm thinking about it.'

'You should be doing more than thinking about it. What says Athena?'

'We talk about it but she doesn't interfere.'

'I thought your father wanted her to interfere.'

'She will if I do anything silly, I'm sure.'

Norah sniffed. 'I suppose you're looking forward to Bournemouth.'

'Why aren't you coming with us?'

'No time, besides I grew out of Bournemouth

years ago. Are you here until you go back to Uni?'

'No, I'm going to see Athena, I think we're going abroad.'

Norah raised her eyebrows disdainfully.

'Are you going to Greece?'

'No, to Rome.'

'Why Rome?'

'They have friends in Rome, Cassie in particular.'

'Isn't that girl married yet? I thought she'd have got married straight out of the school room.'

'Well, you didn't get married, Aunt Norah, so why should it be odd for Cassie not to have married?'

'It's nobody's business why I didn't get married, I had plenty of chances, but I wasn't a flibbertigibbet like Cassie.'

'You don't really know Cassie, Aunt Norah.'

'No. I don't really want to. I've always thought she was the sort of girl destined to break up marriages rather than make them.'

'Well, I don't know that she has broken up any marriage, so you're being unfair.'

Norah grinned. She didn't mind these clashes of opinions with her niece, at least the girl had opinions which was something her mother'd never had.

'Would you like me to make coffee, Aunt Norah?' Selene asked.

'If you like, but I can't invite you for lunch, I'm not eating until I've finished this lot.'

So Selene made the coffee and cleared away afterwards, then with something like relief she made her escape.

Chapter Twenty-Four

The holiday in Bournemouth was predictable and like so many of the others over the years. They stayed in Elizabeth's favourite hotel, one they had stayed at many times before, and around the town various aunts and cousins with their families shared houses and flats. Every day this bevy of relatives descended upon them and in the evenings they went to the theatres.

At some time or another they had all felt sorry for Selene because her parents were dead, but they also envied her because she was the centre of her grandparents' lives.

They envied her clothes, her education and her beauty, and for her part she passed on the clothes she had outgrown which they accepted grudgingly. Two of her cousins were engaged to be married to boys they had known most of their lives, nice ordinary boys, one a painter and decorator, the other a car mechanic. Elizabeth deemed that neither of them would have been suitable for her granddaughter, until her husband pointed out that a local boy would inevitably keep her in the area, while if Athena had anything to do with it she'd find somebody who would whisk her away from them.

They watched the boys who asked her to dance, the boys staying in the hotel who chatted and flirted with her, and as they drove home on the last morning of their holiday Selene heaved a sigh of relief that it was over.

Some parts of the holiday she'd enjoyed, the shows and the concerts, but she had felt stifled by affection. Would her grandmother ever allow her to grow up?

Elizabeth watched her packing her suitcase for her visit to Athena, commenting on her choice of clothes which at one time or another Athena had helped her to choose.

Her grandfather took her to the station and saw her on the train, but still ringing in her ears were her grandmother's strictures that she must be careful with foreigners and not get involved with some Italian boy. In some exasperation she had said, 'Granny, I wish you wouldn't treat me like a child.'

'We only want what's best for you, love.'

'I know, but I really am old enough to look after myself and know right from wrong.'

'That's what your mother always said.'

'Are you telling me that you didn't like my father?'

Elizabeth had looked at her helplessly before saying, 'Of course not dear, only it would have been nice if he'd stayed local instead of taking your mother off to Greece. She wasn't happy there you know, and I still think if she'd remained in this country she wouldn't have died so young.'

'That isn't fair, Granny.'

'It's how I feel, love. She was such a lovely girl, somehow when she came back from Greece she wasn't our Moira any more.'

Her grandmother's words occupied all her

thoughts on the train journey to Devon. There had been so much remembered bitterness in them and they rarely talked about her father. But for Athena he would have remained a wan shadow destined to remain under wraps for ever.

The taxi ride to Athena's house followed the coast and Selene stared out happily at the red cliffs and the azure sea. From Athena's home in the Scottish highlands it had seemed a far cry that she should have chosen to live in the south-west, but Athena and Selene loved it. Cassie was rarely at home.

She could see the house standing on a hillside overlooking the sea, a white house with a pillared entrance door and a long glass conservatory at the side of it, a house of large windows and tall chimneys, with sweeping lawns leading down to the cliff path and as they reached the gates a long low white sports car came zooming down the drive mounting the grass verge to avoid them, and the taxi-driver muttered angrily, 'Stupid young idiot. E'll kill 'imself one o'these days.'

Selene had recognised the car, it belonged to Pierre, Cassie's boyfriend. She had caught a swift look at his face, handsome, dark-browed and evidently very angry and she could only surmise they'd had yet another quarrel. Privately she thought it would be a disaster if they ever married, they were both too volatile, Cassie was spoilt and Pierre was arrogant. She had no doubt she'd soon be made aware of what had caused their latest quarrel.

She paid the taxi-driver who helped carry her

luggage to the door, then she opened the door and went into the hall. Athena was standing just outside the dining room door looking anxiously up the stairs. She turned when she heard the door opening, then she was embracing Selene warmly in her arms.

'Darling, I didn't expect you for hours. I thought you'd be catching the afternoon train,' she cried.

'I was packed up yesterday. I wanted to get away early.'

'Didn't your grandmother mind?'

'I don't think so. Was that Pierre leaving the house in a hurry?'

'It was, and in a fearful temper. He stormed down the stairs slamming the door behind him. They've been quarrelling again, and I think I know what it's about.'

Selene looked at her expectantly.

'He thinks he should come to Italy with us, and I told Cassie I really didn't mind. She won't have it.'

'Why ever not? I would have thought she'd have wanted him there.'

'Apparently not. I can't get any sense out of her. It's gone on too long, off and on, sometimes more off than on, but he keeps coming back for more of the same thing. Do run upstairs, dear, and tell her lunch is almost ready and see if she's upset.'

Cassie was evidently not upset because Selene could hear her humming to herself before she opened the door. The room was a mess with clothes strewn across the bed and suitcases stacked on the floor while Cassie was busy pulling yet more things out of the wardrobe. She turned round and grinned, her pretty face untroubled by anything that had gone before.

'I'm glad you're here,' she said brightly. 'You can help me to decide from this lot.'

'How long do you intend staying in Italy? There's enough here for months.'

'And months might be how long I'm staying.'

'I can't stay for months and your mother won't want to.'

'Not you two, darling, just me. If I stay on with Sophia I can get some modelling work, I've modelled in Italy before.'

'What about Pierre?'

'Well, what about Pierre? He's annoyed because he isn't coming to Rome, but why take coals to Newcastle? Italy's full of divine-looking men.'

'Aren't you in love with Pierre, Cassie?'

'We get along, and that's just it, it's been too long.'

'Then why don't you end it?'

'One day I will. I don't want to marry him. I couldn't live with his mood swings, and he's going off to America soon for his firm.'

'For good, do you mean?'

'Well for some time. I don't want to live in American, my roots are here, I've told him so and he doesn't like it. Here, what do you think about these two? I think the yellow suits me better, but I've worn it several times at some function or another.'

She was holding up two evening gowns, one in

bright buttercup yellow the other in indigo blue.

When Selene didn't immediately answer her, Cassie said, 'You'll prefer the blue. After all, yellow doesn't suit your colouring. If I decide on the yellow, I'll lend you the blue,' then with a bright smile she said, 'On second thoughts, darling, I don't want any competition, you're really far too pretty and younger.'

Selene laughed. 'Oh Cassie, I'll never be any competition for you, I sometimes wish I were more worldly.'

'You will be, that's if you can tear yourself away from those suffocating grandparents of yours.'

'They mean well.'

'I know, but I'm glad they're your grandparents and not mine. Did you enjoy Bournemouth?'

'Yes, it was very nice.'

Their eyes met and both girls laughed.

'I suppose the cousins and the aunts came along?' Cassie said. 'Didn't you meet some nice young man to show you the sights?'

'I've seen all the sights and no there was no young man. Tell me about Rome, Cassie.'

'I'll tell you after lunch. Mother'll be resting and you can help me with my packing.'

'Oh yes, I forgot about lunch. Athena told me to tell you it was ready.'

Athena asked no questions about Pierre, she was familiar with her daughter's arguments with Pierre, instead they talked about Selene's holiday with her grandparents and what they expected to need for their holiday in Rome.

'We should go to the shops, I suppose,' Athena said. 'But I'm sure we can get everything we need in Rome, and things more appropriate for our holiday there. I've arranged for foreign currency and our passports are in order. Is something troubling you, Selene?'

'The money, Athena. I don't think it should be your money which I always seem to be spending. Don't I have some of my own?'

'Well of course, and perhaps it's time I allowed you to see the investments your father made for you. I'm really very surprised how much money he made during those last few years of his life. He had few expenses on the island. Food was cheap, the villa was his and life was simple and uncluttered. One day I hope you'll see it for yourself.'

'I'm not sure I want to go there,' Selene said thoughtfully. 'It will remind me that my father was killed there.'

'Sophia's mother was killed there, in exactly the same spot,' Cassie said, 'but they still have the villa there.'

'Do they ever go there?' Selene asked.

'I think Sophia's brother goes there. I'm not sure about Sophia.'

'How long since you've seen Sophia?'

'Quite often when I was in Rome. They're really very grand, her grandmother's a princess, her brother's a conte, and a very handsome one at that. Don't get any ideas about him, darling. He's reserved and austere and if anybody's going to love him madly, it'll be me.'

'Really, Cassie,' her mother said sharply. 'I hope we're not going to Rome so that you can flirt with Alexander. I doubt if you'd be his type.'

'Well, he isn't married and we get along.'

'You get along with all your boyfriends until one or the other of you fails to get their own way, usually you.'

Cassie laughed. 'Alex is different, I'd be content to go his way. When I was with Alex, somehow it didn't seem so important to get my way.'

Athena looked troubled. She knew her daughter too well, vain, mercurial, spoilt. Ian had spoilt her, more so when he was ill, and because she'd always been bright and witty she'd been popular, too popular with both men and women.

She was beautiful in a bold, colourful way, and looking across the table at the two girls sitting next to each other the difference in them was very apparent. Cassie with her dark auburn hair and green eyes, and Selene's more gentle beauty, pale blonde hair and wide blue eyes, pale porcelain skin barely touched by the sun of Bournemouth.

It was silly that she should be troubled by thoughts on how these two different women would resolve their futures, and even sillier to think that their futures might clash.

Selene might look like her mother but there was more of Mervyn in her character and Mervyn had been unpredictable. There had been something going on between Mervyn and Sophia's mother, not something destined to last, but something very tangible, and very soon she would be introduced to Leonora's children and they might have known if their mother was involved with their neighbour.

Perhaps it was a mistake to be taking Selene to

Rome, but Cassie had been determined to go there and at a time when Selene spent some of her holidays with them.

There had been many times over the years when Athena wished Mervyn had not made her responsible for certain aspects of his daughter's life. The time was fast approaching when she would need to do rather more than advise her on the merits of university life and the sort of future she wanted for herself.

Her grandparents wanted her to become a teacher but Athena knew that Selene had no leanings that way. She had seen some of her work as an artist and it was good. To please the Sheldons she had gone on to accept her place at university and was doing well there, but now all she could talk about was moving on to art school and the sort of career that would offer her.

She talked about dress-designing and she and Cassie talked endlessly about the salons of Paris and Rome.

Cassie had never been academic. With a string of boyfriends behind her Athena had thought she would probably marry young, some boy with a monied background doing something lucrative in the city, who could keep her in clothes and the many luxuries she'd been brought up with. Instead the boys had come and gone. Pierre had lasted longer than the others because he was different, more sophisticated, harder to shake off.

Over the years Cassie had talked about Alex, her friend Sophia's brother, and always when she spoke of him there had been that dreamy haunted look in her eyes so that Athena had been tempted to ask, 'How well do you know him? Has he escorted you about in Rome?'

Cassie had answered her airily, saying, 'He's always abroad somewhere or on that Greek island, and Sophia and her grandmother never go there. After all it has unhappy memories.'

'Then why does Alex go there?'

'He always loved it, that was why his mother kept it on.'

This summer Alexander would be in Rome where the family were celebrating his grandmother's eightieth birthday.

'But why have they invited us?' Athena asked. 'It's not as though I've ever met the Princess.'

'Well I have, and I wanted you to meet her and Alex.'

Cassie was unconcerned that she had quarrelled with Pierre, it seemed that all her thoughts were concentrated on meeting Alex again.

Selene was not a problem. She wanted to see Rome and Italy, she would probably be happy to be left to her own devices, leaving Athena free to concentrate on Cassie.

It was Sophia who met them at the airport, driving a large white Mercedes, her slender red-tipped hands gesticulating this way and that as she steered the car through the streets of Rome. They were driving too fast, Selene thought, affording her only glimpses of sights she had only seen in her history books and yet she was aware that in this eternal city there was a vitality and joyousness she had not known.

Athena sat back in the back of the car looking at Selene's enraptured face, and when the girl turned towards her with shining eyes she said, 'I know, I thought it too the first time I saw Rome. Yesterday, today and tomorrow, it does not change.'

Sophia and Cassie were chatting away in English, unconcerned with the historic buildings and streets they were passing, and then they were driving up a long hill and below them the city with its domes and campanile shimmered in the afternoon sunlight.

Before them stood two great ornamental gates and a long curving drive on either side of which stretched beautifully laid out gardens and one white marble fountain. Sophia brought the car to rest at the foot of a line of shallow white marble steps leading upwards to a wide terrace and beyond it the Princess Cabrodini's palazzo. A manservant came running down the steps followed by a young boy in livery, and Sophia ushered the guests up to the terrace and turning to smile she said, 'My grandmother rests on the lower terrace in the afternoon, I think we shall find her there.'

Cassie was looking round her excitedly, asking airily, 'Has Alex arrived home?'

'Yesterday. We shall find him sitting with Grandmother.'

'Will he be staying here?'

Sophia favoured her with an amused glance. 'Well of course,' she trilled. 'My grandmother wouldn't hear of him staying anywhere else when he's in Rome.'

'Where else does he live?' Cassie persisted.

'He has a flat in Milan where he has banking

interests and he travels here, there and everywhere. My brother is very much a citizen of the world.'

'Does he ever go back to the island?'

'Yes, when he wants to relax, but it really isn't very often these days.'

By this time they had reached the terrace where an elderly lady and a young man were chatting over the teacups. The man rose to greet them and the lady smiled and held out a languid hand.

Selene looked up into a pair of cool grey eyes and at the most handsome face she had ever seen. No wonder Cassie was in love with him she thought.

Indeed Cassie monopolised him throughout the ceremony of afternoon tea and Sophia looked on with some amusement, her grandmother rather less so.

'This is not your first visit to Rome?' the Princess asked Athena.

'No. I have been here a good many times and I love it. This is Selene's first visit.'

The Princess transferred her gaze to Selene saying, 'You will like Rome, you are old enough to appreciate its history and young enough to enjoy its entertainment. I rarely go into the city these days, but I am sure you young people will have something in mind.'

In her mind she was comparing the two English girls, one with a great deal to say and flashing smiles that were attempting to captivate Alexander, and the younger girl, delicate, accepting second place, and she knew which she preferred.

Athena felt tired after the journey. Her arthritis was getting worse and she felt a migraine coming on. The Princess leaned forward to say, 'You look tired my dear. It is very hot today and you have travelled some way.'

'Yes I do feel tired,' Athena admitted. 'I haven't been too well, but perhaps the sun will be good for my arthritis. I hope so.'

'Of course, and you must rest before dinner. I always do. Pietro will show you to your rooms, dinner is at eight. Have you any thoughts about this evening Sophia?'

'Of course, Grandmama. We shall take our guests into the city and show them Rome by night. We have it all in hand.'

'We?' the Princess asked with a smile.

'Nino and I. He's joining us for dinner. I really should have asked him to bring a friend, five is such a terrible number.'

Selene was quick to say, 'Please don't include me. I'll discover Rome tomorrow and I too am rather tired.'

The Princess looked at her with a wry smile. She didn't look tired, in fact she was a young girl standing on the edge of life waiting for it to reach out for her. No, this girl had been well and truly instructed how she was to conduct herself. She was to be no competition for the attentions of Alexander.

Later that evening Selene stood on her balcony looking down onto a city glittering with lights. She could recognise the floodlit dome of Saint Peter's and other domes and towers throughout the city and she thought about the four young people who had sped off earlier in Alexander's open car. There had been much laughter, and the two girls had looked enchanting in their evening dresses. Cassie sat in the front seat next to Alexander and as they drove off into the darkness none of them turned their heads. Selene thought about the words she had exchanged earlier with Cassie, words that Cassie had said airily, even when their meaning was clear.

'I'm sorry you're not coming with us, Selene, but five is a bit of a crowd. I'll have a chat to Alex or Nino and ask them to conjure up a friend for you.'

'There's really no need, Cassie, I'm quite happy to potter around on my own.'

'Well, Mummy's going to have something to say about that.'

'You needn't worry about me, Cassie. Your Alexander is quite safe.'

'I know. I've been in love with Alex since I was a young girl, and this is my chance to get him. You don't blame me, do you Selene?'

'Of course not. But he has to feel that way too.'

'He will. If he doesn't by the time you and Mummy are ready to leave I shall stay on here in the city. I've done some modelling here before, I can do it again.'

'Then I hope it works out for you, Cassie.'

Chapter Twenty-Five

Selene was up with the dawn the next morning and the young maidservant who served her with coffee and fruit stared at her curiously. She knew only a few words of Italian but armed with a map of the city she was soon hurrying down the hill in the direction of the wide thoroughfares beyond.

She decided that first she would go to Saint Peter's and had no difficulty in finding it, for the Dome towered over everything else. So early it was crowded with visitors and she stood in stunned amazement at the statutary and the ornate tomb of Saint Peter himself.

Enraptured, she was standing looking at Michelangelo's statue of La Pietà when a voice beside her said, 'It is magnificent, isn't it? I thought I might find you here.'

She looked up to find Alexander gazing down at her with a gentle smile. Taking her guidebook in his hand, he said evenly, 'Now you can't possibly have covered very much. I drove down here as soon as I realised you had left the house. We'll go to the Sistine Chapel before it gets too busy.'

'This is very kind of you, Alexander, but are you sure I'm not intruding into something else you had in mind?'

'I had nothing in mind, Selene. I like to show visitors my city, particularly visitors who look as though they might enjoy it.'

So for the rest of the morning they wandered through the vast cathedral and absorbed the beauties of the Sistine Chapel. There was too much to take in in one morning and then Alexander suggested that they went out into the sunshine to a small garden where he knew they could get a bottle of wine.

They sat under the orange trees with a bottle of chilled Orvieto, and she listened to him saying how they should spend the afternoon. She felt guilty and was about to suggest that they should get back to the house when he leaned across the table and said, 'You're very like your mother, you know.'

She stared at him in surprise. 'You knew my mother?'

'No, I can't honestly say that, but I did meet her. She came to a party my mother was having. My mother was fond of parties and I remember that your mother appeared rather lost and overwhelmed by it all. We Italians are a gregarious people and my mother was never happier than when she was surrounded by people and laughter.'

'Perhaps my mother was shy.'

'Yes. I was only a boy, but I remember seeing this pretty blonde English woman standing out on the terrace gazing out to the sea. We chatted for a while. I didn't really learn a great deal about her. I knew your father better.'

'You knew my father too?'

'Well yes. He came up to the villa to paint a picture of my father sitting in the summerhouse, then over the years I met him often.'

'Did you like him?'

'Of course. He was very talented. Are you an artist?'

'I'm told I have some talent, I'd like to paint, but whether it's pictures or something else I'm not really very sure. My grandparents would like me to become a teacher.'

'And is that what you want to do?'

'Not really. They've brought me up after both my parents died. Athena has taken a hand now and again but mostly in an advisory capacity.'

'And Athena?'

'She's my father's cousin. They were brought up together. My father must have thought she should be involved.'

Alexander merely smiled. As he looked into her wide blue eyes he was remembering her mother, shy, withdrawn, wishing she was miles away from his mother's guests. This girl may look like her, but there was an independence about her.

'I think we'll forget old ruins for a while,' he said. 'We should discover the city as she is today; yesterday can wait for another time.'

'So we're not looking at ancient Rome today?'

'No. The Colosseum is a sad place with memories of old conflicts and tragedies. We'll take a cursory glance at the Forum but then we'll watch the artists at work in Piazza Navona, we'll climb the Spanish Steps and walk in the Borghese Gardens. I'll allow you to throw your coin in the Fountain of Trevi to ensure your return to Rome, then we will drive to the top of the Gianicolo and Rome will be spread before you in all her magnificence.'

For the whole of that enchanted afternoon Selene forgot everything except that she was totally charmed by the man beside her. She basked in the warmth of his smile, in the low charm of his voice, and when they at last drove up the hill towards his grandmother's house she knew that for good or ill she was in love for the first time in her life.

She thanked him with a blushing face for the happiness his company had given her, and he raised her hand to his lips and gently kissed it.

'We'll meet at dinner,' he said. 'Perhaps this evening we'll see a little of Rome by night.'

It was only when she entered her room and found Cassie standing on her balcony that she came down to earth.

'Where have you been?' Cassie greeted her starkly.

'Alexander has been showing me the city. I didn't arrange it, he found me in St Peter's.'

'I suppose you think you're in love with him?'

Selene decided her question didn't require an answer, and Cassie said coldly. 'I resent you Selene, I always have. I can't even think why your father should ask my mother to concern herself with your future, but my mother took it too seriously. You belong to your mother's family. They brought you up from being a baby and you are not to come into my life now and steal what is mine.'

'That's very unfair, Cassie.'

'It may be, but you won't steal Alex. If it's the last thing I do, I'll stop you doing that.'

Selene turned away. There was no use in arguing with Cassie while she was in this mood, in any case what was there to argue about? Alexander had been kind to one of his grandmother's guests, nothing more than that.

Cassie stormed out of her room, closing the door smartly behind her. It was there she encountered Sophia standing at the head of the stairs, a slow, cynical smile on her lips.

'I can see you offered the proper chastisement,' she said.

'I don't know why she had to come with us.'

'Haven't you thought you might be going about this the wrong way?' Sophia said reasonably. 'Alexander isn't the sort of man to be pushed into anything he doesn't want. You're trying too hard, Cassie. Why not let him discover your charms for himself? As it is, he probably finds you obvious and Selene intriguing.'

Cassie merely glared at her, and with a light laugh Sophia said, 'Oh well, have your own way then. But I promise you Alexander is thinking of ways we can spend the evening and that includes Selene.'

Cassie found Alexander on the telephone in the hall, so she waited nervously for him to put the telephone down. She knew enough Italian to realise that he had been booking a table for eight at some restaurant or other. When he saw her looking at him with raised eyebrows, he smiled.

'We should take a look at Rome from the terrace of Mario's,' he explained. 'I have booked a table for eight.'

'Eight?'

'Why yes. There are six of us here and there is Nino and Uncle Marco. He likes to spend time with us and I am sure he would like to meet your mother and Selene.'

'It was kind of you to show Selene around Rome, Alex.'

'Not at all. I enjoyed it, and it would have been churlish to allow her to stroll around Rome on her own.'

'I suppose so. Particularly as she's recovering from the trauma of a very unhappy love affair.'

'Really. She didn't seem to me to be terribly unhappy.'

'You haven't had to live with her these past few months. She's been unconsolable.'

All the things Sophia had told her about her mother's affair and its aftermath surfaced in Cassie's imagination now. Alex would be appalled at the same sort of trauma that had followed his mother's early romance and he would want no part of it. So her lies about Selene's lover followed faithfully the pattern of his mother's disastrous early love and he listened until she said at last, 'We don't discuss it any more, we want to forget about it.'

'And is Selene prepared to forget about it?' he asked.

'We do hope so. Mother thought this holiday would help, but the affair has left her very vulnerable, I'm sure you can see that, Alex.'

Alex merely favoured her with a nod of his head and a change of subject.

The evening should have been perfect. A warm summer evening under the stars with music and the lights of Rome all around them, yet to Selene it was a disaster.

Alexander was charming and distant. She danced with Nino and with Uncle Marco but by the end of the evening she was viewing the remainder of her stay in Rome with something like despair.

The Princess watched Cassie's behaviour with increasing cynicism. She too was looking forward to the end of the holiday and was devastated when Sophia informed her that Cassie intended to stay on in Rome to do some modelling.

Athena was too concerned with her health to offer advice in any direction. Her rheumatoid arthritis flared up to such an extent that she was unable to walk and was feverish. A doctor was called in, but Cassie immediately said her mother would be better off with her own physician in England, somebody who understood her illness.

Relieved, the Princess said, 'In that case I'll make arrangements for you to take your mother home as soon as possible.'

Cassie and the Princess faced each other, two iron wills in conflict with Athena too ill to care and it was left to Selene to offer a solution.

Logically she explained that she had to give some thought to which way her career was going and she needed to spend time with her grand-parents. Rome had been wonderful, she would never forget it, but she would travel home with Athena and, to Cassie's relief, the Princess seemed to accept the solution.

Athena would spend some time in a private hospital owned by her doctor and an ambulance and nurse would meet them at the airport. It was amazing how quickly everything fell into place, and Cassie was a girl who never looked back.

When Alexander asked if she felt entirely happy that she was leaving the care of her mother to Selene, she replied with a bright smile, 'But of course Alex. Selene is wanting to go home, I know it's entirely deplorable but there's nothing anybody can do about it and Mummy is too ill to be bothered.'

'You mean Selene is going back to be with him?' Alex asked pointedly.

'Why else.'

Alexander drove them to the airport and made all the arrangements for Athena to be supplied with a wheelchair and attendants. When it was all done, he gravely took Selene's hand in his and with the grave smile that stirred up too many emotions said, 'Goodbye Selene, I hope everything goes well for you in England.'

She stared at him curiously. She thought his words were strange. Athena was the one who was ill, yet his words had been for her. Cassie beamed at her and thrust an armful of glossy magazines in her arms, embracing her swiftly and saying, 'Thanks so much Selene for looking after Mummy. Remember me to your grandparents, they'll be so glad to see you home.'

On the flight home Athena slept and Selene thought about Rome and that one day in particular. As for the others, she had discovered Rome alone, jumping on and off trams, discovering all the sights she had only ever read about and in the end Rome had left her with a desperate urge to return.

Back at the palazzo the Princess faced her granddaughter, and Sophia was forced to realise that her grandmother was more than a little concerned with the events of the last few days.

'Your friend should have returned to England with her mother,' she said sternly. 'I think it is quite wrong that she should have left the care of Athena to Selene. Why is she staying on in Rome?'

'She has work here, Grandmama. Cassie's done modelling work for Carvello before, he was delighted that she promised to work for him again.'

'And where does she propose to live?'

Doubtfully Sophia said, 'Can't she stay here for a while, at least until she's had a chance to look around for something else?'

'She's here for Alexander.'

'Oh Grandmama, of course she isn't. In any case Alexander won't be here, he'll be back in Milan.'

'But she knows that he returns often for visits. I heard her asking when he would be back.'

'She was making conversation.'

'And she is aware that he spends some time with us in September, either here or on Capri?'

'Well, if she is working for Carvello she won't be able to visit Capri will she? Besides, I think Alexander wants to visit Greece.'

'When did he say that? I have never heard him say so and he knows I resent him spending time on that island. I find it totally morbid. Surely he can't be fond of a place that cost his mother her life?'

'Oh, Grandmama, the island wasn't to blame for Mama's death. She always drove too fast.'

'I asked Athena if Selene ever went there. Apparently not. She said Selene had never expressed an interest in the island where her father died. Cassie is not the sort of girl I want for Alexander, and I'm not at all sure that Nino is the man I want for you.'

Sophia trilled with laughter. 'I don't want him for me either. He's fun, and he adores me.'

'I once heard those sentiments from your mother, and we all know the sort of disaster that followed.'

'Yes well, Nino isn't like that. He's sane and normal. He's not totally obsessed with me, we're just enjoying life, having a good time while we're young. We'll probably both settle down one day with somebody suitable.'

Their conversation was interrupted by the sight of Alexander's car driving through the gates, and the Princess frowned.

She watched the man and woman leaving the car, walking hand in hand up the terrace steps and Cassie was laughing up into his face, apparently unconcerned that she had just been seeing her sick mother off on her flight to England. Cassie was unconcerned with anything and everything outside Alexander, and already she regarded him with a proprietorial air.

Later that afternoon Sophia advised Cassie to cool her behaviour with Alexander.

'Doesn't she like me?' Cassie asked in some surprise.

'Yes, I'm sure she does, but you smother him,

Cassie, and that's what she doesn't like. She's well aware that you put him off Selene.'

'Surely she doesn't think he was really interested in Selene.'

'Suppose if he was, you told him something that ended it.'

'If he'd really been interested in her, nothing I said would have made any difference.'

'It depends what you said, Cassie. There are deep dark secrets in our family background. Alexander is sensitive, he adored my mother. I never worried about her history, it was over and done with, but Alexander worried that her death might have had something to do with what went before.'

Cassie stared at her in amazement. 'And what about Mervyn's death? Surely he can't think that that was sinister too?'

'I don't know.'

'Oh well, Alex will be leaving soon, so she'll not be seeing us together. I love him Sophia. Until he goes I want to be with him as much as I can.'

They were not to know that at that very moment the Princess was having a serious conversation with her grandson.

'How serious are you about this English girl?' she demanded.

He stared at her in amazement, but undeterred she went on, 'The girl's right enough Alexander, but perhaps not for you.'

'I hadn't realised that you would still be advising me on my love life when I had reached the exalted age of thirty, Grandmother. Do you do the same with Sophia?'

'Sophia is different. She's earned herself a very doubtful reputation with too many lovers and no serious commitments. I've really given up on Sophia, but in your case there's never been any serious woman in your life. When there is, I'd like it to be the right one.'

'And when there is, Grandmama, I can assure you you'll be the first to know.'

'But this girl,' she persisted. 'She's obviously in love with you, she's made that very plain.'

'We get along, she's amusing, and next week I'm leaving for Milan.'

'You know that she intends to stay on in Rome?'

'Yes. She's modelling for some fashion house.'

'And in September, have you decided to come back here as you usually do?'

'I'm not sure what I shall do in September. I have a few weeks, I can take work with me, so I shall need time to myself. I thought I might go to Greece. I haven't been there for several years, the villa needs looking at.'

His grandmother's displeasure was evident in her haughty frown.

'Really, Alexander, I was hoping you'd never go there again. The mere thought of that island gives me the shudders.'

'You never went there, Grandmama, so how can you say that?'

'I can and I do. Why do you keep the villa on, spend money on servants to look after it and gardeners to care for the gardens? Athena told me she had never returned there after her cousin was killed.'

'If we spent our entire lives avoiding tragedies from the past we'd never recover from them, Grandmama, I've decided that this is a tragedy I should face, not run away from.'

'Oh well I don't suppose anything I say will make the slightest difference. You don't go with my blessing, Alexander.'

He reached down and gently kissed her cheek.

'Be nice to Cassie, Grandmama,' he murmured. 'We're friends, nothing more.'

'She's a spoilt and very wilful young woman.'

He nodded. 'I'm aware of it. Shall we go out onto the terrace, it's almost tea time.'

A few minutes later the two girls joined them on the terrace and addressing Cassie the Princess said, 'I do hope your mother will soon be feeling much better. The flight home will not help.'

'She has a very good doctor who looks after her very well. A few weeks in his nursing home will do wonders.'

'Will your cousin be there to visit her in hospital?'

'Perhaps. She'll want to go to her grandparents and there are other people she'll want to see.'

Her eyes met Alexander's and looked quickly away. For the first time she became aware of a spasm of contrition, but it was gone as quickly as it had surfaced.

They'd done enough for Selene. Her mother'd concerned herself with Selene's education, her style, her clothes and the money and investments her father had left for her. Selene's grandparents would have been hopeless, if it had been left with them. Selene would have been the same sort of little mouse her mother had been. No, she'd been right to end any feelings Alex might have had for her. Never in a thousand years would they have been right for each other.

She had to make the most of the few days left with Alex in spite of anything Sophia had said.

Three days later Alexander left for Milan but not before he had informed Cassie that on his next holiday he would not be returning to Rome but intended instead to visit his villa in Greece.

'Why can't we join him there?' Cassie urged her friend. 'You know the island as well as I do, we could have such a wonderful time sailing and surfing there, just like we did when we were children.'

Sophia was unsure.

'Are you thinking about your mother?' Cassie said. 'I could think about Mervyn but I don't. They were accidents, Sophia. It's time to go back.'

'I have been back several times you know, with Nino.'

When Sophia told her grandmother what they planned to do, the old lady was concerned. She did not want Cassie with Alexander, on the other hand she didn't want him on the island alone. She was too old, too old to interfere, nobody would take the slightest notice of her anyway.

Chapter Twenty-Six

It was late the following day when Selene opened the door of Athena's house. She felt weary, with the flight which had been late, and with the trauma of seeing Athena settled into the nursing home. The older woman had been in some pain and was fretful. Selene had left her surrounded by a bevy of attentive nurses and her doctor and although it was summer the house felt cold and unwelcoming.

Davina, Athena's devoted Jamaican housekeeper, came rushing out of the kitchen, her face filled with concern, but Selene was quick to tell her that Athena was being cared for and they would visit her together in the morning.

Davina fussed around, cooking her a meal, putting a match to the fire in the living room. Athena hated gas fires and the grate was always laid and ready for use. She was wishing Athena had a dog so that she could walk across the cliffs with a companion, but Athena had never wanted another animal since Omar her Persian cat had died.

Instead of going out therefore, Selene contented herself by wandering around the house. Athena's taste was everywhere, in the long peach velvet curtains draped at every window and the pale turquoise carpet that covered the floor, in the porcelain vases and china figurines and in the pictures that hung on every wall.

She stood looking up at a picture her father had painted. It was of an azure sea rolling in towards tall cliffs and a garden sloping down to the edge, alive with the colours of summer flowers. Whenever she came to Athena's she looked at this picture, and Athena had told her there were others in a bedroom used as a box room at the top of the house. She never went in there. Athena spoke of Mervyn, but some strange sense of loyalty forbade Selene to speak of him. This was because whenever she spoke of him to her grandparents they changed the subject. They only ever spoke of her mother.

Athena was considerably better the next morning when Selene and Davina went to the nursing home. She was sitting up in bed looking relaxed and pretty in her pale-blue bed jacket, her hair a pale golden halo round her delicate face.

On the table beside her bed stood a huge bowl of yellow roses and seeing Selene looking at them Athena said with a little smile, 'Jonathan sent them. Doctor Pressley telephoned him last night to say that I was here.'

'Why don't you marry him, Athena, it's years since Ian died?' Selene asked gently.

'Oh I don't think so darling,' Athena said. 'We have a very beautiful friendship. Marriage could destroy it.'

'There's no reason why it should.'

'Well we're really very fond of each other but we're also both set in our ways. We should leave well alone I think. You're looking after Selene, Davina. She was so kind to bring me home.'

'What about Cassie?' Davina demanded. 'Why didn't she come home?'

'Oh Davina, you know Cassie. She's got a job in Italy and she's got a young man she's besotted with. Did you like Alex, Selene?'

'He seems very nice.'

'Yes, I thought so.'

She looked at Selene thoughtfully. 'I got the impression that he was rather taken with you, but when he didn't follow it up, I thought I must have been wrong. You're going to be awfully bored in that house all on your own. Have you thought what you'll do?'

'I think I'll go to see my grandparents, just for a few days.'

'What about a job? They'll be pushing you into teaching like their daughter and I don't think you're cut out for it, Selene.'

'No?'

'No. Your father hated it. Are you quite sure you haven't inherited his passion for painting?'

'I do a bit, Athena.'

'A bit! What do you mean by that? Is it any good?'

'I never show anybody.'

'Why don't you take a look in the box room, a great many of your father's pictures are in there. I should sell them, but I was keeping them for you, but you've never seemed interested. I've never been able to understand why.'

'Grandy showed me some pictures mother painted, they were very pretty. He never showed me any of Father's.'

'I doubt if they have any. Selene, they deplored

Mervyn's forsaking teaching to paint pictures in Greece, that's why they never talk about it. Do look at those pictures, darling. They could encourage you. When are you thinking of going to your grandparents?'

'Tomorrow, or the next day. Would you mind?'

'Well of course not. I'm being spoilt by everybody and I'll stay here until I feel stronger. When I go home I've got Davina and Jonathan will be dancing attention.'

At that moment a pretty young nurse came into the room with Athena's medicine and Selene said, 'I'll write to you Athena, and if you want me back here, you only have to ask.'

They embraced each other warmly, then she waited for Davina at the door, listening with a smile to Davina's instructions to Athena, that she must do as she was told by her doctor and insist that Cassie come home.

That evening she climbed the stairs to the attic and sat entranced on an old oak chest quietly, looking at the canvasses her father had painted before she was born. None of them were framed, but the colours were as fresh and true as on the day they had been applied to the canvas. They were of scenes unfamiliar to her. Of gardens and pillared Grecian temples, lawns sloping down to the cliffs and a benign blue sea. There were one or two that were different, a stormier sea, a more rugged landscape, but none of them spoke to her of England, yet as she sat in that empty attic something old and urgent was born in her. Surely something of her father's talent must have been handed down to her.

She thought dismally of the small paintings she had done at school. Her teachers had said they were good, but strangely they had all been more interested in her acumen concerning mathematics and other subjects. Painting was for pleasure, the other things would ensure she could earn her own living.

She had grown up with a desire to please her grandparents, to do what they asked, to make up to them for the loss of her mother and for the way they had always been there for her. Now she was being made to realise that her life was her own, how she lived it, what she made of it and the knowledge that what she was about to do would hurt her grandparents gave her a sleepless night.

She decided against telephoning them to say she would be with them later in the day. Granny would fuss, insist that Grandy met her at the station when she was perfectly capable of making her own way to their house.

She need pack only a small suitcase because the clothes her grandmother liked to see her in were in the wardrobe at her grandparents' house, even so she dressed carefully in a business-like skirt and blouse which she knew they would approve of. Not too much makeup, no strappy shoes and her hair combed into a neat bob. Staring at her reflection in the mirror she was aware that she was looking at a replica of her mother from the host of snapshots she had been shown over the years.

Impatiently she turned away. She was not her mother, even though she might look like her. She had her own thoughts, her own ambitions, the days ahead promised to be extremely difficult.

It was midday when her taxi deposited her outside her grandparents' home and she was paying the fare when the front door opened and both of them ran down the drive to meet her.

Selene looked up with a smile and her grandmother said, 'I was just laying the table when I thought I heard a car pulling up. This is wonderful, Why didn't you say you were coming today?'

'I wanted to surprise you.'

By this time her grandfather had taken hold of her suitcase and she was following them into the house.

There was puzzlement in her grandmother's eyes as she said, 'I thought you were staying in Italy until the end of the month. Didn't you enjoy yourself?'

'Yes Granny, it was wonderful. Athena was ill so we came home early.'

'I suppose Cassie's looking after her mother?'

'Athena's in a nursing home, Grandy, the one she's been in before.'

'Oh well, she can afford these luxuries. How did you like Rome?'

She was glad her grandmother had changed the subject and so throughout lunch she was able to talk about Rome, the Princess's palazzo on the hillside and the wonderful things there were to do in Rome.

Her grandparents were not overly interested. Rome was foreign, Italians were foreign, there were more interesting things to do in England with their own kind.

She was dismally aware that the older she got the wider became the gulf between them. As she helped her grandmother to clear away after lunch the older woman said, 'I've made some scones for Mrs Holly, Norah's next-door neighbour. She isn't well and she's so good to Norah. Will you take them round for me, love. It's a fair walk and my back's been playing up these last few days.'

'Of course, Granny.'

'And do call in to see your Aunt Norah. She's been walking in Scotland but she's home now. Wouldn't you just have thought she'd have been round to see us, but I expect she's busy getting ready for the new term.'

Selene dutifully deposited the scones with Mrs Holly but declined to go inside saying that she had to call on her aunt.

'Well, she's back from Scotland, but I haven't seen top nor tail of her,' Mrs Holly said. 'She's been busy with her garden and her school work I've no doubt.'

Norah received her with an impatient frown and viewing the dining-room table Selene could understand why. It was piled high with school books and manuscripts. Norah looked harassed, wearing slacks and a green sweater, her hair brushed back from her face which wore not a vestige of makeup.

'What are you doing home?' she asked shortly, 'I thought you were supposed to be in Rome.'

'Athena wasn't well, we came home early. Did you enjoy Scotland?' she ventured.

'It was all right. The weather wasn't good.'

'I'm sorry.'

'You can put those books on the edge of the table if you want that chair,' Norah snapped.

'If you're very busy, and I can see you are, I'll come back another day.'

'You're here now, so you might as well stay, I'm busy every day.'

'I suppose you're getting ready for the beginning of term?'

'You'll find out what it's like. Teaching's no fun, I can tell you.'

Selene didn't speak, and after a few minutes Norah fixed her with a pointed look. 'I suppose you are contemplating a teacher's job?' she asked.

'It's what my grandparents would like me to do.'

'Is it what you want to do?'

'No, it isn't.'

There, it was out now. She didn't want to be a teacher, anything but that, and in that split second she knew she was going to disappoint the two people who had brought her up and had such ambitions for her.

Norah was looking at her with raised eyebrows and an expression of cynical disbelief. 'Have you told them?' She asked. 'I can tell you now they'll be against anything else you want.'

'I know.'

'What do you want to do?'

'I want to take a course at the Slade to see if my painting's as good as my father's was. Surely some of his talent must have rubbed off?'

'Well, I would like to be there when you drop your bombshell. Have you spoken to Athena about it?'

'No. She's had nothing to do with my decision. I spoke to one of the masters at university. He helped me apply to the Slade.'

'So it's all cut and dried. You knew about this when you came home?'

'Yes.'

'How have you managed to keep it to yourself?'

'Well, I had to wait to see if the Slade would take me first. I know they'll be terribly upset, but it's something I have to do.'

'Paint pictures you mean?'

'I'm not sure. Some branch of art, there are a great many. But, yes, I think I would like to paint pictures. My father became well known, I think this is one reason the Slade have decided to accept me.'

'Don't artists starve in garrets any more?'

Selene smiled. 'Some do.'

'When do you propose to tell them?'

'This evening.'

Norah opened a large book in front of her and started to read, which told Selene that their conversation was probably at an end. She rose to her feet saying, 'Well, I'll get off home now, Aunt Norah. Shall we be seeing you soon?'

'Maybe.'

'I'll say goodbye then.'

'Close the door when you go out and see that the lock is on.'

She decided to walk through the park on the way back and it was there she encountered two women walking with their dogs. She recognised one of them as her grandparent's neighbour and the other as a teacher who had known her father.

The two women smiled and Selene stooped to pat the dogs.

Marian Adcock surveyed the girl's bent head. She was so much like her mother, had been reared to look like her, act like her. Was there absolutely nothing in her makeup to remind her of Mervyn? Marian had never married, never really fancied anybody after Mervyn, who hadn't been remotely interested in her. When Selene looked up she smiled.

'You've been visiting Rome I believe. Did you enjoy it?'

'Yes, very much.'

'I believe you're interested in going into teaching?'

Selene smiled politely but offered no reply.

'You grow more like your mother every time I see you,' Marian said.

'You'll soon be getting back to school,' Selene said.

'I'm getting ready for retirement, at Christmas I think.'

'Are you looking forward to it?'

'I certainly am. There'll be some teaching posts around here when you're ready for it. At some of the senior schools and the two new schools being built in the town, I should think about making some enquiries. Don't you have a degree in English?'

Selene smiled politely and bidding them good afternoon moved away.

They stood watching her walk across the grass towards the gates.

'She didn't seem too enthusiastic about

teaching,' Marian's friend commented.

'No. I didn't think so. It's what she'll do though. They'll organise her job, her life, her home just like they did with Moira. I never thought Mervyn stood a chance until he sorted himself out.'

'You don't think she will?'

'Unlikely. She's been conditioned too long.'

They moved on with their dogs, unaware how far off the mark their suppositions were.

Her grandfather was busy in his garden when she arrived back at the house and although he waved to her he turned arbuptly away and she stared at him curiously. She could hear her grandmother upstairs but as she closed the hall door behind her, she came hurrying down the stairs and one look at her flushed face told Selene that Norah had got in before her.

'Come into the dining room,' her grandmother ordered. 'Now what's all this about your not wanting to be a teacher?'

'Aunt Norah hasn't wasted any time, Granny.'

'Never mind Aunt Norah, it's you who owe us an explanation. You know it's what your Grandy and me have always wanted for you. I can't take much more of this, first of all it was your wanting us to call you Selene, now it's your future, we have to worry about. I suppose Athena's responsible for all this?'

'No, Granny, she isn't. She doesn't know anything about it, I wanted to tell you first.'

'All these years when we've talked about your becoming a teacher and you've never said anything about not wanting it. It must be Athena, you've never asked any questions about your father, never talked about painting.'

'I know. I didn't think you wanted me to talk about him or his work. It was always Mother you talked about, but for Athena I might never have had a father.'

'So she has had a hand in it?'

'No, she hasn't. She talked about my father, their childhood together, the sort of boy he'd been, but she never tried to influence me either one way or another about the future. This is something I've made my own mind up about. I think I have inherited something of his talent, I have to be sure, that's why I want to go to the Slade. If it's there, I can nurture it there, it's what I want to do.

'Granny, I'm sorry I've disappointed you, but you have to stop thinking that I'm like my mother. I look like her, but I'm a totally different person inside. Somewhere in me is something of my father, there has to be.'

Her grandmother's face dissolved into tears and she sank onto a chair with her head in her hands. Selene looked on helplessly and when her grandfather entered the room, he looked from one to the other in anxious dismay.

Sitting down beside his wife he put his arm round her shoulders gently, 'Now what's all this, nothing's bad enough to bring all this on.'

'It's true Arthur, It's all true,' his wife wailed. 'She doesn't want to teach, she wants to paint just like her father. We've lost her Arthur, just like we lost Moira.'

'Granny, you haven't lost me,' Selene said

softly. 'I love you both just as I've always loved you, and I'll be here whenever you want me, but I have to live my own life, make my own mistakes, decide what my future's going to be. I want you to stop blaming my father for everything that happened to my mother and for what's happening with me. I'm still your granddaughter, we're still a family, and nothing's going to change that.'

'Well, why can't she teach art?' her grandfather said hopefully. 'That's what your father was doing when we first knew him.'

Selene shook her head. 'No Grandy, that's not what I want any more than my father wanted it. I'm not going to teach at all.'

Her grandmother's tears came faster, but her grandfather said firmly, 'Well come along. She's evidently made up her mind and we're not going to alter it. I'll put the kettle on, we can talk over a cup of tea.'

Her grandmother followed him into the kitchen and Selene could hear them setting out crockery, and occasionally whispering together. They returned together, her grandmother pushing the tea trolley and she went forward to help with the setting out of cups and saucers on the dining-room table.

A cup of tea had been her grandfather's solution to every trauma the family had sustained over the years. Great Aunt Agatha's death the birth of Kathleen's twins and Norah's decision to buy her own house. Now, although the atmosphere was strained, at least her grandmother had stopped crying and her grandfather was saying cheerfully, 'Why don't the three of us go to the cinema tonight, there'll be something on that we want to see.'

'You two go, I'm not in the mood,' her grandmother said shortly.

Deciding it was a better idea to talk about the problem than ignore it Arthur Sheldon said, 'Your mother was a nice little painter, she did some lovely flower paintings. They're in your bedroom, love.'

Selene smiled. 'I know, they're lovely.'

'Of course she wasn't in the same league as your father, but if she'd worked at it she could have become really good.'

'Suppose your work's never as good as your father's, will you be able to get into something else?' her grandmother demanded.

'I'm sure I will. I'll still have my degree.'

Her grandmother sniffed. She never used either of her Christian names, Margaret was dead and Selene had never been born.

Selene made an excuse to go to bed early. She'd been up early to catch the train and she wanted to take a bath. Her grandfather wished her a cheerful goodnight, her grandmother merely nodded her head and Selene thankfully escaped from an atmosphere that was far from congenial.

Chapter Twenty-Seven

The week that followed was a nightmare. Her grandfather was anxious, her grandmother distant, making her aware every day of what she considered her treachery.

Aunt Norah called more often than usual since she was relishing the atmosphere and that the much-loved granddaughter had fallen from grace. Selene wished they could talk about it but her grandmother was too proud to ask questions. She longed to tell them that for a long time she'd been interested in her father's work, that she'd been encouraged by friends and teachers to do something about it, now she was being given the opportunity and she wanted them to be happy for her.

Half way through the week she decided she could not stand it any longer. She would go back to Devon and her grandmother's tight-lipped acceptance of her decision was a censure in itself.

'I thought you said Athena was in a nursing home,' she snapped.

'That's right, but hopefully she'll be ready to come home. I need to be there, Granny.'

'She has a daughter. Isn't that enough?'

'Cassie is working abroad.'

'You mean she's not even stayed near her mother?'

'Athena's being well looked after, Granny.'

'Did you say that the art college was in London?'

'Yes.'

'Where are you going to live in London?'

'I've gone into it, Granny. I shall be sharing a flat with two other girls. They were at college with me and now they've both got jobs in London.'

'Well, you haven't a job, so how are you going to pay your way?'

'With the money Father left for me.'

'I suppose Athena's seen to that?'

'Well yes. She was his executor. Granny, please don't be bitter because I want a say in how I want to live my life. I love you, I'll always be here for you, and I'll spend time with you whenever it's possible.'

It didn't get any better but it was left to her grandfather to say, 'Don't worry love. Let us know how you're getting on. Your granny'll come to terms with it and it's your life.'

He was standing on the platform with her while they waited for the Exeter train, and with tears in her eyes she threw her arms around his neck.

'I'll write often, Grandy, I promise.'

He waited until the train had pulled out of the station then he turned away, his face aching from the fixed smile he had maintained for most of the morning.

Several hours later the taxi deposited Selene outside Athena's house and her heart lifted at the sight of the rich red cliffs and the calm blue sea. Another car was parked outside the house and she recognised it immediately as Jonathan

Trevellyan's which meant that Athena was home.

She heard their laughter as she entered the house and then Davina was there to take her suitcase and to tell her that Athena and Mr Trevellyan were in the drawing room. Selene smiled to herself. Even over such a small thing the difference between Athena's lifestyle and her grandparents was apparent.

In Granny's house they sat in the parlour. They thought Athena's lifestyle pretentious and unreal, they had never understood that it was the only life Athena knew.

They looked up with pleased smiles as she entered the room. Athena was sitting in her favourite chair near the window while John was busy pouring drinks at a side table.

'You're just in time,' he said. 'What's it to be, sherry or something stronger?'

'Sherry, please, John.'

'I'm so glad you're back,' Athena said warmly. 'I thought you'd be staying much longer.'

'I needed to sort something out here Athena. Besides, I thought you might need me here. I wasn't sure how long they'd keep you in the nursing home.'

'John brought me home yesterday. I'm much better, but of course it'll come back, it always does.'

It seemed to Selene that Athena never changed – from that first moment when she had walked up the path towards her grandparents' front door and into her life. A tall slender woman with pale blonde hair wearing a pale grey coat edged with arctic fox, her feet encased in high-heeled grey suede shoes. She had seemed a fairy figure to the little girl who had known nothing beyond the down-to-earth normality of the semi-detached house she lived in.

Athena's hair was still that pale spun gold, nurtured carefully by her hairdresser, and her beautiful face remained unlined, her eyes the same intense blue, her mouth exquisitely chiselled, her makeup impeccable.

She sat listening to their chatter until John suddenly said, 'Well I'm sure you two have a lot to talk about and I have a date on the golf course. Shall I call in tomorrow?'

'John, I've told you I'm not an invalid. You have other things to do.'

'Nothing as important as you, Athena.'

She laughed, not at all displeased. 'Well, call if you want to, but I don't want to be a nuisance and Selene's here now.'

Selene smiled. 'She wants to see you John, and I'll be shopping for things I'll need in London.'

Well pleased, John made his departure, turning at the door to say, 'Show Selene the photographs, see you tomorrow.'

Selene noticed a large envelope on the table near Athena's chair and, picking it up, Athena passed it across to her. 'Photographs from Cassie, Selene. She's having a wonderful time in Rome. See for yourself.'

There were about half a dozen of them. Large glossy photographs of Cassie and Sophia by a swimming pool surrounded by several smiling young men. The two girls in evening dresses with different young men, and then one photograph larger than the rest and Selene's heart lurched painfully at Cassie gazing up into Alexander's eyes while he looked down at her with a half smile on his lips.

Athena sighed. 'She's so obviously in love with him,' she mused. 'I wish she wasn't.'

'Why do you say that?'

'Because I don't think he's in love with her. He's intrigued by her as men are with the women who make it plain they find them attractive, but love is something else.'

'Cassie has every intention of marrying him, Athena.'

'Cassie has always believed that she is capable of getting everything she wants. Ian instilled that notion into her head when she was a child and it's never left her. One day she could get badly hurt.'

'Alexander was kind, I don't think he'd deliberately hurt her.'

'Perhaps not, but that doesn't mean he will want to marry her. His grandmother will totally reject the idea.'

'But if Cassie and Alexander want it?'

'Cassie does want it, I'm not sure about Alexander.'

'What does she say in her letter?'

'She's having a wonderful time. She's loving modelling for Carvello and she's going here, there and everywhere with Sophia. Alexander is in Milan but he's closing up the villa in Greece sometime towards the end of October. She thinks they will join him there.'

'Is it very beautiful, Athena?'

‘Yes, beautiful and romantic, but I’ve never really wanted to go there since Mervyn was killed. I’m sure it must have sad memories for Alexander, he was very close to his mother.’

‘I think I might like to go there one day.’

Athena looked at her curiously. ‘Well, the villa is still there and your father’s studio. If you do well with your painting, you could open up the studio. Your father had no difficulty in selling his pictures to tourists. I’m sure you’d do equally well.’

‘I’m not sure I can be as good as he was.’

‘Well, you’re being given the opportunity. How did the Sheldons take it?’

‘Very badly. My grandmother particularly.’

‘Surely you expected that, Selene?’

‘Yes. She made me feel like a traitor. The atmosphere after I told her was terrible, I had to get away.’

‘Surely they must understand that you need to live your own life, make your own decisions and your own mistakes?’

‘They think what I’ve decided to do will be a mistake and Aunt Norah didn’t help.’

‘No, I can see that. Mervyn said she was always resentful of your mother.’

‘And I can understand that. My mother was their favourite daughter. That was wrong too.’

‘She was their favourite because she went away, died young. They expected her to conform, she didn’t, then when she went back into their lives it wasn’t for long.’

‘But you liked her, didn’t you Athena?’

Athena didn’t answer immediately. She had

never really known if she liked Moira, they'd had nothing in common, she had thought her unsuitable for her cousin, but gently she said, 'We never really knew each other very well dear. We lived in Scotland and I didn't even see much of Mervyn. Ian was ill most of the time and then there was Cassie.'

Selene nodded. It was as much as Athena was ever going to say about her mother. She looked down at the photographs again and mused, 'If Cassie does marry Alexander, I wonder if they'll marry here in England.'

'But of course, darling, and you'll be her bridesmaid, probably you and Sophia. I'll have to entertain his family, including the Princess.'

The Princess Cabrodini sat on her terrace sipping her Campari and soda, and watching the antics of the two girls in the pool below. There were several young men all unknown to her in attendance but Nino sat in a long lounge chair with his back to the pool. He was sulking.

Really Sophia behaved abominably towards him and he was a fool to come back for more. She despaired of Sophia. Behind her were a string of lovers airily discarded, two serious affairs with married men including the mention of her name in a particularly scandalous divorce. That men still wanted to marry her the Princess had never been able to understand, apparently a bad reputation was no drawback these days. Sophia was a handful, she had needed a father figure in her life but Giorgio had been an invalid and Leonora hadn't handled the girl well.

Alexander was different. She adored him because he was charming and solid, a grandson to be proud of, not a gay Lothario like most of the young men in the swimming pool. Her eyes narrowed as she watched Cassie climbing out of the pool and sauntering over to join Nino.

She was very attractive with her auburn hair and slender grace. She compared her to a tigress in her animal-skin bikini, a predator, a woman who knew what she wanted. And she wanted Alexander. Fortunately Alexander was busy in Milan and would not be in Rome until Christmas, fortunately too the Princess did not know that the two women intended to join him on the island in October, nor as it happened did Alexander.

Cassie waved to her from the terrace. The girl was friendly and attentive. She was as anxious to please the Princess as she was to ingratiate herself with her grandson. They had all come out of the pool now and when they joined Nino he immediately left his seat and sauntered back to the house. He was a baby, but the Princess spared him an understanding thought. Nino's involvement with Sophia had obviously run its course, she would replace him with some other man, somebody just as unsuitable, and her thoughts strayed to the man in Leonora's life who had caused the family so much grief.

She wondered what had become of him when he was released from prison? Did he have a wife, did he live normally and forgetful of the past?

'You're trying very hard to ingratiate yourself with grandmother,' Sophia said with a wry smile.

'It's essential that she likes me,' Cassie said evenly.

'I'm her granddaughter and she doesn't exactly like me.'

'That's because you've behaved badly.'

'And you haven't.'

'Not since I met Alex.'

'You met Alexander years ago, you mean since you met him as an adult.'

'I'm studying the Princess, I want to be like her, distant and austere, a smouldering volcano with Alex. I want her to like me, I'm going to do nothing wrong in her eyes.'

'She liked your little cousin. She told me so.'

Cassie scowled. 'Well never in a thousand years would she have been suitable for Alex. She's suburban, too ordinary. Her grandparents live in a pre-war semi in a small west country town and they want her to become a teacher just like her aunt. Their minds don't stretch beyond that, can you see Alex marrying a school teacher? Besides, her grandparents would be terrified.'

'School teacher or not, you were afraid of them getting to know each other.'

'Can we change the subject Sophia? You know yourself that that friendship would have gone nowhere. What do you propose to do about Nino? I take it he's not coming to the island with us now.'

'I've promised he can come, he loves it. After that I'll cool it. Besides, he gets along with Alexander, which is more than can be said for some of the men I've burdened him with over the years.'

'Well I'm going up to take tea with your grandmother. I'm going to encourage her to talk about Alexander, she'll enjoy that.'

In London Selene had never been so happy. She was loving her work at the Slade and her teachers were warm in their praise of her. She knew that she had made the right decision and within weeks she knew which direction she wanted her art to take. She did not want to do sculpture or paint models. She wanted to paint landscapes like her father, she even enjoyed sitting out on a windy day drawing some old stone archway or some crumbling pavement.

Her flatmates were amused by her. While they sampled the delights of the theatre or Jazz clubs, Selene painted watercolours of something she'd photographed earlier on. They admired her pictures but couldn't understand her dedication, but when she wrote to her grandparents she was happy to tell them that she was enjoying herself, her work, her life, her friends and London.

To Athena she was more forthcoming. She sent her some of the pictures she'd painted and received Athena's acclaim in return.

When she asked if Athena had heard from Cassie, she was informed that Cassie was on the Greek island with Sophia and Nino. Athena did not mention Alexander, but of course he was there too.

All Selene knew of the island were her father's pictures of it, but she could imagine the green grass on the cliffs, the wandering paths and blue blue sea. The sound of goat bells and the scent of herbs, and in it all she could picture Alexander and Cassie, happy and in love.

If Alexander was surprised when his sister descended on him he showed no surprise: he was accustomed to Sophia and her comings and goings. He was aware that Cassie desired him, it was in her every smile, every gesture and he was intrigued by her with an emotion that was beckoning, but was not love.

The islanders were glad to see that the villa was once more occupied. They had known Sophia and Alexander since they were children, seen them grow up, mourned the death of their mother, now it was apparent they bore the island and its people no grudges, but were happy to return there to enjoy themselves day after day.

They ate in the tavernas and walked across the cliffs. They explored the ancient arena and tiny temple and they swam and sailed in the warm sea.

In the scented darkness once more could be heard the sound of music and laughter floating through the open windows and Sophia issued invitations to old friends to join them.

While she and Nino grew further apart, Cassie and Alexander drew closer together. To Cassie it was not a flirtation, it was real; to Alexander she was merely a desirable woman who openly admired him and was available.

They were sitting on the terrace one morning when he surprised her by asking, 'Do you know if your cousin has sorted out her problems?'

'Problems!' she echoed.

'Why yes. Didn't you say she was being harassed by some man or other?'

Cassie gathered her wits together quickly.

'Oh that. It's gone on an awful long time and she's besotted with him of course. Didn't your mother have some sort of trouble like that?'

'What do you know about my mother?'

'Only what Sophia has told me.'

'We don't speak of it, it all happened a long time ago, when my mother was very young.'

'Well, we're rather hoping Selene will grow out of it, up to now it isn't happening.'

She changed the subject quickly by asking, 'Do you ever drive to the other side of the island?'

'Sometimes. It's very different over there, wilder, grander.'

'I went there once with Uncle Mervyn. I sat in the car while he painted a picture.'

He was staring down at her and she was gazing out to sea, her face suddenly intense, and he knew that she was thinking of the winding road that edged the cliffs and the place where Mervyn and his mother had died. She looked up quickly and meeting his eyes, 'Do you ever go back there Alex? It would frighten me.'

'Frighten?'

'Why yes. That they should both die in exactly the same place.'

'A strange coincidence Cassie, nothing more.'

'You knew Mervyn, didn't you?'

'Yes, he painted a picture of my father. It's hanging in the salon.'

'Wasn't she going to marry Marco?'

'Yes. They'd known each other a great many

years, he was a friend of my father's.'

'I wonder if Mervyn was unhappy about that?'

He stared down at her but remained silent.

After a few minutes she said, 'I remember Leonora, she was beautiful, totally unlike Moira, Mervyn's wife.'

'Moira too was beautiful. Her daughter is like her.'

'Yes, I suppose she is.'

'Why don't we join Sophia and Nino on the beach? The day is too beautiful to waste.'

'Why don't we drive out somewhere instead? I've had enough of the sea and the beach for one day. I'd rather there were just the two of us.'

Alexander smiled. The island was a small one and they had already absorbed all the sights it had to offer. He knew where Cassie wanted to go, to that place on the road where his mother had met her death and in some perverse way he wanted to go there too.

It was quiet on the road and they met no other vehicles. The road had been freshly tarmacked in the early summer and the shrubs that had been torn and ravaged had put out fresh branches and leaves. They stood together looking down into the abyss. The signs of that early tragedy had long gone. New trees and foliage, no signs that once two cars had plunged down the cliff tearing up trees followed by the flames that scorched the earth. They stared in solemn silence, each wrapped up in their own silent thoughts, then with a little cry Cassie turned towards him and he reached out to draw her into his close embrace.

'I hate it,' she murmured.

'You wanted to come here.'

'I know, and now I want to go back. Alex, I want to forget about it, make me forget it. Make love to me. Here on the cliff top.'

Her hands were urgent, tearing at his clothes and then coming nearer they heard the sound of goat bells and suddenly there was sanity and around the bend in the road appeared a young boy and his herd of goats, the bells around their necks making a jingle of sound and Alexander pulled her towards the car.

Her face was sulky but when he smiled she made an effort to find amusement in the boy staring innocently towards them from the edge of the path. At that moment it looked like a scene from the annals of ancient Greece, a land where nymphs and Gods played innocently in the pastureland and benevolent deities smiled gently on their frolics.

The sun was setting in a blaze of glory, turning the blue sea into an expanse of molten gold. Cassie sat beside Alexander in silence. He knew now what she wanted and he would be no different to other men she had known. The only difference was that she loved him, she had loved none of the others.

Tonight she hoped they would have the villa to themselves. Nino liked to dine in the tavernas, he enjoyed the music and the dancing and because this was the last holiday he would spend on the island Sophia was making it good for him.

It was only when they drove through the gates towards the villa that she sat up in her seat with disconcerted amazement. Cars were parked everywhere and from the villa came the sound of laughter and music. She looked at Alexander with dismay and he said evenly, 'It would appear my sister has invited everybody she could think of, we'll have to make the best of it.'

Chapter Twenty-Eight

Cassie went directly to her room to change into something suitable for a party. She was furious. Why couldn't Sophia have told her what she intended to do, she wouldn't know any of these people and she'd never felt less like socialising.

She changed into a green chiffon dress that showed off her tanned shoulders and rich auburn hair, and when she met Sophia in the hallway she hoped her face would not show the resentment she was feeling. Sophia was not fooled.

'We thought it was time we got to know the people living on the island. Mother loved parties, she knew everybody, and since Alexander has decided to keep the villa on it's time he stopped being reclusive.'

'Perhaps he likes it that way.'

'Well, I don't. Come and I'll introduce you.'

They were a mixture of English, American and Greek, rich people, with villas and boats, people who were happy enough to gather on the island during the summer months and disappear to their respective homes whenever they needed to.

Only two English couples and a Greek shipping magnate actually lived there permanently, and she was introduced to Father Sandras who informed them that he had been on the island just four years, after the old priest had died.

'I remember him very well,' Sophia said. 'He came here often, Mervyn knew him too. I'm so glad we decided to have this party, it's so much like the ones my mother enjoyed.'

Cassie scowled. Alexander was standing chatting to three people near the window, his dark head inclined to hear what they were saying, a smile on his lips, urbane and charming, and the pain in her heart was so searching she gasped with its intensity.

Her anger was not lost on Sophia. Over the years Cassie had been her friend but it had always been Cassie who had engineered their meetings. Sophia had always known that Alexander had been her goal.

She was introduced to them but none of them had known Mervyn or Leonora, only the tragedy of their deaths. Cassie wandered out onto the terrace and there she found Nino staring disconsolately to sea.

She had always admired how easily they could all switch from Italian to English, hoping one day that she would be able to do the same. Now Nino addressed her in English and his tone was petulant.

'What did she want to do this for? All afternoon we've been driving round the island with invitations to her party and most of them were able to accept. You look as bored as I am.'

'I am bored. I didn't want this, I wanted a quiet evening with Alex. Just the two of us.'

'You were betting on us being out then?' he said it with a cynical expression in his dark eyes.

'Of course, and that was what you wanted too.'

He looked away but there was no disguising the expression of petulance on his handsome face.

'Look at them. They're both enjoying this, it's like old times.'

She followed his gaze to where Alexander was chatting to the priest and Sophia was enjoying the company of an American whose wife was equally absorbed with the Greek shipowner.

'We don't have to stand for this,' Nino said sharply. 'What do you say to driving out to that new taverna on the waterfront? I doubt if we'll be missed.'

'I don't know,' Cassie said doubtfully. 'I don't want them to be annoyed. After all, Sophia did invite them.'

'She could have asked us first, she didn't even mention it to Alexander. You'll not catch Alexander by being there when he wants you to be, he likes his women to be unpredictable.'

'And you know about his women, do you?'

He smiled. 'Rome is a city that thrives on scandal and the Andoinetos and the Cabrodinis have had their share. Come to the taverna with me and I'll tell you what I know about the scandals of Rome, concerned with the people in high places of course.'

The offer was tempting. After all, what did she really know about Alex except that she wanted him? There must have been women in his life just as there'd been men in hers, but his distance worried her.

Men had wanted to make love to her, a great many of them had wanted something more permanent. Her mother had despaired of her, but her mother had not known that since the first moment she had seen Alex when they were both ridiculously young, she had been unable to take anybody else seriously.

'I'll get my wrap,' she said hurriedly. 'Can we leave quietly without causing too much of a stir?'

'I'll wait in the car.'

She rushed upstairs for her wrap, and on the way out she smiled at the people she encountered, all of whom believed she was finding it chilly on the terrace: Neither Alex nor Sophie were in evidence.

She ran through the garden and found Nino sitting in his car on the lower terrace.

'Meet anyone?' he enquired.

She shook her head. Nino wouldn't have cared. He was aware that this was probably the last time he would be invited to visit the island, his affair with Sophia had run its course.

He drove swiftly through the gates and onto the road, then with a muttered curse he swerved sharply to avoid a man crossing the road.

'The fool,' he muttered. 'What's he doing up here? These roads are private.'

'Italians drive too fast,' Cassie complained. 'You came out of that gateway like a bat out of hell.'

He grinned, speeding down the coastal road with carefree abandon and Cassie saw the lights from the taverna with visible relief.

They dined off freshly caught sea bass and tender new vegetables, then they danced under the lamplight to the exotic beat of the three-piece band.

The men started to dance the spirited Greek dancing, with linked arms and stamping feet, pulling Nino to his feet to join in with them. He had drunk too much wine, his face was flushed but he was evidently enjoying himself. Cassie was wishing she hadn't come. They had both behaved like two spoilt children and she could picture Alex's displeasure. The shutters would come down on that remote handsome face and she could expect little sympathy from Sophia.

When she suggested to Nino that they should leave, he merely filled up their glasses and he was sitting with his arm round her shoulders, hurting her with the tightness of his embrace.

Other diners began to drift away and Nino asked for another bottle of wine.

'They want us to go,' Cassie complained. 'We're the only ones left in the place.'

'As long as we're buying the wine they won't care.'

While he filled up his glass she wriggled free.

'Well I'm going. I'll see you in the car and I'll drive,' she said angrily.

He laughed. 'No need. Demetrius is over there. He'll drive us.'

'Then I'll ask him to take us now.'

She'd walked quickly to the bar where Demetrius and two other men were standing.

'He isn't fit to drive. Will you take me up to the

villa, Demetrius?' she asked, but then Nino was there. 'I'll drive you, no need to trouble Demetrius.'

His words were slurred and Demetrius's face was concerned. Nino waved him aside however, and taking hold of Cassie's hand he pulled her towards the door.

'Let me drive the car,' she said sharply.

'No need. I'm perfectly capable. Here, get in the front seat.'

It was a nightmare drive. Too fast, too careless as they swung from one side of the road to the other, at times teetering on the edge of the cliff, occasionally scraping the side of the car against some jutting piece of rock. He gave a muttered curse as the car's sidelamp caught the iron gates and then they were arriving in front of the house with a screech of brakes and stopping so suddenly she was flung forward against the dashboard.

All the cars had gone and only the beam of a light in the hall shone through the glass windows. Apart from that the house was in darkness and without looking at Nino, Cassie eased herself out of the front seat and ran swiftly along the terrace.

She was unfamiliar with the latch on the door and had still not got it open when Nino joined her. He was tottering unsteadily, brushing her on one side irritably and saying, 'Let me do it.' The catch responded to his probing fingers and they were in the hall. Cassie walked immediately to the staircase but Nino followed her, taking hold of her wrist with devilish amusement, and in a taunting voice said, 'We might as well make a good job of it. Neither of us will be coming here again.'

She struggled but his arms were like pinions and she could feel his hot breath on her face. She was fearful of his words, terrified of him, and yet the more she struggled, the tighter were his arms around her, and he was amused until, unable to bear it any longer, she screamed.

'Stop it, you little fool,' he hissed. 'Do you want to wake the entire household?'

She didn't care, and in the next moment the hall sprang into life and Alexander stood on the stairs staring down at them.

She reeled free, while Nino stared stupidly upwards and Alexander said wearily, 'Go to bed Nino. We'll talk about this in the morning.'

Cassie ran up the stairs and stood staring up into his face. 'Alex I can explain. Please listen to me. Nino's just had too much to drink. Please, please listen to me.'

'Nino is Sophia's friend, Cassie. He must explain to her.'

'But I want to explain to you.'

'It's late Cassie, and there's really no need to explain your actions to me. Whatever they are can keep until the morning.'

With a brief smile he turned and left her, and Cassie felt as if he'd slapped her in the face.

She went to bed hating him, hating Nino and hating herself. She slept fitfully and eventually she sat huddled in her dressing gown watching the first pale rays of the sun illuminating the gardens.

The house was slowly coming to life as she

heard the closing of a door somewhere in the distance and one of the gardeners came into view trundling his wheelbarrow.

It was a morning just like every other morning but for Cassie it was the beginning of a day that had to mean something. She had to convince Alexander that she was not a stupid spoilt woman, even if she had to admit her actions the evening before were hardly on her side.

She would go to see Sophia, Sophia was her friend, Sophia knew how desperately she loved Alex.

A maid was serving Sophia with her early morning tea when she entered her bedroom and Sophia gave instructions to her servant to bring in another cup. Cassie took the chair beside her bed while Sophia looked at her calmly and with a half-smile on her face.

'Sophia, I'm so wretchedly sorry for last night,' she began. 'I'd had such a wonderful afternoon with Alex, I wanted it to go on into the evening.'

'And into the night,' Sophia prompted her.

'Well anyway, I wanted there just to be the two of us and Nino was just as frustrated, he'd wanted the same thing for you two. When I met him on the terrace he was sulky, very angry and I had to placate him in some way or I was afraid he'd cause a scene. When he suggested we went out I agreed, thinking it would only be for a little while. I'd talk to him, persuade him to return, we'd be gone just a little while.'

'Nino was already aware that he would not be coming here again. That was why he was sulking. He knew I wouldn't change my mind.'

'He was drinking too much. He wanted to dance, he wanted a party,' Cassie said bitterly.

'Evidently, but not this party. It's over between Nino and me. My grandmother will be delighted. We're leaving tomorrow anyway.'

'But I don't want it to be over for Alex and me,' Cassie cried. 'Sophia you must help me. I don't know how to face him this morning.'

'Well I know he intends to do some work in the summerhouse, so he'll be busy until lunchtime.'

'Won't I see him at breakfast?'

'Possibly, but you won't be alone together. Nino will be there as well as me.'

'Can't you find an excuse to leave us alone together?'

'Perhaps. We'll see.'

Carrie embraced her quickly then in a happier tone said, 'I'll get dressed. See you at breakfast.'

After she'd gone, Sophia sat back against her pillows with a thoughtful expression. She was thinking of the conversation she'd had with Alexander the night before. Their guests had departed and Nino and Cassie were still out. In some irritation Alexander had said, 'Does Nino have a key to the villa?'

'No, I'm sure he hasn't.'

'Then I suppose I'll have to leave the door open for them. I'm certainly not waiting up for them.'

'Not even for Cassie?'

He raised his eyebrows, and she said quickly, 'Well what about Cassie? You've spent all afternoon together, she came back in a haze of euphoria. Are you in love with her?'

'It's not something I want to discuss at this time

in the morning, Besides it isn't relevant.'

'It's relevant when she's mad about you, Alex.'

'Would you like me to be in love with her, Sophia?'

He had been looking at her with a half smile on his lips. She could understand Cassie being in love with him, his remote handsome face appealed to the madcap girl who'd run through a surfeit of hell-bent young men, and in that split second she knew that she did not want her brother to fall in love with Cassie.

Cassie was dangerous. She loved Alexander now, but when the novelty wore off, she would grow tired of normality, domesticity, respectability. Cassie craved excitement and she was unscrupulous in her dealings with men.

They were two of a kind, and she was remembering how they had giggled together over escapades that would have shocked her grandmother to the core.

Alexander was waiting for her answer, then almost impatiently he turned away saying softly, 'Goodnight Sophia, we'll see what they have to say for themselves in the morning.'

'Alexander wait a moment,' she'd cried. 'No, I don't want you to fall in love with Cassie, and you're right, she is my friend, but I don't want her for you.'

'Why is that?'

'Because she'll go to any lengths to get you. She'll antagonise you against any woman she thinks you might be interested in.'

'Oh come now, how could she do that?'

'She did it with her cousin Selene. Oh I know

you only spent a day with her in Rome, but I think you really liked her. She told you some silly story about some man she was involved with in England, a story that painfully followed the story I'd told her about Mother.'

He had been looking at her very intently, and hurriedly she'd said, 'Oh I know it didn't really matter, Selene was going home anyway, but it would have been just the same if you'd really been genuinely interested.'

For a long moment they'd stared at each other, then quietly Alexander said, 'Goodnight Sophia, like I said, we'll talk in the morning.'

She'd walked before him through the opened door.

Cassie hurried over her dressing, hoping to be the first at the breakfast table, and consequently was annoyed when she saw that Alexander was finishing his coffee and preparing to leave.

He wished her a smiling good morning, and she said immediately, 'Alex. I'm so glad we're alone, I must explain about last night.'

'Really Cassie, there's no need, that was last night. This is another day.'

'I know, but it was dreadful of me to go with Nino. I just didn't want him to start making a scene. He was so hurt that Sophia had told him it was all over, and so very angry, I expected him to do something really drastic. When he suggested going out, I thought it was probably the best thing he could do, and I'd talk to him and encourage him to get back when he'd calmed down.'

'What Sophia and Nino had between them was

never destined to last, Cassie. Nino knew that, he also knew when he came here, that it was probably for the last time.'

'But he wasn't seeing it like that last night.'

'We should forget about it, Cassie. You'll all be leaving soon and I'll be closing up the villa until the spring. When Sophia comes here again, I'm sure it will be with somebody else.'

'I want to come back, Alex. I want to come back to be with you, that's why it's so important to make you see why my going out with Nino last night was a wretched mistake.'

He smiled. 'I'm sure it was Cassie. And now shall we forget about it. What do you intend to do this morning?'

She stared at him helplessly.

'Have you any suggestions?' she said at last, and with a regretful smile he said, 'I want to work this morning Cassie. That, after all, is one reason I came here. I've really done very little.'

'I know, that's my fault,' she said quickly. 'But we'll meet later, won't we, Alex, and we will talk then?'

'We'll meet for lunch Cassie, but not to talk. I think we've done all the talking we need to.'

She watched him walking through the gardens towards the summerhouse and with her usual optimism she thought, 'He wants to forget about it, we'll be together with no more talking. It will be just as if there'd never been last night.'

Sophia and Nino joined her together at the breakfast table, and if at first Nino's expression was a trifle sulky, when Sophia ignored it, he decided to behave normally.

'I want to go down to the village this morning,' Sophia said casually. 'I need one or two things I can get in the market. What do you two intend to do with yourselves?'

'I'll come with you,' Cassie said quickly.

'No need, darling. I want to call in at the garage for Alex to see about his car and I have one or two other errands to do. You'd be bored when you could be spending a morning on the boat or water ski-ing. I'm sure that's what Nino wants to do.'

Nino buttered another piece of toast and didn't answer.

'Why do you need to see about Alex's car?' Cassie asked.

'He's asked me to ask the garage to look after it for him while he's away. Goodness knows when we'll be back here. They look after his car very well.'

'When are we leaving?' Cassie asked.

'I thought the day after tomorrow. Don't you have a job to go back to?'

'I suppose so. Carvello was annoyed that I insisted on coming here at all. Maybe he'll be loath to take me back.'

'Perhaps you didn't think it was worth worrying about,' Sophia said slowly. 'If Alex comes up to scratch, you'll not be needing the job anyway.'

Nino laughed loudly and received an angry look from Cassie.

'Sophia never pulls her punches,' he said wickedly. 'When she finishes with some man or other, or with anybody at all, they're never left in doubt about it.'

Ignoring him, Sophia jumped to her feet saying, 'I'll be back for lunch. It's quiet on the sea today, and calm as a mill pond. You'll have the bay to yourselves.'

She was right. There wasn't another boat in sight and the sea was a gloriously calm azure blue. Cassie's spirits lifted. She loved water skiing and Nino was good with boats. They could tolerate each other for one morning and after lunch there would be Alex.

'I'll go upstairs and collect my things,' she said airily.

'I'll see you at the landing stage,' Nino said, and set off to run lightly down the cliff path to where the motorboat waited.

Chapter Twenty-Nine

Sophia and Alexander stood looking through the window of the summerhouse watching Cassie skip lightly down the cliff path on her way to join Nino on the landing stage where he waited in his boat.

'Why didn't you go with them?' Alexander asked.

'I told them I had things to do in the village and had to see about your car.'

'What possible things have you to do in the village? And Demetrius is coming to collect my car.'

'I didn't want to spend the morning with Nino.'

‘Are you feeling a certain remorse over your treatment of him?’

‘No. He was beginning to take me for granted and I don’t want to marry him. He was boyfriend material, nothing more. What about you and Cassie? We’ll be leaving tomorrow. There’s tonight to be got through.’

‘Leave me to sort my life out, Sophia.’

She laughed. ‘Oh I shall, just remember what we talked about last night.’

After she’d left him he remained staring through the window. The scene was idyllic and his eyes lingered on the graceful figure of the girl on her water-skis in the wake of Nino’s motor-boat. Her dark red hair streamed in the breeze, the bright yellow bikini emphasising the golden tan of her limbs. There was a tigerish grace about her that most men would have found fascinating and she was his for the asking, but strangely he felt he had good reason to distrust the machinations of her mind.

He went back to the table and the work awaiting him but he couldn’t concentrate and after a while he laid aside his portfolios and sauntered out into the sunlight. He wandered along the cliff path to where it led down to the sea and there he stopped to watch the two people below. Nino was weaving a tortuous path through the waves but Cassie was well skilled and enjoying every moment, then from the bend in the cliffs there appeared another boat, a larger and more powerful boat. At first Alexander paid it scant attention and because it was moving so slowly, then suddenly it appeared to be gathering speed and to his horror it bore down on the smaller boat with all the ferocity of a charging rhino.

He called out but his voice was lost on the wind and then he was running madly down the cliff path while at sea the white boat was speeding swiftly away and there was no sign of the smaller boat apart from drifting debris.

Without a second's thought Alexander dived into the sea and swam speedily towards the floating wreck. Then he saw Nino hanging on precariously to a piece of his boat, his eyes vacant, and Alexander searched frantically for Cassie.

Men were running from the house now, gardeners and servants, running down the cliff path, diving into the sea, and he was joined in minutes by helpers. They dragged Nino towards the shore and others joined Alexander as he dived beneath the waves in his search for Cassie. There was a shout from one of the men, and in the next moment they had dragged her to the surface, but one look at her shattered body told them that it was too late.

One moment Cassie had been a beautiful glowing girl enjoying life behind Nino's boat, now she was a sad limp figure, lifeless and spent.

The air was filled with the sound of police sirens and then an ambulance came to take Nino away. He had not spoken a word but remained staring with wide unblinking eyes, oblivious to the people around him, oblivious that Sophia sat beside him holding his hand, her eyes awash with tears.

Cassie too was taken away then Alexander tried his best to describe the white boat, but what had he really seen? Just a white boat like so many others in the conglomeration of harbours dotted round the islands. By this time it could be anchored in any one of them.

Of course they would search for it, but what would they find and a few brushes of paint would quickly obliterate any scratches the boat had sustained.

Sophia wept long and bitter tears but her grief for Cassie and Nino was tampered with a terrible fear.

'This villa is death to all of us,' she cried. 'Father and then my mother, then there was Mervyn and now Cassie. Somebody is out to kill us, Alexander. They thought Cassie was me, she's died instead of me.'

Alexander looked at her sadly. His own thoughts echoed some of his sister's fears, but who on this beautiful tiny island would want any of them dead? And as if she recognised the thoughts passing through his mind she said, 'He haunted my mother for years before he went to prison, he'll be hating and bitter wherever he is, he'll be determined to get his revenge.'

'But that was years ago Sophia. However bitter he might feel it has to end someday. No, I refuse to believe that that man had anything to do with it.'

'What's your explanation then? That he didn't see the boat, in an empty sea he had to crash into Nino. It was deliberate.'

'Well, we have to leave it with the police.'

'And you know how the islanders hang together. We're the outsiders Alexander. We're the foreigners here.'

'They're decent people who won't want something like this to spoil the reputation of the island. So you're leaving as planned in the morning.'

'Yes. I'll go to see Nino in the hospital this evening and I'll get his family to have him sent home. Surely you don't intend to stay on here alone?'

'No, I have to get back anyway. I'll get nothing done here and there's Cassie's mother to contact and her funeral to attend to.'

'You mean we shall have to go to that?'

'I shall go. You must please yourself.'

'Then I'll have to go. Her mother will think it dreadful if I don't.'

He watched her pacing along the terrace but she did not stay there long. 'I hate being in the garden now Alexander, I'm afraid. I'm afraid that somebody is watching us. Tomorrow can't come quickly enough,' she said.

Later that afternoon they were informed that Nino had been taken to the larger hospital on Rhodes but when Alexander suggested they sail over to visit him Sophia shook her head adamantly. 'Not in your boat Alexander, not when there's some maniac out there with sinister designs on us.'

'Then how do you intend to visit him?' Alexander asked reasonably.

'I shall sail across in the morning on the ferry and then go on from Rhodes to Rome. How long do you propose to stay here?'

'A few days, no longer.'

'Alexander, I don't like to think of you here on your own.'

'You're becoming paranoid Sophia. Nothing is going to happen to me.'

'Why don't you put the villa up for sale? Surely you'll never want to come back here. First Mother then Mervyn, now Cassie and Nino. The place has a jinx on it.'

'Well, here is Father Sandros come to commiserate with us. Be very careful what you say Sophia, the islanders are proud of their island. Any hint that somebody here is to blame will not go down well with them.'

The priest was earnest in his sympathy. He remembered the beautiful high-spirited young woman of the evening before and the young man he had seen before on the island.

He informed them that the police were trying to trace the boat but it did not belong in any of the harbours round the island and could have come from other islands, not necessarily Rhodes. He could not believe that the deed had been done maliciously for who would do such a thing? No, there had to be some logical explanation. Lack of concentration, some malfunction in the boat. He would bless the house and the gardens, ask God for protection and for a dismissal of any evil spirit that dwelt there.

When he had gone Sophia stood at the window watching him walking away from the house. Her expression was cynical and looking down at her with a wry smile, Alexander said gently, 'You haven't believed a word of it Sophia?'

'No. I'm still leaving in the morning and I'm never coming back.'

The English newspapers were full of the tragedy of an English woman's death in the warm waters of the blue Aegean and Selene was busily packing a suitcase for her journey to Devon when the telephone rang and one of her flatmates came to tell her that her grandmother was on the line.

'Have you seen the morning paper?' she demanded. 'It was on the early morning news too. There's something wrong on that island when these terrible things keep happening. Have you spoken to Athena?'

'No grandma, I'm going there this morning.'

'What about school.'

'They know about the accident, they know I have to be with Athena.'

'Will they bring her home or will she be buried out there?'

'I don't know any more than you do, Grandma. I'll let you know what is happening.'

'Well at least now it should convince you that the island is no place for you. Your grandfather agrees with me.'

'Yes I'm sure he does. Now I have to get off, Grandma, I'll be in touch when it's all over.'

It was late in the evening when she arrived in Exeter and the last country train had already left so that she had to take a taxi to the coast. It was pouring with rain and as they drove at last on the long coastal road with its lights strung out like jewels, their cheerfulness seemed somehow inappropriate.

Lights streamed out into the darkness from Athena's windows and a long black car which she recognised immediately as Jonathan Trevellyan's was on the drive. At that moment she felt a sudden rush of gratitude for his kindness.

As soon as she entered the room she was aware of Athena's deep distress and she went forward swiftly to embrace her while Jonathan said, 'I'm so glad you've come, Selene. I was hoping you would.'

'Whatever am I going to do now that Cassie's gone?' Athena cried, 'She was so full of life, so beautiful. You won't leave me, will you Selene?'

Over her bent head Jonathan smiled gently at the concern in Selene's eyes.'

It was Jonathan who told her that Cassie's body was to be brought home and that the funeral would take place in the village church.

'I had thought Athena would want her to be buried near her father in Scotland,' she said.

'She considered it, but decided against it. I think Sophia and her brother will be coming for the funeral. I've spoken to Alexander on the telephone. He's making all the arrangements for Cassie's body at their end. They'll be flying here on the same plane.'

'Did he say anything about Nino?'

'He's still in hospital on Rhodes, but recovering slowly.'

Later that night when she was alone in her bedroom she thought about Alexander. She was remembering his smile and the low charm of his voice, the happiness they had shared for just one day before he belonged to Cassie and she was wondering how deeply he grieved for her.

It was Athena who put her thoughts into words when she said, 'Poor Alexander, he must be devastated at losing Cassie this way. I had a letter from her only days before this happened, it was so filled with joy at the holiday, and her time with Alex. They were so very much in love.

'When all this is over, Selene, you and I will go away somewhere, Bali or Phuket. Cassie loved those places, it will be like having her with me.'

'Athena, I'm not sure. I've only just started at the Slade. We could go during the holidays.'

'Oh darling, I need to get away soon. I can't wait for the holidays they're too far off. We'll talk about it later.'

Selene was beginning to feel trapped, not as she had been with her grandparents, but in a more privileged way. Athena was rich, always when there had been trauma in her life, she'd been extravagant with clothes and travel. Cassie had come and gone in her life whenever it suited her, now Athena was busily turning her into the daughter she had never been.

Jonathan was aware of her thoughts. 'Don't worry too much,' he advised. 'I'm a free agent with time on my hands. I'll talk to her.'

'Jonathan's so very kind,' she said to Athena. 'He's like a rock. You should be very grateful, Athena.'

'Oh I am darling. I just don't want to marry anybody, at least not yet.'

'But you can spend time together. It would be good for both of you.'

'We'll see, darling. These next few days have got

to be suffered first.'

They brought Cassie's body home a week later and once more she was dismally aware of her racing heart as Alexander took her hand in his.

'We meet again under very sad circumstances, Selene,' he said softly.

'Yes,' she murmured, then he passed on to meet Jonathan and other people who were at the house. Sophia was pale. She kissed Selene on both cheeks before moving on.

There were a great many people in the tiny churchyard and the flowers were spread out along the paths. Selene was aware of Alexander standing beside her, tall and remote, his expression composed into lines of deep sadness, yet strangely impersonal, while beside him Sophia wept copiously.

Sophia could not have said why grief took hold of her so insidiously. Cassie had not been a terribly close friend but one who had come and gone in her life when it suited her. It had only been Alexander who had drawn them more closely together. Now a feeling of guilt made her more distressed. She had warned Alexander against Cassie, but if she hadn't, could they have found some measure of happiness together?

With Cassie's passing went a piece of her childhood and memories of happier days spent on that beautiful Greek island in the warm summer sun. Then too there was Nino. She did not love Nino any more, it was over, but memories remained. Memories of love and laughter and the good times spent together.

It was early evening and people were beginning

to drift away. Athena pressed Alexander and Sophia to stay but they said they were flying back to Italy the next day and had booked into an hotel in Exeter for the night.

Selene left them chatting together. The sound of their voices followed her up the stairs, where she hoped to find some of her father's pictures in the attic, where she had found the others. There were so many of them, watercolours and oils, pastels and sketches, and she sat on an old chest with one of them in her hands. It was a watercolour of the island and looking at the gentle scenery it seemed incredible that it should be concerned with sudden death and despair.

A gentle tap on the door made her look up startled, and in the next moment the door opened and Alexander stood looking at her.

'Athena said I would find you here,' he said with a smile. 'We're almost ready to leave. I wanted to say goodbye.'

He came forward and took the picture out of her hands, staring down at it thoughtfully.

'He was a wonderfully talented man,' he said at last.

'Yes. I hope I can be as good.'

'You've made up your mind then? Painting as opposed to teaching.'

'They've accepted me at the Slade. I want to take some of these back with me. I promised to show one of my tutors.'

'I'm sure he'll be impressed. Will you ever come back to Rome I wonder?'

He was looking down at her so intently she became embarrassed at the warm colour that flooded her face.

'Perhaps, one day.'

'It seems strange to talk about the island today of all days, but your father's studio is still there on the waterfront, waiting for you perhaps.'

'Perhaps.'

'I'm not giving up on the island Selene. Neither should you.'

'I have a long way to go. I may not be as good as my father.'

'Or you may be better.'

She smiled. 'Will Sophia go back to the island?'

'She says not, but never is a long, long time. I grew up there, I can't think even now that there is anything sinister there. I lost my mother because she was driving too fast. You lost your father in some bizarre, unexplained accident. This last one is the hardest to understand. One minute Cassie and Nino were enjoying themselves in the warm sea, I could hear their laughter, feel their joy, then suddenly there was this big white boat bearing down on them out of the blue. Was it human error, or was it deliberate? I don't know.'

'But to do something deliberate is too horrible to contemplate. Only a fool would do that.'

'I know, a fool, a madman, or a murderer.'

'Will we ever know?' she asked quietly.

'One day perhaps.' He took her hand in his and raised it to his lips. It was a completely foreign gesture, but he held on to her hand for several minutes before saying, 'Goodbye Selene, one day perhaps when all this is behind us we shall meet again. You will come to the island and I shall never be able to stay away from it.'

With another smile he was gone, running lightly down the stairs and picking up her pictures she followed more slowly.

They were congregated in the hall, and Sophia looked up at her with a smile and wave of her hand, then they were gone.

Seeing the pictures Athena said, 'You found what you wanted dear, but surely you're not leaving so soon?'

'I'm a new girl, Athena. I have to get back and I want my tutor to see these. I've talked to him about my father. He wants to see some of his work.'

'I thought we could go abroad, travel a bit.'

'We will one day, Athena, but for now I must get on with my work, I have a living to earn. I know my father left some money for me but it isn't a bottomless pit.'

'But money needn't bother you darling. Ian left me a very rich woman and Cassie's gone, there's only the two of us now, Selene.'

'You've always said if I wasn't careful, my grandparents would take away my independence and I should guard against it. I have disappointed them by going my own way. Surely you don't want me to exchange one sort of dependency for another?'

She smiled. 'I'm being very selfish. It's just that I'm feeling very sorry for myself, I have to pull myself together. Why don't we go into the drawing room and I'll ask John to open a bottle of champagne.'

There was nothing incongruous in Athena

asking for champagne. This was how she had always met the disasters in her life, it was her way of showing fate that it hadn't defeated her.

'Darling, do look in Cassie's wardrobe, and take any of her clothes that you fancy. She would want you to have them, and I want you to have them. I want the drawers and the wardrobes cleared out. Any you don't want I'll send to the local charity shops.'

'I'll look at them in the morning. Then the day after I should get back to London.'

'Sophia said there were gowns and other things of Cassie's in Rome and at the villa. She said she'd pack them up and send them but I told her to take whatever she wanted and get rid of the others. They should fit Sophia, they were about the same size.'

'Did you get to say goodbye to them Selene?'

'Yes. Alexander came up to the attic, he was looking at this picture of the villa.'

'Poor Alexander. He bore up very well even when he must be grieving terribly. Cassie adored him, I'd never seen her so in love. He must have felt the same way.'

Selene thought about Alexander. She remembered his smile and the low charm of his voice. She thought about the words he had spoken regarding Cassie's death and realised that he had said nothing about grief or loving, nor of what her death meant to him personally. Perhaps it was something he felt unable to put into words. Grief to so many people was a personal thing and not something to be wallowed in or blazoned theatrically for all to see.

One day Alexander would learn to love again, but would she ever meet him, in Rome, on the island, and see that awareness in his eyes that she had seen in Rome? Then there had been Cassie. Unless her memory haunted him down the years, there would be no Cassie the next time.

Chapter Thirty

Selene was happy in London, with her days at the Slade and her evenings with friends at their favourite haunts around the city.

Larry Jarvis was a fellow student. He was talented, volatile, good-looking and demanding. From her first few days at the Slade he had pursued her and because she admired his talent and his sense of humour she had been happy to go out with him. Together they explored the museums and art galleries, the exhibitions and the coffee houses frequented by their contemporaries.

Larry was invariably argumentative but he was impatient with life. He wanted to move on, to be famous, and when she showed him her father's paintings he was quick to say they were good but were not for him.

There was times when she felt angry with him. He derided her work because she was happy to paint pictures in what he called the old style, and she had to admit that she didn't always understand his work. It was too new, too unexplained and he grew impatient with her criticism.

'Just because your father painted in the old style doesn't mean there's no other,' he argued. 'Jackson Pollock was every bit as good as Leonardo.'

Selene couldn't see it. Leonardo had painted faces as they were, she would never understand splodges of colour which a bicycle had run over.

Larry scoffed. 'You'll never make the grade, Selene, if you paint like Year One. This is a different age, people want something new.'

She had not told her grandparents about Larry because there was really nothing to tell them. While they were at the Slade they were thought of as a pair. Once they had left, Selene had no doubt they would go their separate ways.

She received postcards from Athena and Jonathan Trevellyan from a great many exotic places and she was glad that Athena was picking up the pieces and learning to live again. Jonathan would be patient with her because he loved her. When she spoke of them to Larry he was caustic. To Larry they were rich aimless people. He would have preferred it if Selene had been short of money because he thought artists should struggle painfully to earn their results in a profession that had too much to live up to.

His portrait painting was like nobody else's, and if Selene could hardly recognise his version of the model in question, she had to admit that he had a flair for colour and design that commanded your attention.

'You'll see,' he said with a short laugh. 'When we leave here it'll be me who gets to exhibit at the

Tate and you who goes on to teach art to indifferent students.'

In the next breath he would apologise but in her heart she saw the truth of his statements. He would get to exhibit because he was different, because the world was changing, because it was crying out for something new, but Selene believed it would come back to the old values and see a picture as being good because it was recognisable.

When she went to stay with her grandparents at Christmas she felt she had never been away. As usual they all came for lunch on Christmas Day and it was Aunt Norah who asked questions about her work.

'Where's it getting you?' she wanted to know. 'You'll need to teach something else besides art, unless you decided to teach in an art college, they're few and far between.'

'I'm not sure what I shall do, Aunt Norah.'

'How do you spend your spare time in London?'

'We go to exhibitions and occasionally to the theatre.'

'London's expensive and I should know. Do you have a boyfriend?'

'Nobody special.'

That had been a mistake. She should have known that Norah would pass this bit of information on at the earliest opportunity.

On Boxing Day her grandmother said, 'Norah tells me you've got a boyfriend. Who is he?'

'Just a friend, Granny, a boy I've met at the Slade.'

'Is he an artist?'

'Yes, he's very good.'

'Is he going to be like your father, wanting to paint for a living?'

'I'm sure that's his idea Granny.'

'We should meet him, Selene.'

'Granny there's no need, it isn't serious.'

'Even so, we need to know who you're going around with. I thought you roomed with three other girls and that you'd all be going around together.'

'We go around as a crowd quite often.'

'Your grandfather and I think you should invite him to spend a weekend here. Does he live in London?'

'He's sharing a flat with two other boys. His home is in Swansea.'

'He's Welsh? Your father was half Welsh.'

'Granny, I'm not sure if Larry will want to come for a weekend, he could well think you're trying to push him into something.'

'That's nonsense. We simply want to know who you're going around with, whether he's decent, and genuine.'

She was irritated with the grin that greeted her when she mentioned a weekend with her grandparents to Larry.

'Wanting to see if I've got what it takes, are they?' he asked pertly.

'They're very protective. It's understandable really, I never knew my parents, they brought me up.'

'I doubt if I'll pass muster then.'

'You will, if you behave yourself. I've explained

that there's nothing serious between us, that after we leave the Slade we'll go our separate ways.'

For a moment his face sobered. 'How do we know that, Selene? I'm going places and you're coming with me.'

'Not with paintings you disagree with, I'm not.'

'So, what are you going to do? England is glutted with people painting pictures like yours. Every art college, every would-be painter on the streets. You've got to do something wildly different to succeed.'

That was the moment she thought about her father's studio standing empty and forlorn on the harbour wall and she knew what she wanted to do. She would not tell Larry. At first he would ridicule the idea, then he would want to go there, and Larry had no place on the Greek Island. One day perhaps she would meet Alexander there. He would see the open doors, see the paintings hung outside in the sunshine, come in the studio to see what it was all about.

'Penny for them,' accused Larry. 'You were miles away. What were you thinking about?'

'Nothing in particular. Are you coming with me to meet my grandparents or not? It doesn't matter to me either one way or the other.'

'Then I'll come. I'll take along some of my work. That will impress them.'

It didn't. The two older people stared at them nonplussed but were polite enough to ask no questions and Selene was amused at their blank expressions.

Not so Larry. When they were alone he said somewhat irritably, 'They didn't understand my work; were they like this with your father?'

'I don't know.'

'Of course, they're a different generation, I didn't think they'd like them, they probably won't like me.'

They didn't. Larry argued with her grandfather about politics and her grandmother about the wallpaper she'd chosen for the bedrooms. She took him round to Aunt Norah's and he was scathing about her concept of teaching young people which he described as stuffy and old hat.

Selene was glad when the weekend was over and they were ready to depart in Larry's ancient open sports car that rattled down the road emitting a trail of exhaust fumes.

She knew her grandparents were already saying a silent prayer that she would have the good sense to end their friendship as soon as possible, hopefully long before either of them had finished at the Slade.

Athena and John arrived back in Devon at the end of March and at the first opportunity Selene went to stay there. Athena greeted her rapturously and she seemed healthier than she had been for some considerable time. Her arthritis had responded to warm sunlight and there was a serenity about her that Selene had always found missing.

They talked about the holiday and showed her snapshots and other mementoes they had gathered. Athena plied her with gifts until Selene said, 'Really Athena, you shouldn't have bought so many presents. I really don't deserve them.'

'Well, of course you do, darling. While we've been out there enjoying ourselves, you've been working hard, and suffering your Aunt Norah. She's a very difficult woman.'

Selene laughed. 'I really didn't see much of her.'

'Still friendly with Larry?'

She'd been able to tell Athena about Larry and Athena had laughed and seen the friendship for what it was.

'I took him to meet my grandparents. Needless to say they didn't exactly get on.'

'Well of course not, darling. Whatever made you do that?'

'They insisted, so I took a chance.'

'They would neither like his work nor the boy himself. Gracious me, they never really approved of Mervyn after he stopped being a school teacher.'

'Athena, what would you say if I told you I wanted to open up the studio on the island after I leave the Slade?'

She stared at her doubtfully, and Selene went on hurriedly, 'If I stay in England, I'm not sure how my work will take off here. I look around at what the other students are doing and mine's no worse and no better, and I don't want to drift into teaching at some art college. Like my father I want to paint pictures. There are tourists who come to the island, and I am my father's daughter after all.'

'I'm not worried about that dear. It's the island that worries me.'

Athena liked to dawdle over her breakfast,

sitting in her silk dressing gown leafing through her morning post, and Selene watched as she laid the letter she had been reading down carefully beside her plate, her expression curiously sad.

'Is anything wrong Athena?' she asked.

'I've had a letter from the Princess Cabrodini. Sophia is engaged to be married.'

'To Nino?'

'No. To some young American from the Embassy in Rome. After the wedding, they'll be going back to Washington, she says.'

'What else does the Princess say?'

'Only that she is feeling her years, that Alexander is well and she hopes the holiday I took abroad has helped me to recover from Cassie's death. I do think about her, Selene. Do you think whoever killed her meant to? Don't you think he thought she was Sophia?'

Selene stared at her in surprise. 'But why should you think that? Why should anybody want to kill either of them?'

'Well, she was very much like Sophia, the same height, more or less the same colouring, and she was with Nino who was Sophia's friend. The more I think of it the more I think of the tragedy that befell her mother.'

'And my father?'

'Oh, I don't really know, darling. I don't really know how deeply he was involved with Leonora.'

'Does the Princess say anything about Nino?'

'Only that he is getting better very slowly, and will probably never be completely well again.'

'Sophia couldn't have loved him, or she wouldn't be marrying somebody else.'

'Of course not. I always thought Sophia and Cassie were very much alike, but at least Cassie really did care for Alexander. I do hope he's getting over her and that he meets somebody else.'

Their time at the Slade was coming to an end. Selene often wondered where the time had gone. All Selene knew was that she had loved it and wanted to paint pictures. So many of them were going into design, industrial and fashion design, but Selene's mind never stretched beyond the desire to paint scenery in watercolour or oils.

She was seeing little of Larry because he was working on his painting which he intended to show at the end-of-year exhibition. She hadn't seen it because he was secretive about it. She saw it for the first time on the night of the exhibition and nobody could really miss it since it occupied almost all of one wall.

She stared up at it trying to guess what it was all about: indefinite shapes, bits of pottery and broken mirror and pieces of what looked like metal piping were amassed into an extraordinary organic growth.

Selene was showing two pictures she had painted, one of St James's Park in the early morning when mist swirled across the grass and the water fowl huddled in groups at the water's edge. The picture of the moorland above her grandmother's house, vibrant with flying clouds and purple heather.

She watched the visitors circling the room and saw their somewhat bemused expressions when they looked at Larry's work. A handful of young vociferous students raved about it. It was something new, something courageous, but the older people who could afford to buy it were notably unimpressed.

One elderly gentleman – an American – stopped in front of Selene's painting of the moorland and stood for a long time with his head on one side then on the other contemplating it, and Selene asked softly, 'Do you like it?'

'Yes I do, very much. This I can understand, but not that huge thing over there.'

He moved closer to look at the signature.

'Hmm. Corwen,' he mused. 'I knew a Corwen once, met him in Greece on some island or other. I liked his work so much I bought several from him, and then when we went back again his studio was closed and nobody seemed to know much about it.'

Selene decided that she would say nothing about her father. After all it was a long story, and the islanders had not wanted to talk about it. Instead she said, 'There are some very good exhibits, I'm so glad you like my work.'

'Tell me something, do you like that thing over there? Do you even understand it?'

'I'm afraid not, but Larry is very talented and he believes in himself. Art is changing.'

'I'm aware of it. I doubt if the world as it is could hope to produce another Leonardo. I rather think the young man who created that would be contemptuous of his work.'

Selene smiled, and her companion went on, 'Is this how you intend to earn your living, my dear? Is there room for all of you?'

'I don't know. I can only try.'

'Well, I wish you the very best, my dear. Find yourself a nice little studio in some beautiful place in the world and you'll sell your pictures. The artist we bought from was selling pictures as though there was no tomorrow, the tourists were clamouring for his work. I still have mine.'

'Were they watercolours?'

'Well yes. We hadn't the time to wait for the oils, but then I like watercolours, they're so fresh and delicate. He had one beautiful picture hanging in his studio of a woman sitting on a stone wall looking out across a garden. The picture was beautiful and so was the woman, I didn't ask him if it was his wife. In any case, it wasn't for sale.'

'What was she like?'

'Very dark, quite beautiful.'

He raised his hat and left her, and Selene was left wondering who the girl in the picture could be. Her mother had been fair, and in the next moment she thought about the picture she had seen in Rome of Alexander's mother. She had been dark, dark and beautiful.

A few minutes later one of the curators came to place a small red dot on the moorland picture, and with a smile informed her that it had been sold to an elderly gentleman who seemed well pleased with his purchase.

Fellow students came to congratulate her, and she was so thrilled she hurried across to tell Larry. He stared at her stolidly for several seconds then, as he turned away, he said, 'Same old has-beens, they don't know real art when they see it.'

'Have you had any offers for it, Larry?'

'No,' he answered shortly.

'Well, perhaps it is rather large to hang in a modern house.'

'It isn't for a modern house, girl. It's for an art gallery or a stately home, somewhere with plenty of space to do it justice. Where will yours be going? To some old buffer's drawing room where he can look at it over his late-night toddy.'

Without answering she turned and walked away. Larry was impossible when he was like this. He was annoyed because his picture hadn't been enthused about and he was jealous that somebody had bought hers.

Later that afternoon he had the grace to apologise.

'I'm sorry Selene. I was frustrated, that's all. But you were patronising me and I don't like to be patronised.'

With an ingratiating grin he said, 'Why don't we set up house together? You can sell pictures to help us out while I'm creating my masterpiece, then when we're millionaires we can get married and show the world.'

'Larry, I wouldn't marry you if you were asked to restock the National Gallery, it would be too traumatic. In the clouds one day, in the depths the next.'

'Oh well, you'll be glad to change your mind when I'm famous. Have you any money? We could go out to supper?'

'I haven't any money for supper.'

'You sold a picture.'

'He paid by cheque, so it's going in the bank.'

'You'll never marry me, Selene. I'm a bohemian, you're a prudent, well brought-up young lady with a strange notion of wanting to be an artist. Artists starve in garrets Selene. They suffer to paint. I suffer. You never will.'

'You're insufferably pompous.'

'And you're insufferably a product of middle-class respectability. You'll settle for a nice modern house in suburbia with well-scrubbed children and a husband with a nine-to-five job in something safe with a pension at the end of it.'

Selene didn't answer him. He was describing the sort of life her grandparents wanted for her, the sort of life her mother had wanted, but handed down to her had been the legacy of her father, unpredictable, a rebel against everything Larry had described.

She did not see Larry for three days and in those three days she said her farewell to London and other friends she had made. She packed her belongings and let herself out of the flat for the last time in the early morning, carrying her suitcase. Larry waited in his disreputable car at the kerb.

She stared at him uncertainly and he grinned, a grin that was totally uncontrite, appealing even, and then he got out and ceremoniously opened the passenger door after placing her suitcase on the narrow back seat.

'It's heavy,' he commented. 'Does that mean you're not coming back?'

'No.'

'Where are you going?'

'To my boringly middle-class grandparents and my future.'

'And what is that going to be?'

'I'll think of something.'

'Can I drive up there to see you sometime?'

'I doubt if I'll be there very long.'

'Oh? Where will you be then?'

'Larry, I don't know, but I'd rather you didn't wait around for me.'

'Oh well, do follow my career with interest, Selene, and have the grace to apologise for your lack of faith in me when I'm famous.'

'I'll be glad to Larry. I sincerely hope you are.'

'You're a nice girl, Selene. You could never have been in love with me, could you?'

She laughed. 'No, but I'm reassured that you're not suffering from a broken heart.'

'You know, I rather liked Athena. She had style, you'd be well advised to throw in your lot with her. Money, lots of travelling about, she could well afford to sponsor you. I'll have to make it on my own but you could be in clover.'

By this time they had arrived at the station and Selene was clambering out of the car. She turned to smile at him while he struggled with her suitcase.

'Thanks for the lift, Larry, and good look with your future,' she said evenly.

'Have you taken what I said about Athena on board?'

'I'm not even considering it, Larry. I'll make it on my own.'

He walked beside her carrying her case and she said somewhat irritably. 'Thanks Larry, I can manage on my own now.'

He bothered her. The expression on his good-looking face, his confidence, she was wishing he hadn't come, then he put the suitcase down and enveloped her in his embrace. His face was unusually serious as he looked down into her eyes. 'You'll make it, girl, and don't mind any of the things I've been saying, it's just me sounding off. Will you let me know what you're doing with yourself? Don't expect a reply, I'm a rotten correspondent.'

'You're hopeless, Larry. Everything with you is so one-sided.'

'I know, that's what's so endearing about me.'

With another impudent grin he left her and she watched him making his way through the early morning crowds. He never looked back.

Chapter Thirty-One

Her grandfather was waiting for her at the end of her journey, his face wreathed in smiles, hurrying forward to take her suitcase, embracing her gently.

'It's good to have you home, love. I left Granny thinking up your favourite meal.'

They talked pleasantries. About the people they knew, the neighbours, Aunt Norah and she knew he wouldn't ask about her future plans until they were all together after their meal.

As soon as the car appeared on the drive her

grandmother was at the door, smiling, waving to a neighbour across the street who was pruning his roses, and with a smile that said, 'We're happy now. Selene is home.'

Reluctantly they now called her Selene, it was their one concession to her father's wishes, but more often than not her grandmother didn't refer to her by name and seemed content to call her 'dear'.

'Did you have a good journey, dear?' she asked. 'Lunch is ready, I was hoping your train wouldn't be late.'

Lunch had been given some thought! Her favourite poached salmon and tender young vegetables were followed by her grandmother's excellent Apple Charlotte and coffee. Then, lunch over, the questions began.

'Have you thought what you want to do now, dear? Norah says you'll have difficulty in getting into teaching since art is really only a sideline in most schools.'

'Let the girl settle in, before we start asking what she wants to do,' her grandfather said tersely. 'Time enough for all that in a day or two.'

'But you're staying here with us, Selene? I've told everybody you're coming back here. I don't want you to live with Athena simply because Cassie's gone.'

'I've told Athena I shall go to see her whenever I can, Granny.'

'Well of course, and I'm sure she's absolutely heartbroken about Cassie, but she was so seldom at home, she was always all over the place.'

Selene decided to say no more. The time would

come soon enough when she had to tell them how she had resolved her future, and they wouldn't like it because her future would not be living with them.

'What has that art college equipped you for?' Aunt Norah asked curiously. 'Is art all you can teach? It didn't help your father, and last week the local college had an exhibition in the town. They set out their pictures around the market place and a great many were sold. Some of them were very good. Will yours be any better?'

'Perhaps not.'

'Well then, where do you go from here?'

Upstairs in her bedroom she packed the three canvases she had brought from Athena's into her suitcase and hid it away on the top of her wardrobe. These were going to the island with her, as well as the things she would need for the work she intended to do.

It was on one of her walks across the park that she came across Uncle Martin, her father's old friend and colleague, who hailed her affectionately.

'I retired in the summer,' he informed her with a broad smile. 'I've just about had enough. I was more of a civil servant than a teacher, now I can spend the day doing exactly as I please. Come back and have tea with us.'

She agreed with him instantly: here was one person she could talk to about the future and know that he remained unbiased.

When she mentioned the island, however, both Martin and his wife looked doubtful.

'Wouldn't it bother you going to the island,

love?' Martin said. 'After all, it can't have very many happy memories for you; your father, and then Cassie. Besides your mother was never happy there.'

'I know, but the studio is still there and the villa. My father's death was an accident and we don't really know about Cassie.'

She refused to admit, even to herself, that there was a chance she might meet Alexander again, but told herself sternly that that was not the real reason for wanting to go there.

'When do you intend to go?' he asked her.

'I'm hoping next spring, by that time my grandparents may have become resigned to it. I need to find a temporary job in the meantime.'

'Any thoughts on what it might be?'

'None at all, but there's sure to be something.'

'One of the women at the college is on maternity leave. I could put in a good word for you there, it's not many pupils who can say they've been taught by somebody who was at the Slade.'

'Oh I really would like that, Uncle Martin. Can you really help?'

'I'm sure I can. Your father did a stint there, Selene. They talk about him. After all, he did make quite a name for himself.'

Several days later the principal of the college called to see her and her grandparents were thrilled when he offered her a post. She tried to tell them that it was only temporary, but all they could say was that one thing led to another. Oh, they weren't pressing her to live with them, they'd look around for a nice little house, similar to the one Norah had, and they'd be happy to furnish it for her.

Consequently her grandmother spent most of her time looking at property, talking to the neighbours to see if they knew of anything, coming up with a great many suggestions about houses that were for sale and all too close to them.

Selene looked at them, but refused to commit herself so that in the end her grandmother became frustrated.

'You've found something wrong with every one of them, Selene,' she said sharply. 'That one on the corner of The Drive was just perfect for you, and beautifully decorated. Didn't need a penny spending on it.'

'Granny, the job is only temporary.'

'They'll keep you on. I was talking to two people who go there and they're quite thrilled with the way you're helping them.'

And helping them was all she was doing. They didn't need a teacher, they had all developed their own style and were reluctant to change it.

At the weekends she went out with them into the countryside where they sat at their easels painting local scenes, and some of their work was very good. They appreciated her help on composition and selection of detail, and any suggestions she had to make about perspective. They enjoyed watching her work on some painting of her own, too.

Some of them would never be artists. They attended regularly, listened to her with some awe and continued to do their own thing. In some way she was relieved when news came that the missing teacher would be returning after Christmas.

'Now what will you do?' her grandmother demanded. 'Didn't they offer you another job?'

Actually they had offered her a temporary post at the college in a neighbouring town, but she had declined on the grounds that she would shortly be going abroad.

That had been a bad mistake, since one of her colleagues was a member of her grandfather's Lodge and informed him of the fact several days later.

She knew as soon as she entered the house that something was wrong. They sat in morose silence with the television switched on and neither of them watching. Selene's heart sank, and her grandmother said, 'We're both very upset, Selene. Grandy's been talking to Mr Bentham, and he's told him you're going abroad to work. You've never said anything to us.'

'I know. I'm sorry, Granny, but I knew it would upset you. I wanted to get round to it gradually. These last few months would have been awful if I'd told you sooner.'

'You let me look at all those houses, and you'd no intention of taking any one of them.'

'Granny, you always knew the job at the college was temporary. How could I possibly move into a new house, when I didn't know where my life was going?'

'And you know now?'

'I think so.'

'I suppose it's Athena's doing?'

'Athena's had nothing to do with it. As a matter

of fact, she's none too happy about it.'

'Why? Why isn't she happy?'

'Because I want to go to Greece, back to my father's villa and studio.'

They both looked at her as though she had taken leave of her senses.

'You can't go there. Think about what happened to your father, to Cassie. Your mother never liked living there. She was desperate to come home. We won't allow you to go there, will we?'

She turned quickly to appeal to her husband, but he sat looking down at his hands clenched on his knees, refusing to meet her eyes.

Selene looked at them sadly. She didn't want to hurt them, but if she didn't make a stand now it might be lost for ever.

'Granny, please try to understand,' she pleaded. 'You only ever see my mother in me, but I'm like my father too. He wanted to paint pictures and so do I. He became well-known there, I want the same thing for me. If it doesn't work out for me, I'll come back and admit defeat.'

'You mean, if you live long enough.'

'Granny, who would want to harm *me?* Nobody knows who I am. Besides, tragic accidents happen to many people all the time. What happened to my father was an accident, nothing more sinister.'

'When do you intend to go?'

'Just before Easter I think. I'll stay with Athena for a few days, so that I can tell her when I'm going, and then I'll come back here to collect my things.'

They had to be content with that. Selene had made up her mind and, like her father before her, there was no changing it.

Athena didn't try.

'I'm so glad you've come,' she said airily. 'I'm invited to a wedding in Rome, and I want you to take a look at my wardrobe with me. It's a highly fashionable affair as you can imagine. I'm surprised that the Princess Cabrodini has invited me, but I suppose it's to do with Cassie.'

Selene's heart raced oddly. Whose wedding? Oh please, not Alexander's, she breathed silently.

Before she could ask Athena said, 'Sophia's fixed the date for her wedding to this American her grandmother wrote to me about. Quite a whirlwind romance, and they're leaving for Washington almost as soon as the ceremony is over.'

She was busy laying out one gown after another across the bed, all of them highly fashionable, together with hats decorated with chiffon, flowers and velvet.

'I thought nothing too flamboyant, Selene. After all, I have to think about Cassie, although she's the last person who would have expected me to wear mourning. I always only ever wear black because it suits my colouring and looks entirely dramatic.'

Selene eyed the gowns thoughtfully. 'Haven't you a preference?' she asked at last.

'Well I do like the black, but I don't want to remind them about Cassie on such a happy occasion, and yet what else is there?'

'You could wear that beautiful black hat with

the white chiffon dress and black accessories. Failing that, what about the navy?'

'I'm not sure. I think the white sounds better. Perhaps we'll ask Jonathan, black and white go so well with the men's formal dress.'

Selene smiled. 'Is Jonathan invited?'

'Well, they do think I ought to have somebody to travel with and it is nice to have an escort Selene. Otherwise I'd have asked if you could go with me.'

'I think Jonathan's a much better idea, Athena.'

'I thought you'd say that, darling. Now tell me about your grandparents. Have you dropped your bombshell yet?'

'Yes, and it hasn't been too well received.'

'You surely didn't expect that it would be, darling?'

'No, of course not.'

'You really do mean to go ahead then?'

'Athena, I have to. I've worked to this end. Now I have to see if it's paid off. Will people want to buy my pictures? Will they see something in my work, just as they saw something in my father's?'

'I'm not at all anxious about that, Selene, but aren't you a little afraid? I know I would be.'

'I try not to think about it. All I see is an island in the sun, the same way I know my father saw it.'

'And if Alexander is there some of the time, you'll feel much safer, I'm sure,' Athena added.

She was not looking at her, but remained totally absorbed in selecting a suitable outfit for Sophia's wedding. She had stated a fact, nothing more. To Athena, Alexander was simply a man who had loved Cassie. Selene posed no threat to her memory, Alexander would be a friend, nothing more.

From her place in the window, Princess Cabrodini watched her granddaughter and her fiancé run lightly up the steps to the terrace above.

She liked the tall young American with his open face and charming smile. For the very first time she could honestly say that she approved of a young man Sophia had brought home, and there had been so many of them over the years. Mostly rich young Italians who drove fast cars and lived aimless lives. Now there was Kevin who came from a prosperous, old Bostonian family, had a good well-paid profession and a steady uncomplicated background.

That he adored Sophia was evident. She was beautiful, mercurial, fun to be with. His family were coming over for the wedding. He got along well with Alexander, and he had absolutely no desire ever to set foot on a Greek island.

Sophia openly adored him.

As they reached her chair Sophia embraced her fondly and Kevin raised her languid hand to his lips.

'You both look very happy,' the Princess commented.

'Oh, Grandmama, isn't this beautiful, Kevin's wedding present to me.'

She held out her arm from which dangled a gold bracelet set with diamonds and emeralds and the Princess raised her eyebrows, well aware of how much the bauble had cost the besotted young man.

'You spend too much money on her,' she chided. 'I'm very much afraid she will expect it to continue.'

He merely laughed, and at that moment Alexander came into the room and Sophia ran forward to embrace him.

'We didn't see you arrive,' she said.

'We were too dazzled by your sister's bracelet,' her grandmother commented dryly. 'Tonight is the first night we are dining as a family. Tomorrow the house will be filled with wedding guests.'

'Did you say Athena was coming?' Alexander asked.

'Why yes, with a man who is an old friend of hers.'

Sophia looked up at him slyly.

'We asked her to bring Selene, but she said Selene was staying with her grandmother, and she would bring Jonathan instead.'

Alexander made no comment.

There would be girls he knew at the wedding, girls he had known for years, He'd taken them to the theatre and to balls, danced with them in nightclubs, sailed with them off Capri and Sicily, even embarked on mild flirtations with one or two of them but none of it had been meaningful.

Alexander was popular with the people of his generation. He was invariably sincere. He didn't say things that were untrue merely because he thought they were things his listeners wanted to hear. He was rich, handsome, and of a serious disposition, and unknown to him most women found him entirely charming.

When he married, it would be to some girl who appealed to him for her sensitivity, her honesty; She would be a woman who could look beyond the material advantages he would give her. Of all the women he knew, he had never really found such a woman. They were all of a kind, they lived in his world, were aware of his affluence, and none of them thought too deeply.

Cassie had been different because she'd been English, a newcomer to his world, but Cassie too had been predictable. Cassie thought she had loved him, and with him all the advantages that went with him and which Cassie craved. Cassie was very like his sister, and things he tolerated in his sister he could never have tolerated in a wife.

On the day before Sophia's wedding the house and gardens were crowded with people. Kevin's family from Boston had brought many of their friends. Even now, as he looked across the terrace, he could see Athena and her escort in conversation with his grandmother and Kevin's mother. They were in good spirits, although on the evening before, when he had taken Athena's hand in his, he was aware of the remembered pain in her eyes.

At that moment her thoughts were all on Cassie and Athena believed his pain was as deep as her own. It had never entered her head that he hadn't loved Cassie.

She introduced him to Jonathan and Alexander sensed the older man's pride in his companion. He loved her, and Athena was as light-hearted about his love as Cassie would have been about the love in her life.

Sophia looked totally enchanting, floating among her guests in gold lamé and chiffon, her auburn hair a shining halo as it fell onto her shoulders, the flash of diamonds in her ears and around her throat. His grandmother too was decked in her jewellery which vied with the dark-blue gown she was wearing.

A handsome woman still, she surveyed the room with her fine grey eyes, her back stiff and erect in her high-backed chair, her slender feet encased in dark-grey high-heeled shoes. At that moment Alexander found himself remembering his mother. She, too, had been very lovely and he remembered the last time he had seen her, waving to her from Marco's yacht as it carried him away from the island and back to school.

He was remembering her words. 'I'll soon be seeing you again Alex, just a few weeks, and you'll be coming to my wedding.'

Athena's opportunity to speak with Alexander came later in the evening, when all the different groups of people had gravitated to their own kind. He approached her with a warm smile and she said quickly, 'Oh, Alex, I do so want to have a quiet word with you and it was impossible earlier.'

'You sound very serious, Athena.'

'It's about Selene. You are still intending going to the island?'

For a moment he stared at her curiously, then she hurried to say, 'Selene has made up her mind that she's going to reopen her father's studio and the villa. Nobody's been there for years, Cassie always stayed with Sophia. I don't think she even opened the door of the other place. Now Selene's got it into her head that she wants to take up where her father was forced by tragedy to leave off. I don't think it's entirely healthy.'

'Because of what happened to her father and to Cassie? It's understandable that you should be worried, Athena, but surely they can have been nothing more than tragic accidents?'

'I'm sure you're right. Will you be going back to the island?'

'Of course. Nothing that has happened will stop me.'

'Then will you please keep an eye on Selene?'

'When does she intend to go there?'

'I'm not sure, but soon. She's had a teaching job for a short while. Now it's finished and she's anxious to start painting. She'll be good at it. I've seen some of her work and she's hoping tourists will perhaps remember her father and see some of his talent in her.'

'I'll gladly help her in any way I can, Athena.'

'Thank you so much, Alex. That really is a weight off my mind just to know that there is somebody keeping an eye on her.'

It was later in the evening when Sophia said to him, 'You were in very earnest conversation with Athena, Alex. Was it about Cassie?'

'No. She told me Selene was opening up her father's studio and the villa.'

'And she asked you to watch over her?'

'Something like that.'

'I know something about the spell of the island, Alexander. The sea and the moonlight, the scent of herbs and the charm of the place. I also know that Selene has a man friend she met at the Slade, an artist. Athena's met him, there's nothing serious, but I thought you should know.'

'Why?'

'Because this is nothing to do with the fairy-story Cassie told you. It was simply the friendship between two young people thrown together in at atmosphere of working in the same field.'

'And I can tell you, Sophia, that none of it has anything to do with me. Athena has simply asked me to make sure she is settled in and happy on the island. Understandable, I think, in view of what happened to her father and her cousin.'

'I do agree, darling. I'm so glad you see it like that.'

After a brief smile she left him and he watched her walking away with a wry smile on his face.

Chapter Thirty-Two

Elizabeth Sheldon stood in the window of Selene's bedroom watching her granddaughter walking down the road. She had sent her out on an errand, an unnecessary errand, but Selene was packing her suitcase and Elizabeth was more than curious.

'I'm sorry, love,' she'd said, 'but the library books are overdue and I really don't feel too well this morning. Would you mind taking them back for us?'

Selene had not minded and Elizabeth had been

quick to say, 'I'll tidy your room while you've gone, and then perhaps I can help you to pack.'

'There's no need, Granny, I've almost finished.'

Now, when Elizabeth surveyed the empty wardrobe and half-empty drawers, she shook her head ruefully. In the suitcase were cotton skirts and silk dresses. She took them out and held them up for inspection then refolded them. Only two dresses she had not seen before and neither of them were dresses she would have chosen. Athena, she thought acidly. They were beautiful, chiffon and intricately pleated, the sort of dresses she'd seen on films and television. Where did Selene expect to wear them on an island Moira had described as very quiet?

Left in the drawer were woollies and warm winter underwear. In the wardrobe only tweed skirts and one winter coat was left hanging.

After making sure that the dresses were put back in the suitcase exactly as she had found them, she started to tidy up the room, folding tissue paper, straightening bedclothes, dusting under ornaments. It was then that she picked up a small booklet which was lying on top of the dressing table, turning it over curiously, dumbfounded to discover it was a driving licence in the name of Selene Corwen. Weakly, she sat down on the nearest chair.

Selene had never told them that she could drive, that she had taken a driving test, but here was the obvious proof. Oh, but Selene was devious, not a bit like her mother. Moira would never have kept something like that from them. Moira had never wanted to learn how to drive.

Angrily she rushed out of the room and down the stairs. Her husband was in the garage messing with his car, but he was instantly aware of her enraged face as she thrust the driving licence into his hands.

'Look at that,' she cried. 'Did you know she could drive?'

'No. Most young women want to drive these days.'

'But did she tell you? She knew we wouldn't like it. This is Athena's doing. Cassie drove, so she encouraged Selene to drive too.'

'You don't know that, Elizabeth. Why put everything at Athena's door?'

'I know what she's like.'

'But do you? Neither of us knows Athena very well.'

'Well, if it wasn't Athena, who was it? That boy she was knocking around with, and in that disreputable car of his? I'm furious Arthur, and you should be too.'

'Elizabeth, we have to learn to let go. Selene's a young woman with a mind of her own. She's not Moira, she'll never be Moira. Tomorrow she's going away, surely we don't want her to go with bad feeling between us?'

'Oh, Arthur, you've never tried as much as me with her. She's not the girl I wanted her to be.'

He put his arm round her shoulders and looked down at her with a strange pity in his eyes.

'Elizabeth, you wanted her to stay close to us, to live in the same town, take up a job you approved of, marry a local boy you liked, watch us grow old. It was never going to be like that. I saw it years ago – you never accepted it.'

'And now she's going out of our lives for good.'

'Of course, she isn't. We'll always be here for her. She knows that and she'll come back whenever it's possible to see us.'

'She could marry some Greek, some man she meets on the island, somebody we'll never understand. He probably won't even speak the same language.'

'Now you're marrying her off before she's even left the house. Here, put this back where you found it. Don't let her think you've been prying.'

Selene sensed the hidden tension for the rest of the day and couldn't understand why it was there. She finished her packing and it was only when she was placing the driving licence in her handbag that she stared at it stupidly. Suppose her grandmother had found it when she tidied the room?

She had never told them she could drive, simply because she knew they would disapprove and worry, particularly her grandmother. Making up her mind quickly, she joined them in the living room, aware that the conversation they were having had ceased instantly when she entered.

'Finished packing, love?' her grandfather asked.

'Yes. I've left all the clothes I'm not likely to need on the island, mostly clothes for English weather.'

'So you'll be coming back to us then?' he said with a wry smile.

'Oh Grandy. How can you think I wouldn't?

I'm not even sure that what I'm doing will be successful.'

Her grandmother's face was set in rigid lines of antipathy, and handing her grandfather the driving licence she said, 'That's another surprise I have for you, Grandy. I passed my driving test in London. I thought it would please you. I passed first time.'

'Who taught you?' her grandmother snapped, 'That boy in that awful car?'

'No Granny. I went to a driving school. Larry would never let me drive his car, it was too precious.'

'What, that awful thing?'

'Yes. It wasn't awful to Larry – it was the most wonderful thing he possessed.'

'I suppose Athena encouraged you to drive?'

'No, but she was delighted when I passed my test. I decided on my own, I am old enough to make such decisions.'

Their eyes met and locked, and as she watched the warm colour covering her grandmother's cheeks they both knew that from that moment on Elizabeth would have to accept that so far and no further would her opinions matter in the younger woman's life.

They both accompanied her to the local airport the next morning and stood staring through the large windows watching her board the shuttle for Heathrow.

They had driven largely in silence. Selene sat in the front seat next to her grandfather, the conversation was spasmodic, and she could feel her grandmother's many hurts as the car ate up the miles. She did not want to hurt either of them, but surely they must see that this was her life? She had to make the most of it.

She embraced them both, aware of the tears in their eyes, and as she stepped out across the tarmac she looked up and waved to them.

She would come back, probably for the winter when the tourists had gone, and she hoped there would be so much to tell them. A success story so that they could be proud of her, but sadly she didn't think it would be enough. It didn't make her like her mother, it didn't bring their little girl back to them: nothing she could ever do would be able to do that.

Settled in the plane she opened up the two letters she had received that morning, the first from Athena to wish her well, the second from Larry. Larry's was brash and good-humoured, concerned with his exhibition and enclosing cuttings that here was an up-and-coming young artist with an original, if somewhat flamboyant, style. She smiled. It was so typical of Larry, so obsessed with his own life he showed little concern for what she was doing with hers.

He ended his letter with the words, 'I'll be in the big time darling, but I promise to spare you several thoughts while you're painting your pretty pictures for holidaymakers.' He made her future sound silly and banal, but that was Larry, cocksure about his own future, predictably scathing about hers.

What a good thing it was that she had never loved him. She felt no sense of guilt in leaving him.

Her grandparents drove back to their home in silence. Arthur reached over and covered his wife's hand with his own. 'Don't fret love. Come the winter and she'll be back.'

'We don't know that, Arthur.'

'Well, of course we do. Do you want to call at Norah's, she'll be wanting to know if she got off all right.'

'No she won't. She's always been difficult, didn't get on with Moira, thought even less of her daughter.'

'Well, she was always like that even as a child, caustic and sassy, too clever for her own boots.'

'But she's done well Arthur. She went to university and got a good degree. She's the deputy head now, we should be proud of her.'

'And we are, love. Perhaps we made too much of one and not enough of the other.'

His wife's expression was sad, and he knew she was remembering Moira. None of it had worked out as Elizabeth had thought it would, and his thoughts turned to Selene's father. He had liked Mervyn but had either of them ever really known him. How Moira had wanted him. That schoolgirl crush for her art teacher had never gone away, but Moira too had made the mistake of trying to mould him into something he wasn't, just as Elizabeth had tried to mould his daughter.

By the time they reached Norah's house the children were coming out of school and they saw her marching down the road, looking neither to right nor left, while the pupils surrounding her maintained an exemplary decorum.

'Hello love,' her father greeted her. 'We thought we'd just call to tell you that Selene got off all right, she'll be on her way to Rhodes now.'

'Did she tell you she'd passed her driving test?' Elizabeth demanded.

'Leave it, love,' said Arthur.

'Well, did she?' his wife insisted.

'No, why should she! We never talked much about cars, or anything else for that matter,' Norah said shortly.

'I found her driving certificate. She went to some driving school in London.'

'I thought that boy would have taught her to drive in that wretched thing he drove.'

'Well no, she'd more sense than that.'

'She's buying a car then?'

'We don't know. Surely she's more sense than to drive on the island, particularly after the way her father died?'

'I'm about to make a cup of tea, would you like one?'

'Well yes, that would be very nice. Why don't you come round for Sunday lunch like you used to? We'd be glad to see you, I'll feel I've nobody to cook for now that Selene's gone.'

'Oh come on Mum. She was hardly ever here of late. Surely you got accustomed to her being away?'

'Well yes, we did, but when she came home, it was just as if she'd never been away.'

Norah's expression was cynical and her father wished Elizabeth would change the subject. With that in mind he said, 'I've heard rumours that there's a headship going at that new school in Darnsbury.'

Norah smiled. 'They've found somebody, Dad, and I wouldn't have been interested.'

'Whyever not?'

'Because it's a way off and unlike some people I don't drive. I'm happy where I am. If Miss Jarvis decides to go, I might just get a look in.'

'You should, love, if anybody deserves it, you do.'

'It doesn't always work out like that, unfortunately.'

She was busy setting out cups and saucers and her mother went to put the kettle on. Both husband and daughter looked at her in surprise when she said, 'I wish you'd come back home to live Norah. I don't like you being here on your own, working at the school, doing all your own housework and cooking.'

'I have Mrs Pearson, Mum.'

'I know, but it's not like being at home, is it?'

In Norah's eyes Arthur read cynicism and desperation. His wife had lost Selene, she wanted Norah back. Norah was not going back, and firmly she said, 'Mum, this is my home, I know you don't think it's much and I'm not in the least houseproud. I don't spend a small fortune on cushions, curtains and carpets, but it is my place where I can do exactly what I want.'

'You could do what you want with us.'

'No Mum, I couldn't. Don't you remember? I had my formative years with you, and we didn't always hit it off.'

'Well of course we did. Every family has its

disagreements, we were no different from all the others.'

'Mum, I'm settled here.'

'I'd like you to get married.'

'Why, for heaven's sake? There's nobody I want to marry. Perhaps one day, if I can find somebody who thinks like I do, is prepared to put up with me, then I might think of marriage. At the moment I'm happy in my home and with my job. I want it to stay like this.'

'I worry about you.'

'Mum, in all the years when you had Selene and you thought she was going to grow up like Moira, you wouldn't have wanted me home, now she's gone and you want another replacement. Well, I would never be a replacement. Ask Dad, he'll tell you it will just be like old times when we argued about everything under the sun because I wasn't like Moira.'

'It wasn't like that.'

'It was. Now come and have your tea. I've only biscuits. I don't bake.'

'I do. Next time we come round I'll bring scones and simnel cake. We thought we'd go to the cinema tonight, why don't you come with us.'

'See those books, Mum, that is homework I have to mark. My job doesn't finish at four o'clock. It'll go on long after midnight.'

'You must get some time off.'

'Well, I'm not in school on Saturday morning, but I am on the hockey field refereeing the sixth-form hockey match against St Celia's.'

'It's too much for anybody.'

Arthur was pleased when it was time for them

to leave. He loved his daughter in spite of her cussedness, but the mere thought of having her back to live with them was unthinkable. Elizabeth must be out of her head to suggest it.

He was only half listening to her as she went on about Norah doing too much for her school and its pupils, and early in the evening he heard her pottering about Selene's room, opening and shutting drawers, or standing forlornly staring out of the window.

Selene was spending her first night in Rhodes having missed the last ferry to the island. She found accommodation in a small unpretentious hotel near the harbour and from her bedroom window she could gaze down on the scene of young couples strolling arm in arm, while laughing children streaked along the harbour wall. She would like to have explored but it was difficult until she became more familiar with the place and she had already made up her mind to take the early ferry to the island.

She was aware of a strange and heady excitement and as she stood at the window, it seemed to Selene that her father was suddenly very close. In her childhood and all the years she had lived under her grandparents' roof it had always been her mother, but now in the soft balmy moonlight, with the scent of herbs drifting in through the open window she could think of her father. These islands he had loved. It was here he had really discovered himself, painted the pictures people had wanted to buy, become known, and if in the end he had met his untimely death here, the past mattered, because it had shaped her future.

She refused to face the fact that she could be disappointed, that, like her mother, she would find nothing to love on the island, that in a very short time also like her mother she would be yearning for home.

She wouldn't go back without giving it a good try. She wouldn't have them say, 'I told you so. Your mother hated every moment of it.'

Selene was conspicuous among the local people who were waiting to board the first ferry out of Rhodes harbour the following morning. They stood with their goats and crates of chickens. Round-eyed children staring at this pale-skinned golden-haired girl who smiled at them warmly so that the men gallantly helped her with her luggage and speculated amongst themselves as to why a stranger should be sailing to the island long before the holiday season had started.

All they could do was exchange smiles. She didn't know their language and they knew little of hers. She stood apart as they neared the island, her eyes eagerly searching the sweep of the hills and the meandering road beyond the jetty.

Again they helped her with her belongings as she stood uncertainly watching them walking towards the cluster of buildings she could see and the squat church tower. A young man picked up her suitcase cheerfully while she carried her sketching material. She smiled at him shyly, 'Do you speak any English?' she asked.

He smiled showing white, even teeth. 'Some,' he replied.

'I need to find the garage. A taxi.'

He grinned and pointed across the road to where she could see a shed and a row of disreputable cars.

She smiled. 'Thank you. It is early, will there by anybody there?'

He shrugged his shoulders, and without another word he marched across the road towards the garage and there was nothing for her to do but follow. Placing her suitcase on the ground he disappeared inside the building, emerging seconds later with a boy of about sixteen. Then with another wide grin he left them together.

The boy looked at her curiously and she smiled. 'Do you speak English?' she asked.

'A little.'

'I need a taxi to take me to the villa.'

'I go for my father.'

He left her and she went to stand where she could gaze up the hill to where Athena had told her she would find the villa. She turned, when a man came out of the garage, a tall muscular man with iron-grey hair a wide moustache.

Demetrius stared at her curiously. He would have known her if he had met her on a crowded street anywhere in the world. It was as if her mother had walked out of the past and into the present, but what was this beautiful smiling girl doing on an island that had brought nothing but tragedy into so many lives?

'Are you Mr Artos?' she asked.

'No. He retired, I am Demetrius.'

'Of course, Athena spoke of you. Is there someone who could take me to the villa?'

'The large villa?'

'No, the small one.'

'You are coming to live here?'

'Yes. And to work here in my father's studio. I suppose it is still here?'

He nodded. 'I take you to the villa and show you the studio, it is not far. How long you stay here?'

'That depends on how many pictures I can sell.'

For the first time he smiled. 'Your father paint many fine pictures and he sell many. It too early for tourists.'

'Yes I know. I hope to have some pictures ready for when they arrive.'

'Come, I carry your case. My son will take the other.'

The taxi was an old one but it was comfortable and he drove slowly, pointing out the street market that was just coming to life and the little church on the hillside, then he stopped the taxi and pointed to a wooden building with large, shuttered windows.

'That the studio. You have key, the priest has one.'

'There will be a key in the villa I think.'

He nodded. Through the driving mirror he could see her leaning forward eagerly with her eyes scanning the road ahead. It was just as Athena had told her, the calm azure sea, the golden sand and the wide sweep of the bay. Demetrius pointed through his open window to where a large white villa stood on the hillside, and jutting out behind the gardens she could see the white summerhouse where her father had painted his portrait of Alexander's father.

It was all coming to life for her, and in the next moment he had brought the taxi to a stop outside a wrought-iron gate and a path that led to a small white villa through an overgrown garden.

They stood together looking through the open gate and Demetrius said gently, 'Nobody live here for many years, not since your father died. The garden is sad, you will need help.'

She nodded. 'Demetrius, I need a small car. Will you be able to help me find one?'

'Of course.'

She was opening her purse to pay him for the taxi ride, but he shook his head gravely, 'See me tomorrow, I will have a car for you to look at then.'

He carried her luggage to the front door and waited while she found her key, then he left her.

Chapter Thirty-Three

She stood in the tiny living room staring around her at the white-washed walls and the wide window-ledges on which stood empty plantpots. A thin film of dust covered the furniture and there was a musty smell indicative of a place that had not been occupied for many, many years.

She was aware of a feeling of excitement as she gazed around her. Why had her mother hated it so? Already she was loving the long chintz-covered couch and the limed oak table on the faded rug set before the empty firegrate. The villa had a charm about it. Above the mantelpiece was a painting of a blue cloud-scudded sky and wide sweeping cliffs, a sea that boiled and churned and she went to look at her father's signature. Where had he painted it? Surely not on this island that seemed undramatic and gentle.

She moved into the kitchen, opening and shutting drawers and cupboards, handling the china and pottery her father had used, the pans and cooking utensils her parents had known, then she went upstairs and into the large bedroom overlooking the sea.

The wardrobe was empty, cleared out by Athena years ago when she gave her father's clothes to the village priest for distribution among his flock. Surely something should remain of her parents? This was a room they had slept in, made love in, she had been conceived in this room. Now it stared back at her like an empty shell, devoid of feeling.

She carried her suitcase upstairs and started to unpack her clothes, hanging them in the wardrobe, placing them in the drawers. As she straightened them out, her fingers made contact with something at the back of the top drawer and she reached in to see what it was. She stared at it in disbelief. How had Athena overlooked this, a photograph of her mother, blonde and beautiful, standing in the garden with another woman, also beautiful, but a woman with long dark hair and a gay smiling face. She knew immediately who the woman was with a face that reminded her poignantly of Alexander's.

She was remembering her name, Leonora.

They had been friends then, her mother and Leonora. Her fingers probed again at the back of the drawer, bringing out more photographs in a large brown envelope and she sat on the edge of the bed and took them out curiously.

There was one of a priest with a long white beard and long white hair, sitting in the garden with a glass of wine on the small table beside his chair. Another of an elderly man sitting in the same place, and turning it over she read, Uncle Bertram aged sixty-two.

There were others of her mother standing on the headland gazing pensively out to sea, in the garden, curled up in a corner of the settee, and then a larger one of her father and Leonora laughing up at him while he gazed down at her adoringly.

She could feel her hands trembling as she laid the photograph down on the bed. Had her mother seen this photograph or had her mother already returned to England? Were they two lonely people, shoulders for each other to cry on, searching for something they had both lost? At the time that photograph was taken, they were happy, living for the moment, unaware of the tragedy waiting for them.

There were other photographs of Alexander and Sophia streaking across the cliffs, a beautiful dark little girl and a boy with a strangely remote grown-up expression in his dark eyes.

She must not fall in love with Alexander. He had loved Cassie and she was not looking for a shoulder to cry on. She replaced the photographs in the envelope and put them back in the drawer.

One day she'd look at them again but for now she had to find somebody to help with the garden and see Demetrius about her car. He'd seemed nice and he'd recognised her. People had always told her that she was exactly like her mother in appearance. There the likeness had ended.

She would have to get help. The water was turned off and the electricity. She only knew Demetrius but he might be able to tell her what she should do.

Demetrius was a tower of strength. He said his wife would find a woman who would help in the house and he had a man who would probably do the garden, somebody who worked at the garage during the holiday season when there was more work to do.

In the early evening the village priest appeared, smiling and kind, offering whatever help she needed, welcoming her to the village. Her spirits lifted. How could they ever say there was something sinister on an island where the people were so friendly and willing to befriend her?

That night she wrote to her grandparents and to Athena telling them all that had happened since she arrived. They needed to be told that there was no danger for her here, that she was as safe as she would have been at home, safer she felt sure.

Athena read her letter with something approaching relief, her grandparents rather less so.

'It's early days yet,' Elizabeth said dourly. 'It'll all come later.'

'Don't be so pessimistic, love,' her husband encouraged her. 'You're busy looking for trouble where none exists.'

On the island Selene was busy opening her father's studio. The floors were swept and the windows cleaned. She discovered oil paints that had dried beyond repair, but she found stacks of canvasses which were as good as new and a hoard of brushes that responded to careful cleaning.

Demetrius was as good as his word. He had found her an old secondhand car, that had done very few miles and was in good condition.

The garden at the villa was improving under the energies of the man who appeared on her doorstep several days after she arrived. He looked about fifty and he was tall, muscular and very handsome. He smiled at her showing white even teeth and he was deeply tanned. He also spoke commendable English and when she asked how much he would charge her for gardening he told her to pay Demetrius who was paying his wages. His name was Paulus.

He was a veritable treasure. Not averse to knocking nails in walls to hang pictures, oiling rusted hinges and any other odd jobs around the house and garden. In turn she made him copious cups of coffee and the mere fact of having him around made her feel very secure.

Every morning she went down to the studio and it was here she did most of her painting from sketches she had done on the cliff paths and the garden.

She was pleased with her work and the villagers came to watch her, nodding their approval. The older people remembered her father, but they spoke very little English and it was left to the priest to tell her what they had said.

Easter was approaching and she now had several finished pictures hanging on the studio walls. The priest voiced his approval and she asked anxiously, 'Do you think they will want to buy any of them? I'm probably nothing like as good as my father.'

'But you are,' he encouraged her. 'After Easter the ferries will bring people every day, they will tell each other and more people will come. In time you will be so busy painting your pictures, you will have time for nothing else.'

It was a few days before Easter when she left the studio to shop at the market stalls and when she returned she stood for a moment looking at an open door she could swear she had closed behind her. Gingerly, she opened the door to look inside. Then she saw him. Alexander was standing in the centre of the room, staring up at the paintings on the walls.

He turned to smile at her, and she could feel the sudden fluttering of her heart.

'You have been busy Selene. All these in just a few weeks?'

'Yes. Are they any good, do you think?'

'They're very good. I'm going to be your first customer and buy this one.'

'Oh, but really, there's no need. I'll do better ones than that.'

'But this is the one I want. You painted it from the hillside?'

'Yes, one very beautiful morning.'

'It's the same view I get from our summer-house.'

'Athena told me my father had painted from your summerhouse.'

'Yes. Tomorrow you must come up to the villa and I'll take you round the villa, the gardens and the summerhouse. If you want to paint there, don't hesitate to come up.'

'Thank you Alexander. Everybody has been so kind to me. I have a girl who comes to clean the villa and a gardener who does all sorts of jobs for me. I can't believe how everything has fallen into place.'

'How did you find a gardener? Who is he?'

'Demetrius found him for me.'

'Oh well, in that case I'm sure he's everything he should be. And the girl?'

'Demetrius's niece.'

'He's been kind to you.'

'Have you only arrived this morning?'

'Yes. I'm now going to collect my car and open up the villa. Do you promise to visit me in the morning?'

'Yes of course. Thank you Alexander.'

With a smile he left her, and she stood in the doorway watching him walk towards the garage. She felt strangely disturbed by his visit. She had known him for such a little time, and yet she had remembered every expression on his cool handsome face, a face that could come suddenly alive when he smiled.

He was chatting to Demetrius outside the garage, leaning nonchalantly against a long white car: tall, graceful and upper crust, the sort of man Larry would have jeered at and her grandparents be dumbfounded by.

She was thinking about all the barriers that divided them and the bonds that united them, the separations that were inevitable, the hungers that could never be.

However much Alexander attracted her, however near she came to loving him, he was not for her. All they had in common was an island in the Aegean Sea and the history of parents who may or may not have been in love.

She would let him show her his villa and the gardens that covered the cliff top, but she would keep her feet firmly on the ground, remembering that he had loved Cassie and was probably still grieving for her.

In spite of all her feelings, however, she fell in love instantly with the villa and its gardens. She looked through the windows at views that enchanted her, and she looked at the picture Mervyn had painted of Alexander's father where he sat in the summerhouse gazing out to sea.

In the salon she stared up at the large portrait of Leonora gazing serenely back at her, her face exquisite, framed by shining blue-black hair, her long, tapered fingers holding a long-stemmed pink rose against the cream satin of her gown.

'She's very beautiful,' she breathed.

'Yes. My mother was beautiful.'

'You must have loved her very much. I wish I'd known my mother.'

'She too was very beautiful.'

'Yes. I think so.'

'You must see the view from the summerhouse.'

They walked slowly through the gardens and

she couldn't help noticing how the large villa dwarfed the smaller one beneath it. Sensing her thoughts, Alexander said, 'It isn't the size of the place Selene. It's the joy one finds there. Your father was very fond of his villa, he did his very best work there.'

Sheltered from the sharp breeze that blew across the headland the summerhouse was charming and she looked around from every window with delighted acceptance that she would paint beautiful pictures from these windows, but when she turned round, she found Alexander staring down towards the sea, a strange, haunted expression on his face.

She went to stand beside him and, after a few minutes, in a small voice asked, 'Is that where it happened?'

He nodded.

Below, she could see the boathouse and the tiny jetty, then her eyes followed the rocks and the cliffs where they jutted out into the sea.

Alexander pointed towards them. 'The white boat was simply moving very slowly round the headland and there, near the shore, Cassie and Nino were frolicking noisily. I could hear their laughter. Nino was in the boat, Cassie was on water skis. Suddenly the white boat gathered speed and headed directly for them. They had no chance.'

'Didn't the boat stop?'

'No.'

'Surely, whoever was steering her must have known he'd hit something?'

'Sophia loved it here. But she will never come

here again. She believes she was the target, not Cassie.'

Selene looked at him in stunned silence, and meeting her eyes Alexander said, 'She may be right. What had Cassie to do with terrible things that happened in my mother's past? If the crime was one of revenge, why not Sophia or me?'

'Did they never find the boat?'

'No. They made good their escape, and there are so many harbours, so many islands.'

'My father was killed here too.'

There was compassion in his eyes as he looked down at her. 'I know, and that must have been an accident, Selene, on a dark windy night on a wet road.'

'Aren't you afraid, Alexander?'

'No. I am watchful, but nothing of the past has anything to do with you, Selene. I am here, and you are well protected by your gardener.'

She smiled. 'Do you miss Cassie dreadfully, will you ever get over her?'

His expression was grave.

'I miss her humour, she was great fun, but I was not in love with her. Given time, I think that Cassie and I would have gone our separate ways.'

She couldn't believe what she was hearing. Cassie had believed he loved her, Athena had believed it, and Sophia, so when had it changed? He was gazing gravely into her eyes, and with a little shake of his head he said, 'I didn't trifle with her affections. Cassie wanted it but two people have to want it, if it is to be a success. Given time, she would have realised that we were not right for each other.'

'She would have been unhappy about that.'

'Perhaps. Cassie was a girl who was accustomed to flirting with life, as you must know. She would have picked up the pieces and recovered quicker than a more sensitive woman.'

'Does Athena know that you didn't love her?'

'No. If she had laboured the subject, I would have had to tell her, but fortunately she avoided the issue. There was a lot of Athena in Cassie.'

'Yes. Athena will want to believe that you were in love with Cassie.'

'I suppose you are spending your afternoon at the studio?'

'Yes. I have a picture to finish.'

'Then will you have dinner with me this evening, either here or at a small taverna on the hillside? I have to make enquiries to see if they are open for the start of the season. If not, we will dine here.'

'Thank you Alexander, I would like that.'

They sauntered back to the villa in companionable silence and he walked back down the hill with her until they reached the gate of the villa below. Paulus was busily working in the garden, and they heard him singing in a musical baritone.

She looked up into Alexander's face. He was standing strangely alert, his eyes trained on the gardener, and with a smile Selene said, 'You surely don't suspect my gardener of dangerous designs on you?'

He smiled. 'Of course not. I'll call for you around eight.' With a short nod of his head he left her and for several minutes she watched him striding up the hillside before she entered the garden. Paulus looked up with a smile and she said brightly, 'I'll make coffee Paulus, I'll bring it out to you.'

She went immediately into the kitchen but was surprised when she came out to find Paulus standing in the living room looking at the photograph in his hands. She put the coffee down on the table top and went to stand beside him and he turned the photograph towards her. It was the picture of her mother and Leonora, and when she took it from him he reached out for the other one of Leonora and her father.

He was smiling, and she said hurriedly. 'Do you know any of them?'

He shook his head.

'My mother, the blonde lady.'

'You like her.'

'Yes, so I've been told.'

'Your father?'

'Yes.'

'And the other?'

'A friend, the lady from the other villa.'

'A lady with much money, fast car, children?'

'Yes. Here is your coffee, Paulus. We heard you singing, you have a nice voice.'

He shrugged his shoulders. 'I like to sing. I not come tomorrow, Demetrius has work for me to do, I come the next day, all right?'

'Yes of course. Whenever Demetrius can spare you.'

He picked up the coffee and with a bright smile took it out into the garden.

Selene stared down at the two photographs. In

some strange way they troubled her. She sensed the secrets behind them, her mother's unhappiness with the island and her life on it, her father's commitment to stay on it, and Leonora, beautiful, rich, the two of them as divided from each other as she was from Alexander. Had they been lovers in spite of their life in different worlds? Or had they taken what was on offer and forgotten the rest?

In the days that followed she saw Alexander frequently. They dined together and swam together. He took her sailing and with him she discovered more of the island, but through it all she sensed a withdrawal.

She knew now that she was desperately in love with him, and when his eyes kindled when he looked at her she tried to tell herself it was reciprocated, and yet his attitude was always circumspect, even when they were alone in the villa or the garden, and, on leaving her, the most he permitted himself was a swift brush of his lips on her hand or against her cheek.

Then he came into the studio one morning to tell her he had to return to Rome, and he had no idea when he would be back.

Hurt, she turned away so that she was unable to see the anxiety in his eyes.

'When are you going?' she asked.

'This afternoon. My plane leaves in the early evening.'

She made herself meet his quiet gaze. 'Oh well, I'll probably still be here when you get back,' she said.

'The pictures are selling well, Selene. I'm sure

you have enough work to keep you here for many months.'

Months, he'd said. Was that how long he intended to be away?

She responded to his smile, then she watched him walking away towards the garage, probably to ask Demetrius to look after his car.

She felt aggravated, annoyed with him, and yet she had no right to be annoyed with him. She wasn't like Cassie who had expected too much from him. She had watched Cassie's machinations, her arm ecstatically through his, the flamboyant embraces, the wide-eyed adoration, she tried to think back on how Alexander had responded.

The resentment within her grew. He wasn't like Larry but he was every bit as bad, concerned with himself and only himself. Then the unfairness of the criticism stung her into realising its stupidity. Alexander did not belong to her, he owed her nothing.

The morning ferry was arriving and with it more passengers than usual. She watched them walking along the jetty towards the harbour wall before she was aware that most of them were heading towards the studio.

Word was getting around. Some of them were coming because they liked her work, others because they remembered her father and saw something of him in her paintings.

The priest had shown her the small cemetery where her father was buried and she'd gone often to look at his grave. Ever since she was a child she'd gone with her grandparents to look at her mother's grave and taken flowers and her Granny had wept a little, pointing out to Selene that her mother was only twenty when she'd died.

Her father had been thirty-two, still too young and buried so far from home. She'd placed her flowers gently against the unpretentious headstone and silently asked his forgiveness for the lost years.

Chapter Thirty-Four

Demetrius was in earnest conversation with the man who worked on Selene's garden but they both turned when Alexander approached them.

'I shall be returning to Rome this evening, Demetrius,' Alexander said casually, 'I'm not sure when I'll be back but I've decided to leave the car in the garage. I haven't much luggage so I can walk down to the ferry.'

'You don't require the taxi?'

'No. I'm not sure which ferry I shall take. It depends on how soon I can get away.'

The other man smiled toothily and turned away, then hesitating he said, 'Are you going alone, sir?'

Alexander looked at him coolly. 'Yes. Does that surprise you?'

'No no. I was only concerned with my work at the villa.' He turned quickly away and walked along the road.

Meeting Demetrius's eyes, Alexander asked, 'I

take it there isn't much work at the garage for him. He seems happy enough with his gardening.'

'Oh yes, he comes, he goes. Artos employed him one year and he came every year after. Sometimes he works on the boats, if we have work here he works for me, otherwise he takes on any job he can find. He works well.'

'Yes. Miss Corwen seems satisfied with him.'

'Will your servants be remaining in the villa, sir?'

'No. They left this morning to join their daughter in Rhodes for a few days. I shall close the villa up myself when I leave.'

'Nothing changes on the island, sir. It will be here waiting for you when you return.'

Alexander nodded, and with a brief smile turned and walked away.

He could see Paulus at work in the garden of Selene's villa, but he walked on up the road, his thoughts concerned with other things.

He had packed a small suitcase which stood in the hall, but he went into the study and stood for a while looking through the window from where he could see down the road towards the village. He surmised that most of the people who had disembarked from the ferry were now clustered inside Selene's studio. At least none of them had ventured along the cliff paths.

He opened a drawer in the small walnut bureau and stood looking down at the button he had taken out of the drawer. It was a brass button off a man's shirt, a workman's shirt and there was a frown on his face when he thought where he had found it.

He and Selene had been happy that night. They had dined at the new taverna in the hills and he had brought Selene back to the villa for drinks. She had talked to him about her childhood, her grandparents and Athena, and he understood that although she had been treasured and cosseted, her childhood had often been lonely and sometimes sad.

He was remembering the curve of her cheek tinged with the glow from the fire and her dark-blue eyes fringed with gold-tipped lashes, her mouth that curved deliciously when she smiled, and the fine golden hair that framed her face.

When they left the villa she had gone naturally into his arms and even as he held her against him, he had been aware of two round shining orbs in the inky darkness of the shrubbery and he had taken their embrace no further.

She had been nonplussed by him, suddenly unsure, and he had been circumspect, so circumspect that she could have had no idea of the passion she aroused in him. Their parting had been friendly but constrained, and their meetings since had hardly been more than congenial.

The following morning Alexander made it his business to look in the shrubbery in the place where he thought someone had been hiding. He scanned the ground for footprints but there had been a heavy dew in the morning and if there had been footprints they had been scraped away. It was while he looked at the ground that he saw something shining in the soil and then he saw the button, new and untarnished, and he knew that some person had stood there watching them and he found himself remembering the times he had seen his mother peering nervously in the direction of the shrubbery.

He had once asked her why, and turning to him with a bright smile, she'd said, 'It's nothing darling, I'm being fanciful, don't take any notice.' Sophia had said she was being silly, always looking for mysteries that weren't there.

Finding that button had made him make up his mind. Whoever found enjoyment in watching him from the shrubbery would find very little to see. The villa would be closed for an indefinite period, standing dark and lonely in the midst of its gardens. Whoever was interested in his movements would soon grow tired of keeping a lonely vigil, staring at an empty house.

He knew the button did not belong to one of his own gardeners. They never went into the shrubbery. For years they had allowed it to run riot while they concentrated on the ordered lawns, flower beds and pathways.

He ran lightly down the stairs and picked up his suitcase, then he let himself out locking the door behind him. He looked up casually at the shuttered windows. Several of the lamps inside the villa were on time switches that would come on at dusk, but otherwise the villa was a dead thing, like so many others on the island while they waited for the people who owned them to return.

He walked quickly in the direction of the harbour, passing the garage and Selene's studio without a glance, and to Selene watching from the window, his very aloofness troubled her aching heart. Her eyes followed his tall figure as he strolled casually along the jetty, waiting with others for the arrival of the ferry, and she waited until it became only a speck on the distant line of the sea.

She wouldn't think about him. He was going back to his own world, to the beautiful eternal city and the life in her squares and streets which he had once contemplated sharing with Cassie. He had said he hadn't loved Cassie but if not Cassie, some other woman, some woman of Rome.

She was glad that the ferry had brought over more people than usual and they crowded her studio looking at the pictures and watching her work. One man in particular seemed more interested than the rest, but although others brought pictures they had chosen to her, he came empty-handed.

He waited until there was a lull in the proceedings before approaching her with a smile, asking, 'I'm looking for a picture similar to one my friend bought many years ago from a man who used to paint here. He bought it from this studio.'

'Then he bought it from my father.'

'Really. Well the scenery was quite different from anything I see in these paintings. Perhaps it was not painted on the island.'

'I think I know the picture you are referring to. It was painted on the island from an entirely different viewpoint to any of these. I've never seen that place, I intend to go there when I have time.'

'Do you have one of your father's paintings for sale?'

'I have seen that picture, but it didn't belong to me. He painted it for a relative and I doubt if she would part with it. I have some sketches he did, if you see them perhaps you will be able to tell me if they are what you're looking for.'

'Do you have them here? I need to get back on the next ferry.'

'Yes, they're here in the cupboard. Like I said they're only rough sketches but they might just give you an idea.'

She produced the sketches and he stared down at them thoughtfully, then handing them back he said, 'Yes, this is the view I want. A rough sea and a stormy sky.' He looked out of the window ruefully. 'From the looks of the weather it seems unlikely to change.'

'Oh but I'm told that it does, and sometimes very suddenly. Anyway whether the sea is rough or not, I can use my imagination.'

He smiled. 'When will you be able to get started?'

'Perhaps next Sunday, it would mean closing the studio, but perhaps I could get Andrea to open it up for me.'

'Andrea?'

'Her mother helps out at the villa. Andrea is her oldest daughter and she speaks commendable English. She attends church in the morning but I'm sure she would enjoy working here in the afternoon.'

'Then will you please paint that view for me.'

'I can't guarantee that it will be as good as my father's.'

'But you have inherited his talent, I can see

that. He must have found you a very good pupil.'

'I never knew him. He died before I was born.'

'I'm sorry. Of course, I heard that there was some tragedy, an accident.'

'Yes.'

'It is brave of you to come here to live and open up his studio.'

'It is something I always wanted to do.'

'Are you here alone?'

'Yes. That doesn't bother me.'

'Is your mother still alive?'

'No. I never knew my mother either.'

There was great sympathy in his eyes, and opening his wallet he took out a card which he handed to her.

'That is my name. I am staying in Rhodes Town for two more weeks, then my wife and I are cruising round the islands. We fly back to the states from Rhodes, but as soon as we get back there I'll be in touch.'

She smiled. 'I think I met your friend in London Mr Travis, at least I met an American who bought one of my pictures at an exhibition. He said he had bought that particular view from my father.'

'What was his name?'

'I can't remember. He bought my picture from the gallery, I didn't speak to him again.'

He chuckled. 'I think I know the gentleman, elderly, silver-haired, sprightly. His name is John Predercost, we live in the same town, play golf at the same club.'

She smiled, and raising his hat he said gently, 'It really is a small world, Miss Corwen. Your father painted a picture many years ago and my friend bought it. Now here we are discussing a picture I am asking his daughter to paint.'

'I hope I shall justify your faith in me, Mr Travis.'

'You will. I am sure of it. These pictures are all very good, it's just me wanting something different.'

She felt strangely cheered by his visit. Whether Alexander had gone back to Rome or not, there were people who liked her work, would buy her pictures. She wasn't waiting around simply hoping he'd come back, she'd got work to do. She told herself that she'd got Alexander's measure. He didn't want her and she wouldn't want him. She'd make that very plain whenever he took the trouble to return.

She decided to take the sketches home with her and work on them during the evening. As she opened the garden gate she saw that Marta, Andrea's mother, was just leaving and she walked up the path to meet her.

'Everything is nice,' Marta said with a bright smile. 'I come here next Tuesday.'

'Thank you Marta. I have to go out on Sunday afternoon. I was wondering if Andrea would look after the studio for me?'

'Sell your pictures, you mean?'

'Well yes, if anybody wants to buy them.'

Marta's face was doubtful, and Selene hastened to say, 'If she would care to spend a little time with me one day she will know what is needed. Would you ask her?'

Marta nodded. 'Yes. I tell her to see you at the

studio tomorrow.'

'Thank you Marta, I really am very grateful.'

As she let herself into the villa she could see Paulus working in the garden. He raised his hand and grinned at her and she thought suddenly, Paulus would know where her father's picture had been painted from, he knew the island well.

Taking her sketches with her she went out into the garden where Paulus was leaning against the wall smoking one of the dark cheroots he favoured. Showing him the sketches she asked, 'Do you know where these were painted from, Paulus?'

He studied them carefully, then with a smile handed them back to her.

'It's a place on the way to Levitus, nothing there, only cliffs and rocks.'

'But could I paint a picture there, similar to this one?'

'Ah yes, there is a leetle path and a ledge. Your father painted from there.'

'You knew he painted there?'

'I know the place. I saw the finished picture hanging in his studio, it was very good.'

'Yes. I hope I can do as well.'

'Somebody want to buy your picture?'

'Yes, an American. How do I find this place?'

'You drive along the cliff road. It is wild and narrow. You see a tiny shrine on the hillside and opposite you can park your car. People stop there to see the view. It very beautiful no matter what the day like.'

'Thank you Paulus.'

As she turned away he asked, 'When you go?'

'Hopefully on Sunday.'

'You go alone?'

His surprise brought the warm colour into her cheeks and almost resentfully she replied, 'Of course. I don't need company when I am working.'

He grinned. 'I thought perhaps the Conte Andoineto be with you.'

'No why should he? In any case, he has returned to Rome.'

He shrugged his shoulders. 'He not stay long, I suppose he will be back?'

'Perhaps. I don't know.'

She did not miss the expression on his dark face. Was it amusement, surprise or sympathy?

Her hurt young pride wanted no sympathy from Paulus. Alexander had gone without a backward glance which showed only too well how little he valued her.

She was dismally aware of the empty villa above her. She had seen Alexander's servants depart even before he had left and he was hardly likely to return while they were away. Faint lights shone from one or two of the rooms in the darkness but she knew they were fitted with time switches. The lighted windows offered her no comfort when she knew there was only emptiness in the rooms themselves.

During the day one or two gardeners worked in the gardens but they departed in the late afternoon when their work was finished. She knew that Alexander's car stood behind the closed garage doors, and Marta remarked gently, 'The Conte has returned to Rome, he not stay long this visit.'

Selene permitted herself a tight smile.

'I remember the Conte's mother. When I married she sent me wedding present, most kind,' Marta said.

'She was very beautiful, wasn't she?'

'Ah yes. Do you know her daughter?'

'I have met her once or twice.'

'She not like her mother at all, the boy was always more like the Contessa.'

'Yes, I can see that from the portraits.'

'It was sad when the Conte died young.' For a moment it seemed that Marta was going to say more but she thought better of it, and turned away to continue with her work.

Selene wished she could ask questions, she longed to know how intensely Leonora and her father had been involved with each other. After her mother returned to England he must have been very lonely and Leonora too had been alone. Alexander would never tell her but she felt that he knew.

Late on Saturday afternoon she was busy packing a case with the things she would need for her trip to the other side of the island when a car pulled up at her gate and she turned to stare at it through the window.

A man was climbing out of the front seat and stood for a moment looking across the garden towards the sea, then he opened the gate and walked up the path.

Selene hurried to the door and stood for a moment with a questioning look in her eyes.

The man smiled. He was tall and casually

dressed, a man probably in his fifties with a cheerful open face, quick to explain his visit.

'I heard that the villa was occupied and I have to confess to being curious. I didn't know that it had been sold.'

'It hasn't. I own it.'

'Really. I'm John Hyams, my wife and I live at the other side of the hill there, I'm just here to open our villa, my wife hasn't joined me yet. You're related to Athena?'

'I'm Mervyn Corwen's daughter, Athena was his cousin.'

'Really. I never knew Mervyn had a daughter. Of course, after that terrible accident everything changed. Athena came here to close it up, and then it stayed empty. We wondered if it would ever be sold, or if anybody would ever realise it was still here and visit.'

'I've opened up the studio and I'm painting pictures.'

'That's wonderful. We did hear that Alexander was here.'

'He was, for a few days only. He's returned to Rome.'

'Really. Oh well, no doubt he'll be back but things are not the same now. We had some wonderful times in the old days. Leonora loved parties and people, she was so joyously alive. How can it be that such a terrible tragedy struck both Leonora and Mervyn down?'

'And my cousin Cassie also.'

'Great heavens yes. I'm not surprised Alexander's gone back. We were here when the accident happened and Cassie was killed and the young man badly injured. They were having such a wonderful time. We could see them in the boats or frolicking in the sea every time we drove along the cliff road. Wasn't Cassie Alexander's girl?'

'I'm not really sure. Sophia is married now and living in America.'

'And the young Italian?'

'Getting well, I think.'

'Oh well, Sophia was always a bit wild, Alexander was the serious one, a lot like his father but with his mother's looks. I hope that nursing a broken heart doesn't keep him away too long.'

Selene smiled politely.

'Can I offer you a drink?' she asked.

'No, really I must get on. I hadn't realised there was quite so much to do, you must have found it horrendous.'

'Actually no. I have a daily help and a gardener.'

'A gardener? Where did you manage to find a gardener?'

'Demetrius found him for me. He works at the garage from time to time, but they haven't much work in at the moment.'

'Oh well, I'll have a talk to Demetrius, he probably knows someone else. I'll take you up on that drink some other time if I may.'

'Yes, of course. Any time.'

'And if Alexander returns, do please tell him I'm here. My wife's joining me in June.'

'I'll tell him.'

They smiled their farewells and she waved as he drove away.

Strangely his visit had depressed her. He too had looked upon Alexander and Cassie as an item, two people who were enjoying each other's company, two people who were in love. Was that why Alexander had gone home? Because he couldn't bear to look across the gardens to the spot where Cassie had met her death? For the first time she began to feel sympathy for him. Tragedy had touched him more personally because he had known the people who had died, the mother he had adored, and Cassie, even her father he had known as a friend.

She was wrong to feel resentment towards Alexander when his tragedies had been more real. He had lost people he had known well and loved, not vague shadowy people other people had talked about in an effort to make them come alive to a lonely searching child.

That night the priest came carrying a carefully wrapped parcel containing the Grecian Urn which Athena had left in his safe keeping, and together they stood looking down at it, admiring its ageless symmetry. The artist in Selene admired its beauty and was aware of its worth, she did not know that her mother had hated it. Turning to the priest she said, 'It's been with you all these years father I want you to keep it.'

'But it is yours Selene, I have no right to it,' he protested.

'I would like you to have it for your museum in memory of my father. I think he would have liked that.'

The priest's face lit up and with a smile he said, 'It will be well cared for, and I will see to it that the gift will be acknowledged in your father's name.'

She watched him carefully wrapping the urn, his fingers caressing it lovingly and at that moment she felt that her father was very close to her, that he approved of what she had done.

Chapter Thirty-Five

Sunday morning dawned golden and bright and Selene ate an early breakfast and departed in some anticipation for her journey to the other side of the island.

All around her were the sounds of church bells but as she drove away from the village she encountered nobody on the road. The good people of the village would be wending their way to church and over the entire countryside there emanated a feeling of peace and well being. The sea was a calm azure blue, the cliff tops ablaze with tiny blue hyacinths and over it all was the smell of herbs so redolent on the island.

It seemed further than she had imagined it, but at last she came upon the tiny shrine on the hillside and opposite the grass verge where she could leave the car. Her eyes followed the narrow cliff path with some anxiety. It was steep, lined with ferns and tiny shrubs, but below she could see a small ledge where she felt sure she could set up her sketching materials.

She clambered down the path carefully, keeping her eyes firmly on the ground and not looking further than she needed to. At last she reached the ledge and was delighted to find that it cut into the rock to give a very good vantage point far larger than she had imagined.

Before her stretched the view her father had painted on a day totally unlike this one. On that day the sea had been rough, the skies stormy, while today the sea was calm, gently meandering in over the rocky bay below and the sky was an untroubled cloudless blue.

She worked tirelessly, drawing the scenery as she saw it, then using her imagination to create something infinitely more dramatic. She paused only to eat the sandwiches she had brought and drink her coffee but she was anxious to press on with her work. She did not notice the sky beginning to darken or that a chill wind was blowing through the ferns that surrounded her. It was the first rumble of thunder that made her look up in amazement while huge spots of rain fell onto her sketching pad.

Hurriedly she packed everything away in the waterproof carrier and she got to her feet to look upwards at the path she must climb. The rain was coming heavier now and water rushed and gurgled down the cliff onto the rocks below. If she stayed where she was she would be drenched and she had no idea how long the storm would last. On the other hand, the path upwards looked slippery and treacherous. She started to climb, helping herself up on all fours, occasionally hanging onto the tough shrubs for support, hampered by the package she was carrying.

She did not look down, and her climb was slow and laborious, but surely she must be reaching the top, she seemed to have been climbing for ever. She looked up, and then her heart lifted with joy at the sight of Paulus's face peering down at her from the cliff top.

She smiled, holding out her hand for him to take, and then her smile faltered at his expression. He did not reach out for her, but stood staring down at her, his eyes cold, and as she placed one hand on the cliff top he stepped forward suddenly and covered it with his foot.

She cried out in sudden pain, and he smiled, the most cruel smile she had ever seen. He continued to press on her hand, and then suddenly he was pulled backward and she almost fell down the path with the realisation that the pain had gone and that some other person had come to her rescue.

Painfully, she pulled herself over the cliff top, then she saw that two men were struggling on the ground. She could not see the other man, but she was aware of Paulus's face convulsed with rage, and then, as she looked along the cliff top, she saw Alexander's car and she knew who her rescuer was.

They were on their feet now, and in Paulus's hand there was the gleam of steel and he was lunging at Alexander and Selene cried out with fear for him. Alexander was unarmed, Paulus would kill them both, and then suddenly there was the sound of a gunshot and Paulus was sinking to his knees, his eyes wide with astonishment, and slowly he turned and slipped over the cliff top while Alexander rose to his feet and went to the edge of the cliff to stare over it.

She ran to stand beside him and she could see Paulus falling through the foliage. For one brief moment his body came to rest on the edge of the ledge where she had spent the morning sketching, then slowly it tilted over and fell with a crash onto the rocks below. Even as they looked, the sea was washing over him and all she was aware of was that Alexander's arms were around her and she was crushed against his heart.

There seemed to be police everywhere, and it was only later that they learned the shot had merely wounded him – the fall had killed him.

That evening she learned the full story.

Alexander had sailed to Rhodes on the ferry as she had thought, but that night he had hired a boatman to bring him back to the island under cover of darkness, leaving him at the jetty, below the villa.

He had stayed undetected in the villa where he could watch the activities of the people below him. He had watched Selene setting out in her car that morning for the other side of the island, and then he had seen Paulus driving one of the cars from the garage along the same road. He had followed, at first leaving his car by the roadside and watching on foot where Paulus sat in his car on the cliff top, occasionally getting out of it to look down the cliff path. Then the skies had darkened and it started to rain. They had both known that Selene would pack her things away and start the uphill climb, and while Paulus waited for her, Alexander went back to his car to bring it nearer.

Paulus had been so intent on what he was doing, he had not heard the car's engine or seen Alexander as he crept towards him. The rest she knew.

'But why did you come back? when did you suspect Paulus might harm me?' she asked.

'From that first afternoon when I heard him singing in the garden. Why does a so-called Greek sing Neopolitan love songs?'

'Why shouldn't he? I know some of them and I love them. Couldn't he have known them too.'

'One day, Selene, I'll tell you the full story. It goes back a long way.'

'But I still can't understand why you were so sure Paulus was waiting to harm me. Why should the singing of an Italian song have put you on your guard?'

'Because he sang it in faultless Italian. I wasn't sure, I only suspected. My mother loved life, she was a truly beautiful joyous woman and yet there were so many times when I saw her looking afraid, staring through the windows into the shrubbery, then I would see her wandering there, staring at the ground, quick to reassure me when I asked her what she was looking for.'

Then he showed her the button he had found, told her about the night they had stood together and he had seen the reflection of two points of light in the darkness of the shrubbery.

Suddenly he surprised her by asking, 'What did you think when I went away Selene? That I didn't care?'

'Yes, that's what I thought, but I couldn't blame

you Alexander. I was never your girl. You wouldn't have left Cassie, that's what I thought.'

'I was not with Cassie on the afternoon she died. I had not expected anybody would harm Cassie. Even now I think it was meant for Sophia, but I did not love Cassie. I stayed here to protect you, because I love you, Selene.'

She knew it was true. There was so much sincerity in his dark eyes, and as their lips clung together, she knew that she had found something that would last.

It was much later when she said, 'I must finish my picture. I promised I would paint it.'

'Then he is going to have to wait a while,' Alexander said. 'Tomorrow the newspapers will be full of today's drama. Your grandparents will read of it as well as Athena. My grandmother will want to see us.'

'We're going to Rome?'

'Yes. We're going to tell my grandmother that we are going to be married. Then I have to meet your family.'

Alexander's grandmother welcomed them warmly. Selene was the sort of girl she wanted for Alexander. Beautiful, talented, loving him truly yet never possessively. They would be good together, yet all through those heady days in Rome, Selene thought about her grandparents.

They would be devastated by the news from Greece. She had reassured them on the telephone that she was well and happy and had promised to be with them as soon as possible, but all through the conversation she had been aware of her grandmother's agitation, her insistence that she come home immediately, that she should forget about Greece and Rome.

She telephoned Athena and it was Athena who promised she would go to see her grandparents to reassure them that all was well. The newspapers had made the most of it. Murderous attack on English artist on romantic Greek island, her rescue at the hands of an Italian nobleman and the police, and the death of the assassin.

It was all a far cry from her grandparents' ordered life, their staid normal everyday comings and goings that neither tragedy nor trauma had had the power to halt.

Athena drove alone to their home but she was not expecting a cordial reception. They had blamed Mervyn for everything that had gone wrong in their daughter's life, and they had blamed her for influencing Selene in so many of her ventures. And now Selene was to marry Alexander whom, she thought, had loved Cassie.

It was natural that she should think about Cassie now. Cassie who had been wilful and capricious, always striving for something that was just out of reach as Alexander had been out of reach. Cassie had loved him, wanted him, but she had never realised that this was one thing she could not have merely because she wanted it.

She drove slowly along the tree-lined road towards the Sheldons' house and sat for a few moments before she got out of the car. The garden was beautifully kept from its smooth green lawn to its vibrant flower beds.

It was Arthur's pride and joy, and even as she got out of the car she could see him trundling a wheelbarrow along the path, wearing faded grey flannel trousers and a soft panama hat that was years old. At the sound of the latch he looked up and bringing the barrow to rest he walked towards her, his face anxious and unsure.

She smiled. 'Good morning,' she greeted him. 'The garden looks lovely.'

'Are you alone?' he asked her.

'Quite alone. I thought I should come to see you. I stayed at the hotel overnight.'

'You should have told us you were coming. You could have stayed here.'

'Well, it was rather short notice. Is Elizabeth in?'

He nodded. 'She is, and none too happy.'

'No, I suppose not. I hope I can bring her some comfort.'

They sat opposite Athena in the living room. Elizabeth had produced tea and scones as always, and she now sat with an expression of infinite misery on her face, while Arthur looked from one to the other in masculine bewilderment.

'Why hasn't Selene come, why you?' Elizabeth asked shortly.

'Selene is still in Rome, Elizabeth. I'm sure she'll come as soon as possible.'

'What's she doing in Rome? She's with that young man who saved her, I suppose.'

'Yes, Alexander.'

'Wasn't he Cassie's young man? I thought Selene said as much.'

'No. He was not Cassie's young man. They were friends, nothing more.'

'I'm sure Selene said…'

Athena's expression stopped her, and in the next breath she said, 'I hope this is the end of it, the island, the studio, she can paint here, teach here, live in England, where nothing like that is ever going to happen to her again.'

'When Selene comes to England, she's bringing Alexander with her. I'm sure she told you that.'

'Yes, but there's no need. I told her we were very grateful to him but we don't have to meet him.'

'Don't you want to meet the man she's hoping to marry, then?'

They both stared at her, Elizabeth's face hard and unyielding.

'Surely she told you?' Athena said.

'She said something, but of course it was all too fresh in her mind. She thinks she owes him something. By this time it'll all have sorted itself out.'

For a moment Athena looked at her in pitying silence, and in the same moment she thought about Mervyn. Why hadn't he seen it before it was too late? They were good people, kind people, people you could trust with your life, but it wasn't enough. Cocooned in their separate lives they would never understand people who didn't live as they lived or thought as they thought. Then Athena said, 'Elizabeth, Selene is in love with Alexander and they are going to be married. She is bringing him here to meet you, but she didn't fall in love with him because he saved her life. It happened before that, during the time she was with me in Rome.

'He's very nice, he's handsome and kind and you will like him. He isn't taking her away from you. That's entirely up to you, but if you love her and want her to be a part of your lives, then you have to learn to let her go.'

'How do you mean, let her go?'

'Live her own life with the man she loves, even if it is in a country other than this one.'

'Isn't he some Lord or other?' Arthur asked. 'It said so in the paper.'

'He is Conte Andonieto. He's a banker by profession like his father before him, and he's handsome and charming. You've got to give them a chance, Elizabeth.'

Neither Elizabeth nor Arthur spoke and Athena, with something like relief, thought she could now conveniently make her escape. It hadn't been easy and she'd done her best, she wasn't sure if either of them had fully understood.

When she rose to her feet Arthur said, 'You're surely not driving to Devon today?'

'No. I'm seeing a friend on the way.'

'You can stay here, can't she Elizabeth?'

'Thank you, but I must be off now.'

She had the strangest feeling that she was seeing them for the last time. They would think about what she had said, they would meet Selene and Alexander when they came to England and they would form their own judgement, she just hoped they would not look upon him as a threat.

They went with her to the front door and Norah, who had seen the strange car standing at the gate, was already letting herself in.

Athena greeted her with a smile. She did not know Norah well. On the rare occasions they'd met, she had found the younger girl irascible and self-opinionated. Now Norah was saying, 'Have you brought news of Selene?'

'Only reassurance that she's well and happy. I'm sure she'll be here to see you very soon.'

'Where is she then?'

'She's in Rome.'

'With that man who rescued her?'

'Yes. With Alexander.'

'You know him then?'

'Yes, I know Alexander.'

She met Norah's inquisitive eyes with another smile, and walked casually to her car. They stood at the door until she drove away, and Athena had no doubt that Selene's forthcoming marriage would be well and truly talked over by the three people she had left.

Indeed as Elizabeth made another cup of tea Norah sat opposite her father asking questions. Arthur was bewildered still by the turn of events and it was hard for him to concentrate as Norah pounded him with questions.

It was left to Elizabeth to answer her daughter, and Norah thought to herself that it was all happening again.

Then, it had been Moira. Not for Moira the boys she met at the school dances and the village hops. For Moira it had to be her school teacher, somebody none of her school friends could aspire to. Now it was Selene and some Italian nobleman no less.

In no time at all her mother would have spread it around. One half of her would deplore it, the other half would rejoice in it, and what came after could be as traumatic as her sister's life with Mervyn.

'What had Athena got to say about it?' she demanded.

'She told us we had to learn to let go, as if we've ever interfered with anything Selene did. He won't want to come to live in England. She'll have to live in Italy. I just hope he allows her to come to visit us often, and on her own. He's a banker, so he'll probably be too busy to do much visiting anyway.'

Norah's snide smile was lost on them. Of course they wouldn't let go, Moira hadn't wanted them to let go, Selene might be an entirely different proposition.

A week later they waited at the airport for the plane that was bringing Selene and Alexander from Rome. They were nervous, but they knew nothing about the apprehension their granddaughter was feeling. As she had always done she hurried forward to meet them and behind her stood Alexander, tall and smiling, holding out his hand in greeting, and then they were walking to the waiting car and Selene knew what was before them. Her grandmother's catering, days of strictures when they had her to themselves, and she knew what she must do.

The opportunity came several evenings later when her grandmother came into her bedroom to say goodnight. She was sitting at her dressing table brushing her hair and her grandmother sat on the edge of her bed.

'You do like him, don't you Granny?' Selene asked with a smile.

'Yes indeed, love. He's very nice, nicer than we thought he would be, but we're not entirely happy about your marrying him. You never mentioned him when you came home from Italy. Now you're saying you're in love with him. I thought it was Cassie he loved.'

'I thought so too, Granny, but I was wrong.'

'Are you sure you've told us everything about what happened in Greece? The papers said it was some man who hated his family and wanted to murder all of them, some vendetta that had gone on for years.'

'The papers don't always get it right.'

'But they get some of it right, love.'

'One day Granny I'll tell you all about it, at the moment there's still a great deal I don't know. I can only tell you that I love Alexander and I'm so happy that he loves me. I want you and Grandy and my aunts to come to the wedding. You will, won't you Granny?'

'But you'll be married here. You have to be.'

'No, we're getting married in Rome. Alexander's grandmother is very frail and far from well. She couldn't possibly make the journey and she's much older than either you or Grandy. Norah will bring you, she's travelled abroad. At least I hope she'll come.'

'Kathleen and George won't come. They never have enough money and there's the children to think of. I'm not sure about Norah either. I've never been one for foreign places. I suppose Athena'll be there.'

'I do hope so. She's all I have on my father's side.'

‘Oh, I don’t know Selene. It’ll mean flying, and I’m afraid of that, and where shall we stay? None of us know Rome. The hotels will be expensive and none of us speak a word of Italian.’

Selene smiled. ‘Granny, I think you will find that most Italians speak English. You will stay at Alexander’s grandmother’s house. It’s very beautiful, on one of the hills overlooking Rome with lovely gardens round it. I’m sure you’ll all fall in love with it as I have.’

‘Well, it’s something we’ll have to think about. I wanted your grandfather to give you away.’

‘Granny he can, but in Rome. I do want you to come.’

‘Oh, love, none of this is turning out as I wanted it to. I wanted you to marry a nice British boy with a decent job and live close by. You’re just like your mother, always hankering after something different, only she knew when it wasn’t working out.’

Selene didn’t speak. There was nothing she could say that would make her grandmother understand. That she loved Alexander wasn’t important, what was important to them was that he was taking her away for ever. A different life in a world they knew nothing about, a world they didn’t want to know.

Chapter Thirty-Six

Elizabeth stared down at the gold-embossed wedding invitation to her granddaughter's wedding with a glum face. Watching her from across the table her husband's heart sank. The past few weeks had been difficult, alternating between fits of anger and tears. Selene had forgotten all they'd done for her. It was Athena's fault with her high-falutin' lifestyle. Why hadn't they seen the dangers all those years ago when Moira was besotted with her art teacher?

Gently he said, 'We can go to the wedding, love. They've said we can stay at the grandmother's house. It's not going to be expensive.'

'I'm not bothered about the expense of getting there,' his wife snapped. 'It's the clothes we shall need. Look at those suits Alexander was wearing. Look at what Selene was wearing, everything will be out of our league.'

'You don't know that, Elizabeth.'

'Oh yes I do. Did you see her engagement ring? It must have cost the earth, and the wristwatch he was wearing. I'm not going all the way to Italy to be made to feel an outsider.'

'I liked him. He was agreeable, and he really did make a big effort to show us that he loved our granddaughter and liked us.'

'Just like Mervyn did all those years ago, and what a disaster that turned out to be.'

'I seem to remember that you made him very welcome, Elizabeth. You did nothing to discourage them.'

'Don't you think that isn't something I regret, that I don't blame myself for not seeing the dangers sooner?'

'What dangers?'

'They were poles apart. She was too young, and then there was that island she hated. We don't know the full story about that and Selene wouldn't discuss it.'

'I expect it's something she wants to forget.'

To her father's surprise it was Norah who didn't see why they couldn't accept the invitation.

'Well, your sister and her family won't go. They won't have the money and we can't very well expect his grandmother to put us all up.'

'She must have the room for us, otherwise they wouldn't have offered,' Norah persisted.

Arthur allowed the two women to argue together, deciding to take no part in it. If they had bothered to ask his opinion, he would have told them that he would prefer to stay at home, let them get on with it. Selene had made up her mind what she wanted, with or without their presence.

Norah's thoughts were on different lines. In the days since Selene and Alexander's visit, she'd begun to look at her life and see it for what it was. A middle-aged woman who lived alone in a house that she had little pride in – a house that was functional and without charm, like her life.

She'd told herself that she enjoyed tramping the

hills of Scotland and travel that had stretched no further than the shores of Brittany, and she'd listened to her colleagues enthusing about holidays spent abroad in exotic countries she'd only ever read about.

She'd treated their stories with cynical disdain and she knew that in the main they regarded her as a bitter and twisted old maid who secretly envied them.

They asked questions about Selene, but she'd always been quick to say, 'Oh, I never know what she's up to, she's like her mother and we never got on.'

Now she found herself telling anybody who cared to listen that her niece was engaged to an Italian conte, whose grandmother was a princess and she was to be married in Rome. None of them could beat that.

The story of Selene's brush with death and her rescue had been the subject of a lengthy write-up in the daily papers and the town's weekly gazette. Often she found the other teachers deep in conversation that stopped immediately whenever she entered the room, and she knew instinctively that they were discussing Selene.

She wanted to go to the wedding. She wanted to see Rome and live for a few days in the palazzo of a Roman noblewoman. She wanted to see her niece marry the Princess's grandson and she intended to move heaven and earth to persuade her parents to go.

It wasn't easy. Her father was reluctant to buy a morning suit, her mother said the price of clothes in the town's best shop were ridiculous and she had to agree with her when it took the whole of one month's salary to purchase a dress and wedding hat.

She had her hair set and styled in the town's most expensive salon and decided on contact lenses instead of new spectacles. Her parents looked askance at the transformation and even her father had to admit to himself that if she'd taken that sort of trouble years before she'd have been unlikely to remain a spinster.

She'd never be the beauty Moira had been, but she had an interesting face, good-looking and intelligent.

They still hadn't replied to their wedding invitation. Every day it seemed that Elizabeth produced one more reason why they shouldn't go. She was afraid of flying, the stupidity of spending so much of their hard-earned savings on a couple of days. The wedding should have been in England, brides were invariably married in their own church.

One other matter was causing Norah some anxiety. Her mother hadn't as yet realised that they were to be married at a Roman Catholic church. Her father was Church of England, her mother was a Methodist and throughout the years there had been one problem after another about weddings, christenings and funerals. She decided to allow her mother to remain in ignorance until they'd booked their flight, otherwise it would be just one more reason for staying at home.

In Rome Selene was rediscovering the eternal

city with Alexander and she was loving every moment. The Princess had jewellers and famous fashion houses arriving at her home, saying she was too old to go down to the city to visit them, and Selene was pampered with beauticians and people only too anxious to show her jewels, wedding dresses and any clothes she would need.

She had dined with Alexander at a fashionable ristorante on the hillside above Rome with the lights of the city shining below and the scent of pines all around them, but when Alexander looked in her eyes he knew that her thoughts were miles away.

Covering her hand with his, he said gently, 'You can't get it out of your mind Selene, but it's over now. He's never going to come back to trouble either of us again.'

For a moment she looked at him in confused silence, then she said quickly, 'I wasn't thinking of him, darling. I hardly ever think of that day. I was thinking about my grandparents, they haven't even answered the wedding invitation.'

'No. My grandmother spoke of it this morning.'

'That means they are terribly hurt and angry. They think we should have been married in England.'

Privately Alexander thought her grandparents didn't want them to marry at all, but reasonably he said, 'It would hardly have been practical, darling. There are so many people coming to the wedding and it is easy to accommodate them in Rome, it would have been very difficult in England. My grandmother has said your grandparents and their daughters can stay with her, and I have offered to pay the expenses of any others who decide to stay in hotels. I don't think we can do any more.'

'I know. I don't care about the others, I hardly ever saw them since Great Aunt Agatha died, but I did want Granny and Grandy to come. You liked them, didn't you?'

'Yes, very much.'

He had liked them. They were kind good people, but he wasn't too sure that they had liked him. He was too foreign, too different and he was taking Selene away.

'I could try telephoning them,' she ventured.

'If you think that would persuade them.'

When her face was still doubtful, he said, 'Athena will be here tomorrow, why not talk it over with her.'

She smiled sadly. 'Athena has always been a thorn in their flesh, they never really liked her, they blamed her for so much, it was unfair.'

'Yes well, time alters many things. Talk to Athena, she's often capricious but she does have a certain aura of common sense.'

Athena arrived the following afternoon and when Selene asked why she hadn't brought Jonathan with her, she said gaily, 'I want these few days on my own, darling. He's coming out for the wedding but I need to think.'

Selene laughed. 'What is there to think about? He's kind, he's nice, and he loves you very much.'

'I know. He's perfect, I'm the one who wants analysing. I was never any great shakes as a wife, Selene. If Ian were alive he'd endorse that. I was vain, frivolous and I always wanted to be on the move. Cassie was a lot like me, it was a great pity he loved me, I didn't deserve it.'

'You were also very young Athena, and Ian was a lot older than you.'

'I know. He was thirty-four going on fifty and I was eighteen going on fourteen. He allowed me to grow up at my own pace. There are times even now when I really wonder if I have grown up enough to marry Jonathan.'

'He evidently thinks you have.'

Athena smiled. 'Now tell me about you and Alex. Cassie always called him that, you never have.'

'No never. I love him, he loves me. I still can't believe that he wants to marry me.'

'Have you heard from your grandparents?'

'Not a word, not even an answer to the wedding invitation. It's the one cloud on our horizon, Athena. They must be very miserable about the whole thing.'

'Selene, they can't live your life for you.'

'I tried to telephone them last night but then my courage left me and I put the telephone down. I couldn't bear to hear them saying they were not coming. I would sense the anger in her voice, see the expression on her face, remember how Grandy had tried to console her for every imagined hurt I had caused them.'

'Then you should let it be, darling. One day you'll see them again, then perhaps they'll accept you've never really left them at all.'

When she told Alexander what Athena had said, he agreed that it was probably the sensible thing to do.

She was not aware that the Princess too was finding her grandparents' attitude hard to understand.

'What is the matter with them?' she asked Athena. 'I have told them they will be very welcome here. Rome is not on the other side of the world and we Italians are a civilised people.'

'You would have to know them to understand,' Athena murmured.

'Are they then peculiar, ignorant people?'

'Ignorant no, unsophisticated yes. They have never set foot outside England. Their lives have been regimented into doing the same thing year after year – holidays, activities, amusements. They are good, well-respected people with little imagination, and I fear they will never change.'

'But if they love their granddaughter, shouldn't they make the effort?'

'I think so, you think so, but, if they are afraid, it can be very difficult.'

The Princess shrugged her elegant shoulders. 'I am not too well and I am old. I wish in my heart that this marriage was over and I can get back to my routine, but I want to witness their happiness and take part in it.'

'Selene hasn't said if they are to live in Milan or here.'

'I told Alexander last night and he will tell Selene himself. I am giving them this villa. It is something that has been long on my mind, but until Alexander married it wasn't practical. Now I have decided that I want to live on Capri permanently. The villa is smaller, and I love it so. Selene and Alexander will be happy here, they will have children I'm sure, and the house and gardens are very beautiful.

'I love Rome. When I was younger I thought there was no city in the world where I would prefer to live. To me everything I love in life was to be found in Rome, but now I rarely go into the city. I sit out there on the terrace and think where I would like to go if I could find enough energy.

'I would like to walk in the Borghese gardens and listen to the fountains in Piazza Navona, enjoy the flowers in Piazza di Spagna, throw one more coin in the fountain of Trevi, but I know that I shall do none of those things. My time has come and gone, Athena. In Capri I shall sit on my balcony overlooking the sea and watch the sun going down on the gulf of Salerno. I have had a good life, I shall be content.'

'Are your other children coming to the wedding?'

'But of course. All of them and their children also. I have been married three times but we are still a close-knit family. Alexander is my youngest grandson, just as his mother was my youngest child. I miss Leonora, she was beautiful and spirited, she loved too well and lived dangerously when she was too young to understand that she may be asked to pay a price for such foolishness.

'It is strange is it not, how that early discretion has brought us all together. Who would have thought that one day that old trauma would take her life and the life of two others also. It almost took Alexander and Selene, only this time it was not to be.'

Athena's face was sad and the Princess reached

and covered her hand with her own. 'Cassie should not have died, Athena, but nor would she have married my grandson. You knew that in your heart, didn't you.'

'Yes, but she loved him.'

The Princess merely smiled but decided not to continue the conversation. Instead she said, 'Sophia and her husband will be arriving tomorrow, then we shall have to listen to her decisions regarding her gown for the wedding. I am pleased that Selene has asked her to be her bridesmaid.'

Indeed Sophia entertained them with talk of Washington and their new home, but it did not alter that fact that nostalgia was raw within her. She had loved Rome, still loved it, and she and her husband spent almost every day renewing old sights and sounds.

With her dark auburn hair she had wanted to wear green for the wedding but the Princess said it was considered unlucky for such an event, and she chose instead a turquoise wild silk gown and said she would wear jewels in her hair.

Somewhat dismayed by this Selene said to Athene, 'Sophia isn't wearing flowers in her hair – or a hat – so where does that leave me?'

'I rather think the Princess has something to suggest, dear.'

It was two days before the wedding when the Princess called her into her bedroom. The wall safe was opened and on top of the bed rested a great many jewellery cases which the Princess was opening one by one. She called to Selene to sit beside her and with a smile said, 'I have a great many jewels that I never wear. Jewels became me when I was young and beautiful. Now, who looks at them on an old woman, unless they are criminals and wonder how they can acquire them?

'I am giving them to my grandchildren. These are what my last husband gave me. I have given some to Sophia, but I want Alexander's wife to have my most prized possessions. Will you wear this tiara on your wedding day, Selene?'

She stared at it in wide-eyed admiration, a beautiful thing emblazoned with diamonds and pearls, and the Princess smiled. 'It will look very well with your veil, my dear. One day I will show you how I wore it on my wedding day.'

She then proceeded to open box after box containing necklaces, bracelets and rings and, while Selene was still finding words to thank her, she said, 'I shall leave them here in the safe. When I have gone from here this will be your bedroom. You will know where they are.'

Guests were now beginning to arrive in Rome, staying largely in the centre of the city in different hotels. In the daytime they came up to the villa with their wedding gifts and Athena thought wryly to herself that Selene's grandparents would have been totally overwhelmed by them. They were Italian, charming and gregarious, the women fashionably dressed and worldly, the men invariably charming and gallant. Alexander knew them all but he stayed close by her side and made her feel protected and loved.

Witnessing the proceedings, Athena thought Cassie would have been in her element among these people. She would have matched their exuberance with her own, been in the centre, laughing, talking, whereas Selene sat beside Alexander, her hand in his, her smile gentle and warm, so warm that they were enchanted by her because she was different.

How strange were the tricks that fate played. Selene had met Alexander only briefly and Cassie had loved him, then Cassie was dead and Selene and Alexander had met again, this time to fall in love.

Alexander had been unable to protect Cassie from the man who had killed her, but he had saved Selene. What strange fate had turned that idyllic island into a tragedy?

They sat on the terrace in the warm summer night on one of Rome's seven hills with the lights of the city spread out before them, and their talk and laughter echoed all around them, but not even Alexander knew that there were many times when Selene's thoughts returned to England and the small county town where she had been brought up.

Everything in her life had changed, and would continue to change, but not all her heart was here. She was remembering people who loved her, the gentleness of her early life, the love that had at times both smothered her and sustained her, and even in the midst of so much joy there was sadness. Why couldn't they have come?

She had been into the city with Sophia for the last fitting of their wedding finery and as they drove up the hill towards the villa Selene was aware of Athena standing on the terrace waving her arms excitedly.

As soon as Sophia stopped the car, she ran towards it and meeting Selene's surprised gaze, she said, 'Selene, they're here. Just after you left. They're in their rooms unpacking.'

Selene leapt out of the car and in amazement said, 'But they didn't answer the invitation. When did they decide to come?'

'Your Aunt Norah's with them. They came in on the early morning flight. Your grandmother didn't enjoy it. She looked a little unsettled.'

'What did the Princess say when they arrived?'

'She was a little taken aback I think, but she soon recovered. Alexander took charge. They're in the rooms overlooking the Italian garden. Norah has the one next door.'

Selene's heart was racing as she ran upstairs and along the wide corridors leading to the rooms allotted to her grandparents. She could hear the sound of their voices, and after a light knock on the door, she flung it open and ran into her grandfather's arms.

Clothes were strewn across the bed and their suitcase lay open on the floor. Her grandmother was sitting in an easy chair near the window and beside her, on a small marble table, was a tray containing a teapot and two cups and saucers.

She went towards her and embraced her, and her grandmother was quick to say, 'We answered the invitation love. It probably hasn't arrived yet.'

Selene smiled. 'Then you've only just answered it?'

Elizabeth murmured, 'Yes well, we had a lot to think about. I didn't think I'd like flying, and I didn't. Then Norah said she'd come with us. She was the one who urged us to come, she's in the room next door.'

'I'm so glad that you're here. How long do you intend to stay?'

'For the wedding, then we're going home. In any case, you'll be going away, won't you, and the Princess won't want us staying on.'

'But we have two days, Granny, to show you Rome. There's so much to see. It's a wonderful city, Alexander will know all the places you ought to see. Isn't this a lovely room?'

'It makes our house like a rabbit-hutch. I'm not surprised you didn't want to get married from home.'

'It simply wasn't practical, Granny. When you've met everybody and realised that they're staying all around the city in different hotels, you'll know we couldn't have coped at home.'

'Did it have to be a big wedding?'

'It was something Alexander's grandmother wanted.'

'Oh well.'

Across the room Selene's eyes met her grandfather's gazing at her with resigned humour, and she smiled. People didn't change overnight. Perhaps her grandmother would never change.

At least they'd made the effort. They were here.

Chapter Thirty-Seven

Whenever there was time Alexander and Selene showed her grandparents and Norah the city of Rome. Elizabeth remembered all the Hollywood films she had seen on the cruelty associated with the Colosseum. Her imagination filled it with wild beasts and tortured Christians, with gladiators fighting to the death and mad emperors exacting cruel deaths from helpless victims.

Nor had her staunch Methodist upbringing equipped her for the splendour of St Peter's and Roman Catholic extravaganza. She did, however, love the piazzas and the fountains, the shops and the sheer exuberance of life on the city streets.

Norah said very little, but in her heart she felt a certain bitterness that she could have used her life better and seen it all before.

Selene walked with her grandfather up the Spanish Steps, while Alexander escorted the two other ladies in front of them, and Arthur said, 'He's nice, Selene. I like him very much. Don't worry about your grandmother, she'll come round.'

'She still isn't so sure, is she?'

'It takes time with Elizabeth. There's a lot of forgetting and forgiving to do before she can look forward.'

'I wish she'd be a little nicer to Athena.'

'I know. She blames her for too much and she's

jealous of her.'

'Jealous! But why?'

'Of her involvement in your life, of her style, and you have to admit Athena's got plenty of that.'

Selene laughed. 'I hope she's going to marry Jonathan. He's so nice and he was marvellous after Cassie died.'

'Wasn't Cassie smitten with Alexander?'

'Yes. It was a crush, nothing more.'

Selene saw no point in embroidering on Cassie's involvement with Alexander. If she did, he would no doubt tell her grandmother and she would convince herself and everybody else that he was marrying her on the rebound.

As they strolled through the gardens Arthur said gently, 'You're not asking me to give you away, are you love?'

She stared at him curiously. 'I thought you would want to, Grandy.'

'I do want to, it was the one thing I wanted most of all, but not here, love. I want to sit in the church next to Elizabeth and Norah, I'd be lost doing anything else.'

'But Granny won't like it.'

'I've told her that that's how it has to be. Nothing she can say will make me change my mind.'

They walked in silence for some time, then Arthur said, 'Who *is* going to give you away, love?'

'Marco will. I've met him several times and he's very nice. He was going to marry Alexander's mother, but she died in that accident.'

'There were too many accidents Selene.

Weren't they all connected with the last one?'

'Perhaps. I still don't know all the full story.'

'But why Cassie? Why your father?'

'Grandy, I don't know. One day I'll know, for now I just keep telling myself that it's over, that I'm young and alive and very much in love. I don't think the past should be allowed to shadow what we have now.'

'No, you're right, love. Your grandmother's going to enjoy telling all and sundry about the Princess and her villa, about the gardens and the fountains and the views from the hill. It'll feel very empty when the old lady's on her own and the guests have all gone. What's she going to do all on her own?'

'She's going to live on Capri. The villa is beautiful but smaller, she'll be happy there.'

'And what about this one? Is she going to sell it?'

'No. She's given it to Alexander. We're going to live in it.'

If she'd said they were going to live in the Vatican he couldn't have been more astonished, but he decided not to comment. If he told Elizabeth she'd convince herself that they'd seen their last of their granddaughter.

Elizabeth slept badly on the night before the wedding. Tossing and turning in her large ornate bed, she watched the pattern of leaves on the ceiling of the room, then the first tentative rays of the sun falling on ivory walls and the pale green carpet, burnishing exquisite figurines and ornate gold pedestals, in the sort of room she had never dreamed she would ever sleep in. She got up and went to stand at the window. Outside the morning sky was awash with pink and gold, shimmering on the fountains cascading into the ornamental pond and the water lilies opening to the sun.

She could hear Arthur snoring gently in the other bed. Men were different, they could sleep through all this, shelve things, convince themselves that everything was normal.

She went into the dressing room next door and surveyed her wedding finery: the pale mauve silk dress and coat that had cost too much money. Why, she could have recarpeted the spare bedroom for what it had cost, and the silly hat with its pink chiffon flowers and delicate straw.

The shop assistant had assured her that there would be nothing more fashionable anywhere, but now that she'd met most of the guests she convinced herself that it was untrue. Those Italian women with their fashion flair and liveliness would make her feel old-fashioned.

She hadn't seen Selene's wedding dress although she'd wanted to. Athena hadn't seen it either and that information had prompted her not to ask if she could see it. She thought about Moira's lace wedding dress folded away in a cabin trunk in the loft, kept lovingly in the hope that one day Selene would wear it, together with the long veil and floral headdress.

Whoever heard of a wedding in the early part of the evening? People at home got married in the morning or early afternoon. Her hat would be superfluous they'd all be there in their jewels and silks and satins. She'd stand out like a sore finger.

Norah was having no such scruples. She'd spent more on her dress than she'd intended, more than she'd ever spent on anything, and if it didn't make the grade it was just too bad.

She sat up in bed enjoying her morning cup of tea. She was enjoying herself, her tour around Rome, being waited on, the opulence of her bedroom, and she was of the opinion that she could hold her own with any of the Princess's guests any day.

Her mother's misgivings had rolled off her like water off a duck's back. She was glad that Selene had had the good sense to cut loose and with that in mind she thought that now perhaps was the right time to have a personal chat with her niece.

She found Selene sitting at her dressing table brushing her hair, and Norah was invited to sit beside her while Selene explained that she was expecting her hairdresser but they had time for a chat.

'Have you seen Granny this morning?' she asked.

'No. She's fallen out with her dress. I couldn't bear to listen to any more of it.'

'What's wrong with her dress?'

'Nothing at all, but she's not sure it's grand enough or if she'll need her hat.'

Selene laughed. 'I'll have a word with her. I doubt if hats will be worn, since we're getting married in the early evening and there will be a ball afterwards. I would have told her all this, but I didn't think any of you'd come.'

'I know. She dithered and dithered. I had to push them into it.'

'I didn't think you'd come, Aunt Norah.'

'Well, no, we've never actually been great friends, have we? But I'm glad I came, it's been the best few days of my life.'

Selene looked at her earnestly. 'Why did we never get on? I did try.'

'Yes I know. It was me, I always resented your mother because she was Mum's favourite. She was prettier than me, sweeter than me, but I was the clever one. That didn't seem to matter. Everything Moira did was wonderful in their eyes, but when her marriage fell apart, they blamed Mervyn, never Moira.'

'Did you like my father?'

'Well yes, he was nice enough. I never thought they were right for each other.'

'Why was that?'

'He was more intelligent, but my God how she wanted him. Underneath all that sweetness, Moira invariably got what she wanted.'

'They both died so young.'

'I know. I think if she hadn't died, they'd have drifted apart all the same.'

'Why do you think that?'

'She was terribly jealous of Alexander's mother. It was strange that they should both die in the same way. Have you never thought so?'

'One day I shall talk to Alexander about it, but I don't think the time is right yet. She was going to marry Uncle Marco, you know.'

'Perhaps it was just Moira being paranoid, or me being too imaginative. I'll call in and see Mum. Hopefully she'll have come to terms with her dress.'

'What are you wearing, Aunt Norah?'

'A pale being silk dress. The woman in the shop thought it was wonderful. I'm not so sure.'

Selene laughed. 'I'm sure it will be wonderful. Why don't you let my hairdresser style your hair.'

'Oh I don't know.'

'I think you should. You have such lovely eyes. I always wondered why you never wore contact lenses. Don't worry about the hat, I can lend you anything in the way of flowers or jewellery.'

'I can't see me in a tiara, or flowers either for that matter,' Norah declared adamantly.

It was later in the afternoon that Selene was allowed to see Norah in her wedding finery. She had to admit that this was an Aunt Norah totally unfamiliar to her. The hair stylist had done a wonderful job with her straight bobbed hair, since now it gently framed her face in soft waves and there were hidden auburn lights in it she had never noticed before.

The dress fitted her slim figure perfectly and hung in a heavy fold about her unusually high-heeled court shoes.

Selene felt a sudden rush of pity for this woman who beside her younger sister had always felt like an ugly duckling. She took great pleasure in fastening a diamond brooch in her gown and diamond earrings to match in her ears.

'But these are yours,' Norah protested.

'They were a gift from the Princess. All the jewellery here was hers, she won't mind my lending them to you I'm sure.'

'Well I don't know…'

'Please, Aunt Norah. I want to lend them to

you, you look wonderful, I'm sure Granny will think so.'

'Well if she does, it's the first time ever.'

Selene laughed. 'Well go along and show her. The next time I see you will be in church.'

Elizabeth sat between her husband and her daughter in the beautiful church of Saint Agnes, surrounded by the other wedding guests. She had watched the Princess being escorted up the aisle, leaning heavily on her ebony walking stick, her arm held protectively by her son-in-law. Her beautiful face etched in ivory was old now, but there were still traces of the charm and loveliness that had brought her three noble husbands. She was wearing French navy, and around her throat were priceless gems to match the tiara which encircled her head.

Norah had persuaded her mother that she should not wear her hat but in the midst of these jewelled women she felt singularly unadorned.

Arthur had assured her that she looked wonderful, and they had both been stunned by Norah's appearance, both of them wondering why they had never seen her potential before.

Alexander exchanged a few words with his grandmother and Elizabeth, looking at his tall elegant figure, understood why Selene had fallen in love with him. The sort of boy she had wanted for her could never have measured up. She only hoped and prayed their marriage would work out better than Moira's had done.

Her thoughts turned to the small, unpretentious church at home and the vicar who had married Selene's mother. There they would have been surrounded by their relatives and close friends. The choir would have sung their favourite hymns and the music the organist played would have been known to them.

She pictured Selene in her mother's lace wedding gown, but the boy she went forward to meet was a shadowy figure. None of the boys known to her found a place in the picture, only Arthur escorting his granddaughter into the church was real. Now he sat beside her, waiting for some other man to bring Selene into the church.

Across the aisle her eyes met Alexander's, and he smiled. His smile was warm, and in that brief moment something like relief flooded her tortured heart.

The music swelled, the sound of singing filled the church and slowly a tall silver-haired man escorted Selene down the aisle and Alexander stepped forward with a smile to meet her.

Tears coursed down Elizabeth's face at the sight of her granddaughter standing beside him, ethereally beautiful in heavy parchment satin with the sheen of diamonds in her hair and round her throat. She remembered little of what came after, it seemed to Elizabeth that memories were more important than the present, until suddenly there was nothing left beyond the sound of music and bells and with the others she was drifting out of the church and into the square outside, to the light of the setting sun falling on old stone and cascading fountains.

She watched from the steps as they drove away in a long white car, their faces wreathed with smiles, their happiness obvious for all to see, and all around them was laughter and cries of joy. At that moment the Princess turned and smiled, then graciously she said, 'Come, I wish you to join me in my car, we are one family now.'

The publishers hope that this book has given you enjoyable reading. Large Print Books are especially designed to be as easy to see and hold as possible. If you wish a complete list of our books please ask at your local library or write directly to:

Magna Large Print Books
Magna House, Long Preston,
Skipton, North Yorkshire.
BD23 4ND

This Large Print Book for the partially sighted, who cannot read normal print, is published under the auspices of

THE ULVERSCROFT FOUNDATION

THE ULVERSCROFT FOUNDATION

... we hope that you have enjoyed this Large Print Book. Please think for a moment about those people who have worse eyesight problems than you ... and are unable to even read or enjoy Large Print, without great difficulty.

You can help them by sending a donation, large or small to:

The Ulverscroft Foundation,
1, The Green, Bradgate Road,
Anstey, Leicestershire, LE7 7FU,
England.
or request a copy of our brochure for more details.

The Foundation will use all your help to assist those people who are handicapped by various sight problems and need special attention.

Thank you very much for your help.